Latitudes of Melt

Books by Joan Clark

for adults

Eriksdottir: A Tale of Dreams and Luck (1994)

Swimming Toward the Light (1990)

The Victory of Geraldine Gull (1988)

From a High Thin Wire (1983)

for children

The Dream Carvers (1995)

The Moons of Madeleine (1987)

Wild Man of the Woods (1986)

The Leopard and the Lily (1982)

The Hand of Robin Squires (1977)

Thomasina and the Trout Tree (1971)

Girl of the Rockies (1968)

For Sandra,
Tully roomie
Newlywed clubber
& 'old' friend
with affection,
Joan Oct. 2,000

LATITUDES OF MELT

a novel

JOAN CLARK

ALFRED A. KNOPF CANADA

PUBLISHED BY ALFRED A. KNOPF CANADA

Published in 2000 by Alfred A. Knopf Canada, a division of Random House of Canada Limited, Toronto. Distributed by Random House of Canada Limited, Toronto.

Knopf Canada and colophon are trademarks.

Pages 3 through 22 of this novel appeared in an earlier form in *The Fiddlehead*, volume 201.

Canadian Cataloguing in Publication Data

Clark, Joan
Latitudes of melt

ISBN 0-676-97288-8

I. Title.

PS8555.L37L37 2000 C813'.54 C00-931421-0
PR9199.3.C52L37 2000

First Edition

Visit Random House of Canada Limited's Web site: www. randomhouse.ca

Printed and bound in the United States of America

10 9 8 7 6 5 4 3 2 1

To the memory of my grandmother
Mary Roche

The sea as it spends itself
can teach us how to grieve—the way
it rushes onto a rock beach, seethes
and sucks back, informationless
the way
it booms under a cliff,
calling all things to their hollows.

Don McKay, "Grief and the Sea"

The polar wastes—no sounds except the grind
Of ice, the cry of curlews and the lore
Of winds from the mesas of eternal snow.

E.J. Pratt, "The Titanic"

The great and mighty sepulchre
plunged downward to her doom,
And the billows closed around her
in the early morning gloom.

And the seagulls chanted requiem
o'er their silent resting place,
Six hundred miles from Boston
and four hundred from old Cape Race.

Collected and arranged by Eric West,
"Sing Around This One"

ONE

Francis St. Croix spotted it first, a black dot floating in an ocean of water and ice. When he and Ernie rowed alongside for a look, they couldn't believe their eyes. There was a baby inside a makeshift cradle on an ice pan, bobbing like an ice cube on the sea. How had a baby come to be in the North Atlantic? Francis wouldn't have been out here himself but for having signed on to a Lunenberg schooner, the Maria Claire. *The fishermen had been hauling trawl lines into the dory when a thick fog rolled in, obscuring their view of the schooner as well as her marker buoys. All day long the men had rowed through fog looking for their ship and that evening, when it lifted and there was still no sign of the* Maria Claire, *decided to head for Newfoundland and rowed all night. Early next morning they came upon the child.*

The cradle was a basket on top of a wooden chair. Black rubber sheeting was wrapped around the basket and tied with some fancy gold rope. On top of the sheeting was a woman's veiled hat. While Ernie steadied the dory, Francis removed the hat and lifted the chair and the basket into the boat, noticing how the sheeting had been rucked up at one end to make a hood. When he pushed back the hood, he saw the baby's face, white as the Virgin's.

A girl, Francis knew it was a girl. Her eyes were closed. Was she dead, or asleep? He held his hand in front of her face, felt a wisp of breath warm his palm. May the Holy Mother keep her asleep. If she awoke they had nothing to feed her except hard tack and a bit of cold tea.

An angel must have been guarding the child, for she slept until the next day, and when she awoke there was no cry, no whimper of discomfort or distress. It was as if she understood that the men were delivering her to land as soon as they could. The sea cradle was on the dory bottom between Francis's legs where he could see the baby as he leaned to the oars. How long had those eyes been open? Blue they were, a clear regarding blue. When he looked again, they were brown. After she had memorized his face—so Francis liked to think—the baby closed her eyes. By the time she opened them again, Ernie was at the oars and Francis was kneeling beside the basket. The baby poked a finger into her mouth and sucked. Francis groped among the cradle cloths to test her warmth and found a jar of sweetened water and a bit of bread wrapped in a lady's handkerchief. This in turn had been wrapped in two flannel napkins and tucked at the baby's feet then covered with rubber sheeting, well away from sharp-eyed gulls.

They were too far out for gulls. So far they had only seen puffins, a small flotilla riding the swell. Though the worst of the ice was behind them, the air was cold. Francis slipped the jar beneath his shirt to warm it. The child was wet. He bent to the task with chapped and calloused hands. When his sons were babies, he had occasionally changed their napkins but he had no skill with such things, much less with a female child. But it had to be done. He chucked the soiled napkin overboard and fumbled a clean one between her legs. Before he bundled her tight, he rubbed her vigorously to bring up the colour but her pallor remained. He softened a pinch of bread in water and slipped it into her mouth. She smacked her lips and swallowed. Then she smiled. She had teeth, four miniature accordion keys. Twelve month old she was, maybe more. She was so little, her age was hard to guess. He fed her more bread and she closed her eyes while they rowed beneath a sky where a celestial compass guided them home. It was a two-day journey to Newfoundland, with each of them taking a turn at the oars while the other dozed.

Francis put ashore in the Drook with the cradle and the hat, and Ernie continued to Trepassey where he boarded a schooner that took him back to Nova Scotia, leaving the dory and the chair behind. Albert Sutton claimed the dory and his wife the chair, a collapsible wooden frame with a woven cane seat. Her mother sat in the chair for years to watch passersby, until a fire destroyed both the chair and the house.

Because no one was expecting Francis, his family was doubly astonished to see him walk into the kitchen with a baby in his arms.

"Mother of God! What have you there?" Merla St. Croix put her hand on the baby's forehead. "Ice cold."

"I found her on a bergy bit."

"A girl, is she?"

"As pretty as you please."

Four sons crowded around while Merla unbuttoned a wool bunting.

"Her little legs are that thin, they're like candle sticks," Merla said.

"She's been without food for a time," Francis said. "She'll be hungry."

No one thought to ask Francis if he was hungry or how he'd happened ashore earlier than expected. All that was told later, after the child had been changed and bundled in the basket, which was put on the oven door like bread set to rise. Merla dipped a cloth in warm milk and squeezed it into the baby's mouth. The child swallowed the milk and went back to sleep. Three days later she opened her eyes, one blue, the other brown, and looked around.

They named her Aurora because Francis had come upon her in a gleaming dawn. When word came from Cape Race that after colliding with an iceberg, a White Star liner, the Titanic, *had sunk southeast of the island with most of its passengers aboard, Francis, thinking that the child might have been cast adrift before the ship went down, gave her particulars to the wireless operator at the Cape who sent them to the White Star office in New York.*

Merla had advised Francis to describe the child as being between one and a half and two years of age. Despite the youngster's size, she was fairly well along, being able to walk and talk, though until now it had been mostly gibberish. It was only reasonable to assume that a child so lovingly entrusted to the arms of the sea had parents, one or both of whom might have survived. There were bound to be grandparents, maybe sisters, brothers, cousins. A youngster as beautiful as this would certainly be claimed.

Father Murphy, the parish priest, placed a notice describing the child—approximate age, sex, appearance—in the St. John's Evening Herald *and requested that information be sent to J. T. Mulloy at Cape Race. Copies of the newspaper were stuffed into suitcases and satchels and carried on trains and ships as far as Montreal and New York where they collected dust in pastorates and libraries. Still, no one inquired about the child and she remained on the island of Newfoundland.*

Though the waters of the island were often filled with ice and its shores hidden in mist, it was not the fabled Vinland or the Island of the Blessed, and it was not newly found except perhaps to an Italian explorer. The island was so large that for centuries fishermen had made use of its shores without even encountering each other or seeing the red people who had sprung from arrows shot to the ground. The shoreline of the island went on at such length and in such a configuration of coves, inlets, harbours, tickles, bights and bays that it was possible for a child who had been rescued from the ice to grow and flourish in splendid isolation.

THE DROOK

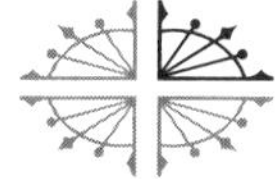

1912

Although I have flickering memories of being at sea, I do not remember being brought to the Drook. Most likely I was preoccupied with a sodden napkin and a raging thirst. I do remember a crude rubber titty being shoved into my mouth instead of the pliant nipple of my mother's breast. I knew I was expected to drink, and I drank. My mother had so often commented on my goodness that even in her absence, I did my best to oblige. And I had taken at once to the woman who urged me to drink the milk provided by an amiable brown cow, whose teats I would later learn to squeeze and pull.

Merla, the woman holding me, was short and sturdy with a surge of unsupported breast far larger than my mother's and covered by layers of impenetrable cloth. One should never underestimate the intelligence of a baby. I knew very well that by being in Merla's arms I had been taken into the bosom of a family. Which was not to say that the St. Croix sons were as delighted as their parents by the presence of a baby girl sleeping near the stove, in a basket mounted on a rusty box that had washed ashore from one of the many shipwrecks along the coast. Shoving and elbowing each other, the brothers peered into my basket as if I were a mermaid or some other rare creature fished from the sea. After the novelty wore off, I was relegated to becoming the daughter their mother and father never had. The brothers were too old to regard me as their sister, except for the youngest, Louis, who at age six was besotted with me.

Though it went against their nature, Merla and Francis at first tried to remain aloof. They told each other that while they would take good care of me, their foundling, they would avoid becoming too attached. There would be no kissing, no petting, no dandling on the knee. In any case there wasn't the time. With summer approaching, there were sheep to shear, the cow must be bred to O'Neill's bull, the fence must be mended, fishing gear made ready. Even so. At nights when Francis sat warming his stockinged feet on the oven door, sooner or later he would slide a fond look at me. He would reach out and touch my cheek. Then he would call to Merla who was washing up after supper. "The baby's cool," he'd say. "Is she poorly, do you think?" And she would call back, "It's better that she's cool than feverish." When it came time to smoke his pipe, Francis would step outside, a consideration, Merla pointed out, that he had never shown his wife or sons.

She was no better, and in the mornings after Francis and my brothers had gone off to their chores, she would carry me into the kitchen and set me on the floor while she rolled pie crust or kneaded dough. To steady myself, I would hold on to her skirt just above the back of the knee—I wasn't used to being on my feet. I knew she liked this for she would scoop me up in her floury hands and nuzzle my neck in the way that I liked. She would tell me that I was as perfect as a doll, that after four sons, I was a gift from God, which I was perfectly willing to believe.

As the months passed, Francis took to carrying me about on his shoulders and Merla sewed me pinafores and hummed me fiddle tunes. A bed was made for me in the upstairs closet. The blond wicker basket that had been my cradle was now used to carry wash to the line. By then I was handing clothes-pegs to Merla, taking them out of the cloth bag one by one while she hung up the sheets, the hem clamped between her teeth to prevent it from dragging on the ground. I was also helping her make pies, patting the crust into a tin pan, heaping the partridgeberries into a glistening mound. I trailed after her as she went about her chores. Though it was uncommon at that time to call parents by their Christian names, I never called Merla Mama or Mom, and I never called Francis Papa or Dad. I don't know why that was. Perhaps they discouraged me from using Mother and Father in the event that my birth parents might show up and snatch me away.

Now that I was part of the family, Jerome and Ben did their best to ignore me. I never really knew my oldest brother, Mike, because when I was about three he left the Drook to work on the boats and eventually moved to Bonavista. Louis and I were close. By the time I was four—more or less—we were sneaking into the tuck behind the outhouse to play dolls, which were clothes-pegs I had dressed in scraps. Playing with a girl was a risk for a ten-year-old boy since it was within the St. Croix cousins' power to make his life a torment if they chose.

My fourth spring in the Drook, Francis sold off the calf and among the sacks of salt and flour he brought home in the wagon was a doll with a mildewed body and a chipped porcelain nose. Merla made the doll a dress using new cloth left over from my pinafores. The doll's shawl was the linen handkerchief that had been in my cradle when I was found. On a corner of the handkerchief the name *Roche* was so finely stitched in white, that it was easy to overlook. Merla named the doll Alice Marie, after a ship that had gone down near Clam Cove when she was a girl.

Once I was old enough to be trusted on my own, I became an outdoors child. I liked to roam about barefoot. It seemed that once my body became accustomed to land, I preferred to have as little as possible between it and myself. Young as I was, I had formed a deep attachment to the Drook, a narrow valley at the bottom of which was a stream fed by ponds and bogs in the Barrens, a wild and for me endless moor beyond the Drook that rolled away like a mossy extension of the sea. The stream flowed into a pond and, after passing the houses of the St. Croix brothers, crossed the black sand and emptied into the ocean. The hills rising on either side of the stream made cosy walls, whose windows faced at one end the sea, and at the other the bent dwarf spruce we called tuckamore. The Drook lacked shelter only from the sky, there being no trees tall enough to support a roof. The small valley might have been created for the purpose of providing a home for the St. Croixs for its hillsides flattened into grassy shelves convenient for houses. These houses were occupied by five St. Croix brothers: Francis, Albert, Bernie, Vincent, Philip, and their cousin Leo Perry. Including wives and children, on my arrival there were forty-two people living in the Drook—I know this because Merla once told me that I was number forty-three. The largest house was Philip and Bride's; it contained the schoolroom where twice a year the priest said mass. Bride ran what passed for a post office, which meant that whenever a bundle of mail was brought from Trepassey, it was sorted on her kitchen table. Francis and Merla's house, where I lived, was on a rise of ground beside the road and across from the landwash where the stream crossed the sand and flowed into the sea. It had been built from wood carried down from Mistaken Point after the wreck of the *Azela* in 1874.

With my coming, there were now three girls in the Drook—the St. Croixs fathered boys, except for Bernie whose daughters were older than me by seven and nine years. At first the girls were curious about me, but by the time I was allowed outside on my own they had lost interest and were most often in the company of girls their own age who lived down the road in Long Beach, a few miles from Cape Race.

I lived in the Drook four years before I realized that except for Merla, Francis and Louis, the St. Croixs were wary of me. I was too young to know that though I had been grafted onto the St. Croixs, I was regarded as an outsider partly because I lacked the panoply of Newfoundland aunts and uncles and cousins required to make me an insider. And I was slow picking up on the fact that I did not look like anyone else. I had little occasion to look at myself and when I did it was in the jagged mirror hanging from a wire over the kitchen sink. What drove me to look was overhearing a conversation between Albert's wife, Lucy, and Leo Perry's wife, Alma. I was crouched behind a rock on a clear summer morning watching an ant making its intricate journey through the grass, when Lucy and Alma passed on the road on their way to Bride's.

Lucy said, "I swear to God if I had a youngster with hair the colour of Aurora's, I would dye it no matter what her age. I says as much to Merla but she won't hear of it. I says, Merla, white hair on a youngster her age don't look right!"

I scrunched closer to the ground and waited for Alma's reply. After her baby died, she had begun kidnapping children to make up for her loss and during her spells, had managed to kidnap every youngster in the Drook except me—none of the parents were bothered by Alma's habit because she treated the youngsters well and only kept them for a day or two. Though I was past the age of being kidnapped, I wanted to know why had I been overlooked.

"Her hair is white because she's a changeling." Alma was so soft-spoken that I could barely hear her.

"Go on. Aurora's no changeling." Lucy's voice rang through the Drook. "A changeling is wizened up and misshapen. Except for her hair, Aurora's a pretty little maid."

"She's got fairy eyes."

"Fairy eyes don't make her a changeling."

I stood up then so they would see me but they didn't notice and began climbing the hill to Bride's, talking all the while.

I didn't know what a changeling was. Nevertheless I went inside and, standing on the kitchen stool, had a close look at myself. There was no denying the colour of the hair—it was as white as the froth on the sea or a field of arctic cotton. I looked at my skin which, though far from being wizened and wrinkled, was most definitely white. Merla often remarked on its whiteness. "I can't get over how your skin never darkens. For all the time you spend outdoors, your cheeks never burns and your nose never freckles. At your age I was all freckles and bites."

Why was it midges and flies never bit me? I could spend hours in a tuck that even caribou avoided and emerge without a bite. I peered into the mirror, taking a long look at my eyes. One of them was decidedly blue, the other brown. I was still on the stool when Merla came downstairs carrying a blanket.

"Have I got fairy eyes?"

"You got different eyes from other youngsters."

"Why?"

"Because you weren't born here but someplace different."

I had already been told about my rescue from the ice. I had also been told not to stray too far from our door on account of the fairies who, Merla said, were wild creatures who kept to the Barrens.

"Have you ever seen a fairy?"

Merla put the blanket in the washbasin and poured in hot water from the kettle.

"No one see fairies, maid. They creep up without you knowing. That's why we never leaves the Drook without our beads and a bit of bread in our pockets."

Merla lifted me off the stool and, handing me the pail, told me to fetch her some wash water.

Drinking water was taken from the spring, wash water from the pond, and with the pail handle squeaking and the sun high overhead, I followed the path to the pond. When I leaned over to fill the pail, I saw a picture of myself in the water and decided that I liked this picture better than the one I'd seen in the mirror. I liked it because it shone and was a shimmering, wavy blue. Did fairies gaze at themselves in ponds like this? If they did, would one of them look like me? The thought pleased me. I wasn't afraid of fairies—perhaps because I had fairy eyes—and fancied that meeting a fairy might be like meeting myself.

When I was five, Merla sent me to school. She said it was time for me to stay indoors and settle down, to what she didn't say. This made me feel that my childhood was moving away from me, steadily burying itself in the past like a clam until the day came when all that was left to remind me that I had once been a child would be a hole in the sand. The teacher, Maggie Mulloy, agreed I could go along with Louis if I would sit quietly at a table at the back. So I did, moving unnoticed between bookshelf and sandbox where I made landscapes too strange to be recognized before they were flattened beneath a boat or a wagon. When Father Murphy, who doubled as inspector, visited the school, he stood behind me and asked me to read from the book in my hand, which I had memorized from listening to the teacher. He allowed me to go on at some length before he reached down and turned the grade three reader right side up. Without anything being said I knew that until then Miss Mulloy and the other children had underestimated me.

Louis didn't like school and wanted to quit but persisted in order to keep me company. He was different from my other brothers and though he had the same sharp features and shrubby hair, he didn't have their scrappiness. He had a loose dreamy way about him, a gaze that wandered off and settled on whatever he fancied. Something in his nature resisted being tied down or boxed in, which was partly why I adored him.

Miss Mulloy was used to fishermen's sons pining to be on the water. A lighthouse keeper's daughter, she herself felt the pull of the sea. While she did not expect most of her students to finish their schooling, she hoped that at least they would learn to read. She wanted them to have the power that came from being able to read bills of sale and written agreements. A passionate Newfoundlander, she knew their history was one of handing over to others what was rightfully theirs. In June, before she left the Drook to marry Wilfred Hunt in St. John's, she marked *failed* on Louis's grade three report card, then put her head down on the desk and wept.

She did not weep for Aurora, though she knew that like many fishermen's daughters, she might leave school without earning her diploma because she was needed at home. At least, this time next year, when it came time to make up Aurora's report card, the new teacher would write *excellent* beside *pass*. The child was already a reader and was utterly unlike the other girls who sat in Maggie's class. At five years of age, she was so quiet and self-contained that it seemed she harboured a wise old woman inside. The other children, contemptuous of her size and age, ignored her. From the day Father Murphy inspected the school, Maggie found herself drawn to Aurora, admiring her for her plucky independence and for her ability to amuse herself alone without giving any sign that, except for Louis, the other children were slighting her. Maggie found it impossible to predict what would happen to a self-reliant, clever child like Aurora, a girl who when she became older, might never fit in. Would she move away from the Drook? Would she go to Trepassey or St. John's? Would she eventually disappear into Canada or the Boston States? Would she, in a manner of speaking, drift away on the sea to the place she had come from?

Louis never asked these questions. He took it for granted that Aurora would stay in the Drook. His wonder was centred not on what would happen to her, but on Aurora herself. He marvelled at how delicately made she was. When she ran along the hilltop, white hair catching the breeze, she might have been a kite the moment it lifts into the yearning blue. He was fascinated by her eyes, which made her seem to be looking at him with one eye while the other one was looking somewhere else. Louis's cousins were wary of Aurora. Paddy St. Croix claimed that Aurora's eyes proved she had the power to lure you away so that you could be lost for days, a comment that Louis answered with his fists.

Another thing Louis noticed about Aurora was that she was never cold. She could wander the hills bare-limbed and never shiver; she could wade through ice water without turning blue. And she had a way of being quiet that was downright odd. Louis would be trouting in the stream, Aurora right behind him without him knowing until he turned. He would be scouring the beach for driftwood unaware that she was watching him from the rocks. There was also the matter of the fox. When Aurora was about seven, she made friends with a red fox. It was shocking to see her walking with the fox as if it was a dog then crawling into its den.

One day Aurora came upon a bird that had blown in from up south on the tail end of a hurricane. It was lying on the beach, its neck limp and its feathers bedraggled. She put it in her lunch pail and carried it to school. Not even Miss Power, who had replaced Miss Mulloy, knew what it was. She said it most definitely wasn't a parrot. It was finer, more delicately made, with scarlet wing bars, a purple breast and a golden tuft on its head. Aurora brought the bird home and made a nest for it inside an old navy blue hat with a torn veil, and set it beneath the stove. Though he would never have allowed his sons to keep the bird, when Francis came in for his dinner, he noticed the hat and lifting it up, tenderly stroked the bird. In no time at all Aurora was walking around with the bird on her shoulder. It stayed until the moment, weeks later, when Louis looked out the window and saw her standing on top of the hill behind Uncle Bernie's, the bird on her wrist. She lifted her arm and flung the bird into the air. It rose, the sunlight catching its wings, and flew south following the edge of the sea.

In April when Aurora was nine or ten—no one knew for sure—a large polar bear strolled off the ice and came ashore in the Drook just as she and Louis were at the table after school having their tea and bread. Merla was sitting in the corner braiding a rag rug. They were the only three at home, Jerome having signed on to a sealer working in the Gulf and Francis and Ben having gone to cut wood. Louis had left the back door ajar after he had brought in the drinking water, but Merla didn't notice because the rubber sheeting, which had been nailed over the doorway since Aurora's rescue, kept out the draft. There was the squeal of an unoiled hinge. When Louis looked up and saw a white bear come straight through the slit in the sheeting, carrying the stink of carrion between its claws, he picked up the bread knife—he would give his life to save Aurora's if it was required.

Merla rose in the corner and lifting her chair, held it like a shield.

The bear stood in the kitchen and lifted its snout, sniffing for meat.

By now Aurora was on her feet. Slowly she raised her hand and pointed to the door.

"*Go*," she said.

Miraculously, the bear shifted his hindquarters and went out the way he had come. And that was that. Aurora sat down and calmly finished her tea while Louis, still carrying the bread knife, reached through the slit and hooked the door. Merla sank to her knees and thanked the Blessed Mother for her merciful intercession. Then she looked out the window for the bear.

The bear was not to be seen, having already left the Drook. He was on his way to Portugal Cove South where he lost no time in ripping the door off a storage shed to get at a ham inside. He then continued to Trepassey, where he entered a house by leaning on the front-room window with both paws until it broke. Ignoring the jagged glass, he stepped onto the wine velour sofa, knocking over the coal oil lamp, which set fire to the Hickeys' wool rug. The fire must have alarmed the bear for he turned and left the house the way he had come. When Catherine Hickey came downstairs with the baby, the rug was burning and the bear was ambling toward the harbour.

The story of how Aurora St. Croix ordered the bear from the kitchen changed the Drook's view of her. Alma no longer talked about Aurora being a changeling and instead claimed that the maid was meant to become a Bride of Christ. By using the girl to banish the bear, the Holy Mother had given a sign that she had been chosen by God. Louis didn't believe this for a second; when Aurora grew up she wouldn't be marrying Christ, but himself.

The story also preceded Aurora's arrival at school in Portugal Cove South. She had finished grade five in the Drook and in the fall both she and Louis went to school in the Cove. Because he had been held back again, they were both in grade six and on fine mornings left the house at seven-thirty, each of them carrying a bucket of lassy bread, and followed the path along the headland, arriving at school by eight-thirty. When winter storms roared down from the north, they stayed home. If the road wasn't drifted in, Francis sometimes took them by horse and wagon.

Merla was pleased that Aurora liked school. It was just as well she was occupied with books for the maid was useless around the house. It wasn't that she refused to work but that she couldn't keep her mind on a household task. If she was told to wash the dishes, she pretended the plates and cups were birds or fish and would play for hours, her hands in greasy water long after it had grown cold. If she was told to peel potatoes for dinner, she would remove large chunks of vegetable with the skin. She seemed unable to separate it from the rest and was so slow that the fish would be ready to go in the pan before the potatoes were set to boil. If she was told to bring in the wash, she might get as far as folding three shirts before she would notice a rabbit running to its burrow and follow it, or she might stop to watch sea ducks skidding across the pond. It was much easier for Merla to do the housework if the youngster was out of the way in school.

Despite the girl's absentmindedness, her pale quiet, her way of disappearing and reappearing, Merla and Francis doted on Aurora. They loved the way she laid her hand, soft as a wing, on their shoulders, the gentle coolness of her touch raising a pleasant shiver to their skin. They loved the way she brushed and combed their hair, brushing Francis's springy grey hair until he fell asleep in the chair, combing Merla's brown hair into a roll or a crown. She wasn't interested in arranging her own hair, which was fine and straight, but she liked Merla to brush it before weaving it into a long white braid.

Merla told Francis that Aurora's combing and brushing was an excuse for her to touch them, that she was a youngster who liked to be petted and stroked. When Merla and Francis were alone of an evening, one of them would remark how fortunate they were that the girl had washed onto their shore. Even Francis spoke about Aurora's arrival in this way though he himself had rowed her in from the Banks.

Jerome and Ben were fond of Aurora in their way but their noses were out of joint because of the way she was allowed to read for hours or to go off wandering somewhere. You couldn't permit that in a maid since it made her useless later on. No man wanted a wife whose head was awash with fanciful thoughts. A man needed a wife who would hoe the garden and make fish.

Life in the Drook was good. The caplin sculled plentifully on the beach each spring and the inshore traps teemed with fish, with the fortunate result that this year Francis didn't have to sign on to a banking schooner—at fifty-four he didn't want the rigours of off-shore fishing. Though she didn't look it, Merla was fifty-five. She was a Bevis from Clam Cove. None of the Bevis women went grey, but the Bevis men, well, they were bald by the time they were thirty. Besides the cow and her calf, Merla kept a pig and a few laying hens. Jerome had bought himself some sheep; he was looking to marry Brenda Martin from Long Beach if she'd have him. The Irish along the coast still looked askance at the St. Croixs though Francis's fore-bears had been fishing this coast long before the Irish and were buried in the same sanctified soil. Using wood from the *Kristioni*, which was wrecked off Cripple Cove, Jerome started building Brenda and himself a house in the Drook near the landwash.

Louis was moved into Jerome's bedroom, giving Aurora a room of her own. On her bed was a quilt trimmed with the tasselled rope that had been used to secure her cradle. It wasn't rope exactly. Rope was coarse and rough whereas this was soft and silky, two pieces of golden cord Merla had sewn around the edge of the quilt.

Aurora entered grade seven, leaving Louis behind in grade six. Miss Kelland, their teacher, was sharp-tongued and strict. She had no patience with a sixteen-year-old who spent most of his time staring out the window. If he wouldn't apply himself in school, he was better off working on the water, especially since most of what she taught went over his head. Louis was both ashamed and pleased that Aurora was so far ahead of him and for the sake of being with her, stuck it out until Christmas, but not even she could hold him after that and he found ways of avoiding school: he had to lay rabbit slips, he had to cut firewood and spell it home on his back, he had to repair the fish flakes before spring. Aurora now walked to school alone. Sitting unnoticed at the back of the classroom, she read *A Child's Garden of Verses* and *Alice's Adventures in Wonderland*. The winter she was in grade eight it was often too stormy to walk to school and during the two months Louis and his brothers were swiling in the Gulf, she stayed home. Because there were no large seal herds on the Southern Shore, if fishermen wanted to make money swiling, they signed on to a ship that took them to the ice, handing over the seals they slaughtered in exchange for cash.

In late April, soon after the St. Croix brothers returned from the Gulf, they went to Mistaken Point looking for seals of their own. At this time of year there was often a scattering of greys on the rocks. Jerome had it in mind to get a pelt for Brenda. He wanted to surprise her with a warm muff, boots, whatever Alma could make—when she wasn't having one of her spells, she could turn her hand to such things and was the best needlewoman between Trepassey and Ferryland. Louis wanted Alma to make something pretty for Aurora. Though he wasn't sure she would accept something made from a pelt, it was the only thing he could think to give her. When the brothers reached the cliffs above the point, they saw a half-dozen greys on the rocks below. Louis had brought along a chunk of drifted timber for a club.

The sea was a deep restive blue, ultramarine—it didn't take much sun to bring up the colour. Aurora had noticed the colour on her way to school. There was something harsh and brutal about the blue. There were no shades in between as there usually were, no pools of grey cast by shifting clouds, no rifflings of green from a rush of wind, nothing at all to soften the colour.

Louis scravelled over the rocks on his way down to the seals while out of habit, Jerome lingered on the cliff taking time to size up the water. He saw that farther out it was heaving against the horizon, a sign that deep in the bowels of the ocean, two massive currents were churning and thrashing, struggling for space. Every few minutes their backs smashed the surface then disappeared, leaving a serpentine ridge of foam behind. About a thousand feet out, two rollers broke loose from the mass of heaving water and charging alongside each other headed for the point. They ran parallel for some distance before one of the rollers pulled ahead of the other and it seemed to Jerome that it would hit the rocks first. Then he saw the other wave rise up and engulf it. Now a sickening wall of steep water was making straight for Louis.

Jerome cupped his hands over his mouth. "Louis! Get up here! There's a big bugger coming! Get up!" Louis was far below on the rocks. All that was between him and the water was a sloping shelf of slippery shale.

Louis didn't hear his brother. He wasn't looking at the water. He was looking at the pup left behind on the shelf after its mother and the other seals had taken to the water. Louis could see Aurora carrying her books and pencils to school in the skin of the seal. He could see her stroking its silky fur and could feel her hand on his arm. The rocks were wet but what odds, the tide was going out. He would be across the shelf and back before he could say jackrabbit. Holding his club in one hand, Louis moved toward the pup.

"Louis! You stupid frigger, get your arse up here!" Jerome picked up a rock and pitched it so it would bounce in front of his brother. The rock landed in the water but it caught Louis's attention. He looked up and for the first time saw the wave. Jerome saw Louis's lips form an astonished O as panic and indecision rode across his face.

Turning his back on the rolling wave, Louis looked at the narrow cleft at his feet and stories of people being saved from a wave by a button or a shoe caught between rocks flitted through his mind. If he jammed his foot into the cleft, would it hold? He looked at an opening between two rocks about thirty feet back at the base of the cliff. The opening was just wide enough to grip his leg. He decided to run for it and gained five feet before he lost his footing on the slippery shelf. The last thing he heard was the hiss of water before the rogue picked him up and slammed him against the rocks. The wave crashed and seethed, spreading over the entire shelf, leaving Louis and the pup lifeless in a glacial foam. The wave retreated then returned to suck up the bodies, shaking them like seaweed before pulling them under.

All this Jerome watched from the cliff top, desperate to rescue his brother but powerless to help. It was not only foolish but suicidal to go down on the rocks until he got a fix on where Louis was. Jerome scravelled over the uppermost rocks, pulling out junks of timber to throw in the water when Louis came up. His brother couldn't swim, none in his family could. Stupid friggers, they should have brought rope. Long Beach was more than a mile away, too far to go for rope. Jerome kept scanning the water but there was no sign of Louis. The minutes crawled by, how many? five, ten? before Jerome saw Louis surface about fifty feet offshore. He was face down, not an arm or leg moving. Jerome heaved his club as far as it would go. It splashed five feet in front of his brother, but he didn't move. Jerome knew his efforts were useless, that Louis was dead. Nevertheless he couldn't stop himself from trying to save him. In a frenzy of grief and rage Jerome chucked out one junk after another until there were no more to throw. The wood bobbed uselessly on the water. While he watched, Louis sank, pulled down by the undertow until he vanished. Jerome stood vigil for more than an hour but his brother never reappeared. He stood vigil, though like all fishermen he knew that a body taken by the sea was rarely given back.

After Louis died, I didn't return to school. I couldn't concentrate on my lessons and I was needed at home. For the second time in my life I was required to reinvent myself. It is my opinion, albeit one formed from a considerable distance, that most of us have several lives. When we are overcome by misfortune, we lose all sense of who we are, the knowledge of ourselves deserting us when we need it most, disappearing from our world like exploding stars. Think of those who crawled out of the trenches of war with identities other than their own, or those who survived the great sealing disaster only to discover that they had left a part of themselves behind on the ice. Think of the people who emerge from the wreckage of a car or a plane or as, in my case, a ship, unable to explain the loss of their former selves.

Young as I was, I lost myself a second time when Louis died. His death stripped my inner landscape so that it was empty of any growing thing and became a wasteland gouged with confusion and pain. At the time I was too numb to find words for my loss. With Merla lying in bed, taking herself through the sorrowful mysteries from dawn to dusk, I did her chores, going about the work like a somnambulist. Come June when Francis, Jerome and Ben returned to the water, I went to the landwash after breakfast to make fish. No one had to tell me what to do. As a youngster I had often watched Merla sprinkle salt on the split fish before spreading it on the flakes, and later dipping the dried fish in the water puncheon to wash off the salt. When I finished making fish, I milked the cow and fed the pig and chickens. Then I went inside and peeled potatoes for dinner and made a pie. On Mondays I did the wash. On Tuesdays and Fridays I baked bread, though not very well—I never did learn the knack of baking bread. In the evenings I went up to the meadow to hoe. I was reinventing myself through women's work. When she noticed, Merla would remark on the change in me. She did this mournfully as if she was not only grieving for Louis but also for the maid I no longer was. It seemed to me that the sea was made of Merla's tears. She took Louis's death harder than any of us. Or so it appeared. Francis kept on working. That was how he grieved. Merla stayed in her bed from April to August. When the sorrow lodged in her head, she was blinded with pain, when it lodged in her belly, she rocked and howled, when it lodged in her heart, she could not speak.

Francis St. Croix had rescued scores of people from the wreckage of ships. He had saved Bob Bartlett when the *Corisande* hit the rocks in 1897, twelve years before Bartlett helped Peary reach the Pole—it was Bob's first shipwreck and he would survive eleven more before eventually dying of pneumonia, a lonely old bachelor in New York. Francis had rescued passengers and crew from the *Kristianiafjord*, and using a bosun's chair had saved the crew from the *Argo* and the *Kristioni*. He had been lowered over cliffs to retrieve corpses and body parts from other wrecks for burial in shallow earth graves, but until now he had never had a son whose grave was the sea. Louis's death shredded Francis's heart until it hung in such tatters that no amount of mending could ever make it whole. Whenever he thought of Louis and felt the wince of pain, he turned away from his family so they couldn't see his face. A demonstration of sorrow was something he couldn't afford, not with his wife lying upstairs. It wasn't that sorrow was a luxury but that it underpinned everything he held dear. For Merla's sake, he never let on that his survival—by which he meant putting his feet on the cold floor every blessed morning—depended on hers.

He also wanted to protect Aurora. Here she was, hardly older than a maid and already she had lost a family and a brother. She and Louis had been close, maybe too close for sister and brother, but there was no point thinking about that now. The fact was that they had preferred one another to anyone else and Louis made up for the friends she didn't have. Francis was troubled about the way Aurora sleepwalked through her work, by the fact that she never smiled and seldom spoke. Often she did not reply to a question, not because she was being crooked or sulky but because she seemed not to hear. When Francis hugged her shoulders, he might have been taking hold of a chair for all the response he got.

Though thick with grief, Jerome and Ben continued to go on the water. After the work was done, their women took them in. On Sundays Ben went to the Cove to court Bridgit Hartery. Jerome's courtship of Brenda Martin had advanced to the point where they planned to marry in late fall after the fish had been sold. Jerome spent evenings building their house, returning to his bedroom after the sun went down, by which time he didn't have to look at Louis's empty side of the bed. Jerome had nightmares of being trapped on the cliff top unable to save his brother from the wave. Jerome's mouth opened but no sound came out. He tried to lift his arms but they were held fast to the bed and he couldn't breathe. When he finally surfaced and caught his breath, he sat up and waited for his heart to steady. Night after night he had a version of this dream and became convinced that the dreams wouldn't stop until he was lying beside Brenda in their new house. How he longed to burrow into the warm flesh of her abundant body. Brenda was in all ways a large woman, a generous, kind-hearted thoughtful woman. No one had to tell her to carry custard and soup to Merla, or to bring him a jug of tea and a slab of pie when he was working on their house. No one had to tell her to help Aurora when she tried to carry a yaffle of fish that she could hardly lift.

Jerome often commented to Brenda on the change in Aurora. It seemed that overnight she'd become a woman. The transformation since Louis's death was nothing short of amazing. Was it sorrow? Aurora was so quiet that it was hard to tell if she was feeling the same sorrow as himself. She must feel something for she and Louis had stuck together like burrs. Now that Aurora was sharing the work, Jerome allowed his fondness for her to show. There was no more of this roaming the hills and hiding in thickets. There was no more vanishing into the tuck with a fox. Wherever you looked, Aurora could be seen doing one chore or another.

Ben also welcomed the change in Aurora. He was reassured by the fact that she now looked almost as ordinary as other women. Her skin had lost its pallor—her face was tanned and seemed darker than it was because of the whiteness of her hair. Her hands were reddened from soap and salt; her fingers were criss-crossed with nicks and cuts. She had taken to wearing one of Merla's oversized smocks made from flour sacking and a kerchief around her head. What a relief it was to have a sister—at last Ben admitted Aurora was his sister—he didn't have to apologize for or try to explain. True, she was quieter than was natural but it was better that she mind her own business rather than other people's as was often the case with women.

One morning in early August, Merla rose from her bed, dressed and went downstairs. The men were on the water and Aurora was at the flakes, which meant Merla had the house to herself. For the first time in months, she set bread to rise. She knew that she had been resurrected as someone else, not because her hair had turned grey and she had lost weight but because she was hollow inside. She had been emptied, all the grief and pain wrung out of her until only the shell of who she'd been remained.

But this morning when she lifted the blind, she saw the Virgin herself rising from the sunlit sea and she felt something gritty inside the shell. It was minuscule, a tiny grain of hopefulness, but it was enough to start her thinking about supper. She would make

Francis's favourite meal, fish and brewis. Dear Francis, who had never once complained about her lying upstairs. Not one word of anger or reproach though she had done nothing to help him through his grief. She would make it up to him, she would. Louis would want it so. From now on Merla would often interpret her good intentions as intercessions from Louis.

Merla had left her bed just when her help was needed most. The summer catches had been so bountiful that Aurora had fallen behind in curing the fish and needed another pair of hands. Throughout August the women worked side by side, taking advantage of fine drying weather. Some afternoons they took their pails to pick bakeapples on the Barrens, that vast wind-shorn land which, away from the sea, became the horizon. Later, they returned for blueberries and in September for partridgeberries. The berries were made into jams and fillings and stored in jars in the space beneath the trapdoor in the kitchen.

That fall, Francis and his sons delivered over five hundred quintals of salt cod to Baird's, the fish merchant in Trepassey. After they had settled their account, making their boat safe for another year, there was credit enough to set up Jerome and Brenda with a bed, dresser, table and chairs so they could marry—a good year for fish was a good year for marrying. Once the fish was delivered, Jerome and Ben found time to drag the sea bottom with a grapple and a wire basket attached to a steel rope. The brothers wanted cash, Jerome for his house and Ben to convince the Harterys to let him marry Bridgit. The Harterys had money but they refused to hand over their daughter until Ben had proved he could support her. On fine days the brothers scavenged the water where ships had gone down: the *Loyalist* and the *Tolstoy* in Bob's Cove; the *Laurentian* and the *Helen Isabel* off Mistaken Point; the *Glace Bay* off the Drook; the *Cyril* in Portugal Cove. Since they'd begun tonging two years ago they had brought up a sextant, an anchor, a large quantity of barrel hoops, two water tanks, a kettle, a brass compass, six washbasins, twelve plates, a brass doorknob, a coal box, two fish tubs, four shovels, all but one without handles, and a metal picture frame that when scrubbed clean looked like gilded paint. Merla was given the frame, Francis the sextant, Aurora the doorknob. The plates were divided between the brothers; Ben kept the compass and Jerome the kettle. The rest went into a pile that would eventually be taken to St. John's where scrap merchants would pay cash in hand. In addition to feathering their nests, the brothers hoped to get enough money to buy a motor for their boat.

With the brothers away so much on the water, Aurora worked alongside Francis, fertilizing the potato beds with caplin, spreading sheep manure on the garden, digging and storing vegetables for winter. Aurora refused to accompany Francis when he hunted partridge or shot eider ducks. She would use the pitchfork to turn hay but not to spear codfish up out of the dory.

In early November Jerome and Brenda went to Trepassey and were married by Father Murphy. Francis hitched the old horse to the wagon and covered the last of the fish with canvas before the St. Croixs climbed on top. The canvas, which had been the hatch cover on the *Helen Isabel*, protected their church clothes as well as the fish which had to be delivered in prime condition. After the wedding Merla stayed in Trepassey with her sister Win. Not wanting to be parted from Francis for long, she only stayed the week, but it was enough for her to learn how to hook wool mats. As Win pointed out, using wool made more sense than braiding rags, since Merla had all those sheep close at hand.

That winter Merla hooked mats as if her life depended on it. Every design showed either the Blessed Virgin or Jesus Christ—who bore a startling resemblance to Louis. There was Mary beaming the dories safely home. There was Christ stilling the waters, filling the fishermen's nets. There was the Holy Mother on the ice glistening like a pillar of salt while her Son washed the swilers' feet. There was Christ in the window above the table around which the St. Croixs knelt to say their rosary. The mats were so cheerful and bright that to look at them you would never guess that their joyfulness had risen from the ashes of grief.

At Father Murphy's urging, Aurora enrolled in a correspondence course using materials sent from St. John's. In the evenings while Francis dozed in his chair by the stove and Merla hooked mats, Aurora sat at the table by the coal oil lamp and learned about the kings and queens of England. Though the St. Croix forebears were Bretons, there were no French books in the house save a battered prayer book. Except for the Wars of the Roses and Joan of Arc, nothing Aurora read shed any light on the St. Croix ancestors. The following winter Aurora took three correspondence courses and finished grade nine. Two years were to pass before she earned her grade ten. By then Aurora was thought to be about seventeen. Her pale fragility had entirely disappeared. In its stead was a strong young woman. The contours of her body were more boyish than womanly, but fine-boned all the same. She was small and slender and would remain so all her life. Her white hair hung down her back in a single white braid which she sometimes tied with coloured wool. Her habit of seeming to gaze in two places at once remained, as did the differing colour of her eyes.

As Francis told Merla, Aurora had always liked to stare at the sea but her sea gazing seemed more apparent now that she was grown. A fisherman all his life, Francis couldn't imagine not living close to the water, couldn't imagine living in a country that wasn't equally made of land, sky and sea. It wasn't that he admired the sea: he respected it, yes, all fishermen did, but the sea wasn't something he admired. It was something that provided work and kept his family fed, but he didn't want to be looking at it after he came home. He would no more sit in the window and admire the view of the sea than he would fly to the moon. When he was snug inside his house, he turned his back on the sea except when he wanted to size up the weather. Whatever it was that Aurora found so fascinating was a mystery to him.

Aurora's fascination was based on wonder. No matter how calm the sea, whenever she was near it, she never took her eyes off the water. She watched it constantly, scanning for waves and currents, for ships and storms, for whales and ice, for sweepings of colour and tricks of light. She was fascinated by the way the sea constantly reinvented itself through motion, never staying still but always shifting and spreading, gathering itself in then letting go, making patterns and shapes as varied and infinite as burning stars.

The summer Aurora was eighteen—so Merla said—she was watching the water when she saw a dory bobbing on the waves beyond the cove. She ran to tell Francis before the boat could drift by or run aground on the rocks. Aurora wouldn't go on the water, so he rowed out and brought the dory in and together they dragged it above the landwash. The boat looked new, its boards freshly painted yellow, blue and red, and it was empty; there wasn't so much as a water jug inside, not an oar or a pail. Francis said that the dory's colours showed it was from St. Pierre.

"Can we keep it?"

"Not yet, maid. We must put the word around and wait."

Jerome and Ben carried the dory to a grassy spot near the house where they could keep an eye on it. It was Francis's wish that it would never be claimed. He wanted to give the dory to his sons, but there was no point in giving it to them if one day it would be taken back and he must wait to see if a fisherman from St. Pierre came to claim it. It was the honourable thing to do, especially since the forebears of the St. Pierre fishermen were from Brittany like his own. The fact that Francis's ancestors were Bretons meant little to him. Despite what the Irish might think, he was a Newfoundlander born and bred.

Though she feared the sea, Aurora sometimes had to fight the urge to fling herself off the cliff and into the water. This wasn't a suicidal impulse brought on by Louis's death, but something quite different. The height of the cliffs filled her with an apprehension that had to be broken, or avoided. Because she didn't know how to break it, she stayed well back from the edge of the cliff, watching the sea, looking not for Louis, but for something she couldn't identify, something unpredictable and surprising. Perhaps she expected to learn something of her origins. Perhaps she expected a piece of her early past to come floating by on an ice pan. When she was younger, Francis had often related the story of her rescue from the ice. He had made the story so magical that she thought of it as a fairy tale, which it was.

By now Father Murphy was encouraging Aurora to become a teaching sister. The Lord knew how much the church needed scholars like her to turn young minds toward reading. Francis didn't see Aurora's future in the church but he was grateful to the priest for encouraging her studies. There was no doubt that the correspondence courses had helped to bring her around. Gone was the vacant look in her eyes and the wooden way of going about the chores. Now she smiled when he put his arm around her. Some evenings she would comb and brush their hair.

Merla didn't see their daughter becoming a nun either. "Aurora will marry a Frenchman," she said. "The deliverance of the dory is a sign that she will be claimed by a man from St. Pierre." Merla liked to think that Aurora had been saved from the sea so that she could marry someone who had the same forebears as Francis. Ignoring Aurora's refusal to go on the water, Merla hooked a mat showing her daughter standing in a dory while the Frenchman rowed her seaward toward the setting sun. "Just you wait," Merla said to Francis, "One day her husband will come for his boat." She put the mat inside the battered frame, which in spite of having been dragged across the sea bottom bore remnants of gold paint, and hung it on the wall at the foot of Aurora's bed.

Months passed and the Frenchman did not come. The following summer Francis gave the dory to his sons and Aurora went berry-picking and met Tom Mulloy.

It was a clear day in July when Aurora and Merla took their pails, one of them containing a jug of water and buttered bread, and walked along the road toward Long Beach. Halfway there, they left the road and entered the Barrens. There, amid the cushioning green, millions of bakeapples shone like orange stars, spreading inland as far as the eye could see, past the blue pond water to the infinite rise beyond. They were a galaxy whose constellations changed as handfuls of berries tumbled into pails. No matter how far the women walked inland, they were never out of sight of the sea. Above, clouds drifted across the blue, riding on the breeze. The breeze kept down the flies. Not that flies troubled Aurora, but they pestered Merla something fierce. Otherwise berry-picking was bliss. There was no better way to spend a summer day than hunkered down in rubber boots picking bakeapples—the berries grew best in boggy ground, the same bogs where purple iris grew. At noon the women sat on a large rock to eat their bread, Merla gazing inland toward the distant hill, Aurora toward the sea.

Merla wouldn't go berrying when thick fog rolled in and the air was windless and damp, for then the flies made the outing pure misery. But Aurora went out, picking steadily until her pails were full. At such times a fox would appear and watch from the disappearing edge where the land became mysterious and unknowable. Once when Aurora was sitting inside an ancient circle of stones, she held a bread crust on her palm for the fox. The fox took a step toward it then swerved away, startled by the clink of a pail handle. Aurora looked up and saw a strange creature emerge from the mist. Whether he was young or old was impossible to say. He had his jacket collar turned up and a scarf wound around his face in a way that reminded Aurora of a picture of an anteater she had once seen in a school book.

The anteater spoke. In a deep, melodious voice, he said:

I met a lady in the meads,
Full beautiful, a faery's child.

And Aurora replied:

Her hair was long, her foot was light,
And her eyes were wild.

There was nothing self-conscious about her response—she'd made no connection between the verse and herself. She had merely dipped into the well of memory and lifted it out. She could have recited the remaining seven stanzas had the anteater spoken the next verse, but he didn't. Instead he unwound his scarf and said, "You must be the girl from the Drook, Francis's daughter."

"I'm not a girl any more than you are an anteater. I'm Aurora St. Croix."

The man laughed. "So you are." He removed his cap. "And I'm Tom Mulloy."

With his head uncovered, Aurora saw that he was about her brothers' age though he didn't look at all like them. Jerome and Ben were wiry and short with tightly curled reddish hair and tidy features. This man was tall and gangly, his lank brown hair flopping over eyes the colour of wet beach stones. His nose was large and beaky, his lower lip fleshy as an earthworm drowned by rain. He was not a handsome man. But he had a relaxed unhurried way about him that Aurora was drawn to. She recognized him as someone at ease with himself. When he crouched down and began picking berries in a manner that suggested they should pick together, she crouched nearby. He was twice her size and they were alone on the Barrens but she wasn't afraid. She trusted him, in part because he seemed familiar. They worked side by side in silence until he asked what poetry she had read.

The question caught her off guard. He assumed she read poetry, which she no longer did since the only book in the St. Croix house was the water-stained prayer book from the *Emmeline*. She didn't tell him that except for Merla and herself, no one in the house could read. She told him that she remembered the poetry she had learned at school.

Tom said his favourite poet was Gerard Manley Hopkins.

Margaret, are you grieving
Over Goldengrove unleaving?

Leaves, like the things of man, you
With your fresh thoughts, care for, can you?

He spoke these words while continuing to pick which made it seem that speaking poetry was as natural as work.

"Go on."

Ah! as the heart grows older
It will come to such sights colder
By and by, nor spare a sigh
Though worlds of wanwood leafmeal lie...

He sat back on his heels. "Would you like to borrow a book of his poems?"

"I would."

After Gerard Manley Hopkins, it was Robert Louis Stevenson, the lighthouse builder's son.

I will make my kitchen, and you shall keep your room,
Where white flows the river and bright blows the broom
And you shall wash your linen and keep your body white
In rainfall at morning and dewfall at night.

After Robert Louis Stevenson, it was Emily Dickinson.

The brain is deeper than the sea,
For hold them, blue to blue,
The one the other will absorb,
As sponges, buckets do.

Aurora was too shy to look at Tom, to risk letting him see what must be written in her face. She was overwhelmed by the fact that this stranger sensed in her a longing for poetry, a longing she had kept to herself until now. She admired the way he seemed to pull verses from the vastness of the Barrens as if he thought they were floating there, waiting to be spoken. She could feel herself being pulled, slowly and surely, into his mind.

Merla was the first to see Tom the next evening riding his bicycle into the Drook—all along the coast people were riding bicycles salvaged from the *Orion*. Through the kitchen window Merla saw Tom catch sight of Aurora hoeing potatoes up in the meadow. He put down the bicycle and climbed the hill, a book under his arm. It was unusual to have a Mulloy come calling. They went by on the road but they seldom lingered for a chat. The Mulloys never had much to do with the St. Croixs except when they wanted men to unload the supply ship, or came to trade flour or sugar for pig or mutton. Once business was finished, they went on home. The Mulloys were different from most people along the shore. They were a bookish crowd, educated people who worked for a regular wage. Jim and Eleanor Mulloy had been keeping the light for years. But Jim was getting on, he was older than Merla. There were four children, two daughters, both married and gone. One had taught school in the Drook for a spell. There was another son besides Tom who was still at the Cape. No doubt he and Tom would take over the light after Jim retired. That was usually the way with lighthouse keepers, they kept the jobs in the family.

Three evenings in July, Tom bicycled to the Drook to pick up one book and deliver another. At that time of day, Aurora would be up in the hay meadow or down by the flakes. From a distance Merla watched Aurora wipe her hands on her smock and walk with Tom toward the house. How small she looked beside him! Merla made tea and invited him in. He turned out to be an easy man to talk to, not at all standoffish or stuck up, and though he wasn't bred to fish he was able to make conversation about the weather and the different shipwrecks in which Francis had been involved. Francis had a collection of telescopes and compasses from places like Spain, Italy, Norway and the Netherlands. Some of these valuables had come from salvaging wrecks, others had been given to him by grateful seamen whose lives he had saved. He had a small bronze bell given to him by Bob Bartlett after Francis rescued him from the *Corisande*. Bartlett had rescued seamen himself. Francis told Tom that when Bob was skippering the *Leopard*, he struck the Horn Head rocks near Cappahayden, but by using the wreck of the *Delmer*, he'd got 151 men safely ashore. These were the same rocks that took the *Florizel*, the ship that carried hundreds of Newfoundlanders to an early death at Beaumont Hamel during the Great War.

In August Merla invited Tom for a Lady Day supper of new potatoes and fresh cod to mark the end of summer fishing. He arrived dressed up, so it seemed to Merla, having replaced his plaid flannel shirt for one with cuffs. Pure white it was too, as if it had been scrubbed with lye.

On September afternoons when the house was tidy and the fish had been turned, Merla and Aurora went to the Barrens to pick partridgeberries. Now that the flies had been killed off by frosty nights, Merla could stay out even if the wind was down. There was no fog that month. The air was sharp and clear, the finest kind for berry-picking and making fish. Sometimes Tom appeared with his pails but, as Merla was amused to notice, he remained off to one side until she moved away herself. Only then would Tom settle down to pick beside Aurora. They didn't talk much, or so it seemed to Merla. Sometimes she caught sight of Tom on his haunches, staring at Aurora while she picked, unaware she was being watched. Once Merla saw Tom's hand reach out as if to touch Aurora's hair but just as quickly it was withdrawn. Merla didn't tell Francis any of this. Her husband liked Tom but he might think less of him if he knew he was out berry-picking in the afternoons. Some men, Merla knew, picked berries but her husband and sons regarded it as women's work.

At the end of October, Tom Mulloy bicycled to the Drook to announce that he was leaving for St. John's and wouldn't be back until December. Merla was outside sweeping the step when he rode up, as usual carrying a book. Aurora was inside washing the supper dishes. Merla tiptoed inside, past Francis sleeping in his chair and sent Aurora out to Tom. While she dried the dishes, Merla looked through the window and saw the pair walk, not down to the water but up the hill. She watched them pass the sheep pound and disappear. They returned after dark, Aurora carrying the book. What had they been doing out there all that time? Aurora had left wearing only a cotton dress and it was a frosty night. Not that she was likely to be bothered by the cold. As expected, she didn't explain what she'd been up to with Tom Mulloy. She merely said he would be staying with his sister in St. John's and that he'd given her another book to read.

A fairy maid, Tom thought when he saw Aurora St. Croix appear through the mist on the Barrens the day they met, *my child bride*, though until that moment he hadn't been all that interested in marrying. He enjoyed the company of women but looking for a wife seemed like too much trouble, something he might eventually do if he felt inclined. Tom was a loner who preferred his own company. He knew that he was too bookish and therefore too strange for the women along the shore but was unwilling to change his ways. The women liked him well enough—so they told him—but were inclined to pass him by in favour of someone else. Not that it bothered Tom. If a woman had shown a romantic interest in him, he would have run a mile. When he met Aurora, he fell so hard and so fast that he couldn't trust himself to think straight and went off to St. John's to decide what to do.

For two months Tom lived with his sister Maggie and her husband Wilfred in their house on Circular Road. He didn't tell either of his sisters—Ruth lived a few streets from Maggie—that he was hopelessly in love, that he had fallen for a woman eight years younger than himself who all these years had been living in the Drook. Remembering the story about the baby Francis St. Croix was said to have found on the Banks, a girl who later sat in Maggie's classroom, soon after his arrival in St. John's, Tom steered the conversation around to the year his sister had taught in the Drook. Maggie said she remembered Aurora as an extraordinary child, not at all like the others, and was surprised to learn that she was still on the Southern Shore.

Tom's sisters assumed he had come to town to find himself a wife and he did nothing to disabuse them of the notion, putting on his new black suit and attending Mr. Pushie's ballroom dancing classes, escorting women to supper dances and the talking pictures, accepting their invitations to card parties and tea. Though he enjoyed the company of these lively and intelligent women, they held no romantic interest for him and when, after eight weeks in St. John's, he bought a copy of Emily Dickinson's poetry at the YWCA's book sale, he knew he had made up his mind. At Ayre's he bought a pair of silk stockings, at Eagan's half a dozen California oranges. To find a Valentine out of season in Wilfred's store, he had to declare his intentions to Maggie. "You're a deep one," was all she said and Tom returned to the Cape for Christmas.

It was the custom with the St. Croix men to cut enough wood to last the twelve days of Christmas. It being the season, they burned wood rather than coal oil and Francis rigged up a barrel stove inside for the fire. On Christmas Eve after Father Murphy had said mass in the schoolroom, Merla baked a molasses cake using a cup of hoarded raisins. There were no gifts or luxuries, not even a bottle of rum. On Christmas Day, after finishing a mutton dinner, they ate the cake. The day after Christmas, the St. Croixs took the curtains from the windows and draping them over their heads, went mummering in Long Beach where they stood in doorways and sat in chairs waiting silently until their identity had been guessed and they were rewarded with a cup of tea and a slice of cake. Aurora didn't accompany them, preferring to claim the house for herself. Perhaps she thought she was strange enough without becoming a mummer. Was she remembering the remarks made about her when she was a child? She didn't say. But she went along to kitchens and danced to the music of the spoons and the accordion, as light as a fairy on her feet.

Tom Mulloy didn't appear on any of the twelve days of Christmas though he might have gone by in a wagon or sleigh. Everyone who went to the Cape by road had to pass the St. Croixs' house and though she was watching, Merla couldn't always be at the window to see who was going by.

New Year's Day, after they had said the litany to the Blessed Virgin and eaten a roast duck dinner, there was a knock at the door.

"That will be for you, maid," Francis said. He had seen Tom pass the window. Aurora went to the door and Francis winked at Merla.

Tom stayed only long enough to give her the stockings, the oranges and the book of Emily Dickinson's poems, then he went on home. That evening, after the others had gone to bed, Aurora sat alone by the fire eating sections of orange and reading. The next day Merla sneaked a look inside the book and read the inscription: *For a lover of poetry, Your Tom.*

Every year on February 14th, Francis tied a valentine—a heart-shaped piece of wood stained red with partridgeberry juice and edged with broken shells—on the clothes line for Merla. This year there was a second valentine on the clothes line and when Aurora came downstairs in the morning, Francis drew her attention to the large white envelope. He watched while she went out bare-armed into the cold, opened the envelope and took out a heart of red lace. When she came in, Merla insisted she read what was inside the heart. Aurora obliged.

My love is like a red, red rose,
That's newly sprung in June.
O, my love is like a melodie,
That's sweetly play'd in tune.

Merla and Francis listened to the poem with satisfaction. Aurora didn't read aloud Tom's inscription but the St. Croixs didn't need to hear it. Tom Mulloy had finally made his intentions clear. "The sooner they marry, the better," Francis said. "Once loving is out in the open, it's time to go before the priest."

But it wasn't until September, after Aurora returned from the Cape where she had gone to meet the Mulloys, that Tom came to the Drook and asked to speak to Francis alone. When the men had walked to the beach and were standing on the landwash, Tom announced that Aurora had agreed to marry him before Christmas and said he'd appreciate having Francis's blessing. "You have it," Francis said and asked when Tom would have the job of lighthouse keeper. Tom said that he and his brother had already taken over their father's shifts and that their parents would be moving to St. John's in November to be near Tom's married sisters.

The wedding of Aurora St. Croix and Tom Mulloy took place on a mild mauzy December afternoon at Holy Redeemer Church in Trepassey. Women along the shore talked about this wedding for years. Flo Kearny, the local reporter who was composing a piece for the paper, described Aurora as *ethereal*, a word she seldom used. *The bride's dress of white satin, had a dropped waist, three-quarter sleeves and a sweetheart neckline. She was wearing a string of pearls, a gift from the groom.* Flo didn't mention the fact that Alma Perry had made the dress or that the groom's sister, who had money, had bought the material in St. John's as well as the bridal headpiece and veil. When writing up weddings she stuck to recording what was in front of her eyes. Nor did she describe the groom, who even in a black suit was downright homely. No one would expect her to. A wedding was, after all, for the bride. *The bride's veil billowed around her head like a sail in the wind.* It didn't hurt to get carried away a little bit.

Following the wedding, a reception was held in the church hall. Guests included the groom's parents, Jim and Eleanor Mulloy; his brother and wife, John and Beatty Mulloy and his sisters and brothers-in-law, Mr. and Mrs. Wilfred Hunt and Mr. and Mrs. Ronald Newhook. Also present were the bride's parents Francis and Merla St. Croix as well as the bride's brothers, uncles and aunts from the Drook.

There wasn't space to list all the St. Croix wives, or their children who were tearing like hellions around the room, swiping sandwiches and spilling tea. Nor was there space to mention those from Trepassey who had invited themselves. Flo wanted to mention six-year-old Edwina and Elsie Bennett, the adorable twins who hung around Aurora as if she were a bride doll, but there was only enough space for a concluding sentence. *Following the wedding the newlyweds will reside at Cape Race where the groom is employed by the Canadian....* Flo scratched out *Canadian* and wrote *Coast Guard*. There was no need to bring Canadians into it.

Overwhelmed by the heat and noise of a hundred or more people crammed into the hall, Merla and Francis had sought refuge in the corner beside the piano. Now that the wedding was over, they wanted to go home, get out of their church clothes, put their feet up and drink a pot of tea, hot tea, not the lukewarm brew that was being poured by the Catholic Women's League.

"It seems like only yesterday that I brought her ashore," Francis said and wiped his eyes.

Merla patted his arm. "Now, now, don't take on. We were blessed to have her with us as long as we did. The Lord gives and the Lord takes," she said, remembering Louis. "He alone knows the way our hearts may be blessed." She made herself think of the mat she would make for Aurora and Tom. There would be a baby in a wicker cradle on an iceberg, and two men rowing toward her in a dory. There would be Mary, arms outstretched, looking down on them from a sky filled with heavenly light.

THE CAPE

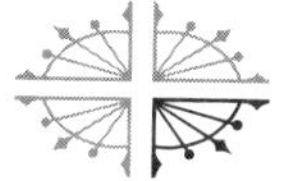

1930

My husband carried me, still in my wedding dress, over the threshold at Cape Race and stood me on the kitchen floor. "Stay where you are," he said and went the front room to wind up the gramophone. Then with his hand on my hip, he waltzed me from room to room to the strains of *Tales from the Vienna Woods*, past the food on the kitchen table, which neighbours had laid out, into the hall and upstairs to what had previously been Tom's parents' bed. We didn't come down until noon the next day when, like shipwrecked sailors, we fell on the cold chicken and roast pork, baked beans and scalloped potatoes, the rolls and pie. Tom said the feast was an indication that the neighbours would leave us alone for a few days, after which they would invite themselves in to meet me. So far, the only Cape people I knew were Tom's brother John and his wife, Beatty. Except for the sound of a crying baby from their side of the house, for three days there was nothing to remind us that we weren't the only ones at the Cape. I discovered the tea-stain birthmark hidden in Tom's groin, the raised cross on his left buttock where he'd sat on a shard of glass. Both of us discovered the amazing strength of my hips and legs. Tom discovered the planes of my belly. He put his thumb on my navel and rotated his palm, stopping at the points of the compass: the promontory of hip to the east, the mound of pale grass to the south, the promontory of hip to the west, the hollow between twin hills to the north until, he claimed, he had circled the world.

On the evening of the fourth day there was a shivaree of banging pots and pans outside before our kitchen door thumped open and the neighbours crowded in, one of them carrying a bottle of Jamaican rum. There were two couples, the Hallerans and the Johnstons, and two bachelor lighthouse keepers, Billy Dodge and Art Spence. My new in-laws couldn't come: John was working the night shift in the light and Beatty had a colicky baby. After the introductions, Tom brought in chairs from the dining room and arranged them around the stove. The man with the rum, Jim Halleran, went to the cupboard, took out glasses and poured everyone a drink. After each of us had a glass, we found ourselves a seat; I wanted to sit between Tom and the stove but Aggie Halleran, the redheaded, busty woman took that chair.

She looked me over and said, "You look like a gust of wind could blow you away. Jim tells me the wind is wicked out here so you wants to hold on." Aggie lifted her glass. "I'm a newcomer to the Cape myself. Cheers to us, girl."

Glasses were raised around the circle.

Jim glanced at me and then at Tom, "It looks to me like you robbed the cradle."

"What do you say, Tom? Own up now." Alf Johnston reached over and clapped Tom on the shoulder.

"She's a pretty little thing," Jim said. "I got to tell you, Tom, that with a mug like yours you could've done a whole lot worse."

For as long as we lived at the Cape this was the way it would be, the men talking about me as if I wasn't there. Not the women, the women spoke to me straight on, dragging their chairs closer, leaning toward me with their questions, their backs to the men. How old was I and was my hair a natural colour? Was I born with different colour eyes? Was it true that my brother was courting Bridgit Hartery from the Cove? Janet asked if I would mind if she and Aggie looked through the house.

I didn't mind, though I hadn't had a close look at it myself. The three of us went upstairs and looked into three bedrooms, which were much the same, each of them having a double bed, a dresser, a table and chair. The door to the fourth bedroom was closed. I didn't offer to open it—I had no intention of showing the women the unmade bed. But when we were downstairs, I encouraged Janet to open the oak sideboard in the dining room containing the blue willow china and glassware. Neither of the women showed any interest in the bookshelves against the dining-room wall, what Tom called the library, but Aggie pounced on the gramophone in the front room. "Mind if I put it on?" Without waiting for an answer, she wound the handle and out came the sound of the Viennese Waltz. "Let's get the men in here for a dance." It occurred to me that Aggie was wearing silk stockings and high-heeled shoes because she'd already seen the gramophone and came prepared to dance. She went into the kitchen and tried to pull Jim to his feet but he wouldn't budge. "What do you take me for? I dance to the fiddle not the violin." When none of the men could be coaxed to his feet, Aggie reached into her husband's pocket and fished out a package of Player's. She leaned against the door jamb, her lips in a pout until Billy leapt to his feet with a match. I was fascinated by Aggie: Francis and my brothers smoked a pipe but I had never seen a woman smoke. It was past midnight when the cigarettes and rum were gone and our neighbours went home.

In mid-January Merla and Francis arrived at the Cape, both of them eager to look around. Although Francis had been coming here for years to unload supply ships, he had never climbed the ninety-six-foot lighthouse with its twenty-five-foot lantern on top. After they walked through the covered wooden passage that ran between our house and the lighthouse, Tom took him up the curving steps to show him the lantern lens. When they came down, Francis had a close look at the coal-fired boilers providing the electricity to run the foghorn and the lantern. Tom took him into the wireless and radio buildings, the one-room schoolhouse and the stable; together they walked past the Halleran and Johnston houses and the staff house for single men, Francis remarking on the high cliffs all around. There was no beach at the Cape unless you counted the coarse gravel at the west landing where, once a year, supplies came ashore.

Merla had been to the Cape several times when she was a maid, but she had never been inside any of the buildings. She didn't know that the Mulloys' house was two houses joined in the middle and went from room to room exclaiming. She was especially taken with the dining room—even Win didn't have a dining room. "The pantry puts me in mind of Baird's!" Staring at the packages and tins on the shelves, the barrels and pails on the floor, Merla remarked that Aurora had her own store under her roof and could pick out whatever she wanted for supper. That night supper was mashed potatoes, cold roast pork with apple sauce and tinned peaches, which Aurora served on Eleanor Mulloy's blue china plates. Merla and Francis were impressed with their daughter's new home, and Merla, in particular, was smitten with Tom. Sitting beside Francis in the sleigh on the way home, she asked if he'd noticed Tom carrying plates into the kitchen after the meal.

"I was pleased to see it," Francis said, though he had never cleared a table in his life. "That's when I knew he would take good care of our maid."

Merla patted his knee. "For all she has, I wouldn't trade the Cape for the Drook."

Francis began to whistle, a sign that he was content. As they came down Drook Hill and saw their particular fold in the valley, he said, "Neither would I. I'd feel like a spider on a plate living on the Cape, but being out there will suit Aurora just fine." Both he and Merla were so pleased with their daughter's good fortune that they were unwilling to remind themselves that with Aurora gone, they were now doing her chores as well as their own.

It didn't take me long to become attached to the Cape, and to marriage. I loved being married, not because I lived in a luxurious house but because I was married to Tom. Marrying him freed me from shyness and restraint. It freed me to do as I pleased. Not that Merla and Francis had been hard taskmasters but they had come to depend on me to do Louis's work, which meant that once I left girlhood, there had been few opportunities for me to do as I pleased. I had married a man who encouraged me to do what I liked. It didn't bother him if I spent the entire afternoon wandering over the headlands or sitting beside the stove reading a book. He had followed his own way for most of his life without concerning himself about what others might think. I knew the neighbours probably didn't know what to make of me, but like Tom, it never stopped me from doing as I pleased. Though my brother and sister-in-law left us alone, Aggie and Janet often found excuses to come to our house: Aggie to borrow the gramophone, Janet, butter or lard or sugar; she was always running short of one thing or another. Once, when she came into our kitchen and saw bread cooling on the rack she asked if it was true that Tom had made it. I told her he made all the bread because his was better than mine, to which she replied that she would never forgive herself if Alf baked their bread.

Tom and I kept mostly to ourselves. Occasionally we went along to bingo evenings at the school but we never went to cards. At bingo one night when Jim asked us why we didn't play cards, Tom replied that I didn't play, that I had never been taught. Jim said that if I was his wife, I'd have learned by now. Tom laughed and said that in the evenings we preferred to stay home and read to each other. Apparently this offended Janet for bunching up her mouth, she fairly spat out the words, "Just wait until you have youngsters, you'll be wanting to be out and about!"

Two, three, four years went by and Tom and I had no youngsters. I knew from her remarks that Merla was disappointed in us even though she already had three grandchildren. Jerome and Brenda already had Louis and baby Francis, and there was another one on the way, and Mike, who had married Betty Sweeny from Harbour Main, had a son. When Merla and Francis came to supper one night, she followed me when I went upstairs to look for some wool I had promised her. While I rummaged in the blanket chest, she stood gazing at the crucifix over our bed. I knew she was wondering if Tom and I were using anything to prevent conception—which we weren't. Before we were married, when she sat me down for a talk, she'd asked if I knew that it was a sin to prevent myself having youngsters. I told her that I did. "Well then, all you need to know is that a happy marriage is made right here." Merla patted the mattress. "You got any troubles, you settle them here, and the Lord will see that you're blessed."

I wasn't bothered about not having babies. I was young and there was plenty of time. Tom and I had no wish to change our lives. We were well suited to enjoying the marriage bed, both of us eager to enter lovemaking as neophyte explorers. Everything I wanted was at the Cape. After the cramped house in the Drook, the Cape house was a mansion. There was an inside privy heated by a coal oil burner and a pantry chock-full of food—as Merla said it was like having my own store. Best of all was the dining-room wall filled from floor to ceiling with books, books by Conrad and Melville, Dickens and Dumas, Stevenson and Twain. *The Complete Works of Shakespeare* and books of poetry and of course the *Royal Readers*. There were books by explorers Amundsen, Shackleton and Scott. There was a small volume with a turquoise cover, *The Wonders of the Ice World*. I read this book first, before any of the others, paying close attention to the engravings of icebergs and glaciers, what the author referred to as laboratories of ice. Though I had been watching icebergs drift through the latitudes of melt for years, I had never viewed them with much interest. I had been brought up with the hard fact that icebergs were, as Francis put it, a frigging nuisance, the way they fouled up fishing nets and traps. I had been unaware that the purest drinking water in the world came from the icebergs floating offshore, or that most of these icebergs came from glaciers in Greenland. I hadn't known that glaciers are constantly on the move, that a boot or a shoe or a pickaxe fallen into a crevasse in Greenland, the Rockies or the Alps could surface years later hundreds of miles away. I had never thought of ice as an archaeological deep-freeze or that it held a future from which both artefacts and water could one day be retrieved.

On the bottom shelf of the library were twenty volumes of *The Book of Knowledge*, each one clothed in a navy blue cover and bearing a torch of gold. Inside on the frontispiece was a drawing of the globe resting on a bed of clouds and showing the lines of longitude and latitude. Every volume was divided into separate sections, the first page of each framed by miniature scenes. The first page of my favourite section, *The Book of Wonder*, showed children gazing up at the heavens. I read these volumes systematically, completing four a year until after five years, I had read them all and knew about tapirs and wombats, dinosaurs and pyramids, about the deepest part of the sea and the highest point of land. I knew that if all the land was flattened, the earth would be covered by sea. I knew about Vermeer and Rembrandt, Genghis Khan and Marco Polo, Thomas Edison and Madame Curie. I knew the origin of coal and the difference between planets and stars. *The Book of Knowledge* was filled with amazing information that had never been in my correspondence course material.

The year after Tom married Aurora, he ordered a bottle of glue, a box of watercolours and a large sketchbook with a coiled spine from Wilfred's store and put them under the Christmas tree. On subsequent Christmases, he would give his wife more of these books, which were sturdy enough to hold moss, leaves, and whatever else she brought home from her wanderings over the countryside. Aurora had never before used watercolours but she managed to paint and draw a likeness of sorts. She drew a large table and covered it with a lace cloth made of white lichen, which she scraped from a rock and glued to the paper. The table was on top of a cliff against a backdrop of painted sea. Beneath the picture she had written "Banquet"; she said she had been imagining a table where sea ghosts came to dine. The strands of horsehair she found on the Barrens became the mane of a white pony in a picture she called "Galahad." The hair was a mystery to Tom who had never in his life seen a horse on the Barrens, let alone a white one. To make "Night Garden" his wife glued tiny marsh marigolds onto a curtain of black paint. Depending on the weather she would take the sketchbook with her on rambles and try to paint a question for which she had no answer. How far does the sky go? Why do whales leap? Why does the sea change colour? Aurora said that even if she knew an answer, it was important for her to ask the question. Some of these questions she gleaned from *The Book of Knowledge*, others she came up with herself. She also wrote down poetry she had memorized *What would the world be once bereft / Of wet and of wildness? Let them be left, O let them be left*, and painted an illustration. Tom referred to these random accumulations as the Book of Wander.

Though Aurora rarely spoke of her origins, Tom thought that by filling her wander books with talismanic bits and pieces, she might be celebrating the miracle of having been rescued from the ice. He had never known anyone with more wonder and delight than Aurora. On long winter evenings he watched her looking through her wander books, lingering over rust-red blueberry leaves, stroking the wing feathers of a bird.

During the early years of their marriage, Tom and Aurora paid scant attention to the passage of time; weeks and months rolled past uncounted like waves breaking on shore. Those were the years when the sharing of chores hardly seemed like work, when working in the house or in the light together was merely a continuation of the movements that took place on the marriage bed; a kiss on the back of the knee when Aurora stood on a stool to wipe a lens, the slow soaping of Tom's back when he hunched in a tub of water in front of the kitchen stove.

On June 10th,1936, Francis St. Croix died at the age of seventy-three. He was on the water with Jerome and Ben when his heart seized up. Because two weeks earlier he had helped bring in the corpses of twenty-five crewmen who had been on the *Marianne*, it was assumed that the exertion of hauling the bodies ashore must have weakened his heart, but in fact it had never mended after Louis's death. Francis might have toppled into the drink if Ben hadn't grabbed him by the collar and laid him on the bottom of the dory. Even with the outboard motor, he was dead by the time they reached shore. After he had been buried in the Cove, Aurora went to the Drook and stayed a month. It was the first time in their six-year marriage that she and Tom had been apart. Every day either before or after his shift, Tom pedalled to the Drook, often staying the night, both he and Aurora sleeping beneath the quilt trimmed with the golden cord.

A week after Francis was buried, Aurora took out the Book of Wander and painted a picture of him in his grave in a meadow of star flowers, his hands clasped on his chest. He was holding a cross made from two slivers of driftwood glued to the page and was circled by the spectre of rescued men. She didn't show Merla this picture knowing she would be upset by what was written beneath, which was "God in Heaven." The title expressed how Aurora felt about Francis: to put it plainly, to her he was in his way as holy as God. Once the picture was finished, Aurora put the book away and set about the chores. Merla was feeling too poorly to work and

Brenda, who was now in her fourth pregnancy, needed help with housework and making fish that might never be sold, since by now the bottom was falling out of the salt fish market and a depression was under way. Like other fishermen along the coast, the St. Croixs were up to their ears in debt. Any credit they had managed to obtain from the fish merchant had long since run out. Philip and Bride had already moved to Peter's River to live with Bride's brother who still had his boat, Philip and Albert having let go of theirs. Albert worked on the water with Jerome and Ben. The St. Croix youngsters were dressed in little more than rags and were listless and pale. Brenda said that once the dole flour ran out, they went to bed with nothing in their bellies but potatoes and porridge. Each time he pedalled to the Drook, Tom brought food from the Mulloy pantry which had been brought to the Cape on the *Erinmore*. Once he arrived with three old coats which had been left behind by his mother and sisters. The coats were moth-eaten and torn but nobody cared since Alma would rip them apart and make something warmer than the youngsters had now.

A few days before Aurora returned to the Cape, Ben announced that he and Bridgit were getting married, and if Merla didn't object, they would move in with her. The news provided Merla with the pick-up she needed and after so long a courtship, she didn't question the hasty marriage, which was just as well. Had the priest found out that Bridgit was six weeks gone, she and Ben would have had to marry in the sacristy after dark, and she wouldn't have been allowed to wear the white dress she'd sewn on her mother's Singer. Father Murray, who'd taken over after Father Murphy died, did his best to prevent this kind of thing from happening, patrolling the roadside with flashlight and cane, but he seldom went as far as the Drook. In any case, the child wasn't conceived in the ditch but on Bridgit's own bed when her parents were out.

During the next three years, Bridgit and Brenda produced two more children. Together with Mike and Betty's youngsters (in addition to a son they now had a daughter), Merla had eight grandchildren and had given up expecting Aurora to produce any. She had come round to thinking that Aurora must be one of these women who for one reason or another was unable to conceive. Wouldn't you know, just when Merla's hopes had been dashed, Aurora announced that she was having a baby. By then she and Tom had been married almost nine years.

The baby's conception occurred on the floor beside *The Book of Knowledge*, after Tom and I spent a July afternoon in the kitchen making jelly from apples that Maggie had sent down from St. John's. I remember how our hot skin, slick with sweat, glistened in the sunlight streaming through the dining-room window. Three months later, it was Tom who identified the rounding of my breasts and belly as pregnancy. Because my menses were intermittent, I hadn't questioned their absence, and there was no morning sickness to warn me. Throughout my pregnancy I brimmed with health and was amorous more often than Tom.

Our daughter was born on March 23, 1939, shortly before the outbreak of the war. Because of my size, the doctor advised Tom to take me to Trepassey for the birth. Fortunately the Cape road was passable, which it sometimes isn't in March, allowing Jim Halleran to deposit Tom and me at the midwife's home in time for a safe delivery within eight hours, with no complications. Our daughter was born perfectly shaped, her skin slightly pink, not a bruise or flaw anywhere.

We named her Nancy Rose after a ship that had gone down off Cape Race in 1880. The naming was Tom's idea. He pointed out that all the family names had been used up and that the prettiest ones were often used on ships. A pretty name for a pretty maid, he said, and like the Book of Wander, it stuck.

I saw my first U-boat as I was walking over the headland with my ten-month-old daughter on my back. The conning tower cut the surface of the sea not five hundred yards away. While I watched, the tower reared up until the deck appeared, water pouring over the sides. The hatch opened and a man came on top. He was dressed in black and was carrying something, I was too far away to see what it was. When he lifted the thing to his face and pointed it in my direction, I knew that he was looking at me through binoculars. The realization that a stranger was invading the wild places I thought of as mine filled me with panic. Sensing my uneasiness, Nancy Rose began to cry and I hurried back to the house, never once turning back. Only after I was inside did I look out the window but the U-boat had vanished into the depths where even shadows disappear.

During the early years of the war, U-boats were a common sight at the Cape. Their commanders must have known they had nothing to fear from us. At night they surfaced below the lighthouse so they could use their generator to recharge the batteries. We could see them from our bedroom window and the sound of their engines often kept us awake. One night on a full moon Tom and I counted five U-boats on the water. Tom said they were hanging around to see when the light would come on—during the war the light was turned on only when a convoy passed on its way to Britain. Otherwise a blackout was maintained. When a convoy passed in daylight, the horizon was black with ships: troopships, supply ships and hospital ships protected by corvettes and destroyers. One morning when Tom and I were up in the light watching, we saw a U-boat trailing the convoy like a shark following a skiff with a corpse aboard. It wasn't long before there was an explosion and a destroyer went down so fast that there wasn't a hope of the crew surviving.

Sometimes the Cape was contacted to look out for survivors. There seldom were any, though their caps sometimes washed ashore; no one survived for long in the North Atlantic, especially in winter. In one January alone, U-boats sank four ships off the Cape: the *Icarion* was so close to shore that it grounded stern up in shallow water. The U-boat commanders were clever, taking cover beneath ice pans and local ships delivering supplies up and down the coast. The third year of the war two boys from the Cape went trouting near Clam Cove Brook and found a striped umbrella and a foreign book (it turned out to be a German novel) concealed beneath some blasty boughs. They ran to the station where the news was wired to Fort Pepperrell. The next day the Cape was swarming with American soldiers.

I no longer rambled over the countryside with Nancy Rose but stayed close to the house instead. In winter I made her snowmen and snow angels and once a snow palace, using icicles for a drawbridge. In summer I set the washtub on the grass and filled it with water to make a splash pool. I refused to tie her to the clothes line or put her in a playpen, which other Cape mothers did, on account of the high cliffs. I thought the war confined my daughter too much as it was. Together we flew kites made from brown paper and crating and raced chariots I'd made from matchboxes and empty thread spools. I also made dolls, using clothes-pins dressed in scraps of cloth, but Nancy Rose was never one for dolls. From the beginning she knew her own mind and was easily angered by any attempt to persuade her to change it. When she was two, her favourite pastime was listening to me read from *The Book of Golden Deeds*. By the time she was four she could read parts of the book herself. She also liked looking at the wander book I had begun for her. The book recorded her progress, height and weight, and the date of her first word, which was Mom. There were half a dozen photographs of her taken outside with the Brownie that Maggie had given us. Photographs of the Cape were forbidden during the war but I ignored the order. A photo of a naked child splashing in a tub or holding on to a kite string was hardly a setback for the Allied cause.

My fondest memories of Nancy Rose were of her sitting on my knee while I read a story or brushed her hair. In those days she allowed me to arrange her hair any way I liked. She had lustrous hair, long and chestnut-coloured. She had Tom's grey eyes. I adored Nancy Rose and found it difficult to deny her what she wanted. I think during the war years that I probably indulged her at the expense of Tom.

Tom didn't know if the alterations in his marriage were the result of parenthood or the war. Most likely it was a combination of both. The alterations weren't serious at first: they were more a series of small misunderstandings and inconveniences than anything else. Until diesel fuel replaced coal midway through the war, Tom would come in from his day shift sheathed in a mix of coal dust and grime and find his daughter playing boats in the tub of water he had come to expect would be warming by the stove. He would have to make do with scrubbing himself at the sink, which only got him partly clean because it took a long soak to get the coal dust out of his pores. Sometimes when he came to bed before dawn, Nancy Rose would be curled against Aurora's breasts, her arms stuck straight out on his side of the bed. He was irritated that once again she had taken over his bed, that Aurora had allowed it knowing he would be too tired to carry Nancy Rose back to her room. Tom folded his daughter's arms together to allow him space to lie down. She sighed and snuggled close to her mother, which was something he wanted to do.

It was the war: the planes droning above the convoys, Spitfires screaming off shore in pursuit of U-boats. Occasionally an air attack succeeded in sinking one but not often though there were rumbled explosions when depth charges were dropped—no wonder Nancy Rose, young as she was, wanted to sleep in their bed. Most of the older children, the boys especially, enjoyed the war. Tom's brother said that his sons would be disappointed when it ended. Every waking hour outside of school was spent scanning the water with periscopes made from mirrors and pipes, whittling wooden swords and guns in case they should come upon a spy; lowering themselves down the cliff to look for something spies might have left behind. The boys had in mind radio batteries, or better still a radio. All they found was an empty bottle of Black Horse from the *Brazildore*, which had been wrecked off Portugal Cove South with a cargo of beer early in the war. John's daughters planted a garden and sold turnip greens and potatoes to raise money for Victory bonds. Tom heard them belting out Vera Lynn songs while they weeded and hoed.

The war had changed the Cape. There were now nine families living here, including the single men working as radio and wireless operators, over eighty people altogether. New buildings including a mess had been built to accommodate them. Like most Cape people, Tom was finding the war a strain. The constant drone of reconnaissance planes, the U-boats, the sleepless nights, the longer shifts (Art Spence had signed up and never been replaced), the news from the radio operators that another ship had gone down or another city was being bombed—all this was taking its toll. Tom didn't sleep for two weeks after he heard the news that Maggie and Wilfred's only child, Peter, had been shot down over Scapa Flow.

Military men were always coming and going at the Cape: Canadians, Americans, Brits, naval men of all stripes. The presence of these men meant there were weekly dances at the Cape which Tom and Aurora occasionally attended. Because men outnumbered women six to one, Tom was lucky if he got to dance once with his wife. In her early thirties, Aurora was still smooth-skinned and unwrinkled. Well, almost. There was some forehead smocking and spider-webbing at the corners of her eyes, but otherwise her appearance was unchanged. With hair the colour of sea spume she would bypass turning grey. Tom had a shingle of grey above each ear, but most people had to expect that after passing forty. At the dances Tom noticed how the young bucks, mostly wireless trainees from Canada, eyed his wife. She seemed to enjoy the attention and would go from one dance partner to another without coming back to him. When they were finally home in bed alone—on these occasions

Nancy slept over at John and Beatty's—Tom would make love to his wife with the urgency of taking back something he had lost. It was during one of these passionate reclamations that Aurora conceived Joseph Stanley.

This time it wasn't an easy pregnancy, especially during the last few months. Aurora had trouble sleeping because her back ached and she couldn't find a comfortable position. A restless sleeper, Nancy was banished to her own bed, much against her will, and for weeks whined and sulked when Tom tucked her in. Later, in bed beside Aurora, he rubbed her back while she lay on her side, hands around her belly as if she was cradling the world—on her slender frame her belly did look like an enormous globe. He washed her hair and put on her shoes. She waddled from one room to another, one hand on her belly, the other on her hip, bluish smudges beneath her eyes. Tom looked past the disfigured breasts and bulging veins and late in the pregnancy he wrote this verse:

Inside
her cave
are sacred pools
and Delphic groves
where a child
may sleep in peace

An unremarkable verse. A failed haiku, but at least Tom had the satisfaction of its being his own. When he was fourteen and began a two-year convalescence from TB, he read every book in the house and began writing verses of his own. He had read enough poetry to know that it was a high calling, one to which he couldn't hope to aspire; he knew he was a scribbler, an amateur, for whom writing verse would never be more than an expression of thoughts and feelings that he was unwilling to trust to anything except a page. Tom wrote in a battered blue scribbler he kept inside a wooden chest up in the light, along with a supply of books and a pair of binoculars. He wrote surrounded by 6,720 pounds of glass—four lenses floating in a mercury bath and powered by a motor the size of a lunch box. The regular turning of the prisms magnifying the lantern flame, reflecting it across an expanse of water and air, filled him with quietude. He liked to think that even with the disruptions of war, the light connected him with the universe.

Heavy with glass, shining with rain
The bright flame signals again and again.
From windowless house, through windowless space,
The prism turns and blinks from its place. . . .

Twice a year the priest said mass at the Cape schoolhouse in the same room where children worked in their copybooks, their backs to the altar. Though Tom went through the motions of prayer, stopping at the stations of the cross mounted on the schoolroom walls, the rituals of the Catholic Church had little to do with what he thought and felt. His spiritual place was inside the light. Up there, 120 feet above the cliffs, was where he looked for God; up there he could look across the headlands disappearing south and west, and across the Barrens rolling north. On good days when the sky was clear and there were no planes or U-boats to remind him of the war, he could look eastward at a horizon as straight and true as a carpenter's rule. He sometimes thought that the island was what the world must have looked like when it was nothing more than water and rock, when God was practising creation and had not yet moved on to greener Edens.

The time Tom spent inside the light was never enough to satisfy him. He always wanted more. Chores kept him grounded. He had to keep the boilers going. He had to clean blackened lenses, alone now that Aurora had Nancy Rose to look after and another child on the way. He had to replace broken mantles, pump kerosene and air and every four hours wind the lantern.

The vegetables had to be planted and buildings scraped and painted—the winter wind blew off the paint. There were always repairs requiring attention: shingles that needed replacing, window frames rotted through, a chimney crumbling onto the roof. Even with Billy Dodge and John taking shifts, there was never time to do all the work. Weeks, months, would go by without Tom writing a word in the scribbler, and when he did it might be a snatch of what he called "real poetry," which, like Aurora, he copied from memory.

My happier world, wherein
To wend and meet no sin:
Above me, round me lie
Fronting my forward eye
With sweet and scarless sky.

When time was short, Tom scribbled a few lines in haste. *Aurora gave birth to a son at 6 a.m. this morning, May 1st, 1945. A long labour. 32 hours. Baby a big bruiser, over 9 pounds. Red and black marks from forceps. But healthy. He made it. Aurora too. Aurora....* Tom began to weep. He couldn't bear the thought of her lying at the midwife's in that everlasting pain. *We are naming the baby Joseph Stanley after a ship that went down here in 1921.*

Six days after this entry, Tom made another: *The war has ended at last.*

Because of the difficult labour, the doctor recommended that Aurora not return to the Cape until she was stronger and for six weeks she remained in Trepassey with Win and Merla, who two years earlier had moved to Trepassey on account of her health. The sisters doted on Stanley and did their best to spoil Aurora, making chowder and soup, beef stew and liver loaf to build up her strength.

Having a newborn in the house suited Merla because she could fuss over a grandchild without having to go anywhere. Nancy, who was in school, remained at the Cape with Tom.

By the time Aurora returned with their son, a major change had taken place in their family that neither she nor Tom could have predicted. During the weeks Aurora was away, Nancy shifted her allegiance from her mother to her father, and there it stayed. Now she wanted Tom to read her stories and braid her hair; it was Tom to whom she showed her school work. If he passed it to Aurora to praise, their daughter left the room. After six years of being an only child, it was to be expected that Nancy would be jealous of her baby brother, but Tom would never have guessed that a six-year-old could be so hard-hearted. Aurora did what she could to woo back their daughter, making her favourite supper—cream of corn soup and chocolate brownies—ordering a red wool coat and hat from the catalogue, which Nancy refused to wear.

One afternoon when Stanley was outside sleeping in his carriage and Aurora was inside cleaning the kitchen stove, Nancy took the baby for a walk. She pushed the carriage toward the school, intending, Tom supposed, to show the teacher her new baby brother. She must have found the carriage too heavy to hold on to, because when she reached the slope in front of the school, she let go. Aggie, who was passing the school on her way home from Janet's, saw the carriage wobbling down the incline and stopped it before it toppled over the cliff. Hauling Nancy by the hand, she brought the carriage back and parked it outside, then marched her into the kitchen just as Tom was returning from the light, and told him in no uncertain terms that his daughter should be walloped. After Aggie left, Tom sent Nancy to bed without a spanking: he never had nor ever would lay a finger on her.

Dad had a massive stroke yesterday. Not expected to live.

September 11, 1948. Dad passed away this morning at 6 a.m. John and I leave for St. John's after supper.

April 1, 1949. April Fool's Day. Yesterday while Smallwood was attending ceremonies in Ottawa and St. John's, making us, on paper at least, the tenth province of Canada, Merla suffered a fatal heart attack. Before the ink was dry, she was dead. The country of Newfoundland was 451 years and 280 days old when it died; Merla, 88 years and 24 days.

Tom had admired his mother-in-law, and some day wanted to write a verse about her. While he was sitting beside Aurora in church listening to the priest extol Merla for her piety and devotion, he decided the verse would say something about her passion for Newfoundland. Merla had voted against Confederation in the 1948 referendum, and before the vote she'd had a lot to say about Newfoundlanders giving up their country—she never thought of it merely as a British colony. She had a lot to say about them learning to run the country themselves, about them standing on their own two feet. Despite her strong opinions, if she'd known about Tom's, she wouldn't have held it against him for voting the other way.

He had voted Yes for Confederation. For years he had been watching people along the shore dribble away, abandoning houses built by their fathers and grandfathers. With the exception of Brenda's father, all the Martins in Long Beach had cleared out for the States, leaving their sheep to forage where they could. Soon after the war Ben and Bridgit had gone to St. Mary's to be close to winter logging around Salmonier. Jerome and Brenda would be next to leave the Drook. They were barely hanging on. The post-war boom, if you could call it that, had petered out and the salt fish trade would never recover. In Tom's view Newfoundland needed Canada's help, and fast.

A year after Confederation, Nancy burst through the door for noon dinner with the announcement that her teacher, Miss Kelly, had assigned the grade-sixes an essay to celebrate the first anniversary of Confederation. This news was disclosed as Aurora was mashing a bowl of boiled turnips. Tom gazed at his wife's back, at the over-sized cotton dress and wool socks pulled up to her knees. She reminded him of a child dressed in grown-up clothes.

Nancy hung up her slicker and washed her hands at the pump without being told. She was wearing a pleated tartan skirt and a red vest, red barrettes in her hair. Now that she was eleven, she ordered her own clothes, she wouldn't let her mother choose even her underwear.

"Dad," Nancy said. "Can you help me with my essay? Miss Kelly says we have to read it before the class. The best one will be sent to Premier Smallwood in St. John's."

"Sure, I'll help you."

"What's the topic?" Aurora said. She must have been miles away when Nancy came in.

"Tonight. Will you help me tonight?"

"Your mother asked you a question."

It cut him to the quick, the way Nancy Rose ignored her mother. With Stanley it was different. He preferred his mother and it was she he called when he awoke at night, and to whom he brought his drawings of icebergs and ships.

"When can Miss Kelly come for supper?" This time she addressed Aurora, who said that Monday would be fine.

Cape parents took turns inviting Miss Kelly in for a meal. She lived at the staff house with a handful of radio operators who called her the "old biddy," though she was a year or two this side of forty. A tall sexless woman with a take-charge air, Miss Kelly was inquisitive to the point of nosiness. Nothing was too small or insignificant to escape her attention: an unfinished crossword puzzle, a photograph of the first lighthouse at the Cape, a new bar of Sunlight soap by the washbasin. All these had been exclaimed over during previous visits to the Mulloys'. She tried too hard, was Tom's opinion.

On Monday when she was sitting in the Mulloys' front room with Nancy after supper, Miss Kelly caught sight of Aurora's wander book on the corner table. Beside the book was a kittiwake feather she had picked up that afternoon, and a jar of glue.

From the kitchen where he was urging Stanley to drink up his glass of powdered milk, Tom heard the teacher ask Nancy if the book was hers.

"It's my mother's."

"Do you think she would mind if I took a peek?"

Tom looked at Aurora who was at the sink pouring hot water into the dishpan, giving no sign that she had heard. Stanley put down his mug and ran into the front room, Tom following. Miss Kelly was at the corner table turning the pages of Aurora's book while Nancy stood at her side.

"Isn't this something," the teacher said, bobbing her head at Nancy. "How interesting that nature's gifts have been made into a book. You are fortunate to have a mother who has taken the trouble to make something like this."

Tom saw his daughter redden—her cheeks were a barometer showing changes in her weather. These days she was never far from a storm.

Aurora carried in the tray and began handing round cups of milky tea. Miss Kelly sipped hers and said, "I've been admiring your scrapbook, Mrs. Mulloy, and would very much like the children to see what you've done. Could I persuade you to bring your book to school one day?"

Tom saw his daughter's hopeful expression. Did Aurora see it?

"It sounds like a good suggestion to me," he said. The invitation would be an opportunity for Nancy to be proud of her mother.

"I suppose I could show it," Aurora said. "But I'd prefer not to speak." She gave Stanley the plate of cookies and nudged him toward their guest.

"You won't need to speak," Miss Kelly said. "Just bring along the book. Would Friday afternoon be convenient? We usually have visitors after our Red Cross meeting."

Friday noon when Nancy came home for dinner, she was obviously pleased that Aurora was wearing the pleated brown skirt and the blue nylon blouse Tom had given her for Christmas. Aurora's braid was neatly pinned around her head and she had put on her wedding pearls. Tom hoped their daughter was thinking the same thing he was, that none of her classmates had a mother as lovely as hers. After dinner Nancy went off to school in high spirits; Aurora followed at half past two.

At half past three Nancy returned from school alone just as Tom was returning from winding the lantern weights and was about to make tea.

"Where's your mother?"

"She's still at school with her stupid book." Nancy dumped her homework onto the kitchen rocker and flung herself at her father's chest. "I hate her, Dad. I hate her!"

Tom thought she meant Miss Kelly who for a reason he couldn't fathom, Nancy tried so hard to please. "Surely hate is too strong a word."

"Mom humiliated me, Dad. I'll never live it down. I'll be tormented for the rest of my life."

It took a few minutes for Tom get a picture of what had happened. Aurora had taken Nancy's wonder book to school along with her own. There had been no problem with her mother's book. The torment began when Miss Kelly was turning the pages of Nancy's book, which showed crayoned pictures and cards, the photographs of her as a baby. Even Nancy's girlfriends rolled their eyes.

The boys snickered. "Aw, isn't that cute!" Ed Pennell said when he saw the necklace of baby teeth. "Look at this, Santy sent a telegram from the North Pole! Shucks!" That was embarrassing enough, but the real shame began when Aurora turned the page showing what she had done with Nancy's hair. Tom remembered the day when his daughter first saw what her mother had done. Using Nancy's hair, Aurora had made a nest with a robin inside. At five Nancy had been delighted; at eleven she was horrified.

"When Mom turned the page where she glued my hair, Ed Pennell looked at the nest and said to Bernie Johnston, out loud so everyone could hear, 'Nancy's dicky bird.'" Everyone laughed and snorted. It was awful. Bernie asked if my dicky bird was brown like the nest. Miss Kelly told the class to be quiet but it was too late.

"I'll never live it down," Nancy put her head against Tom's chest and wailed. "How could Mom be so stunned?" That was the part Aurora heard. The porch door opened and Nancy tore away from Tom and flung herself upstairs. Thump. Thump. Thump, slamming her bedroom door at the top just as Aurora sank onto the daybed. Letting the books slide to the floor, she said, "I should never have agreed to take those books to school."

"If I'd known you were taking Nancy's book, I would have said something."

"But it was you who encouraged me to take them to the school."

"I didn't encourage you to take Nancy's book. It never occurred to me that you would do such a thing." Tom was thinking of his blue scribbler. "It's an invasion of privacy." The astonished look on Aurora's face only irritated him more. "You should know how self-conscious and easily embarrassed Nancy is. You're her mother, for Christ's sake!"

That night I wrote Tom a note and left the Cape while my family was asleep. I had to get away because I was too confused about what had happened to be able to think clearly. I felt that my daughter despised me and that my husband had let me down. Once I got away and had time to think, I realized that because of Nancy's intransigence, I had stopped paying attention to her. If I had been paying attention, I would have noticed how secretive she had become about her body, which had already taken a womanly shape. But I mightn't have noticed her capacity for embarrassment because I have never been embarrassed myself—to me embarrassment is nothing more than a word. But it means far more to my daughter whose life, now that I think about it, appears to be a minefield of possible embarrassments.

Tom came down to breakfast and found Aurora's note leaning against the sugar bowl. *I've gone away for a few days. There's a crock of beans and leftover roast in the cold room. Don't worry about me. Aurora.* No warning, no discussion but an abrupt departure. She hadn't even written *Love*. Tom burned the note in the stove. By the time the youngsters came down for breakfast, he had figured out what he would say. He told them that their mother was feeling tired and had decided to go away for a rest. Only Stanley asked where she had gone. "To Trepassey," Tom said, "To stay with Win."

"I'll expect you to do the dishes," Tom told Nancy. "And help with the meals."

"All right, Dad," she said cheerfully, too cheerfully, he thought.

He was disappointed at her for not being more upset, for not being sorry that her mother was gone. After she left for school, Tom took Stanley with him out to the light. He told him to stop whining and play with his boats while he cleaned and oiled the lantern gears.

Tom saved most of his anger for Aurora. He was angry that he couldn't speak the truth in his own house without her disappearing. How would she like it if he had taken off without saying a word? He was angry that she hadn't said where she was going. It couldn't have been far. She wouldn't have the money to take her far. The only money in the house was in a jam jar they kept in the pantry, and it seldom contained more than a few dollars. Tom wouldn't ask Beatty if Aurora had borrowed any money from her. He wasn't about to admit to anyone, even to dependable, close-mouthed Beatty, that he'd been caught unawares.

After dinner Tom took Stanley for a walk, something Aurora usually did. His son would sleep better tonight if he had a dose of exercise and fresh air. They walked a mile toward Chance Cove and back, Stanley picking up stones and bits of wood to put on his window sill. Though he didn't look at all like Aurora—neither of the youngsters did—Stanley was like her in some ways. He was quiet and self-contained, quick to notice what others missed, at least outdoors.

By the time he went to bed that night, Tom had convinced himself that he wasn't entirely surprised by Aurora's departure. He remembered that in the early days of their marriage he had half expected Aurora might leave him, not on account of anything he'd done but because she'd seemed an ephemeral creature, a will-o'-the-wisp. He didn't think he could hold on to a spirit as free as hers. He kept thinking she might vanish, that she might disappear into the mists as magically as she'd appeared. Sometimes he thought he might have dreamed her, that she was a mirage that would eventually melt away. It had taken a surprisingly long time before familiarity squeezed out the uncertainty and Tom began seeing in Aurora the permanency of a wife.

Although she was self-contained and sometimes remote, until now Aurora had been so steadfast that he had come to think of the two of them as cogs in the wheel that kept the light running year after year; there was a harmonious synchronicity between his wife and himself that gave their life together exquisite precision. Now that the children were becoming old enough to occupy themselves, it was uncanny how Aurora would come to him after he had finished one chore or another, appearing at the corner of the house or on the path with a glass of cold water as he was returning from the meadow, standing at the precise point where their paths intersected, as if she was using the lines of longitude and latitude to track where they would meet. Tom wouldn't have wanted a marriage where he said goodbye to his wife every morning knowing he wouldn't see her again until suppertime. He wanted a wife who surrounded him, who was part of his living, breathing space. Now he had a wife who was lost to him, who had chosen to vanish.

Where has my love gone?
Does she care no more
For this seam riven boulder?
She who is leaf strewn and wild wrought
Will she return to this tower
Where the eye blinks
In its rusting hollow?

By Sunday noon Aurora had been gone twenty-eight hours—Tom was keeping a close watch on the time. At ten-fifteen, Stanley went next door to play with his cousins and at twelve noon Tom set Nancy to work peeling potatoes at the kitchen sink while he began writing up the lighthouse diary. The diary, which was a long narrow ledger called a portage bill, was begun by his father over seventy years ago. The book was mostly a record of weather and shipping news: ships that came and went on their way to somewhere else, ships that sank or ran aground on the rocky coast. The book also recorded when the lighthouse was painted, the garden was planted, the supply ship unloaded. Storms were recorded, high winds, fog, there were hundreds of entries about fog.

This morning there was fog. The horn had started at dawn. Usually Tom paid no attention to the horn's gutteral bass, which sounded like a bull abandoned in a pasture, but today he was drawn to its long mournful note of desertion. He heard a car drive up outside and his heart lifted: maybe Aurora was being driven home.

"We have a visitor, Dad." Nancy put down the peeler and fled upstairs to change her clothes. Tom got up and looked out the window. There was no sign of Aurora, but a man with high coloured cheeks and dark longish hair was passing the window. Probably he was a stray who had followed the Cape road to the end and was now wondering where he was. Tom opened the door and invited him inside. He was young, in his early twenties, and was wearing a windbreaker, dungarees and sneakers.

"Lost your way, have you?"

"I don't think so." He grinned disarmingly. "This is Cape Race. Right?"

A Yankee.

"Right."

The Yankee stuck out his hand. "Patrick O'Connor."

Tom shook his hand. "Tom Mulloy. So what brings you this way?"

"I'm trying to locate a woman in her early forties, a woman my father claims might be his daughter. See, he had a daughter in Ireland who he thought was lost on the *Titanic*."

Tom rolled his eyes. "Not another *Titanic* story." There seemed to be no end to them. You would think there had never been another shipwreck. His visitor hooked his thumbs inside his belt and looked at the floor. "Listen, as preposterous as it seems, I have to say this. Years ago, my father came across an old newspaper ad about a baby girl rescued from an iceberg a couple of days after the *Titanic* went down. He put two and two together and figured the baby might be his daughter. The ad said to contact a J.T. Mulloy at Cape Race."

"J.T. Mulloy was my father." Tom said. "He might have been able to help you but he's been dead for years. I'm afraid I can't help."

"I know the odds are against finding her." Patrick said. "Whoever that baby was, she could be anywhere by now."

"She could," Tom said. "I certainly don't know where she is."

"Dad?"

Tom turned and saw Nancy standing in the dining-room doorway. How long had she been there? In her grown-up voice, she said, "Aren't you going to ask our visitor to sit down?" When she wanted to be, she could be convincingly mature.

Patrick O'Connor looked at his watch. "Thanks but I've got to go. I promised I'd be back in St. John's by three. I don't want our ship leaving without me."

"Patrick O'Connor, this is my daughter Nancy Mulloy."

"Hi, there." Patrick smiled at Nancy. A handsome young man. Which was why, though half his age, Nancy had put on a clean blouse and combed her hair. It wasn't often, these days, that a young man showed up at the Cape. She asked what ship he was on.

"The *Dolphin*, an old corvette that's been converted for oceanographic studies. I'm a summer student working out of Woods Hole. My girlfriend, too. She's waiting in the car." Patrick O'Connor shifted his feet. "Well, I guess I'll be going." He opened the door. "Thanks. At least I can tell my father I tried."

"Be careful of the sheep," Tom said. "In a fog you can't always see them when they wander onto the road."

Nancy went back to peeling potatoes, dejectedly, Tom thought. He returned to the diary. If he flipped back to April 1912, he would find the entry in his father's bold hand, written with a wetted pencil stub. *White Star liner struck an iceberg and went down South of here. She was on her maiden voyage. The report today says 1601 lost, 746 saved. Baby girl found on an ice pan by Francis St. Croix. No account of the* Erna Grace *or the* Beatrice *yet.* Southern Cross *in today.* Tom hadn't read the entry in years but he hadn't forgotten it either. No one else knew it was there. John never looked at the book—he left record-keeping to Tom.

Tom was only slightly disappointed in himself for not showing the entry to Patrick O'Connor, for withholding the story of how his wife came to the Drook. He was far from admitting that the anger he harboured for her had made him mean. Aurora had never shown the slightest sign that she was bothered by not knowing where she had come from, so why should he? When you got right down to it, her origins were none of his business. If she wanted to follow up on Patrick O'Connor's visit, she could do it herself, if and when she came home.

The next day, just before noon, Tom came in from the light and there was Aurora setting the table for dinner, as matter-of-factly as if she had never been away. Tom stood in the doorway, staring at her until she spoke. She said that she'd had to get away in order to think clearly. Surely she didn't expect him to believe she couldn't think at the Cape, that her thinking had been muddled all these years.

"About what?"

"This and that."

The vagueness annoyed him.

"If you decide to do it again, perhaps you'll be good enough to warn me first. You might also tell me where you'll be going and if you'll be back."

When he bent over the washbasin, Tom noticed that his hands were trembling.

Aurora told him she had been at the Drook. She said that when Jerome and Brenda moved to Trepassey, they told her she could use the house any time she liked. This was news to Tom. He supposed he should be grateful that she hadn't gone away sooner than she did. The door opened and Stanley came in. Without saying a word he ran to his mother and threw his arms around her hips. Tom heard him sniffling. Five years old and he was still a mama's boy.

Nancy came in and was so offhand her mother might never have been gone. She didn't speak to Aurora until the four of them were sitting at the table eating fried potatoes and baloney. "We had a visitor yesterday from New York," she said. "His name was Patrick O'Connor. He wanted to know if a woman your age lived here. He had a story about his father wanting to find his daughter who had supposedly been a baby on the *Titanic*."

Tom said, "Why don't you let me tell your mother about the visit when she and I are alone."

"Have it your way," Nancy said carelessly. "But if you ask me it's a stupid story. I don't believe it for a second. Even Patrick O'Connor was embarrassed."

After she returned to school and Stanley was playing outside, Tom and Aurora sat in the kitchen and talked. When he had finished telling her about the visitor, she asked if Tom had told him about her.

"No."

"Why not?"

"What could I say? You weren't here. I told the youngsters you had gone to Trepassey to stay with Win."

Aurora had nothing to say to this. It seemed to Tom that she wasn't all that upset, especially when she disclosed that she might have seen Patrick O'Connor herself. "Yesterday about noon I was coming up from the beach when a man and a woman drove through the Drook. The woman waved at me but the man kept his eyes on the road."

"He told me that he and his girlfriend were in a hurry to get back to St. John's."

That was the last they spoke of it, and though the surface of their life smoothed over, Tom knew that it would never be quite what it had been before, if only because his view of his wife had changed. He had lost his tolerance for her wanderings, her habit of traipsing across headlands and over the Barrens towing Stanley. He was inclined to agree with Aggie when he overheard her asking Beatty why anyone would spend all that time in the fog and the damp unless she had to. Aggie said men fished in weather but it made no sense for a woman to be dragging a youngster through mizzling rain when they could be snug and dry inside. Aurora was no longer Tom's faery bride, a woman with an incandescent face and hair of spun silver, a mysterious, magical creature. It no longer excited him to recall how Keats's verse had once been an intimacy between them. The enchantment was gone—perhaps its disappearance was long overdue. As far as he was concerned, lady in the meads, faery maid were no longer words of affection but reminders that fairies were mischievous, unreliable creatures, up to pranks and unpleasant surprises.

Aurora was to leave the Cape again and again, on average three or four times a year. She never stayed away long, a week at the most. Tom became alert to the signs of leaving: soup and stew placed on the shelf in the cold room; laundry stashed on the dresser, the empty mending basket. She always told him when she would be leaving though not when she would be back. At first he thought she was chafing against the restrictions of the Cape—they had never gone away on holiday and she had never left the Southern Shore—but he revised his opinion when he realized that she never went further than the Drook. He decided her departures were the result of the strain that youngsters, Nancy especially, caused in their marriage, and became used to these forced separations more than he cared to admit. When Aurora was away, he found himself spending more time up in the light, watching a breaching whale or a floating ice palace, or simply resigning himself to the enigmatic blueness of the sea.

The wild abandon of leaping whales
Stops the bog slide into vales
Where broken keels and rusted hulls
Lie deep in sea dust, beyond recall.

When Nancy's crookedness was at its worst, Tom caught himself hoping Aurora would leave. The thought was craven, and he had to admit unfair and disloyal, but he had an urgent and obstinate need for peace, and until Nancy herself left the Cape, his wife's absence was the most expedient way of restoring it. Tom believed that when both their children were gone, he and Aurora could reclaim the life they'd had earlier in their marriage: sharing the chores, reading aloud to each other, waltzing through the rooms, doing jigsaw puzzles, making love in the dining room, pleasures all but forgotten, the blanket they had spread on the floor folded away upstairs. He never doubted that their children would leave—there would be no jobs for them at the Cape. Since the war, the number of people at the Cape had been cut by a third until now only a handful of radio wireless operators were being trained at the station. Fewer ships passed the light and there hadn't been a wreck in years. Once there had been four lighthouse keepers at the Cape; now there was only John and himself and when they needed him, Billy Dodge. One day even their jobs would be gone, replaced by something the government would no doubt refer to as progress. There was only one family left at Long Beach and no one left in the Drook, most people having moved further along the coast to be near the fish plant in Trepassey. Tom discussed these changes with his children, repeating Joey's litany that education was the way of the future and advising them to keep up with their schooling so they could qualify for well-paying jobs. Nancy didn't need to be reminded to study. Since winning the Confederation essay prize (she had received a letter of congratulations from the premier himself), she had made up her mind to become a teacher in St. John's. As much as he dreaded the inevitable wrench of his children's leaving, on some days Tom thought it couldn't happen soon enough and worried that it might be too late for Aurora and him to find their way back to their earlier years of bliss. He knew they would never reclaim the enchantment or all of their wondrous delight in each other, but he wanted to believe that they would retrieve enough of it to keep them both content.

THE TOWN

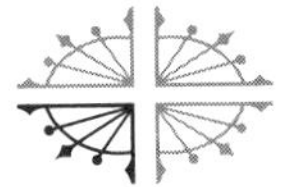

1958

Cape Race, October 16

Dear Nancy,

Instead of a pantry, we now have a bathroom with a flush toilet, sink and bathtub. Unlike the bathroom you're using nowadays, there's no marble or gold but we're proud of it none the less and drew broom straws to see who would have the first bath. Your mother won. The food we took out of the pantry will remain on the kitchen floor until the new cupboards arrive. They're of unfinished wood which we will varnish. We expect to have both the kitchen and bathroom finished by the time you come for Christmas. By the way, Stanley has finished putting together the Viking ship model you sent him for his birthday.

When you write next, be sure to tell us about this term's courses. Your mother will add.

Love, Dad

Dear Nancy,

Tom says Maggie and Ruth have large flower gardens. Could you look around them and pick some flowers for me to press? I know it's late in the season but you may be able to find some I could use. I've collected a few flowers here but need more to glue on the cupboards before they are varnished.

Love, Mom

Nancy put the letter in the top dresser drawer and looked out the bedroom window at the garden behind the house, where flowers bloomed in a rockery. She didn't know what they were but she supposed her aunt wouldn't mind if she picked a few and sent them down to the Cape. She wouldn't tell Maggie what they were for. Her aunt, who had refined taste, would think it odd that her mother wanted to glue flowers on kitchen cupboards, which it was—her mother had peculiar taste. Apart from hanging Grandmother Merla's hooked mats on the wall, her mother's idea of decorating was to drag driftwood inside and pile it in corners; or use a bleached caribou skull as a bookend, oblivious to vermin living inside. Such a thing would never make it across the threshold of the Hunts' house decorated with Chinese urns, crystal chandeliers, silk lampshades and velvet drapes—Aunt Maggie had married old money. On Circular Road, Nancy was offered the occasional sherry, which the Hunts drank from Waterford crystal in front a large fireplace with a Grecian mantel. The walls of their house were hung with landscapes and muted watercolours of fruit and flowers. Wilfred's butterfly collection was in the library along with photographs of Nancy's dead cousin in his christening gown and school uniform—at the age of ten Peter had the pale anxiety of an invalid's face. By the age of twenty he looked more robust, gamely waving a cricket bat at Oxford, which he'd attended briefly before signing up. The last photo taken of him showed a slender young man in an RAF uniform standing in front of a Spitfire.

Nancy didn't ask if this was the plane that had plunged into Scapa Flow. In the year and a half she'd been living with the Hunts, no reference was made to Peter; she was unwilling to disturb this pool of quiet, recognizing the fact that her cousin occupied a place reserved for martyrs and saints. Though Nancy became fond of the Hunts, especially her aunt, during her years on Circular Road she maintained the detachment of a traveller or guest who, despite being coddled and watched over, never quite belonged. She didn't, in fact, know where she belonged but it certainly wasn't the Cape, which in the years before she left it she convinced herself she hated, fearing that otherwise she might never get away, that if she left it too late, she might somehow become absorbed by the Cape's narrow isolation. Now that she had broken away to St. John's, she was embarrassed by its backwardness—not genetic backwardness, the Cape was cosmopolitan compared to places in Newfoundland where people were known to marry their cousins, but intellectual backwardness. Though she knew that if it weren't for her parents' bookishness she might never have left, she had little desire to go home and felt that in her aunt she had found someone like-minded, someone who unlike her mother (Nancy never knew what she was thinking), was passionate and outspoken. She admired the fact that every March 31st her aunt, a staunch anti-Confederate, dressed in black and insisted that the pink, white and green flag be hung at half mast on the Hunts' flagpole where Confederates would be sure to see it. Nancy was fascinated by her aunt's fervour, by the snapping brown eyes and the way she braced her body when she was fully engaged. Barely an inch over five feet, Maggie had the physical presence of a much larger woman. Nancy was flattered when her cousin Cheryl Newhook, Aunt Ruth's daughter, said that Nancy was the dead spit of Maggie, probably because of the thick shoulders and swinging breasts. Though they didn't take the same courses (Cheryl wanted to be a grade school teacher, Nancy a college teacher), they often walked to Memorial together and once a week had tea with Granny Mulloy, who lived with the Newhooks. Cheryl was easygoing and scatterbrained but she didn't condescend to Nancy as some townies did.

St. John's, October 20
Dear Mom and Dad,
I haven't written sooner because I've been too busy. To tell you about my

courses, to put it briefly, three of them are boring. About all my political history prof does is read from his notes. Math is also boring. I don't like it but I am getting good marks, 100% on the last test. Latin is what you'd expect. First it killed the Romans and now it's killing me. But I'm enjoying the survey of English course taught by a woman who was born in White Bay. My favourite course is Settlement of Newfoundland taught by an Englishman.

Mom, I found some pansies and have pressed them in the dictionary. Say Hi to Stan.

Love, Nancy

What Nancy left out of the letter: the Englishman loping into the room the first morning of classes, unaware of his gown trailing on the floor, a carelessness Nancy found endearing. She wanted to pull the sleeve over his shoulder and arrange the gown properly. She was sitting in the front row as she did in every class, having no wish to sit at the back scribbling notes for her seatmates to read. Nancy wanted her professors to recognize her for the serious student she was. Tall and excruciatingly thin, the Englishman folded his body onto the desk facing his students. He took off his shoes and dropped them on the floor, which got a laugh since both toes stuck out of holes in his argyle socks. Swinging his feet back and forth, he introduced himself as Philip Palmer. Not Professor Palmer, one day he would be Professor but not yet. Professor or not, he was their instructor. As the syllabus said, the course was about the history of settlement in Newfoundland. This was a subject dear to his heart, in fact it would be the subject of his dissertation. (Did a master's degree involve a dissertation or was he referring to a doctoral dissertation?) Philip Palmer said he was a recent graduate of Cambridge and was confident he knew more than the class and would, therefore, endeavour to teach them as best he could. Were there any questions? All this was delivered in a plummy English voice that was direct and chummy. It must be his age. How old was he? Thirty? Not as old as thirty-five. Nancy thought he might be as young as twenty-eight.

The first week in October Nancy was in Philip Palmer's office, sitting near the open door, discussing her paper, *Settlement on the Irish Shore*, for which he had given her an A. "I'm curious about why you specified *English* when it's the *Irish* shore," Nancy said, trying to modulate her voice so that it sounded well-reasoned and matter-of-fact, determined that Philip Palmer wouldn't see her as a dumpy schoolgirl.

He came around the desk and leaned against it, his long legs stuck out straight. How tall was he anyway? Taller than Nancy's father by two inches at least.

"Most of the Irish settled here in the nineteenth century whereas the English were in Ferryland in the seventeenth century," he said. "Don't forget the Colony of Avalon. Lord Baltimore and David Kirke."

She had never heard of these men, having studied British history at the Cape, only bits and pieces about Newfoundland.

"Newfoundlanders have always regarded it as the Irish Shore," she said. "Sometimes we call it the Southern Shore."

"Then let us agree to call it the Southern Shore." He smiled and she noticed that for such a tall man he had small teeth; the size of his teeth and the way his lips crooked up on one side gave him a puckish, secretive look. "Shall we drink to that? I was just about to make myself a pot of tea. Would you like a cup?" He reached down and plugged a yellow jiffy jug into the outlet beside the desk.

"I would."

"Then pray. I have a knack for blowing fuses."

They drank their tea with decorum, chatting about the course, Philip Palmer sitting on the desk, leaning toward Nancy in an intimate, confiding way. How did she think the course was going? He was a greenhorn at teaching and any bit of advice she could give him would be appreciated. How strange, how *heartening* to have an instructor ask *her* for advice, but she wasn't so foolish as to oblige. By the end of October, she was visiting his office twice a week, which required her to come up with a pretext that wasn't transparent: a word or phrase needed clarification or a source unavailable at the library; could she borrow a copy of the emigration map he had drawn on the blackboard? Granny Mulloy's cookies and squares were brought as tokens of appreciation and greedily devoured by Philip Palmer over tea.

Cape Race, October 27
Dear Nancy,
A short note before we leave for Trepassey where your mother insists that I see the doctor. I agreed to have a checkup if she would too. Stanley is coming with us though he would rather stay here and work on his science project; he and Kenny Halleran are building a box with screening on two sides to hold glass bottles and jars, some broken, some not. The box will be tied to a rock or tree in Chance Cove and monitored to see how long it takes for wave action to break down the glass. I think the point of this exercise is to test the destructiveness of the sea.
Your mother is mailing you a box of brownies. Trust you are fine.
Love, Dad

Nancy had sworn off brownies: chocolate made her break out in pimples and she was watching her figure. She would give them to Philip who had a sweet tooth.

Cape Race, November 15
Dear Nancy,
Enclosed is a money order for $15.00 to buy Christmas books for Tom and Stanley. For your father I want a good book, with clear maps, of the constellations. For Stanley I would like a book with illustrations, preferably colour, of the underwater world. I'm early with this request because I know you are busy with your studies and won't have a lot of time to shop. Don't bother mailing them, just bring them down when you come for Christmas.
Please give my regards to Maggie and Wilfred.
Love, Mom

Nancy bought the books and mailed them to the Cape along with the pressed flowers; she had already made up her mind that if she could arrange to stay in the city, she wouldn't go home for Christmas. She hadn't yet asked the Hunts if she could stay, but she thought they might be glad of the company. Philip had already mentioned that he would be spending Christmas in St. John's and had asked the class to his flat at the end of term for an evening of wassail, whatever that was. Not only did Nancy plan to be there, but she intended to invite Philip to Christmas dinner at Hunts'.

Cape Race, December 7

Dear Nancy,

Of course we're disappointed that you won't be here for Christmas but we certainly understand your wish to stay in St. John's with your cousin and friends. It will be a boon for Maggie and Wilfred who find Christmas particularly hard since Peter's plane went down on December 22nd. We'll send our presents to town with John when he sees the eye doctor next week.

There's about a foot of snow on the ground here which means your brother more or less lives outside where he and Kenny Halleran have built an igloo. They want to sleep in it tonight but I've said No to that but have agreed to let them have their supper out there, your mother having spoiled them with a basket of food. I must say it looks spectacular in the dark seeing the ice lit up from inside with a flashlight.

Good luck with your exams. Don't stay up all night studying.

Love, Dad

Philip Palmer's flat in Rawlin's Cross was three rooms on the third floor of a wedge-shaped building overlooking the harbour. The living room was furnished with shelves made from apple crates and boards, and a chesterfield stinking of cat piss. The students sat on cushions scattered on the floor; there were nine of them; the rest of the class were either too shy to come or had left for home. Nancy had never drunk mulled wine and was wooed by the headiness of its warmth and by the shadows flickering on the walls from candles burning in jar tops set on shelves and sills. Acutely aware of her attraction for Philip, she staked out a cushion by the window where he could plainly see her as someone separate from the others. She was wearing one of her aunt's hand-me-downs, a red wool dress with a black cinch belt that gave her breasts a voluptuous swell, and had reddened her lips with Scarlet Poppy. Gazing out the window at the buoy light marking the harbour entrance, with the nipple of Signal Hill on one side and the South Side hills on the other, she ignored the conversation of her male classmates who were little more than boys—from their banter and lack of seriousness you could tell that they weren't really men—but she listened closely to Philip who was lying cross-legged on the floor, his head on a cushion. She hadn't yet asked him for Christmas dinner though her aunt had said yes, by all means, invite Mr. Palmer to join us. If only he would get up and go into the kitchen, then she would follow him in and ask—she would never hear the end of it if she invited him in front of the others. And she didn't want to wait until the others had left. That would be setting herself up as someone who was an *easy lay*. That was the way these boys spoke to each other, using words like *broad* and *chick*, *loose* and *pushover*. She also had her aunt's curfew to keep and didn't want to get on the bad side of her by staying out past midnight. Nancy had a fountain pen in her purse but no paper; before it was time to leave she went into the bathroom and, after locking the door, printed the invitation in large blurry letters on a length of toilet paper. When she went into the bedroom to fetch her coat, she put the invitation beneath Philip's pillow. He slept on the floor, on a mattress where they had piled their jackets and coats, which surprised her; she would have thought that someone in his position could afford a bed.

Christmas dinner at Circular Road was a jolly affair. There were Christmas crackers, tissue-paper hats, toy horns and whistles, hard candy, salted nuts and roasted chestnuts. Doorways and windows were trimmed with holly. The twelve-foot tree in the dining room was decorated with candle lights, each one having a tiny rotating shade. Maggie had cooked the turkey herself, the maid having gone home to Harbour Grace. Ruth had brought pease pudding, Granny Mulloy figgy duff pudding with brown sugar sauce and Aurora had sent her version of Merla's cake. There were eight of them around the table, nine after Cheryl's boyfriend arrived. She and Reg sat opposite each other at Wilfred's end of the table while Nancy and Philip occupied the same position at Maggie's end. Nancy felt festive and light-headed, more from being paired with Philip than from drinking pink champagne. Surrounded by laughter and talk, she drifted along with the current of merriment and laughter, bumping into bits of conversation, content to half listen, to float in a reverie of conviviality and good will. But she snapped to attention when Maggie began questioning Philip, drawing him out in a way that Nancy, as his student, was unable to do. He wasn't difficult to draw out and said he was enjoying St. John's "hugely"—another of his words. What a stroke of luck that he was sitting beside Maggie, since she asked the questions Nancy wanted to ask.

His father was the rector in the village of Corfe Castle in Dorset, where Philip and his sister Elaine had grown up. He had read history at Cambridge and intended to return to England some day to complete his doctorate, but first he was eager to try his wings. What better place than Newfoundland, which until recently had been Britain's oldest colony. Added to this was the fact that his mother's family had an early connection to Newfoundland. In 1883, his mother's uncle, Edward Webb, left Poole for Trinity, where he served as curate in St. Paul's for three years, and would have served longer had he not perished on the *Clara Jillian* when she was caught in an April gale on her return from England where Edward had gone for a holiday. Although his uncle's tenure in Newfoundland had been brief, it had affected Philip profoundly; as a boy reading his uncle's letters, he had longed to come to Newfoundland, a place that sounded as rugged and unspoilt as any of the wild places described in the *Boy's Own Annual*. Though he hadn't the slightest desire to become a man of the cloth like his father and uncle—perhaps not wanting to appear maudlin or sentimental, Philip paused and stared into his wineglass—the fact was that, in a curious way, he grew up thinking he had to carry on Edward's adventure. Not duplicate it, that was an impossible feat and he was an entirely different bloke from his uncle and this was, after all, the twentieth century. Nevertheless, he felt honour bound to connect in some way with Edward, whose life had been tragically severed in the flush of youth. Did that sound impossibly romantic and boyish? Not at all, said Maggie.

"Honour bound" was a phrase that would catch up with Nancy later on; for now, she was busy trying to pin down the kind of man Philip Palmer was. She already knew he was unselfconscious and animated, forthcoming, without the reputed English reserve. When he was speaking full tilt, he smacked his lips, oblivious to tiny particles of saliva spraying from his mouth, landing, where were they landing? On his dinner plate, she supposed. When he settled down to his food, he ate with the same smacking sound. A noisy eater—in spite of his Englishness and his height, Nancy was reducing him to a more manageable size. She could see that his boyish earnestness charmed her aunt. Somehow he knew that she expected guests to wear their best caps—in Maggie's view, there was nothing false or wrong in trying to impress, in putting the best foot forward.

They were drinking brandy when the telephone rang. Maggie looked pointedly at Nancy and she felt a guilty jolt as she realized that her aunt knew right away who was calling. Nancy went into the hall and picked up the receiver.

"Merry Christmas, Nancy Rose." Her father was the only one who got away with using her shipwreck name.

"Merry Christmas, Dad. I was waiting until we finished eating to call," she said, though in Philip's presence she had scarcely given the Cape a thought.

He ignored the apology. Being Dad, he sounded unruffled and unperturbed, but so far away. "I forgot that townies dine late." Was he teasing or was that a trace of sarcasm in his voice? "Are you enjoying yourself?"

"Yes, we're having a lot of fun. Guess what. I've been drinking pink champagne!"

"No wonder you're having fun. We've been drinking Beatty's blueberry wine. The Newhooks are there I suppose?"

"Yes."

"I'll talk to Ruth and Maggie later but first your mother wants a turn. She's been standing at my elbow trying to wrench the receiver from my hand."

"Merry Christmas, Nancy."

"Merry Christmas, Mom."

"We just got in from Beatty and John's. We had dinner with them." Her mother sounded breathless and excited. "We enjoyed ourselves but it wasn't the same without you. I miss you, Nancy."

Could this be her mother talking?

"Stanley wants a word."

Her brother's voice was so faint Nancy had to strain to hear. "Would you believe Dad put hoofprints on the roof last night?" he whispered plaintively. "I'm twelve years old and I still have to pretend there's a Santa. Mom says I'll hurt his feelings if I don't go along with it."

"Did you get the telegram?"

"Yeah."

Their father was a believer in family traditions: the telegram from the North Pole, the lump of coal in the toe of the stocking, the carol-sing Christmas Eve, the scrawny spruce in the living-room corner, the boughs on the door and window sills, the partridgeberry garlands, the hoof marks on the roof. The hoof marks were a mystery; ever since Nancy could remember, when there was snow on Christmas morning, their father would take Stan and her up the ladder to see the prints on the roof.

When Maggie came to the phone, Nancy fled upstairs to the bathroom, turned on the tap and splashed cold water on her face in an effort to pull herself together. If she went downstairs with a red nose and bloodshot eyes, Philip would know she was missing home.

To banish homesickness, she imagined a procession of choristers in a Dorset church and a collection of maiden aunts and widowers sitting down to the Palmers' Christmas goose. There was so much more for Philip to miss and if he could overcome homesickness, so could she.

Cape Race, December 29

Dear Nancy,

Thank you for the perfumed notepaper, which you can see for yourself has a flowery smell. Tom and Stanley are pleased with the books you bought on my behalf. I'm rereading Moby Dick *which I haven't read since your father loaned it to me when we were courting.*

The past few months your father has had trouble sleeping, the result of shift work, I suppose. Using instructions from The Book of Knowledge, *I've been hypnotizing him and it seems to be working.*

Love, Mom

Don't you believe it, Nancy. Your mother hypnotized me a long time ago. Happy New Year—Dad

St. John's, January 10

Dear Mom and Dad,

I got my marks back: 100% in Math and Latin, 92% in English, 97% in Political History (all I did was memorize) and 86% in Settlement in Newfoundland. I was disappointed in this mark though it was the highest in the class. At least they are all A's.

Thanks, Dad, for the Waterman's pen and pencil set, and Stan for his original gift. Thanks for the striped sweater, Mom, which must have taken a lot of work.

Love, Nancy

Like their mother, Stan got some kooky ideas. Why did he think Nancy would be the least bit interested in having a replica of a ship's board with *Nancy Rose* painted on it? Stan had the real thing hanging over his bed, well, part of the real thing. Most of the *Joseph* was missing and the paint on *Stanley* was so badly weathered, you could barely make it out. She put the replica in the same drawer where she'd stuffed the sweater: she wouldn't be wearing it, not because she didn't like it but because stripes made her look fat.

St. John's, February 3

Dear Mom and Dad,

Guess what, Uncle Wilfred offered me a few days' work in the store over the Easter holidays so I'll be able to earn some money. He's pretty sure he will have a full-time job to carry me through the summer. Thought you'd like to know.

Love, Nancy

Cape Race, March 14

Dear Nancy,

We are fine though all of us are tired of being housebound. The ground is so icy that your mother can't go on her rambles, which tells you how bad it is. Only Stanley, who as you know admires ice in all its forms, ventures forth, wearing skates of course. He has begun a new science project. (Did I tell you that last year's project was washed out to sea? Not a trace of it anywhere.) This year's project is an arctic science station under glass which will be completely self-sustaining with growing plants to absorb carbon dioxide and produce oxygen.

Your mother passes the time making pincushions for the spring tea at Holy Redeemer, using two of my mother's hats she found upstairs. I've finished the crossword puzzle book you gave me at Christmas (Hint) and am making a large constellation chart to put up in the light.

Love, Dad

Cape Race, April 6

Dear Nancy,

Your father asked me to write and thank you for the crossword puzzle book. He fell on the ice and broke his thumb. It's so painful he can barely lift a spoon. Stanley and I are covering his shift.

The kitchen cupboards arrived and I've finished gluing on the leaves and flowers and will put on the first coat of varnish tomorrow.
Love, Mom

In June, after spring term, Nancy and a classmate, Gerry Morgan, spent an afternoon inspecting the construction of the new university campus. They hadn't set out to do this together but met by chance on her afternoon off—she was now working full-time at the store. Gerry had a harmless cocky manner she appreciated. Now that she was seeing more of Philip, it was a relief being with a male who didn't set her heart thumping, who didn't make her sweat and flush.

The new campus was being built on what had once been farmland, on the north side of the avenue. Though so far there was nothing to see but concrete foundations and steel girders, there were a dozen or more people wandering about the site, taking advantage of the warm windless weather. Gerry said that Joey planned to connect the buildings with underground tunnels so that students could walk to class without going outside. How money was flowing into Newfoundland! Smallwood couldn't spend it fast enough.

"The theatre will be in the arts building. Just think, girl. You and me will be the first class to climb the steps to Joey's new stage." Gerry reached out and gave Nancy's ear lobe a playful tug. When she bumped him with her hip as she used to do with Stan, knocking him over, he grabbed her hand and pulled her down on a patch of grass. They rolled onto their backs, looking at the wide blue sky, flinging their arms at their sides and laughing. When she sat up, Nancy was dismayed to see Philip loping away from the campus in the direction of Rawlin's Cross.

The next morning Philip arrived at her uncle's store, coming in droopily, damply out of the rain; he looked like a stork or an egret, some long-legged, long-necked, ruffled bird blown off course by a storm. Nancy, her sunburnt face shiny with Noxzema, was at the back of the store, taking stock of the school supply section. She was used to seeing Philip turn up at the store to buy supplies, a notebook, envelopes, pencils, he seemed to be always running out of one thing or another. He didn't look for anything today, but came straight to the aisle where Nancy was sitting on a stool, writing *8 scribblers* and *5 erasers* on a clipboard; putting a hand on a shelf, he leaned over so that she was at eye level with his leather jacket buttons. "Tell me," he said, his voice barely audible, "Is Gerry Morgan your lover?"

Nancy didn't laugh though later—years later—it occurred to her that laughing was exactly what she ought to have done. In fact she was never able to remember precisely what she had done. Did her jaw drop a fraction of an inch? Did she bite her lip, run a hand through her hair? It didn't occur to her to tell Philip to mind his own business or ask if he'd been spying on Gerry and her; she didn't know how to say *bugger off*. What she said in a small voice was, "No."

"In that case, I would like the privilege."

Her heart didn't stop, it only felt like it had; her ears were blocked against the sounds in the store: footsteps, the door opening and closing, her uncle's voice. But she could think. Did Philip mean he wanted to marry her, that he was in love with her, or merely that he wanted to sleep with her?

He touched her lightly on the shoulder. "There's no hurry. Take your time deciding." He loped up the aisle and out of the store, then doubled back to buy a package of file cards.

Nancy counted the rulers twice, then twice more again: there were eleven but she couldn't trust herself to write down the number. What should she do? If she pretended she hadn't heard Philip's offer, she might be able to face him after this; she wouldn't be taking any courses from him in the fall and perhaps could avoid him until then, at least until the confusion cleared. She was disappointed that rather than their becoming lovers in a moment of passion, Philip had put lovemaking on a rational basis, making an offer she could either refuse or accept. She wanted to accept, yes, she did, she was nineteen, old enough to make love to a man—Philip was twenty-seven, Aunt Maggie had extracted his age—but you couldn't sleep with a man without taking precautions. When Nancy began menstruating, her mother had made a vague, oblique reference to sex, but in her preoccupied way had neglected to mention birth control. How was she to know that her parents had never taken precautions, that her and Stanley's births had been random collisions of egg and sperm? She would have to ask Cheryl, who she was certain was doing it with Reg.

St. John's, September 28
Dear Mom and Dad,
I'm sorry I won't be able to make it down over Thanksgiving weekend. It isn't the fare—I have enough money saved up from my job. I know I promised but I have three assignments due by the middle of October—that's two weeks. It's important that I keep up my marks.
Love, Nancy

Nancy and Philip became lovers on Thanksgiving weekend. Cheryl had finally been consulted: a diaphragm was supposed to work, but to get one Nancy would have to be fitted, and if she went to an RC doctor for a fitting the visit would be immediately reported to Maggie (who hadn't converted when she married Wilfred). It would be hard to find an RC doctor who wasn't under the thumb of the priests and Cheryl didn't know any doctors who were Prods. She advised Nancy to take her chances with French safes, as she and Reg were doing. Philip bought the safes, condoms he called them, saying he would be responsible for taking precautions whenever they made love. Nancy was so nervous and tightly wound that the first time Philip entered, tears smarted at the corners of her eyes. Philip assured her that making love improved with time. She assumed that this was the voice of experience speaking since Philip seemed to have a clear idea of how it was done, dragging the mattress into the living room because he liked making love below the window sill where a candle burnt off condensation, making a porthole through which, if either had looked, they would have the sheen of the harbour. He preferred Nancy on top, straddling his hips while he held her breasts; knees bent, he heaved his buttocks off the mattress then thumped hard against the floor. Nancy thought about what the elderly man who lived below must be thinking, and never left the flat without worrying about meeting him on the stairs. She was a fallen woman, a man's lover, a mistress. The words were exciting, clandestine, adding a dimension of risk and danger to the affair.

Keeping a lover required energy and concentration, Nancy hadn't realized how much. She had wanted love, sexual love, so badly that she had never questioned the cost. Her grades began to slip: she made a B in chemistry and in psychology—for the first time in her life—a C. When she told Philip that she would have to cut back their trysts—another of his words—until she pulled up her marks, he put on a long face that lasted until she agreed to meet him twice a week, on Saturday and Wednesday nights, after the library closed. So it was that she became one of those students who "did" it, riding an arrow aimed straight into the heart of adulthood since by taking a lover she had moved herself beyond all possibility of reclaiming the innocence of girlhood, no matter how much she might sometimes wish its return.

Cape Race, November 25

Dear Nancy,

Your father and I are excited that you'll be coming for Christmas. By all means bring a guest. Wasn't he the instructor who taught Settlement in Newfoundland? If you don't mind, I'll send you a list of items to bring down when you come. Later, after I've given it more thought. Here's your father.

Love, Mom

Hi Nancy,

I think arthritis set in my thumb after the break. You can see from the scrawl how stiff it is. Just want to add that we look forward to seeing you at

Christmas. You realize that it will have been two years since you were here. Though your mother and I haven't said so, not wanting to hold you back, we think two years is much too long to go without seeing you.

Love, Dad

Nancy and Philip agreed to forgo lovemaking during their week at the Cape, and not to give any indication that they were more than acquaintances. Philip said that as the son of a rector he understood the necessity of keeping one's sex life underground. The pretence would be a continuation of their life in St. John's since they now avoided each other on campus in order not to draw attention to themselves. Philip never touched her unless they were on his mattress, which Nancy viewed as considerate, even virtuous.

Because her father knew the history of the Southern Shore, Nancy had imagined that during the holiday he and Philip would have long discussions at the kitchen table, but it didn't happen; her father was distant and formal with Philip whom he addressed as Mr. Palmer and seemed to avoid, staying up in the light or going upstairs to bed for a nap after his morning chores were finished. Perhaps it was a matter of his being older—he was fifty-seven—and needing more rest. Her mother was more hospitable, packing a lunch of sandwiches and tea, accompanying Philip, Nancy and Stan to Clam Cove Brook to see where fishermen had buried one hundred drowned corpses retrieved from the sea after the wreck of the *Anglo Saxon*. The bodies of 137 more—steerage passengers emigrating to the Canadian prairie—had never been found. Her mother also went with them to Mistaken Point to see the Precambrian fossil beds where Stan listed twenty-two ships that had gone down off the point, rattling off dates and ports of call, and later after they returned to the house, showing Philip a map he had drawn of all the known shipwrecks along the coast.

Philip was impressed with the Cape. He said that in some ways the coastline reminded him of Cornwall: both had windswept moors and rocky shores, but the Cape was wilder, harsher and he thought more primitive. He scrambled over the rocks and loped across the Barrens, a white scarf wound around his head like a bandage, his hair sticking out like black straw. Beside him, wearing Tom's oversized parka, her mother looked elfin, walking demurely alongside their guest, hands deep in her pockets, smiling at his lavish enthusiasms. Philip was courtly with her mother, deferential to the point of fawning, going on about how much he liked the kitchen cupboards with their border of pressed flowers. When Nancy and Stan went skating on Middle Pond, he declined to go, saying he preferred to sit in the kitchen rocker and talk to their mother while she prepared supper. Though he didn't skate, Nancy was peeved at him for not coming along, and she was peeved at her mother. It wasn't that she was flirting or leading Philip on, but she wasn't doing anything to discourage his attention. At least her father didn't embarrass her by climbing the ladder on Christmas Day, or showing off the library, which seemed narrow and dated compared to the Hunts'. To his credit her father took Philip to Chance Cove to cut a tree and boughs, carrying an axe and a thermos of cocoa; Philip was beside himself with excitement, swinging his arms as they strode across the headland. While they were gone Nancy hung wreaths her mother had made from sphagnum moss, bunchberries and red ribbon. She thought the wreaths made the windows look cosy in a ye-olde-country way and said they would suit the windows of houses on Circular Road.

"Then I'll make more for you to take back to Maggie and Ruth," her mother said, and inquired about Nancy's courses, asking if she a clear idea of what she wanted to do after graduation. She didn't inquire if she had a boyfriend or if she and Philip were more than friends. On this visit her mother's self-containment worked to Nancy's advantage; she answered Philip's questions politely but didn't offer unwanted information. She did not, for instance, mention the embarrassing fact that her children had been named after shipwrecks. Stan was also well behaved; he didn't tease and spared Philip the ridiculous story about their mother being rescued from an ice pan. On the morning of Nancy and Philip's departure, her parents accompanied them to the Cove to wait for the taxi from Trepassey. When it came, Nancy's father hugged her tightly and told her that he had enjoyed having her home. Philip hugged her mother and shook hands with her father, thanking them yet again before getting into the car. He thanked Nancy, too, three hours later as their taxi was coming into St. John's. "Christmas at the Cape was an extraordinary experience. I wouldn't have missed it for the world. Your mother is enchanting. I think I have fallen in love with her." He sighed and tipped his head against the window. Knowing that after a week's holiday it couldn't be a sigh of exhaustion, and that it must be a sigh of longing and regret, stunned Nancy into silence. She could think of nothing to say that wouldn't make her look childish, and had no intention of demeaning herself by telling Philip that his remark was thoughtless and cruel, all the more so since he had never once said that he had fallen in love with her. How easily those words about her mother had tumbled out of his mouth!

For the next three months she began finding excuses to avoid his flat: she was having medical problems, nothing serious, but she preferred to wait until she was feeling better before meeting him at Rawlin's Cross; she was behind in her work, which was certainly true. She needed to graduate with first class honours in order to go on to postgraduate work. It wasn't so much a recognition that she must ultimately depend on herself that was making her single-minded about her future as much as it was her inclination, when stung, to turn away. It would be years before she recognized that with regard to Philip, her habit of withdrawal began that day as their taxi was entering St. John's, establishing a pattern that would recur whenever she felt slighted by him.

By Easter she was again meeting him in his flat until Cheryl told her that Philip was also seeing Catherine Wright, a second-year history student; Cheryl had known about Catherine for some time but hadn't wanted to say anything for fear of hurting her cousin. Once again Nancy found excuses to avoid Rawlin's Cross. It was easier than admitting jealousy, which Philip would regard as immature. This period of abstinence was much longer, lasting through the summer and into early fall, and didn't end until October when she and Philip attended the opening ceremony of the new university campus. Standing in the crowd outside the Arts and Adminstration Building listening to the loudspeaker broadcast the speeches taking place inside, she felt someone lean on her shoulder and, turning, caught sight of the familiar scarf trailing from the sleeve. Bending over and putting his mouth close to her ear, he vowed that he would be on the stage one day soon. She was astonished by this naked declaration, by how badly he wanted to be one of the professors in black robes and satin plumage who earlier had passed them in solemn procession. Though she wanted to become a professor (she wasn't sure of what), Nancy hadn't once imagined herself sitting among the dignitaries on stage.

He surprised her again, when they were lying on his mattress at Rawlin's Cross. He told her that when he went home for Christmas he would be visiting Cambridge to make arrangements to begin work on his doctoral thesis next year, and suggested that when he went back again in the spring she might return with him. In England, he said, they could live together.

"Wouldn't your parents object?"

They need not know, he wrote in the air.

"I have no money. Can you afford it?"

Two can live more cheaply than one.

Nancy interpreted the invitation as proof that he had given up Catherine Wright in favour of her.

Cape Race, December 10

Dear Nancy,

As you know, Maggie and Wilfred invited us to spend Christmas in St. John's. John has agreed to take my shift and I will take his when he and Beatty go to Brigus for New Year's. Your mother has already ordered us new clothes so we will look presentable in town. Stanley is plotting how he can look around the university. He particularly wants to see the science lab.

Love, Dad

St. John's, December 14

Dear Mom and Dad,

I'm writing this in the library where I've come to study. The Hunts are having the bedrooms repainted this week so it's much too noisy to study there. I'm fine, hard at work as usual and am looking forward to your being here for Christmas. I spoke to Dr. Butler, my last year's chemistry teacher, about Stan being able to look around the lab. He said he didn't think it would be a problem.

Love, Nancy

P.S. Tell Stan to bring his skates.

Nancy's mother arrived at Hunts' wearing an Eaton's catalogue coat and matching hat—she must have known that in town most women her age wore a hat. Nancy noticed that beneath the brim her mother's hair had been cut and that when she removed her coat she was wearing a respectable grey suit. Looking at her sitting in the velvet wingback chair sipping sherry, her legs elegant in silk stockings, Nancy had to admire her, thinking that no one would guess this was her mother's first visit to town or that she had spent her life on the Southern Shore. She didn't embarrass Nancy by gawking or gaping at the luxurious furnishings. Was she unimpressed or merely taking the opulence in her stride? Nancy thought she looked more at home on Circular Road than her father and Stan who were wearing grey flannels and new blazers that didn't quite fit. Both of them were obviously uncomfortable in their new clothes, and after dinner removed their ties and exchanged their jackets for sweaters. Not her mother who wore the same outfit for the four whole days she was in St. John's. It was as if, once she had chosen her outfit, it became a uniform to be worn everywhere in town: to the Capitol to see a movie, to the basilica for mass and to the hotel for luncheon; she even wore it sitting in front of the Hunts' new Marconi television.

No one, not even Cheryl, asked about Philip. He had told Nancy not to expect him to write, that he would be back in St. John's before a letter arrived. Nancy had obligingly put him into a box and set him on a shelf, anticipating that when she lifted the lid in January, he would pop up like a jack-in-the-box and snatch her up. In the meantime, she and Stan skated to music at the Stadium and went sliding on Robinson's Hill. She smuggled her brother into a club where he made a half-hearted attempt to dance the twist. After he and her parents returned to the Cape, she went to bars with Cheryl and Reg, and on New Year's Eve to a house party in the Battery where she danced with Gerry Morgan, who had returned from Heart's Content early, after he and his girlfriend had a falling out.

St. John's, January 5

Dear Mom and Dad,

Last term's marks have been posted. You'll be pleased to know that I got straight A's. I can hear you both saying "Was there any doubt?" Believe me, there was.

We had a good time at Christmas, didn't we? I feel like I've been attending parties ever since. Now I'm ready to settle down for my final term. Only four months to go before graduation.

Love, Nancy

Though Nancy buckled down to her courses and Philip to writing a research outline for his Cambridge supervisor, they still managed to meet twice a week in Rawlin's Cross. She became pregnant in late February and by mid-April when her breasts became sore and her skirts were too tight, was shattered by the realization that she would be nearly three months along at her graduation. She calmed herself down, though only slightly, by the assurance that if she was careful about what she wore, she might get through it without anyone noticing. As soon as they met at his flat on Saturday afternoon, she broke the news to Philip, who put his hands to his face and moaned, "Oh no!" But he recovered without Nancy needing to remind him that he had been the one looking after birth control. "We'll marry," he said, taking charge. "We'll marry after your graduation, before I leave for England. That way we'll arrive in England a married couple. Your parents are coming to your graduation, aren't they?"

"Yes."

"Then it should work all right."

What a relief that the problem had a convenient solution, one moreover that would allow her to live in a country she longed to see. It didn't matter that Philip hadn't asked if she would marry him, that he'd assumed she would; what mattered was that her family wouldn't know about the baby until after she was married and living in England, thereby rescuing her from disgrace.

St. John's, April 17

Dear Mom, Dad & Stan,

This will come as a big surprise to you, but Philip Palmer and I are getting married. I was going to phone you the news but it's easier for me to tell you about it in a letter. We've been friends for some time but have kept it a secret because of the situation (his being an instructor and me a student). Because I'll be accompanying him at the end of term when he returns to England for further study, we've decided to marry the day after my graduation, which should work out well since you will already be here.

Aunt Maggie and Uncle Wilfred have agreed to let us be married at their house by Wilfred's cousin who, as you know, Dad, is a United Church minister. With Philip's father being an Anglican rector and me a Roman Catholic, it seems the best way to do it. Aunt Maggie kindly offered to look after the wedding arrangements so that I can concentrate on my studies.

I hope you will be as happy as I am about this news.

Love, Nancy

Happiness flowed through Nancy like air, aerating her flesh, lightening her bones, making her feel unencumbered, uplifted, as if she were floating through the ether on feathered wings. Except for morning nausea, she didn't give the baby a second thought. It, too, had been put into a box and shelved until after her graduation and marriage. Oh, then, she and Philip would be off to England! What could be more exciting than a honeymoon in England?—which both she and Philip would certainly deserve by the time they finished their term.

Nancy enjoyed studying for exams, enjoyed cramming information into her head. She liked the dry sweetish smell of books, the reassuring arrangement of sentences on a page, the tidy margins and numbers telling her where she was. She liked the alignment of her notes, the lists of books she had read, the orderly proof of all she knew.

Cape Race, April 11

Dear Nancy,

As I mentioned on the phone we were surprised by the news of your marriage and as parents naturally worry about you whether or not you want us to. The misgivings I expressed on the phone should be seen in that light, as a father's understandable wish to protect his daughter as best he can.

Rest assured, I will be there to give you away to the man of your choice.

Love, Dad

Dear Nancy,

I think Maggie's suggestion that you wear a hem length veil over your graduation dress is a good idea. Do you want to use my wedding veil? Tell Maggie I will make the wedding cake (using Merla's recipe of course). If there is anything I can do to help, let me know.

I am happy for you. Love, Mom

Once again, Nancy was overwhelmed with gratitude, this time for her mother. It was she, not Nancy's father, who had written the needed words, *happy for you*.

Unlike her solemn graduation the day before, the wedding was a burst of vernal optimism, a familial rite of spring. The fireplace mantel on Circular Road was banked with tulips, daffodils, hyacinths, primulas and forget-me-nots to make a backdrop for the ceremony. With the addition of the veil, Nancy's graduation dress, which fortunately still had a waist, was transformed into a wedding gown. Philip wore a brown suit, the cuffs of his shirt folded back to offset the shortness of the jacket sleeves. Nancy had never seen him in a suit and thought it made him look inexperienced and vulnerable, which was oddly reassuring—until now it hadn't occurred to her that he might be terrified at becoming a husband and a father, taking home a bride his parents had never met.

After the ceremony, they went into the dining room to drink champagne and cut the wedding cake, which Aurora had iced, arranging a wreath of yellow forsythia around the base of the cake. By now the forsythia had wilted and looked more like a crown of thorns than a circlet of flowers. Nancy scarcely noticed—apart from Philip, she wasn't noticing much. But when Wilfred gave the toast to the bride and joked about Philip having courted her right under his nose in the store, she blushed at the thought that her uncle might have been watching when Philip asked if she would become his lover. She wondered, briefly, what else he and Aunt Maggie knew.

Later, after Nancy had changed into one of her aunt's tweed suits, the family squeezed into cars and drove to the train station where they rained confetti on the newlyweds. As the train carried them away Nancy felt she was riding the twin rails of excitement and satisfaction; here she was, a university graduate sitting beside her husband on their way to Halifax where a ship would take them to England. Think of the rosy future that lay ahead! Still no thought of the baby.

By the time she was lying on the lower bunk of the *Poseidon*, a rusting Greek liner bound for Southampton, the stench of her vomit rising from the pail, the future was the last thing on her mind, which was fogged with exhaustion and misery—she had been throwing up since leaving Halifax two days ago. To get away from the stink, Philip spent most of his time walking around the ship and going to the bar, from which he returned smelling moistly of ale. Nancy cheered herself up by reviewing how happy she'd been a week earlier. She'd been happy during her graduation, sitting in the fifth row of the auditorium beside Gerry Morgan, who told her she looked beautiful in white—no one had ever called her beautiful, not even her father. She'd been happy walking on stage and shaking hands with the chancellor who handed her the degree and then the Governor General's Medal for the highest marks, all this in front of her father and brother sitting below in their new blazers and flannels, her mother looking trim and respectable in her city clothes. After the graduation ceremony, while Maggie was taking photographs outside, Nancy put the medal on the palm of her father's hand and curled his fingers around it. "It's for you and Mom," she said and he wept and hugged her with a fervour that wasn't repeated on her wedding day.

Tom was disappointed when he learned that our daughter was pregnant; Maggie said she wouldn't have told him if he hadn't been so dead set against the marriage. He had telephoned his sister to ask if she thought Nancy could be talked out of marrying Philip, whom he seemed determined to dislike, all the while insisting that his objection to the marriage wasn't based on dislike but on his disappointment that for all her cleverness and ability, Nancy had allowed herself to be seduced by one of her instructors. Though I reminded him that at twenty, she was the same age I was when we married, and told him how I wanted to be carried along by her evident joy, he insisted that she was far too young to marry, to throw away her plans to become a college teacher. I knew that it would be some time before he got used to the idea that Nancy was married, and was unsurprised that he wept when she placed the medal in his hands.

"What shall I call your father?" Nancy and Philip were on the train between Southampton and Poole where his parents would meet them with the Austin. "Shall I call him Reverend or Mr. Palmer?"

"Wait and see what he suggests."

Nancy caught sight of his parents first through the window. Because of his collar, she picked out the rector right away: like Philip, he was long-shanked and thin. Beside him, Philip's mother was short and almost square, wearing a coat that wouldn't button; on her head was an unbecoming hat, its sunflower, if it was meant to be a sunflower, crushed almost beyond recognition. At the sight of the hat, Nancy felt a giddy reprieve; Philip had said that his parents were ordinary people but she hadn't believed him and had expected a commanding, austere couple, not this red-faced wheezing woman and unprepossessing man. His mother immediately kissed her cheek and said encouragingly, "You must call me Lucy." Taking his hand from behind his back, his father bent over and offered it to Nancy. "Arthur Palmer."The intense pained expression vanished the moment he smiled. "Welcome to England."

England, the Mother Country; she had set foot in it at last. Once the luggage had been stowed in the boot, they were on their way, Philip chatting with his parents, Nancy staring out the window at the hedgerows and stone walls on either side of the winding road as they sped by hosts of trees: beech and elm, hawthorn and chestnut. Bursts of green were everywhere: copses, closes, greenswards, commons, meadows and fields: England was truly a green and pleasant land. After the barren rockiness of Newfoundland, its openness to the sea, its vast empty spaces, England had the intimacy of a garden. Everything Nancy saw was in miniature; the narrow streets, the row houses, the tiny shops (the butcher, the baker, the candlestick maker) might have been part of a child's play village.

The rectory, however, was enormous. A wide U-shaped stone

building dominating an acre of walled garden, it was dark and chilly inside. With Philip's sister Elaine at Oxford, there was no attempt to heat the unused rooms. Doors were kept shut and a tapestry curtain hung over the front door to block out drafts; the Palmers came and went by way of the kitchen porch, which served as a cold room. A coal fire burned in the small sitting-room grate next to the kitchen and another in Arthur's study at the end of the hall; upstairs the Palmers made do with electric heaters and hot water bottles. Philip's parents' bedroom was above the study; the newlyweds were given a large, drafty room over the kitchen that had the advantage of being off by itself.

Philip looked at the green wool carpet on the bedroom floor and remarked that someone must have died. "Remember when Stan was telling me about how many houses along the shore had been furnished from shipwrecks? It's the same thing here. When an old wreck in the parish dies, he or she wills various goods to the rectory. That's why there are so many mismatched pieces in the house." He was in high spirits, glad to be home, to have the nightmare voyage over with, to settle down to his doctorate.

In the morning, Lucy Palmer brought them tea and biscuits in bed, knocking discreetly before opening the door. Nancy sat up while Lucy, a white apron over her navy blue dress, carried in the tea tray, which held a daffodil in a bud vase, and put it on Nancy's lap. "Breakfast in an hour," she said.

Nancy tapped her husband on the shoulder. "Philip, is this an English custom or is your mother spoiling us because we're newlyweds?"

"We always have tea and biscuits in bed. Pour me a cup, will you?"

How grand to be sitting with her back against the pillows, pouring tea into porcelain cups. Elation cancelled out any thought that very soon, she would be the one carrying in the tea tray. Some brides wanted to honeymoon in hotels and resorts; they were the same brides who wanted diamond rings, furs, crystal and silver ordered from Birks. Nancy had never wanted any of that; what she wanted was exactly this, sitting in a real English bed drinking English breakfast tea whilst looking at an English daffodil, albeit a late daffodil with wrinkled edges.

After breakfast, she and Philip walked up to the Corfe Castle ruin and climbed over tumbled walls and through rock-strewn passageways, peering through stone arches at the landscape below, where cottages and farms looked like a picnic spread on a quilt. From up here the village was a jumble of grey stone and slate roofs tapering into a road that disappeared into the Dorset countryside. How quaint, how charming, words that never could be applied to the Cape. Unlike Newfoundland, which was raw and untouched, there was something finished about England, as if everything that needed doing had been done and now it rested, fully imagined and complete, every inch of it having been thoroughly examined.

In the afternoon Philip went off in the Austin with his father to the Steeple Church and Nancy accompanied Lucy to choir practice in St. Edward's, which was along the road from the rectory. The Church of St. Edward, King and Martyr, had vaulted ceilings and a spacious interior, a stalwart plainness that seemed appropriate for the Palmers. There were eleven choir boys, unruly lads who jostled each other up the aisle then poked and prodded each other as they arranged themselves in a ragged line. Nancy sat at the rear of the church and listened to Philip's mother coax and cajole them through the singing. Though the boys' minds were no doubt on the playing fields, bit by bit Lucy brought them around to singing the Twenty-fourth Psalm with an earnestness and concentrated purity that was sublime.

Corfe Castle, June 6

Dear Mom and Dad,

At last we are here, after a wretched crossing during which I was seasick the whole time, but I am now wholly recovered. Philip's parents met us at Poole and brought us to Corfe Castle where we are staying with them at the rectory which is enormous (12 rooms) with hidden corners, the sort of mansion where you might expect to see a ghost float down the hallway, if you believe in that sort of thing which I don't. Philip's parents, who insist that I call them Arthur and Lucy, are unpretentious and down-to-earth. Lucy's passion is music—she's mistress of three choirs and teaches piano lessons as well. Arthur's passion is the garden in which he grows what he calls Shakespeare's flowers: lady smocks, long purples, columbine. Corfe Castle is like the pictures of English villages in The Book of Knowledge*: narrow winding streets that seem to have been here forever. Tidy front gardens with stone or wrought iron fences. Roses. Imagine roses growing in gardens in June! I could go on but Lucy has begun making tea which is really supper and I must go and offer to help. This is short, I know, but you can see I am well and enjoying myself hugely.*

Love, Nancy

Nancy and Philip's first married quarrel took place in the rectory kitchen after his parents had left for evensong and Nancy had made the tea. Philip slurped a mouthful of tea and announced that tomorrow he would begin interviewing people in coastal villages: his thesis supervisor had suggested that he include a chapter about possible connections between families in southwest England with their relatives in Newfoundland. Nancy asked what could he possibly expect to find after 150 or 200 years.

"Folk memory. There may be a few old-timers who have some knowledge of family connections with Newfoundland. At any rate, I intend to browse around villages and see what I can find."

She wiped her hands on a tea towel and sat down. "That sounds like a delightful way to spend a honeymoon." Philip had yet to suggest one. Perhaps the trip over had been his idea of a honeymoon.

"Actually, I wasn't intending that you would come."

"What were you intending I should do while you traipse around the country? Stay here with your parents?"

"Why not? You get on well together and my mother could use the help."

"I didn't come all the way to England to live with your parents!" Nancy was standing now and shouting. She had never before shouted at anyone except her mother.

"Calm down. Calm down. I swear there's nothing worse than an hysterical woman." Philip shook his head in disgust, got up, loped down the hall to his father's study and slammed the door. Within minutes he was back, bracing an arm against the sink and looking gloomily out the window at the mizzling rain.

"All right, you can come. But pregnant or not, you will have to sleep in a tent. I can't afford to put up in hotels. Even a modest inn is too dear for my pocketbook. My savings won't stretch that far."

"I thought you said two can live cheaper than one."

"I didn't say three can live cheaper than one. With a baby on the way, we have to be frugal. I won't ask my parents for another penny. My mother has already spent her inheritance sending Elaine and myself to university. If I am to finish my degree, you will have to shape up."

Nancy shaped up, but as someone who had recently had ironed laundry laid on her bed by a maid, she found that married life in another country took some getting used to. She learned to cook after a fashion on the two-burner stove in the small furnished flat the Palmers had rented above Peake's Chemist Shop in Salisbury. Philip had found a part-time job teaching at the South Wiltshire Grammar School for Girls. She washed clothes in the sink and dried them on the wooden rack hanging from the kitchen ceiling. She darned socks and patched jackets and pants. She sewed a baby layette entirely by hand and prowled through second-hand shops for a crib, which she scraped and painted, now thinking of little else but the baby, who had long since been taken out of the box. When she broke the news about the pregnancy to her parents, her mother wrote back immediately to say that she was pleased, but her father made no mention of it in his letters. For the first time in her life, Nancy missed her mother and wanted her near: she would understand Nancy's terror of the impending birth and would know afterwards what to do with the child. When she was most homesick for her mother, Nancy would wet her finger and write in the air *I am not afraid*.

On November 5, 1961, after a two-day labour, Nancy delivered a long-limbed, black-haired daughter slimy with mucus and blood. Since the baby was a girl, Philip said Nancy could choose the name; she chose Sheila, a Newfoundland name that as far as she knew had never been used on a ship. Philip telephoned the news to the Cape.

By the time Philip telephoned us with the news, Tom was anticipating the birth as much as I. We admired Nancy for making the most of a difficult situation, for carrying the child all these months in a strange country, even if it is the country where she wanted to be. When Philip said she had endured a bloody awful labour with pluck, I didn't point out that considering the loneliness and fear I knew she must have felt, courage would have been a better word.

Corfe, December 27

Dear Mom and Dad and Stan,

I was disappointed in the terrible connection on Christmas Eve. I'm sure I heard only half of what was said. Even hearing your voices through that static made me weepy but I am often weepy these days. The baby is fine and has lost her redness and only cries when she's hungry. Thanks for Sheila's quilt, which I told her was made by a ninety-seven-year-old Newfoundlander named Alma Perry, but I don't think she took it in.

Philip's sister arrived in Corfe Castle on Christmas Eve. I must say I don't know what to make of her. She's a haughty, opinionated person, though friendly enough to me, but she seems bored with everything so I doubt she'll stay long. I would stay here for weeks being spoiled, but the day after tomorrow Philip and I are returning to Salisbury where he begins teaching full-time (replacing a pregnant teacher).

Happy New Year from the three of us.

Love, Nancy

Salisbury, January 16

Dear Aunt Maggie,

Philip and I want to thank you and Wilfred for the generous gift of a pram, which I use when I take Sheila out for her daily walk. Now that I have got the hang of breastfeeding, she is sleeping through the night—I'm told this is exceptional for a child this young. Philip's parents took some photographs of her at Christmas and as soon as they are developed I'll send you a picture. Thanks again.

Love, Nancy

Salisbury, March 15

Dear Mom and Dad,

Now that Sheila is weaned, I've taken a job, working downstairs for Mr. Peake who needs someone to mind the cash while he fills prescriptions. His wife used to do this but she has some problem with her legs and has been ordered off her feet. Mr. Peake is getting on himself and sort of shuffles when he walks. The job isn't challenging but it will pay the rent, and has the advantage of me being able to see Sheila at noon—I have a childminder to look after her here while I'm at work.

Love, Nancy

Cape Race, June 20th

Dear Nancy,

Thank you for the recent photos, which your mother has tacked to the wall above the kitchen table. I can see, proud grandfather that I've become, that

Sheila is a very pretty maid. (Your mother predicted this would happen.) With that black hair she certainly looks like her father, but then your mother claims that most firstborns look like their fathers and Sheila certainly bears this out.

I've begun scraping and painting the house, which took a beating last winter; your mother is painting the trim. We are back to sharing chores just as we did in our early married days. Stanley will help us paint once he finishes his exams.

Did I tell you Beatty's mother died and left her the house in Brigus? By the way, Wilfred has been diagnosed with Parkinson's disease.

Love, Dad

Dear Nancy,

Your father has covered the news so I will ask you to give the baby a kiss from Gran. Tell her I am making a book for her birthday.

Love, Mom

Nancy had already begun keeping a book for Sheila in which she recorded information under its proper heading: *three months, six months, one year*, being careful to avoid details that might embarrass her at some future date. Already she was fiercely protective of her daughter, a feeling that had caught her unawares, probably because before Sheila was born she hadn't known anything about babies and had never been the slightest bit interested in them. If she hadn't become accidentally pregnant, she might never have had a child, but now that she had Sheila, she was unwilling to contemplate a life that didn't include this dark-haired, blue-eyed baby with whom she was enthralled.

Salisbury, November 10

Dear Mom and Dad,

Mom, many thanks for Sheila's book. I showed it to her straight away. I am touched by your thoughtfulness. She took her first steps and will be walking soon.

Love, Nancy

Sheila's birthday book wasn't at all what Nancy expected. On its cover her mother had printed in bold letters: *Where My Mother Grew Up*. Inside were scenes from the Cape, watercolours mostly, on which her mother had glued foil (the lighthouse), string (the clothes line), cotton wool (snow) and grass, which had shaken loose on its transatlantic flight. Her mother had drawn pictures of Nancy as a baby, then as a toddler, a girl, and so on.

As soon as Mr. Peake lowered the blind on the shop door at five o'clock, Nancy bolted upstairs, put Sheila in the pram, and took her out for an airing, something the childminder refused to do. By that hour most of the shops were closed, but the bakery on New Canal Street stayed open an extra half hour and there were usually books to return to the library. This was Nancy's favourite time of day, pushing the pram along the streets, watching the woman in an angora sweater and white gloves cycling past as she did every day, and the war veteran on his way to the pub followed by a waddling bulldog. On weekends Nancy walked past the houses of the well-to-do, admiring the huge Victorian mansions with their bevelled glass windows and elaborate roof trim. Sometimes she walked around the cathedral close, stopping at intervals to admire the soaring magnificence of the church.

These days she and Philip saw little of one another. Through the good graces of the headmistress, he had been given the use of a school library for evening study and spent most of his free time there, returning to the flat after Nancy was asleep. In the mornings, she set his tea tray on the dresser beside the bed before she went downstairs to work. In the evenings, after Sheila was settled in her crib, Nancy put the bread board over the exposed wire spring in the seat of the lumpy velour chair and sat down to read beneath the yellowed fringed shade of the floor lamp.

Salisbury, February
Dear Mom and Dad,
This is a dreary time of year. Nothing but rain which means I've not

been able to give Sheila her daily airing. When we go out, there's no more of this lying down in the pram. Now she sits up and looks around, like me, taking in the sights. Fortunately she's easily amused and when it rains is content to play inside.

While Philip works in the evenings I read my way through Jane Austen and Thomas Hardy. Though we are more or less in Hardy country, I've yet to visit his house. I must say it is exciting to live in a country of great writers. Last Christmas when we drove through Bowerchaulk on our way to the rectory, Arthur Palmer remarked, as casually as you please, that William Golding lived in the thatched cottage to the left. Philip did much the same thing on our honeymoon, pointing out John Fowles's house in Lyme Regis. The English are offhand about this as if it's to be expected that a writer lives down the lane.

When the weather improves, I will scour the second-hand book shops for copies of Austen and Hardy and send them to you.

Love, Nancy

Cape Race, May 3

Dear Nancy,

We haven't heard from you for ages and hope that means you are busy. Your mother says that now that Sheila is walking, you probably don't have a minute to sit down.

Some changes are in the offing here. The wireless duties are being transferred to St. John's and the radio station is being closed next year which means the supply ship will stop coming. The Hallerans are moving to Trepassey and the Johnstons to the Cove. There's talk about automating the light and the fog alarm; when that happens your mother and I will retire to Trepassey and John and Beatty to Brigus.

Stanley is studying hard for exams to qualify for one of Joey's scholarships. Everything will be paid for at Memorial if he can keep up his marks, which I'm confident he will. His friend, Kenny, quit school; he was so far behind that he knew he wouldn't graduate.

Your mother sends her love.

Love, Dad

Salisbury, October 6
Dear Mom and Dad,

I appreciate you wiring me about Uncle Ron's death. How sad for Aunt Ruth.

Philip was to have gone up to Cambridge to see his supervisor this weekend but had to cancel due to lack of progress on his thesis. He's been laid low by a bout of pneumonia; it's all he can do to drag himself off to school.

Sheila has become quite a chatterbox and loves to draw. I included some pictures with the books I finally mailed off to you last week.

Love, Nancy

Salisbury, November 9
Dear Mom and Dad,

Two deaths in one month! Poor Aunt Ruth, first losing Uncle Ron and then finding Granny Mulloy dead in bed. I think Philip is as upset as I am by the news. He still talks about Granny Mulloy's baking. Now that he's feeling better, he has made some headway with his thesis, and we'll spend Christmas here so that he can get more done over the holiday. Lucy and Arthur will be visiting us on Boxing Day. They really are most awfully kind.

Love, Nancy

Philip sometimes asked about Aurora. Give your mother my love the next time you write, he would say, tell your parents I was inquiring about them (not once had they inquired about him), but Nancy never passed on his remarks.

Salisbury, March 23rd
Dear Mom and Dad,

Just a note to tell you that in a fortnight I'm going to Cambridge with Philip for a few days. Sheila is coming with us. This will be our first holiday since our honeymoon when we hitched rides and often pitched our sodden tent in some farmer's field beneath a dripping tree. This time we go in style, travelling by train and staying in residence digs. Philip says April is the loveliest month in Cambridge.

Love, Nancy

During the train ride to Cambridge Philip and Nancy took turns reading to Sheila from their sack of library books. At three and a half she was far more interested in the illustrations than in the story and would spend hours gazing at pictures. She was an even-tempered, accommodating child. Philip doted on her—it was he who insisted on bringing her, saying he didn't see enough of his daughter. Nancy watched him hunched over a slate, drawing funny pictures for Sheila; she hadn't known he could draw or that he possessed the patience to entertain a restless child, twisting waxed paper into bits of furniture and making animals from twine by weaving it around his fingers and between his hands. When they stepped down from the train in Cambridge, he hoisted the child onto his shoulders, where she squealed and clung to his hair. Walking behind, carrying Aunt Maggie's wedding luggage, Nancy felt tears leaking down her cheeks. Why should the ordinary sight of a child straddling her father's shoulders make her weep? Was this happiness, or regret that their family spent so little time together?

The next day, after Philip finished meeting with his supervisor, they were scheduled to meet Elaine at the banks of the Cam. Elaine was driving up from Oxford in her lover's Morris Minor. Her lover was a dentist separated from his wife. None of Elaine's lovers were Oxford dons—Elaine didn't believe in mixing business and pleasure. So she had told Nancy when they'd met at the rectory at Christmastime. (The dentist spent Christmas with his wife and children.) Though two years Philip's junior, Elaine had already defended her doctoral dissertation, a comparative study of the translations of William Blake in German and French. She was also fluent in Italian and Spanish, supporting herself by giving occasional lectures and working as a translator for the university press.

Elaine met them beside the Cam, carrying a picnic hamper and a hand-wound Victrola. She had the sinuous body and studied indifference of a fashion model, and always appeared in costume. Today it was a tuxedo and a top hat. She was given to tossing off outrageous statements, not to provoke discussion, which she never encouraged, but to shock and impress: England had become a boring museum: anything of interest in the country had happened in the past. For energy and excitement, one had to go to America, by which she meant the United States; Canada, she said, was mindlessly dull, nothing more than a smattering of tedious provincial cities strung north of the border. Nancy thought Elaine's arrogance and dismissiveness was in some way connected with her education, with having graduated from the most prestigious institution in the English-speaking world. If Elaine had graduated from an institution in a colonial backwater, would she have held onto this unshakeable confidence in herself, or would she, like Nancy, be besieged by inarticulate doubts and wavering opinions? If their situations been reversed, would Nancy have become as recklessly opinionated as Elaine?

Philip didn't object when Elaine insisted on poling the punt. Relaxed and lazy after a successful interview, he preferred sitting at the opposite end from his sister, with Sheila between his knees. Nancy sat in the middle beside the Victrola, which was on top of the picnic hamper.

"Wind it, will you, Nance?" Elaine said. "There's a dear."

Louis Armstrong's gravelly voice floated out over the Cam. "*I see trees of green, red roses too...*"

Elaine put a hand to her breast and sang along.

The punt wobbled dangerously.

"Watch it, Elaine. There's a child on board."

"Yes, bro."

Elaine poled inexpertly beneath King's Bridge, past students sprawled on the grassy embankment.

I see skies of blue and clouds of white,
The brightness of day, the darkness of night.

They were beneath Trinity Bridge when Sheila announced that she needed to pee and Philip instructed his sister to manoeuvre close by the stone wall. After he and Sheila went off in search of a toilet,

Elaine turned off the Victrola and set it on the bottom of the punt. She opened the hamper and brought out Stilton and pâté, malt cake and red wine, corkscrew and glasses. Nancy sipped her wine and lifted her face to the sun. How extraordinarily perfect the day was.

Postcards from Cambridge

April 7

Dear Mom and Dad,
Cambridge is as lovely as Philip said it would be. Everywhere you look there are masses of flowering trees. This morning while Philip met with his supervisor, Sheila and I went to St. Boltolph's Churchyard. She played on a stone bench while I admired primulas and narcissus and an apple tree whose blossoms were as big as pom poms. This afternoon we went poling on the Cam.

Love, Nancy

April 7

Dear Maggie, Wilfred and Ruth,
Imagine poling on the Cam listening to Louis Armstrong sing "It's a Wonderful World." That's how Philip, Sheila and I spent a lazy afternoon, drinking wine and drifting along, the sun pouring down. Idyllic. Philip's sister Elaine was with us. All I will say about her is that she is a character, what a Newfoundlander would call a piece of work.

Hope you are well,
Love, Nancy

What Nancy decided to overlook:

Elaine removing her top hat and fingercombing her short black hair. Uncoiling her body, then leaning back on one hand:

"So, Nance, how is bro behaving himself?"

"Shouldn't you be asking Philip that question?"

"No, it's you I'm thinking of. A word of sisterly advice: you have to keep Philip on a short lead."

"Oh? And why should I do that?"

"Because we're PKs. Preacher's kids."

"What's that supposed to mean?"

"PKs have an overactive sex drive, which comes from all that repressed sex, in Protestants especially. Catholics deal with it better by encouraging people to enter little boxes and confess their wicked craving for sex, amongst other things. Philip and I were brought up to pretend sex didn't exist."

"It doesn't appear to have harmed Philip. Our sex life is fine, thank you very much."

"I'm only trying to help." A sweep of white arm, an elaborate yawn, a wave. "Ah, the wanderer returns."

Nancy thought that since coming to England Philip might have had a liaison with another woman, possibly one of the teachers at the school, or a librarian. Philip spent a great deal of time in the library. Nancy had no proof of his infidelity, none at all; it was a fleeting suspicion that came to her whenever there was a waning in his sexual appetite, which happened periodically and could just as well have been attributed to lack of sleep, worry about money or preoccupation with his thesis. The suspicion was dispelled as quickly as it came. She didn't, of course, tell Philip about Elaine's warning. He would likely have attributed it to bitchiness; though fond of his sister, Philip admitted that he could only tolerate her company in small amounts. He said his sister was someone he thought he would like better when she grew too old to compete with everything that walked and talked.

Cape Race, July 22

Dear Nancy,

Thank you for the pictures taken in Cambridge. They are with the others on the kitchen wall. Sheila has become a little maid.

Stanley has been down two weekends since Easter. He has taken up diving in a big way and every weekend is spent with his diving buddies, looking for shipwrecks along the coast.

Tom and I have been out twice picking bakeapples, trying to get enough for Maggie and Ruth—we'll be in St. John's next week for Tom's doctor appointment. Did I tell you that Wilfred is now in a wheelchair?

Hugs for Sheila.

Love, Mom

Cape Race, October 15

Dear Nancy,

Now that the potatoes and turnips have been dug and the garden kelped, your father and I are making items to raise money for Holy Redeemer; he is making replicas of the Cape lighthouse from jam jars and plumbing pipe and I am making tea cosies using wool from a knitted blanket Aggie Halleran discarded last year. Lately we've become more involved with the church, and usually go to mass in Trepassey with Beatty and John. They go in twice a week to pick up mail and groceries. We finished reading Mansfield Park *but didn't like it as much as* Persuasion. *Tom asked me to tell you that if you see a second-hand copy of Hardy's poetry to please send it along.*

I mailed a parcel for Sheila's birthday yesterday.

Love, Mom

Cape Race, November 30

Dear Nancy,

We've decided to go to St. John's for Christmas again this year. With Ruth at Cheryl's in Corner Brook and Wilfred so poorly, we'll spend it quietly with Maggie and Wilfred who can no longer speak. Stanley has his driver's licence and will fetch us in the Hunts' car. We'll stay in St. John's an extra day so that your father can see the specialist about the headaches he's been having.

Love, Mom.

Corfe, December 1

Dear Stan,

Surprise. Surprise. A letter from your long-lost sister. The reason I'm writing is to inquire about Dad. He used to write most of the letters but now

Mom is writing them, though sometimes he scrawls his name at the end. She mentioned him seeing a specialist when they go to St. John's for Christmas but she didn't say what kind of specialist. Do you know how Dad is? Could you check it out at Christmas and let me know?

Thanks, Nancy

St. John's, February 5

Dear Nancy,

Yes, I'm late answering your letter but neither of us can claim to be close correspondents.You spoke to Dad on the phone at Christmas so you know he's okay. The specialist was a neurosurgeon but as far as I know nothing came out of the appointment. Apart from occasional headaches Dad seems to be fine. He's slowing down but you have to expect that at his age. Mom is the same as ever.

Stan

In July, Nancy received a telegram from Maggie telling her that her father was critically ill in St. Clare's and advising her to come home at once—she would wire the fare. Nancy flew home to stay: she and Philip had decided that it would be better in the long run for Sheila and her to move back to Newfoundland. He would resign from his teaching job and move to the rectory where, without any demands on his time, he would be able to finish his dissertation within six months. Once that was done, he would come to Newfoundland where he was assured of a teaching position. Nancy was easily persuaded to return to Newfoundland. What was the point of staying in Salisbury when she and Philip hardly saw one another? She hadn't seen much of England either: she hadn't been to London or Stratford or even Stonehenge, though it was close by, on the Salisbury Plain. In Newfoundland she could find herself a teaching job: there was a shortage of high school teachers with university degrees in St. John's. Sheila would be four in November, old enough for nursery school and Nancy would rent a flat near the campus and begin working on a master's degree by taking geography courses at night. It was time to get on with her own education.

Until the prospect of returning to Newfoundland became a possibility, Nancy hadn't realized how much she longed to go home, to return to the place she once felt she had to live down. Long before moving to England, she had become a snob, embarrassed by her origins and determined to purge herself of the rough edges of the Cape. It was precisely those rough edges that she now missed; she had probably been missing them all along, but could only admit it now that she was going home.

She knew that in Newfoundland she could come closer to having the kind of life she wanted, a life that could make a difference in a way it never could in England. Instead of denying Newfoundland's rough edges, she could, as Philip said, help shape them. For too long she had resisted his enthusiasm for the Cape and for Newfoundland, having been too close to it, she supposed. Before leaving, she had never thought about the challenge of living in a wilderness so immense that it was impossible to tame, but now she saw that the island needed Newfoundlanders like herself to map its wildness and give it a voice, to deliver it to the world now as it was, elemental and untrammelled.

Tom Mulloy died of brain cancer two weeks after his daughter and granddaughter came home. He was conscious enough to squeeze their hands but was so heavily medicated that he couldn't open his eyes, and the day after they arrived, lapsed into a coma. He was buried in the Holy Redeemer graveyard in Trepassey. After the wake, Nancy and Stan drove to the Cape while their mother stayed behind at Brenda and Jerome's, not wanting to return to the Cape.

The Cape road was worse than Nancy remembered, deeply gouged and strewn with boulders that kicked against the muffler of the borrowed Chev. Stan eased the car around the worst of the ruts. How odd to be sitting beside her grown-up brother with his thick shoulders and hairy forearms, a science graduate who would soon be an engineer, a stranger, though no more than anyone else Nancy had left behind. After her years away, she was swept up in rushes of violent recognition followed by plunges into uncertainty. At least the landscape was the same, the blue reaching without limit or direction, the Barrens starred with bakeapples, the ponds winking back the sun. The colours were vibrant and distinct. Nothing Nancy had seen in England could match the clarity of Newfoundland's landscape on a fine summer's day.

But there were changes at the Drook. Two of the houses were missing, and the second storey of her grandparents' house had been removed, so that what remained was no more than a cabin. Long Beach was also empty, though the houses were intact.

"You won't recognize the Cape," Stan said. "Houses have been torn down. It's like a ghost town. That may be why Mom wouldn't come back."

"Leaving us to pick up the pieces." Deafened by grief, Nancy didn't hear the sharpness in her voice.

"Going through Dad's things is the least we can do for her, considering how seldom we came to visit her and Dad."

"She certainly managed to keep his illness a secret from us," Nancy said. She was surprised by how much it hurt her that she hadn't known about the tumour, thinking of the blinding pain their father must have suffered in silence out here on the Cape.

"He didn't want us to know. He didn't want any fuss. The doctors wanted him to have chemotherapy and radiation, but he said no, he'd rather stay out here with Mom until the tumour had run its course. You know how devoted they were to each other."

Yes, she knew, she knew better than Stan about their devotion, which had been particularly noticeable since she and Stan had left.

"Do you know what caused the tumour?" he said. "Maggie told me. Fumes from the mercury bath. Apparently it's an occupational hazard for lighthouse keepers."

Of her own possessions, their mother wanted only her clothes, an ancient porcelain doll, Grandmother Merla's wall hangings and a tin chest. She had instructed them to dispose of their father's clothes as they liked, but to bring back his books, including *The Book of Knowledge*, and the replica he had made of the lighthouse. They could help themselves to whatever furniture they wanted; the rest would remain in the house. Nancy taped her name to the oak sideboard, which she would arrange to have trucked to St. John's later on. Opening it, she asked Stan if their mother wanted what was left of Granny Mulloy's china and glassware. He said he doubted it, that their mother had said she wanted to start all over again. Nancy decided to help herself, knowing that as soon as she got back to St. John's, she'd be looking for a place to live.

When they were finished in the kitchen, Stan went out to the shed for more cardboard boxes and Nancy went upstairs and opened the night table drawer on her father's side of the bed. Her mother had insisted that she bring back a blue scribbler, a journal belonging to their father. Nancy found the scribbler and was carrying it downstairs when a piece of paper fluttered loose. Picking it up, she saw that it was a sheet of notepaper, the same kind of notepaper on which her father had written letters. This wasn't a letter but a poem written in her father's scrawly hand, which had deteriorated almost to the point of being illegible, the result of the tumour, she supposed.

Stan came into the kitchen carrying a cardboard box and a broom handle. "Look what I found in the shed!" Two caribou hooves dangled from the top of the handle.

"So that's how he did it."

"Do you want them for Sheila?"

Nancy shook her head. "Somehow I can't see Philip getting up on a roof," she said. "Did you know Dad wrote poetry? Listen to this." Stumbling and squinting, she made her way through the poem.

The soul inhabits the starry beyond,
It moans in the wind; it sighs in the rain.
What will I be when I'm gone?

Will I hear the whisper of a faery maid?
Will I heed her cry? Will I take her hand?
Or will I wander far from home?

She began to weep. She wept for having put so much energy into trying to smash her parents' devotion, especially her father's adoration of her mother, some of which she had wanted for herself. She wept for the absence of devotion in her own marriage, knowing that unlike her mother she wasn't the kind of woman to inspire devotion, perhaps because she didn't fully understand what it was. Was devotion something that grew between two people like a rose that was nourished and tended, or was it present when lovers first met, an angel of annunciation anointing lovers' heads?

Before leaving the Cape, they climbed up to the light and looked across the ocean with its curtains of purpling light. Today the sea had a watchful intensity, and Nancy thought that for her father, the sea had been a universal eye. Today it returned her gaze, as it had his, holding it so long that Stan had to remind her that if they didn't leave soon they would be driving Drook hill in the dark. As they drove west, toward the sinking sun, Nancy conceded that their mother had been wise not to return to the Cape, that Trepassey was a better place for her to be. It was certainly providential. Even before this shore had been settled, Trepassey had been known as the bay of trespass, the haven of souls, the river of roses, the place where for centuries fishermen came ashore to bury their dead and mourn their passing. Nancy told Stan that she remembered being told, it must have been by one of her teachers, that on stormy days in Trepassey, the voices of the dead could be heard in the wind.

Like so much else, Trepassey had changed while Nancy had been living away. It was much larger than she remembered. Designated as one of Joey's fishery growth centres, it had a new church and a new regional high school, and everywhere she looked there was a smattering of new houses. Its population had been increasing steadily since Confederation as people moved from places along the shore to work at the fish plant. What had begun as a settlement of thirty-four fishing masters and two hundred Irish servants four centuries ago had become a prosperous town of over a thousand that now had two masters: Fishery Products, which processed fish; and the Government of Canada, which put UI money into pockets when the fish ran short, as it often did. At last people had money to buy themselves televisions and refrigerators, toasters and electric frying pans, trucks and cars; now they could drive into St. John's to shop in city stores. There was talk of paving the road all the way down to Trepassey from the city. It seemed that all the energy that had drained away from the Cape and the Drook was now flowing through the town.

While her brother drove, Nancy looked at the places that were being erased from the map, the vanished houses and emptying landscape, and imagined the flakes and the dories that were no longer here. For hundreds of years these tiny settlements had been tucked into the folds of the island, ever since fishermen had emigrated to this shore. Now most of them were gone. The draining away had begun when she was still a girl living at the Cape but she had been so determined to leave that it hadn't mattered to her. But it mattered now and she wept with abandon, not only for the loss of her father, but also for the loss of people and places that would never return.

TWO

TREPASSEY

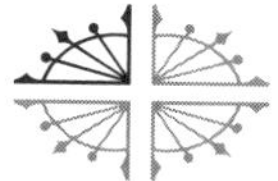

1965

The month after Tom passed on, I stayed with my brother and his wife in Trepassey, sleeping in their daughter's bedroom, where every morning I waited until after they'd left for work before getting out of bed. Jerome and Brenda worked in the fish plant alongside their youngest son, Gary; their youngest daughter, Fran, had a summer job looking after Alma Perry, the widow of Francis's cousin, who lived in Biscay Bay. Their five older children had jobs on the mainland, except Norman, who was stationed with the military in Germany. Though the house was empty during the day, I spent most of my time in the graveyard with Tom; I wasn't ready to give up his body even though it was lying beneath a mound of gravel and dirt. Sometimes I went down to the landwash to pick up small stones and bits of shell, which I used to decorate his grave—I hadn't yet chosen a marker—but mostly I sat on Otto Tobin's stone and tried to talk to Tom, reminding him of how contented we'd been together. When we were first married I'd thought we could never be happier, but after the difficult years between, I found that we could, though in a more settled, muted way. What I was missing now, and struggled to keep alive, were the conversations we used to have, but I was too numb to remember. Instead I sat in dull contemplation of the water, which I could see from Tom's grave. When I wasn't sitting on Otto Tobin's stone I kept to my room, though I knew it worried Brenda; she tapped on my bedroom door every morning and asked would I like to go some place with her after work: to the store, to a neighbour's or for a drive along the shore.

One night I awoke in the darkness of the bedroom and heard Tom say that he had to turn on the light because a convoy was on its way. I heard him grope for his pants and pull on his sweater; before he left he urged me to go back to sleep, telling me that after the convoy had passed, he would come back to bed. I was so comforted by the sound of his voice that I did. When I opened my eyes to the summer morning, I noticed that his corner of the blanket had been thrown back on the spread as it always was when he got up at night.

Twice a week, Brenda drove the second-hand pick-up two miles down the road to Biscay Bay to check on Alma and Fran. The winterized cabin where Alma lived had plumbing and electricity but no telephone, which meant she relied on Brenda to bring the groceries and what little there was in the way of mail. Alma, the only person along the shore with a letter from the Queen, had been a widow for seventeen years and by the age of 101 had been living on her own for five years—ever since her brother-in-law Bernie died of emphysema. Because there was no nursing home in Trepassey and Alma had no youngsters to take her in, Brenda felt responsible for her, and whenever she went out to Biscay Bay she invited me along. I refused until one Saturday morning when, on impulse, I said I would go; it was a clear August morning, the kind of day when Tom and I used to pick berries on the Barrens, which may have been why I said I'd go. I knew Alma lived beside the Barrens in a cabin only slightly larger than the tilts built out there by caribou hunters.

As soon as we went into the cabin I noticed the Queen's letter, with Her Majesty's red seal, which had been framed and hung on the wall facing the door where a visitor like myself couldn't fail to see it. Then I noticed Alma sitting by the window in a cotton house dress—though bird-boned and skinny, like me she was unaffected by the morning chill. Brenda said, "Alma, you remember Aurora."

"Of course I remember Aurora. Not long ago I made her granddaughter's quilt, and once I made her wedding dress." She looked at Brenda. "Sit down. Fran is in the kitchen making tea. I told her you'd be along."

"Did you now," Brenda said, easing her bulk onto the couch, leaving me the chair on the other side of the window.

"And I knew Aurora would be with you." Alma reached out her hand and I took it. I felt like I was holding a nest of paper and grass. "I was sorry, girl, to hear about your Tom."

I averted my eyes. Alma had a penetrating stare and I didn't want her to see my longing for Tom, preferring to keep it to myself.

"Last night I prayed to the Blessed Mother to bring you out here. I think we could help each other, Aurora. I still miss Leo though he's been dead a while. And I miss Bernie too." Her hand fluttered away when Fran came in with the tea and a plate of buttered toast. Fran, a fair-haired slip of a girl, didn't look at all like her mother, who was heavy and dark. She waited patiently, holding the plate while Alma shook out an embroidered serviette and spread it on her lap before taking a slice of toast. When she came to me with the toast, Fran said, "Alma has a proposition for you, Aurora."

"What would that be?" I looked at Alma but she seemed not to hear and gazed out the window.

Giving the plate to her mother, Fran went over to the old woman and shouted in her ear, "Isn't that true, Alma?"

Alma turned and said "That's true, girl, but as you know I'm far from deaf, so there's no need to shout." She began rocking back and forth—which she could do without spilling a drop of tea—and said, "You tell her."

Fran looked at me. "Alma wants to know if you'd be interested in living out here with her when I go back to school in a couple of weeks."

I was so surprised that I nearly said, why would I live with Alma?—we hardly know each other. But I didn't, because I immediately thought, why not? I couldn't go back to the Cape and I had to live somewhere. Why not live out here beside the Barrens with Alma? I said I would try it for a while and see how it worked out.

Brenda explained that except for cooking and being helped in and out of the bathtub, Alma didn't require much looking after, and offered to drive me to Holy Redeemer every Sunday, for which I was grateful—I wasn't thinking about mass but visiting Tom.

The first thing Alma did after I moved into the cabin in Biscay Bay with my clothing and cartons of books was to assign a third chair at the table for Tom; there were already chairs for Leo and Bernie, which left exactly two, one for each of us. If Tom came to visit me again, I didn't think he would sit in the chair, but because Alma had set him a place I thought it would be easier for him to find me in Biscay Bay.

As Brenda had said, Alma didn't require much looking after. For a woman her age she was in remarkably good health, dressing and feeding herself and keeping up with her needlework. Though I had grown up with the notion that Alma was slow-witted, a "lame duck," Merla once said, I saw no evidence of it and decided that she was probably a lot smarter than many people half her age. I appreciated the fact that though she seldom went outside, she never objected to me walking across the Barrens or down to the beach.

We quickly established the habit of sitting on opposite sides of the front-room window to sew and knit; we spent most of our time working there, intermittently watching the rollers breaking on shore. In the evenings I turned on the lamp and read aloud from *The Book of Knowledge*. Alma couldn't read but she had a curious mind and enjoyed listening to whatever I chose. One evening, after I'd finished reading a story about a frog prince, I asked if Alma remembered thinking I was a changeling.

"I remember. It was soon after I lost my infant daughter to the fairies. They took my beautiful healthy baby out of her crib when I was outside pegging wash to the line and put an ugly old fairy baby in her place. I took care of it, hoping the fairies would return my baby but they never did. After a while the changeling died."

"I'm sorry."

"I wasn't. I was glad to see it go."

"Was I ugly and old?"

"No, but you had that white hair and these queer eyes. You didn't look like anyone in the Drook."

"Neither did you."

Though her hair was grey, Alma's eyebrows were black and her eyes dark, without the milkiness common to the aged.

Her parents, Dolores and George Baikie, had lived in a shack in the woods behind Clam Cove, well away from the other livyers. When Alma was ten years old, her father drowned after getting himself tangled in a fishing net. Some months later, Dolores disappeared for nearly a week. People went into the woods searching and calling but there was no sign of her. When she finally staggered back to Clam Cove, her clothes were raggedy and she was half naked and bitten, but she cleaned herself up and settled down to looking after Alma. No one knew where she had been and she never said. Alma claimed the fairies must have got her mother because nine months later she gave birth to a fairy son who was dwarfish and clubfooted. One of the Bevis women hotted a shovel and whacked it across his backside, but it didn't cure him, and he died when Alma was sixteen, not long after she married Leo Perry.

"I was some glad to get away from Clam Cove with its fairy paths every which way. You could scarce leave the landwash without stumbling onto one."

The second time Tom came to me it was here in Biscay Bay on an August afternoon when I was walking on the beach—I needn't have worried about him finding me. It was unusually hot and dry, so dry that I heard the sun sucking moisture from the sea and felt puffs of hot air like a bellows against my cheek. I heard an unexpected splash of water—unexpected because it was past the time for whales and seals—and shielding my eyes against the glare, I looked up and saw Tom wading through the water about twenty feet away. I was startled to see him in the sea; I had never seen him in the water; he couldn't swim, neither of us could. I asked him what he was doing and he said, "Don't be afraid of the sea." Then he vanished, there wasn't so much as a shadow on the water, no spindrift against the blue, nothing to indicate that he'd been there.

A month later he came to me again when I was asleep in my room next to Alma's and I woke with the certain knowledge that he was standing beside the bed; I didn't see his shape but I felt his presence. "I'm leaving now, but you go on. Remember we're travelling in the same direction," he said, and not another word. In the morning when I was spooning out her oatmeal, Alma said that she'd heard me calling Tom during the night. I told her that he'd come to say goodbye before he left. I was as certain of this as I was of the steam rising from the kettle; I felt as if the string I'd been holding had slipped from my grasp, and like an airborne balloon Tom had been carried up and away.

Alma reached for my hand. "He'll come back on All Souls' Night and sit right at this table with Leo and Bernie."

I had no sense of Tom being at the table on All Souls' Night but I wasn't disappointed, perhaps because I had by that time moved to another level of mourning. I was no longer Tom's wife or Mrs. Mulloy. I had taken the vow of widowhood and now at the age of fifty-five, I was Aurora Mulloy, a woman reinvented on her own, a woman who for the first time in her life undertook the financial responsibility of looking after herself. It never occurred to me to look to my children and in any case they were in no position to help: Nancy was maintaining Sheila and herself on a teacher's wage and Stanley was a university student. Because I wanted to stay on the

Southern Shore near Tom, working as a housekeeper-companion in exchange for room and board—which was the arrangement I had with Alma—allowed me to put his pension toward the purchase of a house. I was determined to buy my own house, a place with a view of the water and a garden with which I could do what I pleased.

In December Alma agreed to stay with Brenda and Jerome so that I could spend Christmas in St. John's with Nancy, Sheila and Stanley. With Philip still in England, all of us stayed at the Hunts'. Maggie was finding Wilfred's illness a strain and badly wanted company. On Christmas Eve Stanley climbed the ladder and put hoof marks on the snowy roof for Sheila, who like any five-year-old was beside herself with excitement when she saw them on Christmas morning. I made snow angels with her as I used to do with Nancy, and on Boxing Day watched her draw pictures in her first wander book. When I returned to Biscay Bay, Alma wanted to know everything I had seen. It was a source of pride with her that she had never been to the city, which she regarded as a degenerate yet fascinating metropolis. The city didn't fascinate me; I told Alma that I would have liked St. John's better in the days when I could have wandered past finger wharves, beneath flakes woven like baskets above my head; I would have liked to have smelled the curing fish and heard the horses clip-clopping along Water Street. I told her that the city builders were piling up ugly monstrosities of brick and cement all over downtown, and that I'd never seen such trash littering the streets, broken glass, cigarette butts, cardboard, plastic and paper, that it was a relief (this was what she most wanted to hear) to return to the clean open spaces of Biscay Bay.

In February, Nancy called to ask if I thought Alma would agree to be interviewed for a term paper she was writing about Newfoundland superstitions and beliefs—as well as holding down a teaching job, she was taking an evening course in folklore. Nancy said that Alma, because of her advanced age, would be a valuable source of information, and asked if I could advise her about how to proceed. Alma didn't like the telephone, so I suggested that Nancy write her request in a letter, which I would read aloud. I advised her to avoid using the word *superstition*, which like me, Alma was likely to regard as an offensive reduction of the truth.

Alma didn't want to be interviewed, but she said Nancy was welcome to visit. On Good Friday morning Nancy and Sheila arrived in Biscay Bay and stayed with us overnight, sleeping on the horsehair couch in the front room. While the women talked, I took Sheila for rambles along the beach and over the Barrens, showing her foxholes and rabbit paths and rooms hidden inside the tuckamore. When we returned, the two of them were still circling one other. Alma, who was suspicious, wasn't going to say anything until Nancy had earned her trust, and it wasn't until Saturday morning that she decided to talk. She told Nancy about putting her infant daughter's clothes outside on the step on All Souls' Night, and a plate of carrots, turnip greens and potatoes on the table for Leo, Bernie and Tom. She told her about one of the O'Neill sisters at Long Beach being dragged across the Barrens by the fairies and dumped into Middle Pond.

"Where we used to skate," Nancy said.

"The same," Alma said. "You didn't know that pond was on a fairy path, did you?"

"No, I didn't."

"You aren't like your mother."

"No."

"She knows the fairy paths. She's one of the enchanted."

"You don't say." Nancy grinned at me.

"You don't believe me," Alma said reprovingly.

Nancy's cheeks coloured. "It's not that I don't believe you. It's that it's hard for me to think of my own mother as enchanted."

The answer seemed to displease Alma for she gripped the arms of the chair and began rocking furiously.

"I think of you and Mom as perpetual outsiders. I mean in most settlements there are one or two people who for various reasons don't belong, people who defy ordinariness, who aren't like the others, who are off to one side."

Alma sniffed. "Is that what they teach you in school nowadays?"

Nancy stood her ground. "No, it's what I think myself."

Did Nancy know about the little girl who waited for a week in a shack in Clam Cove, hungry but not daring to forage for food, wanting to be there when her mother came back, afraid that if she went berry-picking she might cross a fairy path? Had Alma told Nancy any of this? Did she know how much of an outsider I had been as a child? I had never told her about being ignored by the other children, but she may have guessed that like Alma I was an outsider. I suppose I shouldn't have been surprised by her intuition, but I was.

As Nancy was getting ready to leave for St. John's, Alma got out of the rocker, took hold of her wrists and said something I knew myself. "I'll tell you something important, girl. It's this: if we live long enough, we circle around to what we were."

Like Alma, I knew there was a point where I had stopped going up one side of my present self and began going down the other, that somewhere along the way the direction of my life had changed and I was now moving back toward my childhood. It was as if the directional signposts of my life had their arrows reversed; I didn't know when it had happened—the reversal of their arrows had been so subtle that I might have been brushing my teeth or peeling potatoes or sleeping when the journey down the other side of myself began. I didn't see the change in direction as a sign of regression or senility, rather as taking another and more interesting route back to the place where I began the ascendancy of my years. It seemed entirely natural that I was now asking myself: who was that child on the ice?

Nancy summed up Alma Perry as a 'find.' In a word, that was how she described her, months later, when she was talking to her brother in St. John's.

"I don't know that I could have written my paper without her. Well, I could have written it but I don't think I would have made an A. Until I met Alma I hadn't realized the effects of extreme isolation, how it can alter perception, turning benign belief into something frighteningly real."

She and Stan were drinking beer at the Stardust. It was smoky and noisy, though neither of them cared, since they were in a celebratory mood. Stan was elated to be back in Newfoundland after having spent a sweltering July in a prairie trench fourteen miles east of Winnipeg where he was finishing up a summer project on ice scour in what had once been a glacial lake; after two years on the Mainland he was home to stay because, luckily, before finishing his degree in Halifax, he'd been offered a full-time job with ERI, the Engineering Research Institute at Memorial, where research relating to the engineering aspects of the North Atlantic was being developed and sold.

Nancy's spirits were high because she was anticipating Philip's return at the end of the month; he'd handed in his thesis at last and had a position as a geography professor lined up at Memorial; she'd even found them a house to rent. Everything, she said, was falling into place, including their mother who had found herself a niche living with Alma.

Stan didn't remember Alma but expected to meet her this coming weekend when he and his buddy Warren Sullivan would be driving down the shore. He asked Nancy what she thought their mother would do when the old woman died.

"She says she plans to buy a house."

"Maybe she'll buy Alma's house."

"Maybe."

"She says she wants a place that she and Sheila can enjoy during the summer holidays. The two of them are thick as thieves."

"Do you think Mom is over Dad?"

"She's over the mourning, if that's what you mean, but I don't think she'll ever be 'over' Dad. She refers to herself as the Widow Aurora. I never knew she had a sense of humour."

"Maybe you didn't recognize it."

Throughout the summer and fall Stan went diving along the Southern Shore, stopping before or after a dive to visit the cabin in Biscay Bay, where he usually he found his mother and Alma doing handwork in front of the window—as Nancy said, between them they supplied half the sale goods for the Catholic Women's League. Visiting Biscay Bay always made him feel good, mainly because the women were so pleasant and polite with him and with each other that it was like being with a pair of fairy godmothers. After his years in engineering school, he figured he needed a benevolent influence like theirs.

In November Wilfred Hunt died, and Fran stayed with Alma so that Aurora could attend the funeral in St. John's. She had been back in Biscay Bay a scant three weeks when Alma passed on one night in her sleep—her heart simply stopped. Her passage was silent and though the two women slept with their bedroom doors open, Aurora heard nothing, not even a sigh. It was as if, day by day, Alma had been emptying her lungs of air, so that on the night she died only a hush of breath remained.

The previous afternoon when they had been sewing together, Alma had folded the tablecloth she'd finished hemming and held it in her lap.

"This is the last bit of handwork I'll be doing in this world," she said, patting the cloth.

"Why is that?"

"I'll be leaving soon."

Alma had spoken of her death before, though not, Aurora later realized, with the same finality.

There was no question of Aurora staying in Biscay Bay. Without Alma, she had no wish to remain, and in any case the cabin now belonged to Bernie Perry's daughter, who lived in St. John's and would be using it as a country place. A week after Alma was buried beside Leo, Aurora moved to Trepassey and began looking after Albert Sutton who was paralysed on one side and needed live-in help.

Albert had been married twice. His first wife Hilda had fallen down the cellar stairs and broken her neck twenty-eight years to the day after she had claimed the deckchair from the *Titanic*. Hilda Sutton had the idea that one day the chair would be worth a fortune and had never got over losing it when her house burnt to the ground. Albert's second wife, Ida, had electrocuted herself by poking a kitchen knife into the toaster to loosen a slice of bread. The accident was after the electricity came in, before people got used to using kitchen appliances. After his stroke Albert had been looked after by a succession of young women who stuck with the job only until they found better paying work in the fish plant.

Aurora accepted the job after Albert agreed to pay her $100 a month over and above room and board. When Aurora told Nurse Archibald that she would only stay a year, two at the most, Nurse Archibald said that at ninety-one, Albert probably wouldn't live that long. She was wrong; Albert held on for four more years. For two of those years Aurora kept him going, cooking his meals, changing his sheets, doing his laundry and housework. Though she pretended otherwise, she disliked Albert Sutton. She disliked his congested face and insinuating leer, most of all she disliked his sense of entitlement, that he should imagine her as a wife. She heard him tell Nurse Archibald, when she came to assist him with his weekly bath, that he had every intention of getting better so that he could marry his housekeeper. In the evenings when he was finally asleep and she had time alone, Aurora reminded herself that it was foolish to dwell on her dislike. Dislike was an indulgence she couldn't afford, and Albert had to be tolerated until she was able to move on.

On summer weekends when Stan began diving on the Southern Shore, he would ask his diving buddy Warren to drop him off at Albert's for an hour's visit. The old man didn't like him coming and glared at him whenever he tried to speak to his mother. Stan couldn't say two words without Albert butting in with mumblings and grunts meant to pass for speech. How did his mother put up with the old goat? How did she stand being shut up day after day with sour piss smells and the gloom of impending death? During one of his visits in July, the old geezer started going on about how Hilda, his first wife, would be mad at him if she knew that he was living with a younger woman. Albert winked at Stan and shifted his balls, which made Stan want to take his mother straight out of the house. When he heard Warren tooting the horn in the camper, Stan took her by the hand and pulled her toward the front door.

"Has Albert ever laid a hand on you?" He looked like a man who could whack his mother with his cane if he felt inclined.

"I'm careful never to get too close."

"If he tries anything you, let me know."

"If he tries anything, I'll leave."

Stan went outside and got into the camper, knowing that though his mother would stand in the doorway watching until they had driven out of sight, she would never try to detain him, to make him feel guilty that he was leaving her behind.

Windows down, elbows on the door, Stan and Warren headed for Portugal Cove South, the offshore breeze rushing through the cab, whipping their hair and fanning their cheeks; if either had spoken, their words would have been snatched away and carried out to sea. They gave themselves up to blue water, blue sky, not a cloud in sight; landward the open barrens stretched green and shining. There was a sheen over everything, as if sunlight had wrapped the landscape in cellophane.

When they reached the Drook, they cooked a supper of fish and potatoes on the beach, afterwards sitting around the fire and talking about tomorrow's dive. Stan wanted to find the mother lode of the *Corisande*, Bob Bartlett's first shipwreck. He remembered his father's story about his grandfather Francis rescuing the barkentine's crew after she had foundered off Mistaken Point. On previous dives he had found his namesake ship but not his sister's, which had also gone down off the Cape; the *Nancy Rose* wasn't anywhere near where she went down; like many of the older wrecks she had probably been dragged away by scouring bergs, then scattered by currents and tides.

Stan's interest in wrecks wasn't to collect artefacts; nowadays he couldn't bring up so much as a beer bottle from Newfoundland waters without registering it with to the government to whom it belonged. Even the artefacts given to his Grandfather St. Croix by grateful seamen were now in the museum. Gone were the days of wreckers drinking champagne out of tin pannikins, which they did when the *Aquitaine* ran aground off the Cape with a cargo of wine. When he located a wreck, more often than not there wasn't much to see; the blurred outline of a keel and scattered debris was about all he could expect to find in shallow water (the best-preserved wrecks were in deeper water); often there wasn't even enough there for him to be able to mark an X on the wreck map tacked to his bedroom wall. For him, diving was an obsession that began when as a boy he wanted to know what was beneath the surface of the sea, and he had imagined a sea bottom littered with shipwrecks, schools of fish hovering above broken masts and spars, a giant squid folded inside a damaged keel. He had fished off the Cape the odd time with his uncle John, but there had never been any question of entering the water; to a fisherman the undersea was as alien as Jupiter or Mars.

In the morning they went a few miles up the road to the point and by then were suited up—they always timed their dives between ten and two to make the most of vertical light. They carried the tanks to the fossilized rocks, and after synchronizing their watches, strapped on their air tanks and jumped into the abyss to begin their descent. Colours disappeared, red first then orange and yellow until they were down to blue and green. At thirty feet they checked their watches and again at sixty. A diving instructor, Warren was a stickler for checks and Stan was safer diving with him than with anyone else. Warren took a photograph of him hanging above the sea bottom shelving into darker green before continuing down, following the contour of the land, yet far enough out to avoid the solitary, long-jawed wolf fish whose territory was the rocky slope; they had run into it before when they'd inadvertently gone too close to its lair, and it had lunged for Warren's arm and might have bitten it off had Stan not jerked his buddy away in time. The bottom rose up to meet them, sudden, immense. Stan felt a rush of adrenalin as if he was about to slam onto pavement. Impossible. Down here movements were slow, balletic, mimed; voices were sibilant releases of air. The silence and slow motion were restful, hypnotic. A rubber tire hove in sight in the middle of a scallop bed and Warren raised his camera. A marine biologist whose main interest was to record how a wreck altered the sea bottom, he had a series of photographs intended to show how the sea bottom was being changed through man's intervention.

By now they had been down thirty minutes; it always amazed Stan how time was shortened during a dive. There was a logical reason for this illusion; the weight of bodies kicking through water slowed movement, tricking them into thinking speed equalled time. Warren tapped his wrist, a signal to begin the slow ascent. As was usually the case, most of the first dive had been spent on photography.

On the second dive Stan located an anchor, about ninety feet down and a hundred feet beyond a deep sea scour where an iceberg had dragged itself along the bottom before floating seaward. The anchor was fuzzed with silt and so corroded with rust that when Stan touched it, a flake of greenish lichen floated away. There was nothing else, no debris, no other signs to read, to tell him if this was the *Corisande's* anchor. They must have been bulldozed away by ice, leaving him to settle for possibility not fact, a ? not an X.

By midafternoon they had packed up and were heading north. Before going on to his girlfriend's, Warren dropped Stan off at Nancy and Philip's house for dinner. The Palmers lived in a prefab on Whiteway Street built during the war. It was poky and small but serviceable: two bedrooms upstairs, a study for Philip off the entry and another for Nancy in the basement. Except for the oak sideboard at one end of the living room and a Wedgwood tea service Philip had brought from England, the house was furnished with odds and ends picked up in second-hand stores and through newspaper ads. Philip had bookshelves built in every room except the bathroom and was proud of the house, which he said he could never have afforded to buy in England. It looked like a place whose its occupants did as they pleased; cups and plates were put down on top of magazines and books, slippers were tucked beneath chairs. When she ran out of clean dishes, Nancy churned through the rooms, scooping up mugs and plates and dumping them into the sink. If she had the patience, she assigned Sheila this chore, but she took forever; Sheila was ten, at an age when she often drifted from room to room with no particular purpose in mind. She had her grandmother's gift for removing herself. Like her father she had small white teeth, long slender bones and shining black hair that she wore well past her shoulders. When Stan came in and kicked off his sneakers she came over to him and gave him a hug. Philip, who was in the corner chair, put down his book and pushed his glasses to the top of his head.

"You're looking well, Stan," he said. "How was the dive?"

"Good." Stan took a book off the rocker and sat. "I found an anchor that might have belonged to the *Corisande*."

"Did you see Aurora?"

"We had less than a half hour together," Stan said. "Which was all I could take of Albert Sutton. I don't know how she puts up with the man."

"Your mother's an angel, so patient and understanding." Philip sighed wistfully.

Stan glanced toward the kitchen. "Where's Nancy?"

"Where she usually is, downstairs in her cubbyhole. Sheila, tell your mother that her brother is here." Philip pursed his lips. "I've been told I must barbecue our dinner. It's not a chore I relish. When it comes to cooking, I'm all fingers and thumbs."

There was a thud of feet on the cellar stairs.

"The charge of the Light Brigade," Philip said.

Stan, who was facing the basement door, stood up and held out his arms so that Nancy could step into them. A bulky woman in a skirt and blouse, with bare legs and two-inch wedgies on her feet, when she put her arms around his waist the top of her head barely reached Stan's chin. Over the past few years Nancy had been putting on weight, until now her underarms swung and she had saddled hips. She rarely used lipstick and wore her hair short at the sides and straight across the forehead, which gave her a severe, puritanical look. Stan wondered if she had given up on some part of her life and become too discouraged to care about her appearance. Nancy was now a geography instructor in the same department as Philip. Though she and Stan had become close during the past few years, she had never said a word to him about the fact that Philip was often in the company of good-looking women young enough to be his students.

"What were you working on down there?"

Nancy plunked herself on the chesterfield. "I was transcribing interviews collected last summer in Ferryland. Would you believe it's taken me this long to get them onto paper?"

She was recording oral accounts of immigration, relying on folk memory to establish a pattern of settlement from Ireland to Newfoundland in much the same way Philip had looked for Newfoundland settlement patterns in Dorset and Devon. She had begun her research by interviewing people in Bay Bulls and intended to continue the process all down the Southern Shore.

She asked Stan if he wanted a beer.

"Sure."

"I'll have one too," Philip said.

Stan followed his sister into the kitchen, and she told him she'd invited a guest.

"Of course," Stan said. This wasn't the first time his sister tried to set him up with a woman.

"It's not what you think. She's the new secretary in our department. She's homesick so I asked her over. I'm not trying to fix you up with a date."

Sometimes Stan wondered if his sister knew he was a virgin. How could she, when nobody knew? Twenty-eight years old and he'd never fucked a woman. All those engineering brawls he'd attended, all those jokes about tits and ass, those lusty renditions of Godiva riding naked through Coventry, Christ, what a laugh, he'd never even laid a hand on a woman's breast. Pathetic. But he was good at keeping up his end of the jokes. When he went out for a drink with the guys from work, he made sexual insinuations and references, how this broad went for his balding head, how another remarked on the bulge of his crotch. Lies, all of it lies.

The secretary, whose name was Alana, already had a boyfriend in Port Saunders and in any case she wasn't Stan's type, if he had a type. She didn't seem to be Philip's either. Stan would have thought he'd take to her, on account of her caramel-coloured hair and long slim legs, but he paid her little attention and after the meal was over excused himself to go into his office and read. An hour or so later Stan walked Alana to her room on Freshwater Road, not because she needed protection but because he thought she was a girl who counted on male attention: he'd never gone to bed with a woman, but he prided himself understanding women, probably because he spent so much time thinking about them and wondering what made them tick. He walked slowly alongside Alana, hands in his pockets, studying the cracks in the pavement, while she told him about her boyfriend who was helping his father make a go of the shrimp fishery in Port Saunders. If it didn't work out in three years, he promised to move to St. John's to look for work. She held up her charm bracelet and showed Stan a miniature gold ring. "We're engaged." She seemed too young to be engaged; to Stan she seemed scarcely more than a child. Walking her home made him remember the evenings when he was asked to babysit Sheila and used to read her stories before tucking her into bed.

Whenever Stan managed to get his mother out of Albert's clutches for an hour or two, they drove around looking at houses. Stan had bought himself a second-hand station wagon and would drive to Trepassey on Sunday afternoons. Aurora wanted a house on the edge of Trepassey and was particularly interested in Daniel's Point, where at long last a nursing home was being built. She said she wanted to work there when she left Albert, and already had her eye on a white bungalow a quarter of a mile away, on the same side of the road as the nursing home. The house was larger than Alma's but like hers it backed onto the Barrens and faced the bay, in this case Trepassey Bay. The place was empty, its owner having found work in Alberta. Like many Newfoundlanders he hadn't boarded up the house but had simply locked the door, leaving the furniture inside. Twice his mother insisted on getting out of the car to walk around the house and peer in the windows, though the curtains were drawn and she couldn't see much.

Stan took her interest as a sign that she was preparing to leave Albert, which she was. She said she was tired of being blackmailed, tired of the way he carried on whenever she told him that she might take a few days off, warning her that her departure would bring on another stroke. Now that she had some money saved, she told Stan that she was no longer willing to miss out on life. She'd missed the Christmas pageant in which Sheila played the Virgin Mary, and she'd missed seeing Nancy receive her master's degree. (Nancy had missed it herself, saying that she didn't want to haul her fat body onto the stage for a roll of parchment when she could keep the memory of a slim young graduate intact.)

Eugene Fitzgerald owned the house in Daniel's Point. At Stan's urging his mother telephoned Fort McMurray and asked Mr. Fitzgerald how much money he wanted for the house. Eugene said he wanted four thousand dollars. Aurora said she'd take the house, and he told her the key was in the convenience store across the road. George Waddlington kept it in the cash register. She should feel free to go into the house and have a look around. First thing tomorrow he would have a lawyer draw up the papers.

Stan advised his mother to have someone present when she broke the news to Albert that she was leaving.

Albert sat in front of the window on the colonial chesterfield at the opposite end from Nurse Archibald, the cane propped against his knee. The noon sun magnified the hollows of his cheeks and heightened his florid, blotchy face, making it look like a jelly bag with the juice squeezed out.

Aurora pulled the rocker close, so that he couldn't pretend not to hear, as he sometimes did.

"Albert, as of today I'm giving notice that I'll be leaving your employ in two weeks. I've bought a house and intend to apply for a job at Ocean View Home."

Albert said nothing.

"I'll be moving to Daniel's Point."

Still nothing.

"If you are concerned about who will take over from me, Nurse Archibald is willing to look for someone. With summer holidays beginning next week it shouldn't be too difficult to find a young woman to come in."

Not a word.

Albert didn't speak to Aurora for five days, which in a way was a relief. When he finally spoke at the breakfast table on Thursday morning, he said she should pack her bags and leave immediately.

He had phoned his son in Toronto, who promised he would come to Trepassey tonight, and he didn't want her here when he arrived. Aurora didn't believe his son was coming; he rarely called and Albert needed her help using the telephone. "Off with you. You're no use to me any more," he said and swung his cane, reminding her of an ancient, impotent king whose only power left was to humiliate and abuse. It was too bad, she thought, that he hadn't known that dignity would have served him better.

Leaving the dishes in the sink, she walked out of the kitchen and called Devereaux's taxi and went into the bedroom to collect her things. By the time the taxi arrived, she had her cartons and boxes piled in the driveway for Clarence to load. She had him stop at Waddlington's to pick up the key. Though she had mailed off a certified cheque to Eugene Fitzgerald, she still hadn't been inside the house and was pleasantly surprised to see that there were beds and dressers in all three bedrooms, a sofa and chairs in the front room, and a stove, refrigerator and chrome set in the kitchen, as well as a bathroom the same vintage as the Cape's. Eugene Fitzgerald had left the bedding and curtains, even a kitchen clock. There was no telephone, and from the water stains on the ceiling she knew the roof leaked; the air smelled mouldy and there were mouse droppings everywhere, but the place was hers. The Widow Aurora had found a home.

Nancy drove down with Sheila for the weekend to help her clean, arriving in a Volkswagen crammed with boxes of groceries, pots and dishes, kitchen utensils and various cleansers. By the end of the weekend they had cleaned the inside of the house end to end, and washed the curtains and bedding. The linoleum floors had been scrubbed and polished until they smelled of soap and wax. The last thing they did was hang Merla's mats on the walls. Stanley came down the following weekend and replaced ripped screens and broken boards and restrung the clothes line. He cleaned out the well and oiled the pump and arranged for the roof to be reshingled.

Two weeks later when Chuck Butler began working on the

roof, Aurora asked him to build a widow's walk in the middle of it. She also hired his son Johnny to dig up the quack grass and weeds behind the house where the ground was hilly, with large rocks that looked as if they had rolled out of the earth in some prehistoric upheaval. Beyond the rocks the land gave way to the Barrens where the tuckamore had been humbled by the wind into a shelter for rabbits and foxes. It was here on the edge of the wilderness that she decided to make a fairy garden, and while Johnny hauled stones from the beach to make a fairy circle, she planted fairy flowers: forget-me-nots, daisies, shooting stars.

A month after she moved to Daniel's Point Aurora began working as a caregiver at Ocean View. Her job was to help feed and bathe residents and do their hair. When these chores were done she sometimes read aloud to them, and when necessary lent a hand in the kitchen. Now she had everything she wanted: a place of her own, an occupation she enjoyed and plenty of time to do as she pleased.

Her children visited her often that summer, usually arriving at midmorning and returning to St. John's in the early evening, but twice Sheila stayed for the weekend. The following July, when Aurora had time off, her granddaughter spent two weeks with her at Daniel's Point. She would do this every summer until she finished high school and left Newfoundland.

My Favourite Place
by Sheila Palmer

My favourite place in all the world is my Gran's house at Daniel's Point. Inside hanging on the walls are my great-grandmother's mats. On the window sills are pretty stones and shells my Gran and I have picked up on the beach. On the roof is a widow's walk, which is not for decoration. My Gran built it so that the two of us can look at the stars. On clear nights we climb a ladder and open a trapdoor to the roof to look at the constellations like my grandfather used to do. I can pick out both Dippers, the North Star,

Orion and Cassiopeia. My friend Cindy says the widow's walk looks foolish on top of a bungalow. I notice people driving by on the road stop to poke fun at it, but I don't care what they think and neither does Gran. She doesn't care about my bedtime either and lets me stay up until she goes to bed. She makes me fried baloney and toutons, which my parents hate.

Gran has a fairy garden. It has an ugly toadstool that my uncle Stan bought at a yard sale, and a fairy ring made of stones, in case the fairies want to dance. Gran doesn't think they will. She says they have been sleeping inside the rocks in her garden for hundreds of years and probably won't wake up. Every afternoon Gran and I have tea in the garden. We paint out there and work on our wander books. Gran mostly helps me with mine. If a rabbit comes in the garden it will stop and look at Gran. Its nose will twitch in a way that looks like it is talking to her. The rabbit isn't the least bit afraid of Gran. Neither is the fox. There is something magical about my Gran which is why I love her and her place.

ICE

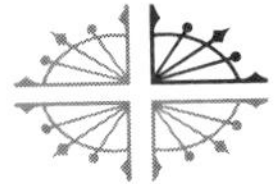

1979

From *The Book of Knowledge*:

"At what point does ice freeze?"

"What percentage of the globe is covered with ice?"

"What is pack ice?"

Before he was seven, Stan had known the answer to these questions and as far back as he can remember has been fascinated with ice. His earliest memory is being bundled into a snowsuit and pulled across a frozen pond on a sled, his mother leaning down to break off a piece of fringe ice to show him its frazilled design. When he was older, he and his sister skated on the pond, or rather *she* skated while he knelt to peer at the ice, noticing how the skate blades sliced the milky surface, making razor-thin incisions rimmed with shavings whose crystals were finer than sugar or salt. He remembers spending hours watching pack ice tame the ocean, imprisoning the waves until they moaned to be free. There was one Cape winter when, after weeks of freezing and thawing, the surface of the sea was transformed into an anomaly that Stan now thinks of as a desert of broken columns and friezes, pyramids and sphinxes caught in its grip. As a boy he never tired of making snow forts and igloos and once he and his buddy Kenny Halleran built a rink by carrying drifted snow and packing it down before flooding it with water. It hadn't mattered if the rink couldn't be skated on—they could always skate on the pond—Stan's interest had been in observing how snow could be made into ice. Intrigued by the fact that it could be transformed by temperature and movement, he and Kenny spent afternoons every spring breaking ice with crowbars in an effort to channel melt water down the cliff. Stan still remembers the satisfaction of being able to manipulate ice behaviour by breaking it into smaller pieces, and in that way controlling the speed of melt.

Ice was Stan's birthright and even before he'd known the profession existed, he had wanted to become an ice engineer. His timing was excellent, since drilling for oil on the Grand Banks had begun a few years after he finished his engineering degree, when he was working on his master's. Stan and ERI were perfectly positioned to take on the biggest engineering challenge in the North Atlantic, which was how to manage ice.

Stan was now renting a house in Beachy Cove, and one cold December night he got a call from his boss at ERI telling him that he was being sent to the Arctic to undertake tests on the polar cap, where a camp had been set up for the purpose of research. By early February Stan was aboard a Twin Otter flying low over the polar ice, so low that he could make out the ice sails where pressure ridges had formed, their keels thrusting into the Arctic Ocean, their snaking ridges reminding him of miniature mountain ranges.

The ice camp, a handful of insulated huts that looked as if they had been tossed like dice from a plane, was more or less over the Lomonosov Ridge, which, rising several hundred metres above the ocean floor, was a likely spot for oil exploration. The location explained why it was petroleum companies that were financing this line of polar research. Most of the scientists had been in the camp for several months; as newcomers, Stan and Art Stander were assigned a hut that was farthest away from the mess hut. While Art went off to the mess, Stan, tired from the trip, stowed his gear beneath the lower bunk and went to bed. Though the ice drift was imperceptible and erratic, shifting direction with polar currents, sounds of moving ice permeated his dreams. A light sleeper, he awoke whenever the ice rumbled below or there was a sharp explosion, as if firecrackers were going off inside the ice.

He heard similar noises during the day, and after a week at the camp couldn't tell nocturnal and diurnal noises apart. In any case, with the absence of natural light he sometimes forgot if it was night or day since it was as dark when he got up in the morning as it was when he went to bed. At noon, when the rim of the sun rolled above the horizon, the sky was briefly lit by a footlight, but by midafternoon the sky was again an indeterminate, fuzzy grey. Stan and Art used their strain gauges and tiltometers and sonar apparatus beneath fluorescent lights—all of the huts had electric lights and kerosene stoves—working in T-shirts because although it was forty below outside, it was seventy above inside. When they wanted a break, the camp scientists, nine men and one woman, wandered from hut to hut discussing one other's test results, and after supper sat around the mess hut talking about Peary and Cook and Franklin or the whereabouts of two ships, the *Breadalbane* and the *Phoenix*, both of which had gone down while looking for the *Erebus* and *Terror*. Sometimes they played checkers or cards.

Barbara, the only woman in the camp, was a Calgary geologist whose husband Bill was the camp director. She liked to amuse herself by reading cards and one night instructed Stan to lay out the cards in a particular order, after which she shifted them around. No one took this seriously; her card reading was nothing more than a distraction from science, a bit of harmless fun. After studying Stan's cards, Barbara looked at him over her glasses and remarked that he was a loner.

Stan grinned—noncommittally, he thought.

"But that will change."

"When?"

"Soon. You will be taking a trip."

"She tells everyone that," Bill said. "How can she go wrong? One of these days we'll all be flying out of here."

"This trip is to someplace warm."

"Hawaii?" Stan asked, "Tahiti?"

"You will meet a stranger, a woman."

"Now you're getting somewhere."

"She will become important to you," Barbara said and swept up the cards.

(In spite of himself, for months after he left the Arctic, Stan reviewed her corny forecast, as if thinking about it could make it happen.)

Bill put Stan and two others to work opening an ice hole with ice chippers and chainsaws. In some places the ice was several fathoms thick, but not where they were working; Bill had selected a spot where it was only seven feet thick, so that the hole could be made wide enough for a diver to descend and guide the camera as it was lowered toward the sea bottom. For two weeks Stan neglected his testing program, instead making himself useful inside the diving hut, all the while keeping an eye on the television monitor, which showed enormous chunks had broken off the pressure ridge keels and embedded themselves in the sea bottom where there were clams and sea stars, anemones and sea urchins. The ice hole was kept open by a cluster of light bulbs that had to be checked and frequently retaped—another chore that Stan took upon himself, in addition to untangling cords and manning diving tethers.

On an afternoon in late March when a flaming sun rolled briefly onstage, Stan was rewarded with a dive and slipped through the ice hole, following Bill through the slush of frigid water. After clearing the bottom of the hole he began adjusting the air in his suit: when he added too much, the top of his head bumped the ice; he did this twice before he let out the right amount of air to keep him level with Bill. Then he double-checked his mouthpiece, knowing that in water so piercingly cold, one slip-up would freeze his larynx, allowing panic—a diver's worst enemy—to set in. Though they were tethered the men stayed within sight of the ice hole, where an enormous triangle of light hovered above like a dangling lampshade; when they descended and looked up through a current of swirling plankton, the shade seemed to sway from side to side. At fifty feet Bill motioned Stan to follow him to the edge of the shade and switched on a flashlight, their gaze following its beam upward as it jumped and pulsed through plankton until it reached a cave carved from the bottom of the ice; they could see stalactites flashing like prisms in the sunlight shining through skylights, where wind had blown away snow from the surface ice.

The weight of the neoprene suits made it difficult for the divers to swim any distance; they hadn't gone far, yet already they had been down twenty minutes and it was time to go up. When they reached the bottom of the ice hole, Stan pointed to a hairline crack in the ice that originated at the ice hole and extended several feet before seeming to disappear. Did it end there or had it merely changed direction? Bill, a marine geologist, wasn't concerned about the crack—ice was full of cracks; what was one crack more or less? Nevertheless, Stan mounted a strain gauge over the crack and wired it to a monitor inside his hut so that he could measure how much stress had been caused by forcing a hole through the ice. He was scheduled to leave the Pole in three weeks, which was hardly enough time to gather conclusive data, but at least he could measure the early indications of stress.

In April, five nights before he was due to leave the camp, he was awakened by a thundering boom from deep in the ice. The hut walls shuddered as if they were being pulled apart.

"What was that?" Art said from the bunk above.

It was 3 a.m.

Stan's feet were already on the floor. He peered out the window and saw, beneath the polar moon, the unmistakable glitter of open water.

"The ice has opened up."

He and Art pulled on their arctic gear and went outside and saw a channel of black water six feet from their door.

"Jesus," Art said and shook his head. "A good thing neither of us walks in his sleep."

Bill was already outside, showing others how close the crack had come to the mess hut. Stan went to the diving hut and saw one corner of it hanging precariously over the water as if the ice had been wrenched apart at precisely this point. The crack might not have originated inside the diving hole, but the width of open water by the hut was certainly a strong indication that the hairline crack had caused the rupture.

The data he collected before leaving the camp supported the conjecture, for it clearly demonstrated that the crack had opened into a fault line that gradually widened until the ice suddenly split apart. As soon as he was back in Newfoundland, he intended to calibrate the results; he might even work up a paper. His boss at ERI was always hounding him about writing papers, pointing out that a body of published research would go a long way to establish Stan's credibility as an ice man, which was what they had taken to calling him at ERI.

"The Iceman returns!" someone shouted when Stan came back from the Pole. Stan was flattered—the Iceman was what they had called Captain Bob.

Stanley told me that his friends at work had taken to calling him the Iceman, which he said was probably inevitable, considering the fact that his mother had been found on the ice. When he returned from the Arctic, he brought me a jagged piece of ice about the size of a spearhead that looked as if it had been chipped into that particular shape by a prehistoric tool; he said had taken the ice from beneath the polar cap when he was wiring one of the instruments he uses to measure stress in ice. After I had shown the ice to the residents of Ocean View—quickly, so it wouldn't melt—I put it back in the freezing compartment of my refrigerator. Though I have taken it out for my own enjoyment many times since, the ice is as clear and crystalline as it was when Stanley gave it to me, its constellations of air bubbles unchanged.

In June, a year after returning from the North Pole, Stan entered the Piazza Santa Maria in Florence one morning, on his way to a conference. Though it was a few minutes past eight, there was a hum of traffic on the Via Della Scala and behind him the buzz of a Vespa. Except for an old man in a cap dozing on the church steps and a couple of backpackers having a morning wash in the fountain, the square was deserted and he crossed it quickly, wanting to arrive at the conference early. He had never before attended a geotechnical conference, much less made a presentation, and his paper, *The Effect of Hairline Cracks on the Fracturing of Ice*, was scheduled for the first session at nine. At the corner of the piazza, he checked the map before continuing along the Via del Belle Donne, a narrow, winding, claustrophobic street, a terracotta maze where flowers spilled from wrought iron balconies, and shrines to the Holy Virgin were niched above doorways. The morning air was cool and reflective, and somewhere close by a church bell tolled. As he passed an open courtyard, there was the scent of oleander mixed with gasoline. He came to a corner and stopped to take his bearings.

The girls leapt at him from one side; they must have heard his footsteps and been waiting for him to enter the intersection; there were three of them; agile and slight, they flew at him with quick darting hands, one of them waving a package in his face, the others plucking at his arms and chest.

"Buy, meester, buy!"

"Five dollar. You take!" The package flapped against his glasses. "Five dollar!"

He felt his ear being yanked, and trying to drive his attackers off he yelled, "Stop that!" One of the girls grabbed his glasses and, too late, his hands shot up to retrieve them. He felt a hand inside his pants pocket and dropped his elbows, but again he was too late and the girl ducked away. He heard footsteps behind.

"Basta! Basta!" A woman's voice. He turned and saw her swinging a fist at the girls. "Movimente!" She shoved one of them hard so that the girl holding his glasses was knocked down by the others.

Quickly she got up and holding the glasses behind her back, said, "Ten dollar."

The woman put out her hand. "Policia."

The girl threw the glasses at the woman's feet and ran down the street after the others. "Ladro!" the woman screamed after them. "Ladro!" until faces appeared in windows and doorways.

The woman picked up the glasses and looked at them sorrowfully. "They are broken, signore." She gave them to Stan. He saw that one lens was shattered and carefully put the glasses inside his shirt pocket.

"These thieves make life difficult for everyone: Florentines and visitors alike," the woman said. "Did they take your money?"

He patted his right hip, relieved that his wallet was still buttoned into the pocket along with his folded paper.

The woman clucked her tongue. "That is not a good place to keep your money, signore. You should keep it here." She patted her waist. "Inside."

Myopically, he looked at her waist then above, at the rise of breast beneath a black fitted top.

"You are confused."

"Yes." He reached into his pants pocket to check the time. "They took my watch." He looked at the woman. "The strap was broken so I took it off."

"With men, they go for the pocket. With women, they go for the purse."

"What is the time?"

"Fifteen minutes to nine."

"I'll be late." He was frantic.

"Where are you going?"

"To a conference near the railway station. I'm supposed to read a paper at nine."

"I will take you there pronto." The woman put a hand beneath his elbow. "Your conference is only ten minutes from here." While she steered him across another piazza and onto the Via Valfonda, he was aware of the warmth of her hand and the space she occupied beside him; she was about his height and had a firm, brisk stride. At the corner of Via Nazionale, she stopped in front of a large grey building and pointed to the conference poster taped to a glass door. "This is it. You are where you should be and on time. Will you be able to read without your glasses?"

"No," Stan said.

The woman reached into his pocket and took out the glasses.

"For now you could tape the broken side." She had long wine-coloured fingernails.

"Yes," Stan said. "I could do that." He began to pull himself together. "Thanks for your help." He stood there, not wanting to be late but unwilling to leave.

The woman laughed and he saw her large gleaming teeth. "I am not finished with you. You are to meet me here at five." She pointed across the road. "I work in the train station over there. I will come for you after work and take you to get your glasses repaired. Okay?"

"Okay." Her kindness overwhelmed him and he wanted to keep her talking but she was already on the curb. He watched her plunge into the traffic on the Via Valfonda, ducking Vespas and cars. On the other side she turned and waved and through the wavering air, he noticed the abundant dark hair sitting on her shoulders like an ancient headdress. How regal she was!

At a quarter to five, he was on the corner of the Via Nazionale and the Via Valfonda; he was early because he wanted to see the woman before she saw him and was relying on one lens to see. He watched her come up the station steps and cross the road, swerving around cars and trucks, oblivious to shouts and car horns, her hair bouncing wildly. She rushed up to him breathless and smiling, an angular, hook-nosed woman with high cheek bones and deeply recessed eyes. He was determined to ask her name and extended his hand. "Stan Mulloy."

Folding his fingers onto his palm, she cupped his hand between both of hers then amazingly held it between her breasts and told him her name. "Anna Crump."

Stan glanced at the station. "What do you do over there?"

"I work in the tourist centre." She asked if he had been able to read his paper.

"I stumbled through it."

"Were you pleased?"

"Relieved." In fact he was pleased that three people had commented on the innovative aspect of his research, though he couldn't remember exactly what they had said. He'd spent the day attending presentations and panel discussions, scarcely hearing a word because he'd been thinking about this woman, worrying about whether she would turn up, and if she did what he would say to her.

Now he said, "I would be honoured if you would allow me to buy you dinner." Did that sound too formal, as if he was more interested in returning a favour than in her company? Maybe he should have simply asked, would you have dinner with me? But asking a question gave her a chance to refuse, which she might do in any case.

His hand was still being held between her breasts. "If you will be honoured then I will be too." She dropped his hand and took his arm. "But first we must see about getting your glasses fixed. I know an optometrist on the Via degli Speziali who will repair them within twenty-four hours. It is about a fifteen-minute walk from here."

"Shall I hail a cab?"

"At this time of day it is faster to walk," Anna said.

They didn't talk much on the way to the optometrist. Anna chose a route that took them across crowded intersections and along streets so narrow they walked single file on a strip of raised concrete. When they were crossing the Piazza della Repubblica side by side, she remarked that the square had once been a Roman forum. "Now it has cafés and shops that cater to tourists like yourself." When he protested that he wasn't a tourist, she laughed and patted his arm. "There, there, Signore. I should have said visitor."

At the optometrist's, he took out the broken shards of his lens, which he had carefully wrapped in a Kleenex. While his eyes were being checked, he was aware of Anna sitting to one side turning the pages of a magazine and rotating a foot; he could see the toe of her shoe going round and round and hear her humming, a light insubstantial hum that sounded as natural as breathing. It reminded him of his niece; when she was sweeping the kitchen floor or drying dishes, Sheila would sometimes hum in a tuneless, meandering way, not an unhappy sound, not at all. It was the sound of self-absorption, of gathering in, of patient hope.

When the optometrist had finished, Anna took him to a nearby restaurant in a cellar lit by candles that cast flickering shadows on a wall hung with paintings and plates, but all he saw was Anna's shadow soaring and diving behind her as she talked. While she studied the menu, he studied her. She frowned, deciding what to order, her features hawkish and fierce; abruptly she laid the menu aside and asked Stan if he was sure he wanted her to order for him. The waiter came and she smiled at him, her head tilted up as she explained what they wanted, capelli d'angelo, bistecca al sangue, melanzane alla parmigiana, vino rosso, her hands moving as she spoke. The fierceness had entirely disappeared and she was now animated, relaxed. Not a pretty woman, not good-looking in a conventional way, but magnificent, splendid.

She was the daughter of an American soldier, born during the last year of the war, three months after Stan. She had never met her father, who was married when he met her mother, but throughout her growing up years he regularly sent money (though never an address), which paid for clothes and lessons in English, riding and swimming. Her mother, who had been brought up by an aunt in the village of Monteriggioni, worked in a glass and china shop on the Via del Moro.

"Where the wealthy visitors shop."

Her mother had never married.

"Have you?" Stan said.

"Have I what?" Anna put a piece of steak into her mouth.

"Have you ever married?"

She took her time replying, chewing slowly (seductively, Stan thought), taking a sip of wine.

"No. I have never married. But. ..." she paused. "There have been a number of men." She put down her fork and leaned on her elbows toward Stan. "Now, Signore, you must tell me about yourself. Are you married?"

"Me, married?" Stan laughed and shook his head.

"Have you ever been married?"

The question struck Stan as hilarious, but he could see her look of consternation, that she was confused by his laughter. Weirdly, he told her the truth.

"I'm a thirty-five year old virgin," he said, "though not by choice."

Her look changed to one of incredulity but in an instant she recovered.

"You, Mary and Joseph." She smiled. "You are in good company, Signore."

"Yes. Yours."

They looked at each other, both of them larger than life, their shadows leaping and dancing on the wall. Why had he told her? Because she had rescued him once and he needed rescuing again? Because he thought she was a woman he could trust? Because in a strange country he could throw caution to the wind?

She knew every street and public building in Florence, having conducted hundreds of visitor tours. After they left the restaurant, she led him toward the Uffizi "Which you must see while you are here," and on past the Ponte Vecchio. "No visit to Florence is complete without a stroll along the Arno in the moonlight." The Arno was unlike any river he had seen: bathed silver by the moon, it eased between city walls like mercury through a tube. At the Hotel Loggia they took the rackety elevator cage to his third-floor room, which was small and functional: wardrobe, bed, dresser, desk, chair. Anna undressed Stan slowly and nudged him onto the chair before undressing herself: black top and black bra, black belt and checked skirt, black stockings and underpants. Her breasts were high and round; beneath them he saw the rib bones clearly, the hollow between her hips, the coppice of black hair beneath her navel. She straddled his thighs and eased his cock inside and he came at once. She hadn't, apparently, expected otherwise for she crooned, "There, there," into his ear. They moved to the bed and Anna told him what she wanted; she was patient and gentle as if his eagerness to perform needed calming. He was surprised by her ardour, by the power it gave him to please her—he wanted to please her, to make her feel his euphoria—he was euphoric and flying.

In the morning, after she had left him at the conference centre, he sat in one room after another, grinning abstractedly while he waited for five o'clock when he would see her again. He passed the final day of the conference in much the same way. That evening after dinner she took him home to meet her mother who lived in a second-floor apartment in the Via Santo Spirito: four small rooms with a glass door opening onto a balcony where red geraniums bloomed in copper urns.

Luisa Crump looked like a well-kept widow or wife: she was a woman who took care with her appearance: hair dyed cherry red, cherry lipstick and fingernails, a tailored, rust-coloured suit, a gold wedding band. Obviously used to meeting strangers, she greeted

Stan with amused curiosity, and while Anna made coffee she inquired about what had brought him to Florence; he thought she already knew the answer but was asking out of politeness. When he said he intended staying in Florence another week if he could find cheaper accommodations, Anna poked her head out of the kitchen and asked if Silvano could help. "I will ask," Luisa said. "I am sure something can be arranged."

Silvano Antinori, Luisa's lover, was a desk clerk at the Loggia Stazione. Estranged from his wife, he slept in the hotel on those nights when he wasn't with Luisa. After he had made Silvano's acquaintance and settled into a room that was even smaller and more spartan than the one he had left, it occurred to Stan that this wasn't the first time Luisa's lover had been asked to put up one of Anna's acquaintances; his impression was based on the smoothness of the arrangements, how easily they had been accomplished and on Silvano's knowing smile. Stan didn't care what men Anna might have brought to the hotel. He could hardly expect a woman of her splendour to be a virgin like himself. While she was at work, he obediently took himself to the Uffizi, the Galleria dell'Accademia, San Marco. He spent a day in the science museum in happy absorption, studying quadrants, compasses, astrolabes, clocks and microscopes. How exquisitely crafted the early instruments of science were! Gleaming brass sextants incised with complicated motifs, gold-embossed leather telescopes, beakers of delicate glass; in the map room Stan found ancient globes twinning sea and space: a world map where monsters ruled the oceans and a celestial map where creatures of the zodiac ruled the heavens. Removing his glasses, he squinted at the varnished surface of the world globe, now darkened a mahogany brown, until he located a blurred wobbly shape surrounded by water. Newfoundland.

One evening Anna took him to hear a Gregorian chant echoing through the cloister of Santa Maria Novella and on another evening, while soft amber light illumined the nave window, he found himself facing the altar of Santa Croce listening to a Bach organ recital; afterwards Anna showed him the tombs of Galileo and Marconi at the back of the church.

"Did you know Marconi received his transatlantic signal from Newfoundland?" he said, while they were eating antipasto di pesce.

"I knew it was from a hill somewhere." There was a dismissive wave of the hand.

"It was in St. John's. There was also a Marconi station at Cape Race where I grew up." This caught Anna's attention and she leaned across the table. "Dearest Stanley, it seems the places of our birth were joined by Guglielmo Marconi."

"Will you forget me when I'm gone?" He was leaving the day after tomorrow.

"Not if you write to me and telephone."

She insisted on taking the morning off from work in order to accompany him to the airport, sitting in the taxi weeping and dabbing her eyes, and when he checked his luggage, leaning disconsolately against the wall, hands shoved into her jacket pockets, her nose red and her cheeks pale—after their lovemaking at dawn, there had been no time for applying make-up.

Nancy met him at the airport.

"You look pleased with yourself."

He grinned.

"Like a cat that swallowed the canary."

"That's me."

"A woman?"

"You betcha."

"What's she like?"

He tried to describe her and failed. "Her name is Anna."

They stopped at Gordon's for fish and chips, which they ate in his kitchen.

"Guess what," Nancy said. "I'm going to spend next year in Ireland. I've been offered a sessional in Cork. Sheila will be coming with me. She finishes high school in June. The sabbatical will fill a hole in my research and, to be honest, I want to take a year to decide what to do about Philip, whether I should continue putting up with his peccadillos or end the marriage."

So she knew. Stan asked about their mother.

"She's the same as ever. She really likes working at Ocean View. You have to admire her for the way she's landed on her feet."

"I do admire her."

"Without a formal education or employable skills, she's managed to keep herself employed."

"Mom has plenty of employable skills."

"I know," Nancy said humbly, "I know."

On Stan's first day back at ERI he began working on a proposal for the Atlantic Geoscience Centre. He was hoping to go aboard *Pisces* IV, which would be diving off the Labrador shelf in the fall; when he finished the proposal he went to Halifax for a first-hand look at the submarine. He didn't phone Anna; instead he scribbled notes on postcards, sending her pictures of Bell Island's rugged cliffs rearing out of Conception Bay, the bleak stone tower on Signal Hill, pack ice rammed between shore and sky. He deliberately chose rock, sea, ice—images that were barren and cold—wanting her to understand how inhospitable and unyielding his homescape was.

When he thought of her, he remembered them lying together in an olive grove overlooking the Tuscan hills bathed in soft auramine light, the air mild and soporific. After wandering around the Roman baths and ruins, they had shared a picnic supper of bread and cheese. The gates had closed at dusk (of course, Anna knew where to climb the wall). She also sent postcards, pictures of Fiesole, the Arno, Santa Croce, places they had been together. Judging from his postcards, she wrote, Newfoundland seemed to deserve its name, and she claimed to be fascinated by its wildness. Was she really? She told him that she missed him, which made him wonder if she meant that he hadn't yet been replaced.

In October Stan was inside an untethered submersible with Henrik Linderoth, dropping four hundred feet below the sea's surface to the Labrador shelf. *Pisces* IV was equipped with strobe lights, an external camera and a manipulating arm that could manoeuvre rock samples and debris into a basket. On the bottom he found evidence of scours and boulder dumps where icebergs had broken up, depositing debris that had either been scraped from the sea bottom or embedded in a berg's keel. Manipulating the arm to avoid a green plastic bag and a tin of Campbell's tomato soup, he transferred samples of rock and debris to the basket. All this was done with the help of strobe lights; without them, the sea was an impenetrable greenish black.

It was during the slow ascent that he thought of Anna, remembering her standing in the airport looking exhausted and forlorn. Why didn't he remember her rushing toward him smiling, or leaning urgently toward him across a table? Thinking of her sadness in the darkness of the ocean spooked him. Why should he remember her in this way, and down here of all places? Had something happened to her?

As soon as he was back in Beachy Cove, he picked up the telephone and dialled her number. It was 2:30 a.m. in Florence.

"Stanley, is that you?" Her voice was groggy with sleep.

"It's me."

"Are you okay?"

"I'll be okay if you marry me."

"Stanley. I will come to Newfoundland and then we will see."

His heart leapt. "You'll stay with me?"

"Yes."

"When?"

"Two weeks, maybe three."

"Hurry."

"Yes."

They were married during a storm on Valentine's Day, 1981, in Holy Rosary Church in Portugal Cove North. They had no way of knowing that in exactly a year, on their wedding anniversary, a far worse storm would sweep eighty-four men off the *Ocean Ranger*, the platform drilling for oil roughly two hundred miles offshore on the Grand Banks. This year's storm didn't ride the sea into mountainous waves; there were no waves large enough to smash the glass porthole in the ballast control room, or to wash over the platform floor; this year's storm brought the most common kind of winter weather in Newfoundland, freezing rain; even so, the black ice made the St. John's–Trepassey road treacherous enough to prevent Stan's mother from attending the wedding.

The Saturday following their marriage, the newlyweds drove to Daniel's Point, where Aurora served them a wedding dinner of roast chicken, dressing and gravy, potatoes and peas, and for dessert fruitcake decorated with white icing and a plastic bride and groom from the convenience store. She had placed the cake on one of her crocheted doilies with a white candle on either side and tied a large paper bell to the overhead light fixture. After they had eaten their meal and drunk their toasts with blueberry wine, his mother gave them a bulky brown paper package tied with white ribbon; inside was a blue tent with a red and white striped awning. Anna was delighted with the tent and said she had always wanted to sleep in the wilderness. Stan told her that in four months they would be sleeping beneath the stars.

"No so long as that!" She had a way of challenging while at the same time imploring.

"Four months. Our winters are long."

Stan need not have worried about how she would take to a Newfoundland winter. Anna was unfazed by the pack ice tight to shore, the freezing rain on woods and fields, the mournful bleat of the Cape Spear fog horn; she claimed that Newfoundland was exotic. He laughed and said, Newfoundland, exotic? Come on now, Italy is exotic: the ochre-coloured stone, the fragrant air, the church bells ringing over red tiled roofs, *they* were exotic. Yes, yes, they were, but so was the blinding purity of ice, the silvered fences and trees, the fogged voices of the drowned. Anna didn't miss Florence, she missed her mother, yes, that was to be expected, but she didn't miss Florentines who were *snobistico*; they had become so used to looking through tourists that they ignored everyone. People in Newfoundland were not like that; they looked her in the eye, they nodded to her on the street, they spoke to her in shops, they called her "love," which was *affascinante*. No, she didn't miss Florentines or Florence. You had to be rich to enjoy Florence. Otherwise, living there was like ... what was the word for those drums that go round and round? A treadmill, yes. Newfoundland was not a treadmill. No, here in this new land, you could go in different directions, here you could be yourself.

Anna took diving lessons from Warren, and Stan bought her diving gear so they would be able to dive together when summer came. She also took driving lessons and in three months had her licence. She cooked tortellini, rigatoni and ravioli, made jars of antipasto, marinated olives and artichokes in garlic wine and learned how to bake foccacia. She stocked their kitchen with homemade pasta, olive oil, balsamic vinegar, grew oregano and basil under fluorescent lights, made up cards: ANNA'S ITALIAN CATERING, put an ad in the newspaper and waited for the phone to ring. It took a while—this was before pasta became big in Newfoundland. All the time she was building up a business, Stan was boarding icebergs.

Of the ten thousand icebergs calved in Greenland each year, about one-tenth crossed the latitude of 48 degrees north; half that number made it to the latitude of 46 degrees; few of these would make it past the tail end of the Banks at the latitude of 43 degrees. Because Newfoundland was roughly between 46 and 51 degrees north, it was smack in the middle of the latitudes of melt. Every year, icebergs drifted down the Labrador Current to ground in the island's coves and bays.

For an ice man, the size and variety of bergs were a scientific and strategic challenge, which was not to say that Stan ignored these temples of beauty, their supple elegance and fluid grandeur, the way they had perfected the art of becoming anything under the sun: a Roman bath or a tropical lagoon; an alpine cliff or an Arizona canyon, the Taj Mahal or the Colossus of Rhodes. These wonders of the world weren't replicas or imitations but sculptural abstractions, monuments of artless splendour. Nominally Catholic, Stan didn't regard himself as religious, but he found something profoundly spiritual in the ice. The purity of the white, the gleaming symbols—the holy rood, organ pipes, cathedral spires—the soaring shapes that had nothing to do with innocence or evil filled him with exhilaration and wonder. But as a scientist, he knew the beauty was incidental, that icebergs weren't works of art, spectacular chunks of alabaster quarried into the sea, but remnants of the Ice Age, stored water, frozen weights on a spinning globe. Let loose on the sea, they became destroying angels, monstrous and unpredictable, instruments of chaos and ruin, so lethal that in spite of the iceberg watch begun after the *Titanic* disaster, the best advice he could give to anyone travelling or working in the North Atlantic was to tell them stay out of an iceberg's way. Impossible of course, which was why so much of ERI's research was focused on how ships, boats and now oil-drilling platforms and pipelines could be protected against ice.

Stan avoided highly sculpted bergs; he and Art Stander boarded low, modest-looking bergs, what Stan called savoirs, which on the surface were undistinguished, flat, snowy fields sawn from land that sometimes presented a pleated sylvan pasture sloping gently into the water, or a shallow cliff onto which an ice ladder could be hooked. One berg provided a wharf ribbed with pelagic planks; there was even a hitching post for them to tie up—a boulder scraped from the ocean floor. Before boarding a berg, the men circled it in the Zodiac, looking for signs of movement, knowing that an iceberg's balance was constantly being changed by underwater melt and that it was impossible to predict when one would roll. Before it rolled, an iceberg sometimes rocked, swinging its hips furiously from side to side. But even a motionless berg that was more or less flat and gave the illusion of being stable, could suddenly turn. They once boarded an innocuous-looking berg that had crouched on the water like a sleeping sea serpent, its tail curled around its feet, while they bored holes in its back and took their measurements, but they had been off it less than ten minutes when the monster shook itself awake and turned belly up, presenting an underside shaped like a lumpy keel that looked like it had swallowed wreckage from the sea bottom. Art Stander caught the turning on film, snapping one photo after another, proving that the transformation from serpent to keel had been accomplished in twenty seconds.

By July when the bigger bergs had either broken up or continued their southward drift, Stan analysed test results and on weekends he and Anna camped and dived, eating tortellini around the campfire, bread torn and dipped in vinegar and oil, shrimp marinated in wine—she hadn't yet landed a catering job and cooked for the weekends. "I am a failure, Stanley," she said, her hair and eyes reflecting the fire, making her look tragic and morose. "People here do not want an Italian caterer." Stan assured her that come fall, when the townies closed up their cabins and hauled their trailers back to the city from the gravel pits where they'd been parked all summer, her business would pick up.

That summer they pitched their tent on the Ferryland Downs, the Drook, St. Shotts, wherever there was access to diving or they could use a boat. At first they didn't dive beyond thirty feet. Until Anna was more experienced, Stan didn't want to take her deeper. Once, in August, when they were diving in Conception Bay, Stan thought he heard humpbacks singing. He'd heard whale songs before when he was diving, but he'd never seen whales below. In November when it became too cold to camp, they took the ferry across to Bell Island and dived off Lance Cove, where they heard the shrillness of the ferry whistle underwater. There were three world-class wrecks in prime condition off the island, ore carriers torpedoed during the war, two of which lay too deep to show Anna, but the third, at seventy feet, she could see, the water so clear that he could show her where icebergs had broken and broadcast the ship, and where a fishing net had been caught in the stern. The day before Christmas, they made their last dive before winter with Warren and his girlfriend, Peg. Following a tradition of Warren and Peg's, they took a fir tree below in Middle Cove and anchored it in a concrete block; the plastic balls tied to its branches floated upward like buoys, and the four of them exchanged gifts sealed in jars as if they were miniature ship models inside glass.

Stan was soon on the ice again, this time in Pond Inlet, North West Territories, with Art and an American engineer, Twyla Byrd. Working out of a small cabin facing Bylot Island, during the day they assessed the properties of sea ice using radar and acoustical equipment, recording strain meters and thermistor probes; at night they listened to Art play wineglasses—he had brought along a briefcase filled with glasses, which he used to make music, rubbing their rims to make thin airy tunes, what he called fairy music; meandering and ephemeral, it was the kind of music that fairy believers at home might claim they heard on the Barrens when they became lost and disoriented. The thought of the Barrens made Stan homesick for Newfoundland and for Anna—he didn't like being away from her and longed to fall asleep with her body enclosing his, longed to feel her hair on his cheek when she leaned over his shoulder to read; she never sat down to read the newspaper, preferring to scan it over his shoulder while she filled clients' orders. In a modest way her business was taking hold and she was now catering receptions. Her clients wanted finger foods, not full-course meals, and she served antipasto tarts, gingered shrimp, fig pastries, saffron eggs, food Newfoundlanders had never eaten before, food no one had eaten before—the recipes were experiments from her kitchen. Her standbys were miniature pizzas and wafers made with olives and cheese and arranged on platters, served by Anna herself in a long wine-coloured dress, a black fringed shawl, wine knee boots and dangling filigree earrings; with her terraced hair, hawkish nose and sunken eyes, she looked like a Mesopotamian goddess. One of these receptions was in the art gallery, another in an insurance company boardroom, the rest took place in people's homes. After she had banked enough money to buy the equipment, she intended to sell containers of pasta and pasta sauce. Stan was beginning to realize that he had married a shrewd businesswoman.

When he telephoned from Pond Inlet Anna wasn't home; she was at Murray's Pond catering a fiftieth wedding anniversary, Nancy told him. She'd been living with them since her return from Ireland last summer, alone—Sheila had remained in Cork with her boyfriend, an Irish playwright.

Nancy said, "You'll be pleased to know I'm moving out at the end of the month."

"Why would I be pleased? You know how much we like having you there." His wife and sister had hit it off from the start and there would be sadness and weeping when Nancy moved out. "Anna will be desolate."

"I've taken advantage of your kindness long enough. An old college friend, Gerry Morgan, found me a rent-to-sell house on Dick's Square. I can manage the payments but not much else." Nancy laughed. "Can I borrow a mattress?"

"Sure, anything you need."

"Well, maybe a chair. The house has a table. I won't ask him for anything. I'd rather do without than ask him." *Him* was Philip. "He says that as a rector's son, he is honour bound to resist divorce. Can you believe it? I passed him in the corridor last week and he was barely civil."

Stan had never liked his brother-in-law, but then he'd been predisposed to dislike him because of the affairs. While Nancy and Sheila were in Ireland, Philip had taken up with Tina Murphy, a psychology professor whose Volvo Stan often saw parked in the early morning in the Palmers' driveway. Someone, a neighbour or a colleague, must have contacted Nancy in Ireland, because she'd known about the affair and before returning from Cork had decided to leave Philip.

"Do you need any money?"

"No. Thanks. Listen, this is costing you a fortune. Why don't you call back at eleven? Anna will be home by then. She has news."

The news was that Anna had lined up two big jobs: a June wedding rehearsal party and a reception aboard a boat during a medical convention.

"For that I will wear a bathing suit."

Stan wrestled with the picture of his wife in a bikini passing snacks around a boatload of doctors, most of whom he assumed would be men.

"I think you should wear a dress."

"It was a joke, Stanley. Don't you know that you are stuck ...is it stuck?"

"Yes."

"Stuck with me for life."

In March Anna left to spend a month in Florence with her mother while he stayed behind to work on the final report on the Pond Inlet experiments. How he enjoyed going to ERI in the mornings, walking down iceberg alley where photographs of icebergs he had boarded were mounted on the wall, along with the map pinpointing icebergs drifting through the latitudes of melt. Stan's office was next to the Victor Campbell room with its artefacts from Scott's Antarctic expedition: books and skis, a sextant and transit, photos of the five doomed men. For recreation he painted the inside of his house before moving on to paint Nancy's, and twice he drove to Daniel's Point and stayed with Aurora, who took him to Ocean View to visit his Aunt Brenda and Aggie Halleran, his old buddy's mother, whose hair his mother had done that morning—she did all the hair at the nursing home.

In June, after the algae bloom had run its course, Anna and Stan began diving again, mainly along the Southern Shore; they didn't go far from St. John's because he was working on an ice scour project for Petro-Canada and she was preparing for the medical reception and wedding rehearsal party. One of their favourite places to camp was above the beach in Mobile Bay, where

Stan usually came to watch whales during the caplin scull, which was late this year on account of the ice. In July there were still icebergs cruising offshore and, closer in, a small berg—more of a growler than a berg—floating in the bay. It seemed perfectly balanced on a pair of wings, one on either side of a sloping breast, which inspired Anna to call it the Winged Victory. While they drank the last of their morning coffee she asked if Stan had ever dived beneath a berg, and he told her that he never had or would, though Warren had done it once, dived down a berg's gleaming flank then around the keel and up the other side.

"Once I dived into the aquamarine water surrounding a berg."

"It must be like swimming inside a jewel," Anna said. "I want to do it, Stanley, I want to dive into that beautiful colour."

The Winged Victory was mounted on a flaring pedestal, which made the surrounding water an astringent turquoise. Because the underwater spread was so wide, Stan thought it would be possible to swim through it while keeping a safe distance from the berg, and agreed to give it a try. While they were suiting up, he warned her to expect poor visibility because the aquamarine was, in fact, a barrier of frigid water and once they entered it, ice crystals would coat their masks, making it difficult to see.

Did he say too much? Or not enough? Why hadn't he trusted his instincts and refused to take her anywhere near the berg? There was no point rationalizing or trying to explain it to himself. It happened, that was all that could be said. Chance. Luck. Circumstance. It came down to that. The whale, God, how he hated the whale. If his family hadn't kept a close eye on him afterwards, like Captain Ahab he might have tried to hunt it down. Irrational of course; the humpback was intelligent and elusive, not a hunter of humans; the sea was its element, not theirs, and they had gotten in its way. Because it was accidental, Stan could never be sure exactly what had happened; no matter how many times he reviewed the dive, he couldn't figure out what had gone wrong; there were too many pieces missing. The whale had appeared to be alone, which was unusual, and it had swum toward them though whales were known to scrupulously avoid divers. Warren's theory was that the berg must have blocked the sound of their approach; he said the whale must have sounded and gone under the berg just as they reached the other side. Warren's eyes blinked when he said this; he had a faint V-shaped scar over one eyebrow; odd that after all their years together, Stan should only notice it now. He told Warren that he'd been surprised to see the whale but not afraid, knowing it would veer away rather than come close, but Anna wouldn't have known that and must have thought it would come right up to her. It was a big one, the roll of its wake slamming against Stan, bouncing him on a wave. Right away he had looked over his shoulder for Anna but she wasn't beside him in their usual formation which was to swim side by side, Stan slightly ahead. Wiping the ice crystals from his mask, he had turned his body in a circle, but she wasn't in sight. He found her drifting thirty feet behind, blood trickling from her nose and mouth.

"She must have panicked when she saw the whale swimming toward her," Warren said. "She didn't know it would never touch her, that it would sound."

"I lost her," Stan said. "We should have been tethered."

"At thirty feet in open water? We never tether at that depth."

"But I knew about the poor visibility."

"Don't blame yourself. It was a fluke."

As soon as Stan got Anna on top, he took off her mask, which by then was pooled with blood. Rivulets of blood had seeped into the eye sockets, turning the balls a fiery orange.

"Lie back, sweetheart. I'm towing you in."

She was conscious. A lung had burst, but he thought he could save her though it took forever—fifteen minutes—to get her ashore. A man was there, standing in front of a camper with his dog, a sheltie. Strange what he remembered. He didn't remember anything about the man, didn't know his name. They laid her in the back of the camper and drove to St. Clare's Hospital, speeding all the way, Stan kneeling beside her, the sheltie whimpering and trying to lick her face. She lived two days in a coma. There was a battery of doctors, one of whom, Stan didn't remember his name either, said it was just as well, Anna was brain dead. Christ, brain dead! He didn't believe it.

Over 150 people attended the funeral—in less than two years Anna had touched that many people. There was no burial; she had disliked graveyards, claiming they were a waste of beautiful earth. That was the way she'd put it one day when she and Stan were walking along Quidi Vidi Lake past the Forest Road Cemetery. Somehow he managed to retrieve every word of her conversation from his jumbled brain. Anna said it was better to plant trees and flowers than gravestones, that graveyards should be made into parks. She was cremated, her ashes placed inside a six-inch pottery jar. That Anna, his Anna, should be inside something so small was preposterous, a cruel joke, a cosmic game that he, the messenger boy, was playing out. He went along with it, playing the role doggedly, ritually, what choice did he have? He got on one plane, then another, then into a taxi, the jar cradled in his hands, all the way to Luisa Crump. When he had phoned her from the hospital, she had broken down, saying she couldn't come to Newfoundland, no, she couldn't. Stan promised he would come to her, that he would bring Anna back.

The roots of Luisa's hair were grey and her nails were chipped. She wore a black dress and didn't have the energy for polite cordiality, but she didn't blame him. "With you she was happy," she said. She had Anna's shrine in the corner near the balcony, a high brass table draped with lace cloth. Between two candles was a terracotta urn decorated with a Grecian woman striding forward, her arms held high, bearing a platter of food, her hair streaming behind. Luisa lifted the cover of the urn and placed Anna inside. On the wall behind was a picture of her at twelve: a tall, buck-toothed, gawky girl in a confirmation dress squinting at the sun. Before Stan left, Luisa folded his hand between her breasts, just as Anna had. "You come visit her any time you want."

When he got home, his mother was waiting for him in Beachy Cove. She stayed with him for two weeks, answering the phone, making meals he couldn't eat, keeping her distance while watching his every move. Her presence was so unobtrusive that he hardly noticed when she left and was surprised to see that his sister had arrived.

I had a hard time leaving Stanley, but I was expected to return to my job at the nursing home. I told Nancy that I was thinking of leaving Ocean View altogether in order to stay with Stanley, but she wouldn't hear of it. She said she would move to Beachy Cove and wouldn't leave until he was ready to return to work, which she didn't think would be very long.

Warren asked Stan if he wanted to see what remained of the wreck of the *Florizel*, which was off Cappahayden; this was a dive they had often talked of doing together.

"I won't be diving again."

"They say when you fall off a horse, you should get back on again."

"No more diving."

"What about going back to work? You can't sit out in Beachy Cove forever."

No, he couldn't, but he understood why his mother had refused to leave Trepassey after his father's death, why she had wanted to stay close to the Bay of Souls. Though he'd taken Anna's ashes to Florence, she was still here, in the cries of the seagulls, in the mist and the fog. Any day now she would walk out of the water, wild-eyed, with seaweed tangled in her hair, a merwoman recovering from amnesia.

A month after Anna died, Jeff Jones, the engineer who had taken a submarine beneath the polar ice cap, called from the Scott Polar Institute in Cambridge to say he was looking for a Ph.D. student to undertake ice research in the Antarctic next year. "Are you interested?"

"I'll think about it." Once Stan had wanted a Ph.D., and he'd wanted to work out of the Scott Polar; now he didn't care if he ever did.

"Don't think about it too long. I can give you a week to decide."

It was Nancy who decided.

"You'd be a fool not to take him up on it," she said. "It would give you a chance to spend some time in Cambridge and it would be good for you to get away. You could visit Sheila in Cork."

He was thinking that if he left Newfoundland, he would have to give up the house in Beachy Cove, and wondered what he would do with Anna's things. He couldn't bear to part with her things.

"Stan. I'm talking about Sheila. I'm worried about her."

"Why?"

"She's throwing her life away on this Irish writer, keeping house for him and some students. I don't want her making the same mistake I did."

The thought made him wince: was Sheila a mistake?

"If you were in Cambridge, you could nip across to see her. You could let me know how she is. You could tell me what you think of Kevin Byrne."

"It would depend on when I go to the Antarctic."

"I'll help you with Anna's things. You can keep whatever you want at my house."

He kept the pasta and cappuccino maker, the jars of oil, the cookbooks, but gave her clothes to the Harbour Light and sent her jewellery to Luisa Crump except for her wedding ring, which he wore around his neck.

He went to Cambridge but didn't stay long. Jeff Jones had an Italian wife, a Venetian, and though she didn't look at all like Anna she had an extravagant, passionate nature that reminded him of her, and so he moved on, crossing the Irish Sea.

He intended staying only one day in Cork, but Sheila talked him into staying three, saying that with Kevin away and her students gone she'd be alone in the house. The house, which belonged to Kevin, was high on a hill off Sunday's Well Road. It was lime-green, painted concrete like the other houses on the street, and had tall windows, a narrow strip of unmown grass and a rose garden gone wild—the garden had been Mrs. Byrne's. Two small windows had been built at either end of the roof below the chimneys, and Stan slept in one of these rooms. The other was Sheila's studio, as he discovered the first morning while she was downstairs making breakfast. He looked in and saw an unfinished painting on the easel—at least, it looked unfinished to him; it seemed to be nothing more than strips of green and blue, with a small figure midway between. It wasn't until he saw a painting on the floor showing an iceberg floating on a strip of band, a small black dot marking one end, that he had some idea of what she was trying to do.

"I'm painting a series about Gran," she explained. They were sitting in the kitchen and she had poured Stan a second cup of coffee from a dented metal pot that, like everything in the room, had seen better days. In the gloom of the kitchen her face was milk pale, probably because she wore no make-up and was dressed in a black sweater and pants. A long black braid fell over one shoulder and her hands fluttered like doves while she talked.

"The series began with an assignment I had last year when I was trying to visualize Gran's life in pictures." Sheila was a student at the Crawford School of Art and Design. "Before I can finish the series, there's a lot more I have to find out."

"Such as?"

"How Gran got on that ice pan."

"So you don't agree with Nancy that our mother's rescue was a story to cover up something else."

"No, I don't, and I intend to prove it."

He heard the determination in her voice; for a dreamy kid she showed a surprisingly strong will, but of course she wasn't a kid any more, she was a self-possessed young woman.

"For what it's worth, I don't either."

"A few years ago Gran sent me a handkerchief that she said was in the basket when she was rescued and had been on a doll all these years. I think the name, Roche, stitched on the handkerchief, might have been my great-grandmother's. Roches are thick on the ground in this country so it will take time to track her down and I won't be able to work on it this summer. I'll be taking a landscape painting course in July and I promised Kevin I'd go to the Edinburgh Festival with him in August."

"It sounds as if you live a busy life."

"Oh yes, I do."

"I'm supposed to ask when you're coming home."

"I have no plans to go home." Again, Stan heard the determination in her voice. "Apart from Kevin, I have other reasons for wanting to stay here."

Before leaving Cork Stan mailed two letters home, one to his mother, the other to his sister. Although Nancy stayed in close touch with her daughter, he wanted to reassure her that she didn't need to worry about Sheila, who as far as he could tell was very much in command of herself. He said he was impressed by her determination to continue painting, and didn't mention her pursuit of the Roches, or that he hadn't met Kevin who was in Dublin staging one of his plays. He wrote much the same thing to his mother.

From Ireland Stan went to Antarctica, to the bottom of the world, where he was assigned lab space and a room at Scott Base, a cluster of green aluminum buildings on McMurdo Sound beside the Ross Ice Shelf. For nine months Stan went out on the ice and checked his instruments—he was measuring the rate of ice flow, an area of ice scour research that was virgin territory. Most of the world's ice was in the Antarctic and the world's largest icebergs were in the South; Trolltunga, a former glacier tongue, had been a hundred kilometres long and fifty wide until, after eleven years of bumping along the coast, it finally calved, birthing a berg as flat and tabular as itself. The ice he was working on was more or less flat, not difficult to travel across compared to the northern pack ice; there were fissures to avoid, but even in the winter dark they were easily identified by the lights mounted on the Ski-Doo he used to get to his instrumentation site three kilometres away from the base. It took him thirty minutes to reach the site, including the time it took to ram poles into the ice—a sight line of poles was essential when the wind blew snow into whirling eddies that obscured the camp. He prided himself on going out in all weathers, and so far there had been only two days when a screaming blizzard made it impossible for him to work outside.

Scott Base suited Stan. Twelve men worked in their cells like monks, living a celibate, cerebral life, coming together only for meals then dispersing to follow the orders of holy science. The year began in October, the last flight out was in February and the first air drop was in June, which meant four months when the light was underwater murk. Those were the months when the moon moved up the sky and nowhere did abide. Stan was inside an ice vault at the bottom of the world, where sorrow weighed on his shoulders like a slain albatross. On July 12th, the day a year ago when Anna died, he rode the Ski-Doo out to the instrumentation site and, like a zombie, noted the readings in his record book.

He grew a beard that, given his thirty-nine years, showed a surprising amount of grey. He repaired an old bicycle he found in one of the sheds and rode it aimlessly around the ice. Until one of the scientists raised the alarm, he hunted skuas with a bow and arrow and brought a penguin to the kitchen, asking the cook to make penguin stew, which he ate under eleven pairs of reproachful eyes.

"If it's good enough for Victor Campbell," he said, "It's good enough for me."

Victor Campbell and his men had survived the Scott expedition by eating penguin and seal meat while holed up inside an ice cave for eight months; Campbell eventually moved to Newfoundland.

"Campbell was starving," the biologist said.

"It tastes like seal meat," Stan said, to rub it in—he had no use for people who were against hunting seals.

"I suppose you'll be eating dog meat next?"

Soon after his arrival at Scott Base, Stan had befriended Fram, a sled dog named after Nansen's ship, which had brought Amundsen to the Antarctic. Ski-Doos had put sled dogs out of work and it was a sore point with the biologist that the half-dozen dogs penned behind the camp were growing fat on seal meat.

Fram enjoyed racing the Ski-Doo to the instrumentation site, and when the snow around the base melted down to gravel, the dog slept in a tent with Stan. No one complained. They had decided to avoid the eccentric Newfoundlander, who stank, having gone weeks without changing his clothes.

In September, when he returned to Newfoundland with the dog, Stan shaved his beard, shed his filthy clothes, rented a house in Tor's Cove and went back to work. Now that he was near the top of the world, remembering who he had been at the bottom, he knew how close he had come to doing himself in; he knew that if he had switched off the light on the Ski-Doo and opened the throttle full speed he would have eventually rammed into a jagged serac or catapulted into a fissure. Or—he clearly remembered thinking this during a raging storm—he could have gone outside and like Oates, one of Scott's doomed party, wandered off and disappeared in all that ice and snow. The twilight had made it seem easy and in a way inevitable, but in the end he had refused to become a martyr to grief.

Stan had lost the haunted look and was older and greyer. He wasn't the same man who had left for the South Pole. Something deep inside him had shifted. Ice was solid but not immobile, and beneath the ice cap it flowed ceaselessly, imperceptibly opening up fissures and crevasses. Somewhere inside him, a subterranean widening had taken place, a seam shadowed and deep where fresh water had leaked in and frozen. The ice was crystalline, jewelled. It held a wrenching, violent beauty created during a time of fiery upheaval, when seams of ruby and aquamarine were brutally laid down.

THREE

THE QUAY

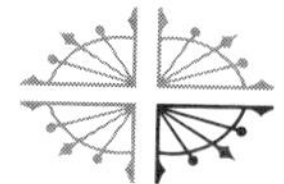

1910

I was conceived in my father's room in Coal Quay, shortly after my parents, Mary Roche and Owen O'Connor, were married. The room was one floor above a fish-and-chip shop and faced the Lee, which meant the womb more often held river noises than the clamour of the street. Though she decried its filth, my mother had a sentimental attachment to the Lee because it was there on the quay that she met my father. After their marriage, my parents lived apart, which didn't trouble me as long as my home continued to be the warm broth of my mother's womb, where I turned in circles with my fists pressed like earphones to my head. Through them I heard the reassuring thump of my mother's heart and sometimes, only sometimes, intermittent messages, rustlings, coded whispers from outside.

Until I was halfway to being born, my mother continued her occupation as a millinery assistant at number 7, North Mall, where she was required to live in a room behind her employer's shop. Because my father was away six days a week working the coal boats between Queenstown and Cardiff, my mother and he agreed that it was sensible for her to continue receiving an income, modest though it was, for as long as she could. She decided to leave her employer only when her wedding suit no longer buttoned over her belly, knowing it was only a matter of weeks before she would be dismissed: one of the conditions of her employment was that she be a 'respectable' woman by which her employer meant Protestant and unmarried, neither of which my mother was.

Her departure from her employer's premises was carefully planned, and for some weeks she had been moving her belongings to my father's room. She had posted a letter to her mother, Louise Burke-Davis, at Annakisha, my mother's home in the country, a letter timed to arrive after she and I were safely out of reach in Coal Quay. She had also written to her employer to apologize for leaving without notice, and expressing the hope that another millinery assistant could soon be found. On Sunday, while her employer was visiting her brother after church, my mother placed the letter on the folded counterpane in the bedroom behind the shop. Then she picked up her handbag and cane and we went out to await my father in Knapp's Square.

Mary had chosen to meet Owen in Knapp's Square because it was close by and was a safe place to wait unnoticed—Owen was never on time. He had been thirty minutes late for their wedding, making her wait in Carey's Lane dressed in her wedding clothes, the same wool suit and hat she was wearing now. She had spared no expense with the hat, a broad-brimmed navy blue felt, trimmed with a wide satin band and a veil of the finest Belgian weave, that could be draped over the crown as it was now, or lowered over her face as it had been when she and Owen exchanged vows in the sacristy of the church of St. Peter and Paul. When he'd finally appeared at the end of the lane that day, with a red rose snitched from a garden on Wellington Road in the lapel of his brown tweed jacket, Mary had nearly swooned with relief, for by then she'd been convinced that he'd changed his mind about marrying her.

Owen's looks alone were cause for swooning: despite the long hours he spent shovelling coal, his skin was uncommonly fair, and his hair a silky flaxen white. Tall and slender, he moved with a leonine grace and except for his square, quarried hands, in his good clothes looked almost elegant.

He sauntered toward her now in Knapp's Square, only twenty minutes late, hands in his suit pockets, whistling, grinning, not a care in the world. When matters were proceeding the way he liked, there was no sunnier disposition than his. Mary knew better than to chide him for being late since even gentle teasing met with a sharp retort. Instead she remarked that it was almost teatime. "There's raisin buns at home," he said, and picking up the valise, took her firmly by the arm.

Mary thought one of the pleasures of marriage was being led by her husband. She liked the way he gripped her elbow while propelling her along, making the use of her cane unnecessary. He steered her over the bridge and up the stairs to a grubby room he was evidently proud of, since he often praised its location and its window view. To someone whose bedroom window had once overlooked a country meadow, barges and tugs hardly constituted a view, but at least the window had an outside box attached that provided a convenient place to store butter and cheese. He was also proud of the bed, though its metal frame was skewed and the decorative knobs that might have given it some charm were missing. In addition to the bed, there were two straight-backed chairs and a scarred drop-leaf table for which Mary had embroidered a cloth. She had already added a tea set and a coal-oil lamp to the room. An electric light bulb left over from the building's warehouse days dangled from the ceiling, but it didn't work. The place had been made over into rooms and flats, but nothing had been done to improve the electricity or water, and Owen said a complaint to the landlady only resulted in a warning that the rent would be increased.

He bolted the door and she was about to suggest he light the burner when he put down the valise, unpinned her hat and hung it on the peg. Placing his hands on her shoulders, he put his cool, scaly lips to hers.

"First things first," he said smiling—he smiled without showing his teeth. He unbuttoned her jacket and began fondling her breasts.

Mary would have preferred to have tea first. She liked the ritual of setting out saucers and plates, lining up spoons and knives, pouring milk into the little shamrock jug, more than she liked making love. So far in their marriage, she had enjoyed the anticipation of coupling—the word she used—more than the coupling itself. But she didn't resist; she couldn't expect her husband to wait until after tea, not after months of hurried Sunday afternoons together. Owen removed her skirt and chemise without fumbling and while she rolled down her stockings, took off his clothes. He stood before her in his bare feet, his member erect, and for the first time they regarded each other's nakedness—there had never been time to undress before. Mary was startled to notice that the skin below his neck was whiter than her own. He didn't lead her to the bed; instead, taking hold of her buttocks, he hoisted her up and held her back against the door. He entered her that way, heaving her up so that with each thrust her head arched on her neck knocking her forehead against his chin. She was shocked by the violence and scandalized that it was taking place, not within the discretion of bedclothes or darkness, but in broad daylight, at teatime, while she was pregnant with me, no less. It seemed vulgar and improper. She felt shamed, and was offended that Owen hadn't warned her of his intention beforehand. When it was over and they were resting on the bed, he put his hand on her belly and grinned. "Think of it, an O'Connor inside a Roche womb," he said, in a way that made me wonder if I had been indecently conceived.

Mary heard the defiance in his voice, the look-what-I-did. He was proud of having made her pregnant—one would think the union of Catholic seed and Protestant egg was an accomplishment, and in a way it was. The mixture of defiance and pride mitigated the shock of having been held against the door. Lying beside her husband, she considered making a confession to the priest. Would he disapprove? Would he be shocked by what she had allowed Owen to do? If they could imagine it, her mother and stepfather would be shocked, but that would be only one of many shocks, the first one being the news, when it eventually reached them, that she had run off with a Catholic coalman. There was no telling what Harold Burke-Davis would do when he heard the news. He was capable of breaking down their door, regarding it as his duty to rescue her from an unsuitable husband. Her mother's response would be to forbid the mention of Mary's name within Annakisha's walls—if she was so foolish and ungrateful as to choose a life of ruin and disgrace, then she could expect to be disowned. Last year, when at the insistence of her husband, Louise had agreed to send Mary to find employment in Cork, she had hoped that her daughter would in time be courted by a respectable Protestant, a notary or teacher or perhaps a banking clerk, a man of modest means and aspirations who, despite Mary's lameness, would consider himself fortunate to be marrying a Roche.

By marrying Owen, she had not only thrown respectability away, she had become an exile, giving up her younger sister Rose and beautiful Annakisha in exchange for this ugly room with its grimy window and smoky walls, a window and walls she would have to wash herself since she had also given up servants. So be it. She knew her situation was the result of being rash and impetuous. Before he died, in her thirteenth year, her beloved father had warned her that her nature might some day lead her astray. He said that in a child impetuosity was to be admired because it showed a youthful spirit, but that in a young woman it needed restraining since it often led to serious mistakes.

High-spiritedness had compelled Elsa and her to fling themselves into the Blackwater the July they were ten. Pulling off their dresses, they had run yelping and laughing into the river, gleefully splashing and ducking each other. The mud oozing between Mary's toes, the willow branch tickling her back, the eel slithering past her thigh, all of it had been thrilling and dangerous. Not real danger, not the danger that came afterwards, but imagined danger that made her shiver with delight.

Owen never again held her against the door and she didn't make a confession to the priest. Instead, reminding herself of the church's teachings that love was forgiving, that forgiveness cleansed the soul, she forgave Owen and herself. She wanted to believe that forgiveness expunged unwanted feelings and made way for love, that love overcame wrongdoing and made her clean and pure-hearted; love made her a dutiful wife.

A month after she moved to Coal Quay, she wrote to her brother Will in New York. A few years ago Will, who was a journalist, had published an article on land reform in the *Cork Examiner*; their stepfather had disagreed with Will's views and they had a falling out that led to Will's decision to emigrate. Of Mary's two older brothers, he was the one of whom she was fond; she had no fondness for Thomas, who was unyielding and opinionated. In his view, Ireland's worst enemy wasn't the English but the Irish, by which he meant the Catholic Irish. The Irish wallowed in their troubles likes pigs in muck instead of getting themselves out of the mire. The Scots were the same. The Celts were a grievous lot who suffered from a perverse enjoyment of misery. A good thing the Roches were bred from Anglo-Norman stock. This condemnation of the Irish never failed to drive Will from Annakisha's dinner table; he would pace back and forth in the garden until he had calmed himself enough to return to the dining room where he would attempt, once again, to refute his brother's proclamations. A waste of time: trying to change Thomas's mind was like attacking a fortress with a hat pin. This was how Mary sometimes thought of

Will, as a knight trying to rid the world of narrow-mindedness and bigotry. She knew that he was loyal and trustworthy, and could be counted on to keep a secret. He had always been, and still was, her closest confidant.

Now she confided in him about her conversion, marriage and pregnancy, being careful to explain that she became pregnant *after* her marriage, but had kept her condition a secret to enable her to continue working as a millinery assistant. She told him that she had written their mother about the marriage but had omitted the news of her conversion and pregnancy. She wrote that Owen's plans were uncertain but that he was contemplating emigration to America because there was no future in Ireland for his line of work, which was the transportation business. She asked how Will enjoyed living in New York and requested that he send his reply to Mary Roche O'Connor in care of the Cork post office.

In October, when I was seven months along, my mother took herself out to the Lying-in Hospital on Western Road, walking slowly, stopping often to lean on her cane—my added weight was making her short of breath and her limp more pronounced. Though we were otherwise in good health, she wanted a doctor's assurance that our pregnancy was proceeding the way it should. She also wanted to see the hospital beforehand, or thought she did. Because Owen's work required him to spend considerable time in Cardiff it was likely that when my birth began, we would have to find our own way there.

Mary hadn't for a moment considered entering the Cork Lying-in or the Victoria Hospital because in a Protestant hospital she would risk being recognized by someone acquainted with her mother. Far better she come to this Catholic hospital, a three-storey concrete building with dormer windows on the roof and a fire escape along one side. The building looked as bleak as a barracks and as dreary as a poorhouse, which it was, but it had the advantage of being safe from the Burke-Davises. Though she had spent most of her savings, had no prospect of an income and was entirely dependent on Owen's meagre wage, Mary, who had a proud, resilient disposition, didn't think of herself as one of the poor. Poverty was a temporary situation which in time would pass. She had no clear idea how her situation would improve but having enjoyed a privileged upbringing until her father's death, she was confident that it would, most likely through emigration to America, a possibility she brought to Owen's attention as often as she could.

Inside the hospital Mary sat on a long wooden bench, waiting her turn to speak to the frail whiskery nun who was writing down particulars at the desk. There were two women ahead of her; hugely pregnant, their bellies bulbed over their thighs like rounded fruit. Sometimes Mary thought of her belly as an enormous melon, the kind of melon she had once seen on a silver tray in the dining room of the Hotel Metropole.

The woman being interviewed was little more than a girl, and when the nun asked her about the child's father, Mary was shocked to hear her say, in a rush of bitterness and fear, "The man of the house." Was she a servant? Did she mean her employer or her father? Mary tried not to listen; it was improper to intrude on another's privacy; instead she concentrated on the plain wooden crucifix on the opposite wall, which was identical to the one Owen had hung over their bed. She put her hand in her pocket and fingered the beads. *Hail Mary, full of grace. The Lord is with Thee; blessed are Thou among women. Blessed is the fruit of Thy Womb, Jesus.*

This wasn't her first time inside a Catholic hospital. Stricken with infantile paralysis after her frolic with Elsa in the Blackwater, she had spent ten weeks in the Cork Union Hospital, a place her mother, shuddering as if a mouse were running up her back, called the "workhouse," since it was where Catholic paupers were nursed. Certainly it was no place for an upper-class Protestant girl. But her father had insisted that if she was to make a full recovery, Mary would have to be in the orthopaedic ward with the other polio cases under Dr. O'Connell's care; he was the only doctor in Cork who treated patients stricken with paralysis. After inspecting the ward, her father had reported to her mother that the Sisters of Mercy operated a first-class hospital; gone were the days when children suffering from various diseases slept five to a bed on vermin-infested mattresses, their shaven heads smeared with ointment to cure the itch. Their daughter would have a cot of her own, sharing a room with other paralysed children. Bed linen was changed twice a week and the commode emptied every day; meals were spartan but adequate.

When her mother learned that Mary had not only married a Catholic but had become one herself, she would be convinced that her conversion was the result of her stay in the Cork Union Hospital, and would insist that with their usual Catholic arrogance the nuns had worked zealously to convert her to what they regarded as the one true faith. The Sisters of Mercy had done no such thing; while in hospital Mary herself became a willing novitiate to Catholicism and almost immediately fell in love with the Virgin, whose statue was in an alcove between her and Kathleen's cots. While Kathleen, who was paralysed from the neck down, said her novenas, Mary repeated them, her fingers travelling a necklace of imaginary beads, her eyes on the Holy Mother dressed in pale blue, her head tilted to one side as she gazed at the white lily in her hands. She might have been a doll except that dolls did not have a sorrowful expression. On either side of the Virgin were candles that were lit when the priest came to say mass.

Her mother would have been appalled if she'd known about the mass. Fortunately, she never arrived during mass since the priest came in the mornings and her mother in the afternoons. The first thing her mother did when she came into the ward was to ask one of the sisters to place a screen around Mary's cot, "to have my daughter all to myself" was the way she put it, though Mary knew it was to shut out the Catholic girls in the ward. Her mother brought baskets of fruit, pears and apricots from Annakisha's orchard, lady fingers and slices of ginger cake. Mary noticed how her mother kept frowning at the bleeding Jesus hanging from the cross above her bed, her mouth puckered as if she had a cherry pit in her mouth and was waiting until such time as it could be delicately removed. Mary's father and brother also visited, Will more often, since he came to the city three times a week to attend classes at the university college. Neither of them had requested the screen or taken notice of the crucifix.

For Mary the crucified Christ held the terrible fascination of a fairy tale; the bloodied Christ was a disguise for a Heavenly Prince who would one day come down from the cross and rescue Princess Kathleen from the chains of paralysis that she suffered without a word of complaint. Kathleen was sixteen, the perfect age for a princess, and though her skin was badly pocked and her scalp like the top of a salt shaker where her hair had fallen out, one kiss from the Prince would prepare her for Heaven, making her cheeks rosy and smooth, her hair shining and thick. After Mary had been discharged from the hospital and Dr. O'Connell was examining her leg, he told her that Kathleen had died saying her novenas and Mary knew that she had been rescued at last.

Now the girl who had blamed "the man of the house" for her pregnancy went into the doctor's examining room, and the woman beside Mary moved to the chair beside the desk to be interviewed by the nun, leaving the acrid smell of unwashed flesh behind. Mary didn't move along the bench to the place the woman had vacated but remained where she was, at a further remove from the smell. She noticed red welts around the woman's wrists. Were they birthmarks or some kind of skin disease? The woman's uneven hair looked as if had been sawed with a bread knife.

When it was Mary's turn to sit at the desk, the nun asked her age.

"Nineteen."

"Is this your first pregnancy?"

"It is."

She placed her left hand on the knob of the cane where her wedding ring could be seen.

"Why do you use a cane?"

"My right leg is lame from polio and is two inches shorter than my left leg. I wear a corrective boot."

A notation was made of this.

"If possible, when your times comes, you are to bring a change of underlinen, bedclothes and the child's napkins and gowns, all of it initialled to avoid confusion."

Dr. Donovan was younger than the nun, though not by much. A shambling, bulky man with yellowing hair, he had a drinker's porous nose and his hands shook when he undertook the examination, but he was kindly and well-intentioned. He said that both mother and child—meaning me—appeared healthy, and after inquiring about what my mother was eating, advised her to undertake regular daily exercise. Then he asked if my father had work.

"He is employed in transportation six days a week."

"That is fortunate for you," the doctor said. "Tell him for me that from now on there are to be no intimate relations, and none for three months after the birth. Can you tell him that?"

"I can tell him."

"If you require my assistance in that way, you will call upon me?"

"You can be sure my husband will behave as a civilized man."

"Very well then, that's settled."

My mother spent most of her travail walking the second-floor corridor, past women who like her kept one hand on their bellies, the other on the railing. When she passed the stairwell, she heard the moans and screams of women in labour one floor below. She heard a woman cursing the child's father, shouting oaths of vengeance and recrimination. The foulness of the language troubled my mother; it upset her to think that the woman hated the child's father. My mother was naive; even I, viewing the world from the inside out, knew there were all kinds of women in the hospital, women who lived an entirely different life from my mother's.

Nell Pye, who occupied the next cot over, had eleven children and was now carrying twins. The doctor had ordered her to bed after she had started showing blood at seven months. She had been in the hospital one month and had one month to go. Lordy, how she missed her little ones. A grey dishrag of a woman, Nell talked on, telling Mary more than she wanted to know about the randiness of Mr. Pye.

Owen didn't know Mary was in hospital. He had tried to persuade her to go to the Lying-in before he left on the Cardiff run, but she had refused. The nun had made it clear that because of the shortage of beds, she mustn't come to the hospital before the pains began or her waters broke. Finally her water broke early Wednesday, and she hired a hansom to bring her in. For two days she walked the hospital corridors, scarcely aware of the winter storm raging outside. On Friday morning, she was lowered onto a table and a mask was held over her nose. She wanted to fling it across the room but her arms were strapped at the wrists and she had no choice but to inhale the bloom of sweet gas. The ether streamed into her nostrils, clung to the hairs, poured down her throat, invaded her mind until she saw her father's coffin being lowered into the ground on a rainy afternoon. She couldn't see Owen though he claimed that he and his brother had been in the graveyard during the burial. He said that after they had dug her father's grave and his coffin had been lowered inside, he saw one of Mary's aunt's—Emmeline?—pass Mary a flask, and had watched as she took a swallow before it was taken away. She could feel the whisky now, trickling down her throat.

I have only a vague recollection of my birth. I recall the broth draining away leaving me slumped against a wall that thumped and quaked before coming to a shuddering stop, stalling me in a bloody crevasse for so long that my limbs were cramped and my eyelids gummed shut like a wizened bog creature's. I heard a man outside giving orders and felt cold hard tongs grab me by the head, but I was too weak to protest as I felt myself being dragged through the crevasse and out into an astonishing shower of light as dazzling as the Milky Way, and accompanied by a whoosh of alien cold that knocked me senseless for many days.

When Mary awoke, she was back in her cot, her body throbbing from exhaustion and pain. Nell reached across the narrow space between their beds and patted her arm.

"You have a girl."

"A girl." Mary smiled. Owen wanted a girl.

"How is she?"

"Sister said she was fine. You're the one that's worse for wear. You've had a hard go."

A wave of vomit rose in Mary's throat and she retched into the pail beside the bed. Nell rang the emergency bell.

Sister Beatrice came at once. She wiped Mary's mouth and held a glass of water to her lips.

"It's the anaesthetic."

"Can I see her?"

"She's sleeping now, but when she wakes you can feed her a bottle of sugared water. That's what we'll give her until your milk comes in." The nun had a friendly, reassuring manner. "Sister Ursulette, who assisted at the birth, says she could tell from your daughter's eyes that she's been here before."

Mary was alarmed. "What do you mean? Is she sickly?"

"I mean she's what sister calls a wise child, and she ought to know. She's been assisting at births for fifty years." All the while she spoke, the nun was dabbing Mary's face with a damp towel. "You needn't worry. Your daughter's perfect. Do you have a name?"

"Annie Rose."

Owen had insisted that a girl be called after his mother, Annie. She was the only one in her family to have survived Black '47, when people in Cork County were dying of famine fever by the thousands. At the age of ten, she left the corpses of her three brothers and her father—her mother and sisters had died earlier that year—and walked twelve miles from their hut on the Nagle estate to the workhouse in Mallow, where she became one of 802 paupers. Before she met Owen's father, Annie stayed in the workhouse for five years, scrubbing floors, tables and benches, boiling clothes, pounding corn for gruel and soup.

Mary had no wish to name her daughter after her own mother, who in her view had remarried too soon after her father's death to a man who was cruel and harsh, whose narrow opinions and army habits dominated a home that had once been benevolent and kind. Instead, she preferred to name the child after her younger sister, Rose, to whom she had been especially attached. She liked the idea of choosing two names, one from each side of the family, of uniting the two families through me. It somehow made up for the wrong Harold Burke-Davis had brought to her family. And she hoped it would soften Owen's hatred of Annakisha; when the hag was on him, he would say the house should be blown apart, insisting that it had been built on the backs of the starving poor—as in fact it had, having been built during the worst year of the potato famine.

Mary had only half expected Owen to come to the hospital the previous night because on Saturdays he didn't get back to Cork until nine, by which time the hospital doors were closed. She was certain that he would visit this morning. Breakfast came and was eaten, after which the priest arrived and said mass. The doors opened to visitors and Nell's husband, a small bandy-legged man, came in and sat on the stool beside Nell's bed and handed her a bunch of battered calendulas that had survived the storm. "Norry found them."

"Bless her heart."

Mary couldn't bear it. She turned her face to the wall and resolved not to cry—Owen mustn't see her with swollen eyes and mussed-up hair. In spite of the soreness of her body, especially now her breasts, she had made an effort to be clean and neat. At noon she swallowed what she could of the boiled beef dinner and between two and four, when the ward doors were closed, she napped. When they reopened, Owen still didn't appear, and by five o'clock tears were streaming down her cheeks.

"There, there," Nell said. "Never you mind. He'll come. Some men go on a tear when their wives have a baby."

"Owen isn't a heavy drinker."

"Then it must be something else."

Mary's silence brought a reproof: "Count your blessings that you have a husband," Nell said. "There's women in here that aren't so lucky."

That night she cried herself to sleep. In the morning, while breakfast was being served, Sister Beatrice appeared beside her bed and in a hushed voice informed her that her husband had broken into the hospital during the night. He had come up the fire escape and entered a window, but Sister Margaret, who was on duty, wouldn't allow him to come into the ward. "He asked sister to give you this." Sister Beatrice handed Mary a small parcel wrapped in brown paper.

The parcel contained a carved wooden spoon with two hearts at the top of a handle. Attached to the handle was a link that Mary supposed was for hanging on the wall. She wrapped up the spoon and tucked it beneath her pillow.

"A message from your husband?" Nell said.

"Yes." Mary laughed, giddy with relief. "Yes."

"Didn't I tell you he'd come? But you wouldn't believe me." Nell was peeved but Mary didn't care. Owen had come at last and when he returned on the weekend, Mary would be looking better and the forceps bruises would have faded from the baby's temples.

How proud Mary was when Owen appeared Sunday morning, tall and splendid in his tweed jacket. She saw how the other women watched as he walked between the rows of cots until he reached hers, where he leaned down and kissed her on the mouth before sitting on the stool between the beds, his back to Nell who had enough manners to turn away.

"Do you like the Welsh love spoon?"

"I do."

She didn't tell him that she'd been afraid he mightn't come, that her trust in him had wavered. Shyly, she slid the spoon from beneath the pillow. Owen traced the outline with his forefinger.

"These two hearts are us. The link is the baby."

"Have you seen her?"

"They let me have a peek on the way in. She's grand."

"She looks like you."

There had been a collision near Cardiff during the storm. Soon after their old coal bucket, as Owen called it, had cast off, it was rammed by another steamer and had to return to port for repairs. By the time the coal boat reached Queenstown, it was midnight. At home, he found Mary's note telling him she was in hospital, cleaned himself up and came to see her before returning to work. But getting into the hospital had been tricky business—the first-floor windows were barred and he'd had to swing free of the fire escape in order to reach the second-floor window. Luckily the window was unlocked, but in trying to get it open he'd lost his grip and had to hold on to the sill with one hand. Hearing his adventures, the risks and difficulties he'd undergone to reach her side, impressed Mary deeply. Her husband wasn't one to use endearments and his lovemaking was more functional than passionate, but she must remember that he was someone who showed his fondness by swinging from a fire escape in order to bring a love token all the way from Wales.

I was carried home in a bed that had been woven by the blind in St. Monica's Home on Infirmary Road. It was a basket of blond willow, lightweight yet large enough to accommodate a child much larger than myself. To make a cradle, my father placed the basket on a set of rockers my mother had bought from Mrs. Henchy in the Corn Market.

Mrs. Henchy was a tiny woman who wore a stiff white bonnet and had cheeks as round as a Toby jug. When my mother's confinement ended, a chat with her became part of our daily outing. With me in the crook of her arm, my mother would spend as much as an hour walking between market stalls, where women wearing striped aprons and knitted shawls sold crockery jugs and bowls, metal teapots, scarred tables and chairs with missing rungs, roll ends of wallpaper and carpets, occasionally a dresser. Mixed with this flotsam were piles of cabbages, turnips and potatoes, jumbles of clothes and mismatched shoes, sometimes a rat.

Mary bought very little at the market. Owen's room was adequately, though sparsely, furnished, and she was saving the five pounds sewn into the hem of her skirt against an emergency. In any case, their present living quarters were temporary; soon she and Owen would be moving to more satisfactory accommodation. Her single daily purchase was made at Brophy's bread wagon—she didn't know how to bake bread and there wasn't an oven in Owen's room, only a small coal burner for cooking and heating water. Twice a week she went to the post office to inquire about a letter from Will. On Fridays she went to the fish market to buy sprats, which she fried, setting aside half for Owen's Sunday breakfast. There was little likelihood of her being seen by one of her mother's Cork friends in these markets because their servants bought the fish and Annakisha's produce was bought in Mallow. Once a month her mother came to Cork to shop on Patrick Street and Grande Parade; there was always some item she wanted: a pair of embroidered hand towels, a jar of candied oranges, a small packet of rice for the salt shakers. Annakisha's cupboards and drawers were crowded with unnecessary items, and it was only after marrying Owen that Mary understood how little in the way of goods was required to live.

In November, her visits to the post office were rewarded by a letter from her brother, who wrote that he was relieved to hear from her since there had been no mention of her in their mother's letters and he'd been wondering how she was getting on. Will assured her that he understood the delicacy of her situation with regard to their mother and stepfather and would divulge nothing about it or her whereabouts. He told her that he missed Ireland, but not so much as she might suppose, probably because New York was full of Irish and there was none of the doldrums of home. He encouraged her plans to emigrate, saying he would do his best to help—if she required financial assistance, she need only ask. As for her husband, if he was interested in the building trade there was no shortage of work in New York, which was being built by the Irish.

Mary replied to his letter the same day, acknowledging receipt of his new address and thanking him for his kindness. She said that she and Owen hadn't fully settled their future plans but if they decided to emigrate to America, as she hoped they would, she would keep his kind offer in mind. She finished the note by telling him that Annie Rose was a darling child—which of course I was.

When Owen came home late on Saturday night and Mary told him about her brother's letter, she was disappointed by his lack of interest in Will's offer of help. He seemed more enthusiastic about the used pram he was carrying than he was about starting a new life in New York. He said he'd lugged the pram all the way from Cardiff, where he'd stopped a man from pitching it off a wharf, and as soon as he found replacements for the broken wheels, they would air the baby in Mardyke Park. Mary said she couldn't go to the park; she couldn't risk seeing her mother, who sometimes brought Rose along when she came to Cork to shop, and took her walk in the park before returning to Annakisha.

What was she afraid of? Accusations that would reduce her to tears; her mother's turning away; Rose's confusion and hurt about her sister's wordless disappearance. How could Mary explain what she had done in a way that an eleven-year-old would understand? Mary was also afraid that seeing her family might arouse a longing to return to Annakisha, and she didn't want to make herself unhappy by pining for what she could no longer have. As it was, not a day passed without her remembering the luxury she had left behind; when she covered the chamber pot with a cloth and carried it down to the communal toilet for emptying, she couldn't help wishing she had a toilet with a china handle pull like the one in Annakisha; when she filled her water buckets at the cold water tap, it was impossible not to be reminded of the gold-plated taps in the Hotel Metropole where at the age of eleven, she had been Aunt Emmeline's guest on the occasion of the Royal Parade.

On the day of the parade, standing in her aunt's hotel room window, Mary had watched the King and Queen go past in a coach pulled by tasselled horses on their way to open the Cork Exhibition in Mardyke Park. The day after the parade, Mary's father had taken her to the exhibition and spoiled her by buying the small shamrock jug she'd admired in an Irish novelty house. Afterwards he sat beside her in the summer house, enjoying the way the breeze shook the tiny electric lights and made them flicker like fireflies in the summer dusk.

Aunt Emmeline, a woman who enjoyed fashion and society in equal measure, was childless and liked to spoil Mary, taking her to elegant shops to buy blouses and skirts and lace underwear, to the Palace to watch Little Daisy Palmer dance and sing, to Madden's for tea and to the Tivoli to watch the races. Her aunt liked betting on the horses, something she could never do in England since it was unthinkable that a Salisbury banker should have a gambling Irish wife. When Emmeline came to Cork, she never stayed at Annakisha with her sister Louise. She didn't care for country life and preferred the privacy of the hotel where she could drink Power's whisky and visit Louise without the company of the dreadful Harold Burke-Davis.

It was Emmeline who encouraged Mary to leave Annakisha and apprentice herself to an accredited milliner with an impressive clientele; her niece was artistic, and amongst the wealthy there was always a demand for a stylish trimmer. Millinery hadn't been Emmeline's first choice for her niece's occupation; she had tried, unsuccessfully, to interest Mary in becoming a governess to young children, a profession that would have had the virtue of being respectable without taxing the girl's health—Emmeline always referred to her as "the girl." The girl was a quick learner and had a lively intelligence, but was by no means a scholar—which was just as well. Emmeline didn't encourage intellectual pretensions in females.

Owen was forever bringing home an assortment of broken goods from others' trash: a dented copper tea kettle, a parasol with bent spokes, a cracked flowerpot for the day when they had a plant to go inside. These objects distressed Mary, who was still smarting from her husband's indifference to Will's letter. She feared that he had lost his resolve to emigrate and was prepared to go on living indefinitely in this cold, waterless room.

In early February, Owen returned from Cardiff with the news that a million Welsh miners had gone on strike for a minimum wage and that he had been laid off. Steel mills had ground to a halt, sailings and trains had been cancelled and coal boats tied up, no one knew for how long. Transportation had been brought to its knees. Owen held out his hand and said that all he had to show for years of backbreaking work was this, and he tossed three shillings onto the table. Before Mary could say a word, he went out and was gone for most of the afternoon. Though the rain had stopped, she decided to occupy herself inside, knowing that she was less inclined to worry if she kept herself busy. While the baby slept near the open window, she washed the floor, the window, the table and chairs, for the second time in the week. She might have washed the walls had Owen not returned carrying a fish that Muckley had given him for their supper. Muckley owned the punt Owen was using the day he and Mary met on the steps of Pope's Quay.

"We won't starve living beside a river," he said, "and since there are no jobs for me here, I was thinking of putting you to work instead." Though he was grinning at her, Mary knew that he wasn't joking. "As I was going through the Corn Market, I noticed no one was selling hats. Boots and shoes, dresses and suits, blouses and shawls but no hats."

Why hadn't she noticed that?

"I was thinking that if you bought plain straw hats, you could trim them up and sell them for more."

The next morning, Mary threw caution to the wind and went to the Munster Arcade and scarcely giving her previous employer a second thought (*her* millinery goods were ordered from Dublin and London), purchased four plain straw hats, lace, ribbon, piping and feathers. In the afternoon Owen foraged the streets and lanes, coming home with a torn velvet dress and a broken fan edged with tiny seed pearls. Mary worked far into the night trimming hats by candlelight. Each hat was different in some small way: a velvet band decorated with a cluster of pearls or a brocade ruffle, a lace flower or a brace of feathers. As an apprentice she had been required to trim a hat so that it not only complemented a lady's attire but also flattered her eyes and the line of her chin. These were details afforded by wealthy women, whereas the hats she was trimming now would be worn by the women she saw in the Corn Market: servants, fishwives, hawkers, the kind of people who sat near the back of the church during mass.

In the morning, Owen took the hats to the market; by noon they were sold and Mary returned to the arcade to buy more hats. Owen was seldom home. He didn't like being cooped up and was given to brooding if he was idle, and so kept himself occupied scavenging for something that was useful for Mary's trade. He roamed the lanes behind the mansions of Montenotte, where he retrieved a pair of discarded lampshades, curtains and a fringed stool, which he knew Mary would in some way put to use, for she was becoming skilful at ripping apart furniture in order to salvage valuable trim. Now she was trimming up to six hats a day, all of which sold within a day or two. The profit bought them milk and bread, carrots and cabbages, apples and cheese, but there was never enough to pay the rent.

A fortnight after Owen had been laid off, Mary snipped the thread from the hem of her skirt, removed a pound note and resewed the hem, leaving four notes inside. Though the priest had preached that husband and wife must keep no secrets from each another but must share all things, she hadn't told Owen about the money. When he was working the coal boats, she had to be prepared for the possibility that he might become stranded in Wales, and now that he was without work she thought if she told him about the money, it might be quickly spent. She went downstairs to the fish-and-chip shop and paid their landlady the rent.

Owen returned in good spirits. "My lucky day." He was holding two pram wheels in good repair. "I found them beside the railway tracks."

While he attached the wheels to the pram, Mary went out to buy more hats and bread. By the time she got home, the pram had four working wheels. Over tea he announced that the time had come for a family outing to Mardyke Park, where rich people aired their children, and winter or not, they were going.

Mary set her apprehensions aside. With the colder weather, her mother was unlikely to take Rose walking in the park and by now Mary had some confidence that she could move about without being recognized by her mother's friends. These past weeks she had been on Patrick Street many times without encountering any of them, and she knew that in her black skirt and shawl she looked like hundreds of other women on the street.

The next day, a blustery Wednesday, my parents made their way down Crawford Street and along Lancaster Quay to Western Road, my father pushing the pram, my mother carrying the picnic basket. They walked with their heads bent to the wind, his cap pulled low on his forehead, her shawl draped over her face, while I was snugged inside a blanket, looking up to the sky where bits of cloud broke loose and sailed away like drifting ice. The sun was pale and intermittent, the sky flickering with phantom light.

As anticipated, because of the weather no one else, rich or otherwise, was in the park. My mother laid apples, cheese and bread on the flat rail and she and my father ate their picnic while stomping their feet on the cement floor to keep them warm. My mother tried to coax me into eating the bread and drinking the sweetened water she had brought along, but I wasn't interested in food or drink because I was entranced by a small bird with a red breast and purplish wings that had dropped out of the sky and perched on the rail, eyeing the crumbs my mother had put in my hand. To my delight the bird hopped toward me and tickled my palm with its beak as it ate the bread. It stayed for some time and when it flew away, I laughed, but my mother began to cry and said this was the first time her poor baby had seen a thrush. My father's response to her tears was to plunk me into the pram and push it toward the river where he lifted me out. In a while my mother followed and stood beside us on the stone embankment. We were directly across from Sunday's Well, a pool of sheltered water that returned a perfect reflection of an old tamarack stooping over the river. Behind the tree was a large house with a glass room attached to the back; inside, a maid was offering a tray of food to men in pressed suits and women in pastel frocks who sat laughing and talking with the carelessness of those who could forget the cold February wind blowing outside.

"Some day, we'll have a house like that," my father said. He jiggled me up and down. "Won't we, Annie Rose?"

"What do you mean, some day?" my mother said. "Not so long ago I lived in a house with a glass room. Now it's further away than it ever was." She had spoken sharply, without warning, surprising herself. She was tired, tired of hauling water upstairs and emptying the chamber pot four times a day; tired of trimming hats with others' cast-off goods and worrying how the rent would be paid when the money ran out. Most of all she was tired of trying to persuade my father to go to America. Gone was the fervent desire to be a good wife, to be loving and pure-hearted; all that had been trampled underfoot with the endless grind of degrading work.

"A man can dream, can't he?"

"Dreaming doesn't put food on the table. What happened to the dream of emigrating to America? Where did that go? I'd like to know that."

"Stop."

"I won't stop."

"Stop."

"Before we were married, you were full of plans about where we would go and what we would do. Now you never mention how we will better our daughter's life. You've given up."

"It's easy for you to say, born with a silver spoon in your mouth. Everything looks easy to you."

"It isn't easy. I never thought it would be this hard. I might never have married you if I'd known it would be this hard."

Without saying a word my father put me into the pram and wheeled me away, leaving my mother to limp back to Coal Quay alone.

The next morning, Owen was gone. He had left early, before his family was awake, and had tossed Mary's skirt over a chair where she would be sure to see the unravelled hem. He had left her two pounds and a badly printed note saying that he had gone to Southampton to see about hiring on to an ocean steamer once the coal strike was over. He said the only way for him to get to America was to work his way across and that she should get the fare from her brother in New York, and soon, in case he got lucky. If she wanted to write him back, she should direct the letter to the port authorities in Southampton.

Mary was distraught. Owen had thrown their future, her daughter's and her own, into her lap, and all because she had tried to impress upon him the necessity of changing their situation. What had possessed her to marry him? Had the empty Sunday afternoons been so lonely that she'd accepted the first man she came upon? All she'd wanted was someone to love who would love her in return, and she thought she'd found that in Owen. She'd had no idea that love would require her to bear hardship in silence, to bury her longings and fears, to shoulder difficulties without complaint. As a recent convert to the Catholic church, she'd thought faith and the Virgin's blessings would make her strong enough for love.

She imagined herself returning to Annakisha and begging her mother's forgiveness—never Harold Burke-Davis's. She even imagined her mother welcoming her home, standing up to her husband, insisting that he allow her daughter to reclaim her rightful place—but then Mary stopped and chided herself for thinking such foolish thoughts. She would never be welcomed back to Annakisha and there was no way of reclaiming what she had lost. There was only one thing to do.

Taking out paper and pen, she wrote to Will telling him that she and Owen had decided to emigrate as soon as the coal strike was over, and with that in mind her husband had already gone to England to see about getting hired on an ocean steamer since he had no choice but to work his way across the Atlantic. She told him that she had decided to accept his kind offer to advance her the fare, which she would endeavour to repay once she was established in America. She would be grateful if he could send the money as soon as possible.

The day after posting the letter, she was fetching water from downstairs and was coming through the dark passageway which was gloomy at all hours of the day, when she saw a tall figure standing in the doorway leading to the street. The figure itself was dark but around it was a spray of wing-shaped light that made her think that something terrible had happened to her husband and that in some way he had come to warn her.

"Owen!" She put down the pail and steadied herself by flattening a hand against the wall.

"I'm Eamon," the figure said and came along the passageway, the winged light disappearing as he moved. Though his words said otherwise, as he proceeded toward her Mary was still convinced that he was her husband; he wasn't wearing Owen's clothes but he was unmistakably Owen.

"You must be Mary."

The mention of her name confirmed her fear that the man was a corporeal vision of her husband. She backed up, passing the entrance to the second-floor stair until she was in the corner.

"I didn't mean to frighten you."

"I'm not frightened. I wasn't expecting to see you is all."

"I brought you this." He stretched out his hand, while keeping his distance. He was holding a loaf of bread.

"What is it?"

"Owen told me you liked soda bread."

At last she understood. "Are you a brother of Owen's?"

"I am. Owen asked me to look in on you."

Owen had once spoken of having a brother but only in passing. She'd been under the impression that his brother lived with their mother in Macroom.

"Are you visiting Cork?"

"I live just around the corner on Merchant's Quay."

"Do you now."

She was embarrassed by her ignorance and furious that Owen

hadn't told her about the proximity of his brother. The fury was surprising, considering the amount of relief that followed the realization that the man in front of her wasn't a premonition of her husband's death. But she collected herself and invited him upstairs for tea, leading the way while he followed with the water.

"I'll put the kettle on," she said, and he took a seat at the table. In the window light she saw how closely he resembled his brother; he had the same well-shaped nose and mouth, the same amber-coloured eyes, the same pale flaxen hair.

"You and Owen look enough alike to be twins," she said, slicing the bread for tea.

"We are." He even sounded like Owen.

"I can't think why Owen didn't tell me that he had a twin living close by."

"Owen never acted like a twin."

"And why was that?"

"According to our mother, it was the way we were born. I put my hand out and knowing we were twins, the midwife tied a bit of red thread on my finger, but Owen shoved me back in the womb so he could come out first." Eamon laughed. "You could say that at birth he was off to a running start. He was always dashing off somewhere whereas I was a stick-in-the-mud."

Though his voice sounded like Owen's, he didn't talk like him. Owen never offered personal disclosures; he needed to be drawn out. There were thoughts and feelings he would never admit, even when prodded. Mary found it odd to be sitting opposite a man who seemed to occupy her husband's body, yet was so very different. Eamon said that he wasn't adventurous like Owen; he wasn't one to strike out in different directions, which was why he'd been baking Mr. Brophy's bread these past nine years.

"I buy my bread from Brophy's wagon! To think all this time I've been eating bread made by yourself!"

Their laughter woke me. My mother came to my cradle and picked me up. I sat on her knee and stared at Eamon.

"A few days ago Owen came to see me. He said he wanted me to keep an eye on his wife and child." Eamon laughed. "That was the first I'd heard of you. He said that he might be gone for months and wanted to know someone would look out for you." Eamon spread his hands. "So here I am."

He seemed so familiar to me that I held out my arms and he lifted me onto his lap.

My mother said, "Do you have little ones?"

Eamon laughed. "Me? Little ones? When you work nights, there's not much chance of meeting a wife, let alone fathering children." He kissed the top of my head, which I liked.

On Tuesday, Eamon came to tea bringing half a dozen cinnamon buns. He came again on Thursday bringing caramel cakes. He visited twice the following week, coming midway through the afternoon after he had slept, which allowed time for an airing before he went to work at six. With Eamon at her side, Mary stood on the Lee's south channel watching stately windjammers from America being towed upriver to unload timber and grain: the *Falls of Garry* and the *Maid of Kintale*, a three-master and a four-master with tightly furled sails. The sight of these seagoing ships cheered Mary, bringing the faraway shore closer in spite of the fact that nowadays people emigrated under steam, not sail.

Mary and Eamon went to the horse fair on Anglesea Street. This was the sort of place where she could expect to encounter her brother Thomas or Harold Burke-Davis, which was why she stood on the sidelines, her head concealed beneath a shawl and the mended parasol. She had been brought up in a riding family (her father had twice ridden in the steeplechase between Buttevant and Doneraile), but there were no racehorses at today's fair, only swaybacked workhorses she saw every day on the city streets. Even so, she felt refreshed by the outing, which she wouldn't have undertaken on her own.

She was relieved that Owen didn't know about these outings or the affinity she felt for his brother but couldn't explain, not even to the priest. There was something blunted and soft about Eamon, and when he appeared at the door with his baked offering, his clothes lightly dusted with flour, a gentle, patient expression on his face, she was overwhelmed with affection and wanted to put her arms around him, an impulse she justified by thinking of the two brothers as two halves of a whole: the closed half, the half she wanted to know was Owen; the open half who would love her passionately if they were wed, was Eamon.

On March 14th, Mary picked up a letter at the post office from Will. The letter was bulky, a good sign. Wanting to read it before going home, she made her way to St. Peter and St. Paul, where she lit a candle to the Holy Mother before sitting on a bench at the back to read. She slit the envelope with her fingernail and drew out a letter and a receipt. The receipt, made out in her name, was for a berth in a second-class cabin on a White Star liner called the *Titanic*. How generous of Will to book her into second class when she would have been grateful for third! Will wrote that he had booked her passage on the *Titanic* because he had been told that by using American coal, it was assured of making its maiden voyage in early April; from all accounts the ship was large, much larger than the *Mauretania*, the ship on which he had sailed. It would be stopping in Queenstown, where a ticket would be waiting for her in the White Star office, and when she arrived in New York, he would meet the ship and she could stay with him until she was settled. Did the invitation include Owen? She sat in the church for another half hour rereading the letter and staring at the receipt with its white star at the top. In the window's filtered light, the star looked like a beacon that would guide her across the sea.

Eamon tried to be pleased. She could see that he was trying, that he wanted to be caught up in the excitement of the occasion and share her happiness.

"'Tis grand news, Mary."

"You'll have to come and see us," Mary said. "When we're settled."

"That I will. Now that I know you I could hardly stay away."

She averted her eyes. What had she done to him? "I'm sure you'll forget Annie Rose and me as soon as we're gone."

"I will not."

That night she wrote to Owen, telling him that Will had booked her passage on the *Titanic* sailing from Southampton in early April, and that she would board the ship in Queenstown. She said she hoped he would be able to find work aboard and that she was looking forward to the new life they would have together in America. She gave him Will's New York address and sent the letter in care of the Southampton port authority, though with the continuing coal strike she had no confidence that the letter would reach him before the *Titanic* sailed in three weeks' time. She knew that if she didn't hear from him, she could cash in the ticket and book passage on a later ship, but she was unwilling to continue living in a situation that Owen might refuse to change. Far better that she take advantage of Will's generosity and emigrate while she could, because once she was in America there would be more incentive for Owen to come across.

Will advised her to bring the proper documents: birth certificates, passport, vaccination records. When these were in order, she bought wool and knitted booties, mittens, sweater and bonnet, a hooded bunting—it would be cold on the North Atlantic. She hemmed napkins and embroidered handkerchiefs and bought a wicker valise. She also continued selling hats, not wanting to part with her remaining pounds, and took the coal oil lamp and most of the crockery to Mrs. Henchy to sell—the furniture would be left behind in lieu of rent.

Eamon insisted that when she left Cork on April 10th he would take two days off work in order to accompany her to Queenstown. He had booked a trap to take them out, since Mary had been advised to arrive in the White Star office in Queenstown early to pick up her ticket and find overnight accommodation.

Two days before she was to leave Cork, Owen's letter, dated April 4th and written in another's hand, arrived at the post office. Reading it inside the church, Mary was certain that her husband had undergone a change of heart, because he said he was pleased she had a ticket on the *Titanic* and had put his name down for standby crew on the ship; he was number five on the fireman's list. To work as a fireman he needed a certificate of continuous discharge, which he didn't have but had a good chance of obtaining. One way or another he would be on the ship, but she mustn't expect to see him aboard until they arrived in New York, because firemen didn't mix with passengers and he would be working deep in the hold while she would be a mile away on one of the upper decks. He had seen the *Titanic* and said that she looked like a floating hotel. Mary folded the letter into a square and sewed it into the hem of her skirt.

On the afternoon of April 10th, the three of us travelled to Queenstown. By the time the driver dropped us off at the shipping line office, there was already a queue of some thirty people on the quay. While I held on to Eamon's hand and showed him that I could walk (I had been practising all week), my mother procured the ticket and arranged for our luggage, including my blond wicker cradle, to be tagged and checked. The White Star clerk suggested that as second-class passengers we might wish to stay at Adherne's, where for three shillings shared accommodation and a breakfast egg would be provided. My mother found us a cot in the women's quarters and Eamon in the men's and that evening while I dozed in Eamon's arms, he and my mother climbed the steep hill to the cathedral behind Adherne's.

The climb was arduous, but Mary was determined to light a candle and pray. Inside the cathedral were mosaic shrines where gold and coral tiles had been shaped into flowers and leaves framing the Holy Mother's face. Mary was humbled by the Virgin's shimmering beauty, and was grateful that she had embraced a romantic and elaborate faith, a faith that allowed her to explore its mysteries through ritual and prayer. The mosaics, the candles, the rosary beads brought a comfort she had never found in the plain grey church in Doneraile.

In the morning when Eamon appeared in the dining room rumpled and haggard from lack of sleep, Mary thought that it had been a mistake for him to have stayed in Queenstown overnight, that she ought to have encouraged him to return to Cork after she had settled in yesterday. She couldn't bear the sadness in his eyes which reminded her of the sadness she had felt when she left Annakisha. She didn't want to be dragged down by sadness, to spoil the anticipation and excitement with regret.

By eight o'clock, we were on the White Star quay where gas lamps burned through the hazy grey light. Two tenders, paddle steamers, the *Ireland* and the *America*, were tied up at the dock. There were two queues, one for second class, one for third. The third-class queue was already the length of the quay. Ahead of us in the second-class queue was a large, handsome older woman wearing a dark green coat and a green felt hat, a hat so plain and severe that I thought it would benefit from my mother's skilful hand.

Mary was relieved that Eamon's good humour had rallied—thank heavens he had shed his woebegone expression. By nine-thirty all of the passengers were on the quay yet there was no move for them to board the tenders. When Eamon questioned an official about the delay, he was told they were waiting for the mail; at ten past ten the mail arrived and was loaded on the *Ireland*, along with 113 third-class passengers.

At last it was time to go. Eamon kissed my face all over while I smiled and laughed. Then he turned his full attention to my mother and wished her well, after which he kissed her for a long time on the mouth. "Goodbye, Mary," he said and walked away. He may have lingered to watch and wave, but I didn't see for I was soon passed to my mother who had stepped into the *America* where six other second-class passengers waited for us. Also I was straining to hear, above the thrashing of paddles, the tune a piper aboard the *Ireland* was playing.

The ship was anchored two miles out, off Roche's Point. Mary caught sight of it as soon as the tender cleared the harbour. Even from a mile away the *Titanic* looked gigantic: black hull, white decks, row upon row of windows. Owen was right, the ship was a floating hotel. As the tender was closing the last quarter mile, she saw a man's head appear at the top of one of the yellow stacks, and she watched as he pulled himself up and sat on the edge with his legs dangling down, which made it seem that he was halfway inside a barrel. As the boat came closer, Mary saw the man, who was dressed entirely in black, doff his cap and wave at someone on the *America*. He was looking down and waving at someone. It took her a moment to realize that he was waving at *her*. Was that Owen up there, blackened with coal dust from climbing up the stack and signalling her that he was aboard? Remembering his gallant climb up the hospital fire escape and through the window, she became convinced that the man in the smokestack was Owen.

"Look!" she said to me. "Look, Annie Rose. That's Papa up there!" She pointed to the stack and waved.

Obediently I looked up, but all I saw was an enormous black wall coming straight toward us. I don't think I knew what it was. All I knew was that I was frightened for I had never before seen anything so impenetrable and immense. At that point I think I must have felt, in the unequivocal way of babies confronted with unwanted change, the first stirrings of self-preservation. This is not to say that I sensed the blind terror that was just ahead but that I knew my life was changing quickly and in a way I wasn't sure I wanted. I did what most babies would do in that situation. I opened my mouth and screamed.

My mother held me against her shoulder beneath her hair. "There, little one, there." I heard her tell the others that I was a good child and hardly ever cried. I was crying now. I was fit to be tied. I was in such a state that I refused to be consoled and putting my head on my mother's shoulder, I wept as if my heart would break.

THE SHIP

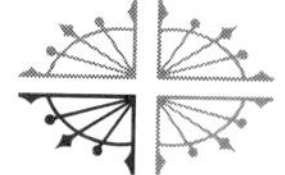

1912

When Stella Flynn, along with the five men in the tender, boarded the *Titanic*, they were directed to follow the passageway to the lift where they were instructed to wait for the seventh passenger so they could all be taken to their quarters together. Stella was annoyed that she was expected to wait in front of the lift—*elevator* was the word on the overhead sign—until the young woman who was limping down the passageway toward them caught up. A further annoyance awaited Stella: when the steward showed her to cabin D43, it was clear that she was expected to share accommodation with the lame woman and her child. Although the child didn't look old enough to get its sticky hands on Stella's things, babies did fuss and cry. She would have to speak to the purser about moving to another cabin; he was bound to understand that trying to sleep with a squalling infant was not anyone's idea of a holiday.

Like the passageway, the inside of the cabin had been painted a vitreous white, yet despite this unfortunate choice of colour (green would have been more restful), the room had a certain cosiness, aided by floral chintz curtains enclosing two mahogany berths and the upholstered tandem, what Stella called a bedsitter. Between the berths was a mahogany combination of dresser and commode containing a porcelain sink bowl and two soap dishes, drawers, cubbyholes, even a hinged table for holding one's spectacles and book. Except for the matter of the child, the accommodation was entirely satisfactory, and Stella removed her hat and placed it on the lower berth, thinking that if other accommodation wasn't available, she would at least insist on having the lower berth.

The young woman sat on the tandem, the child on her lap, and looked around.

"Isn't it grand?" she said. "Everything is so fresh and new."

It was an ingenuous remark, a gesture toward friendliness and conversation that was steadfastly ignored by Stella, who sat on the berth and took a book out of her reticule, intending to read while waiting for the delivery of the luggage, but instead keeping her eye on the woman.

The young woman unpinned her hat and placed it beside her on top of her purse; the child looked at the hat but made no attempt to touch it, though the yards of veil, which in Stella's view cried out for removal, must have been tempting. Stella couldn't abide veiled hats and disliked the notion of concealing one's face, having seen far too much of it in the asylum, patients who pulled hair over their faces, hid themselves behind splayed hands, and when they could get hold of them, inside paper bags. Unless she was grotesque why would any sane woman hide behind a veil? This woman looked entirely sane and was far from grotesque for she had the benefit of a country complexion, abundant hair and remarkably clear eyes; otherwise her prettiness was common and Stella had seen thousands of Irishwomen with her kind of good looks, young women with doubling chins and thickening waists who would be fat before reaching middle age. Stella herself was hefty and big-boned; her hips broad, her thighs thickly padded, but she didn't regard herself as fat—when she regarded herself, which was seldom. She wasn't a vain woman except for her hair, which despite her sixty-six years was a sturdy, gingery red.

After ten minutes went by and the luggage still hadn't come, Stella decided that no harm could come from being civil and, setting her book aside, announced that her name was Stella Flynn. "And your name?"

"Mary O'Connor."

A Catholic name inconsistent with the good quality suit and educated voice. Stella was used to spotting Catholics, for she had been raised in Belfast and, for a time, had nursed in Dublin.

"And this is Annie Rose."

I studied the woman named Stella who, no doubt was referring to my mismatched eyes, remarked that I was an unusual child.

"She's a good baby. She never cries," Mary said loyally, then—noticing Stella's quizzical expression—went on, "except when we were approaching the ship. I don't know what got into her."

"Are you visiting relations in America?"

"No, my husband and I and the baby are emigrating."

"Didn't I see him on the quay?"

"Oh no," was the hasty reply, too hasty, Stella thought, "that was my husband's twin. My husband is a fireman aboard. As we came alongside, did you not notice a man waving from the top of the smokestack?"

"I can't say that I did."

"That was my husband."

"What an interesting place for him to be."

Their conversation lurched along at a desultory gait and by the time the luggage arrived I had nodded off—in those days I had a predilection for sleep.

Stella directed the steward to place her luggage on the lower berth and gave him a half shilling. Mary O'Connor provided no directions as to where her luggage should be put and became agitated, looking for her purse which she seemed not to remember was under her hat. A nervous, flighty woman, Stella thought after the steward left without Mary O'Connor's tip. She decided to go in search of the purser, and walked down one passageway after another, then rode the elevator one floor up, which brought her to a carpeted reception area furnished with wicker chairs; from here a passing steward directed her to the purser's office where, it was explained, second-class single occupancy cabins were available at a higher rate than the fare Stella had paid. There were some empty berths available in occupied double rooms but the purser was uncertain how many of these were suitable for females. Could she possibly wait until later when he had time to check the reservation books? The fact was that Mr. Ismay, the White Star's director, was aboard and had asked him to arrange a tour of first-class accommodations for second-class passengers, and the arrangements would require his attention of the next half hour. Perhaps Miss Flynn would care to join the tour? It was a rare opportunity offered only because this was the *Titanic's* maiden voyage. All this was said in a clipped, staccato voice meant to pass for civility and efficiency. Hardly efficient, if the tour was only now being arranged, Stella thought, but she told the purser that she might as well join the tour.

"Very good," he said. "The stewards will be advising passengers to meet in half an hour on the second-class deck. Now, if you will excuse me."

She was amused that he supposed that he had the power to dismiss, that he could gather in people then let them go. Clearly he was the Napoleonic sort, small and self-important. After thirty-three years as lady superintendent at Richmond Asylum, she was used to summing up people in this way; she did it habitually, using people's gestures and facial expressions to assess their personalities. It wasn't a habit one wished to carry into social occasions, but then she didn't often indulge in social occasions.

She went outside and stood looking down at the three hundred or more passengers on the third-class deck, who were listening to the piper playing Erin's Lament. Some of the women were weeping, wiping their eyes with the edge of their shawls, reminding Stella, as if she needed reminding, how sentimental the Catholic Irish were. She was thinking that it was far better they weep than drink and fight when she felt her arm being touched and immediately jerked away as a mute in a herringbone vest and cap pointed to his basket of postcards and pencils. To get rid of the hawker, she gave him a penny and selected a card showing a picture of the Queenstown quay which she would send to her sister in Belfast. The hawker moved on, and she resumed observing the people on the lower deck. Many of them were speaking a foreign tongue that might be German or Swedish or Norwegian—to Stella's ear, all Northern Europeans sounded more or less alike. A steward was rounding up the hawkers on the third-class deck and ordering them into the bumboats tied alongside. The piper was now playing Lake of Pointrain.

Stella was close enough to the stern to see the water behind the propellers froth and churn as the engines deep inside the ship accelerated. As the ship moved forward, she stood at the rail, watching the Irish mountains recede. By now there were about forty people, most of them men, assembled on the second-class deck waiting for the tour to begin. It occurred to her that many of these men might be occupying a double berth cabin alone, which might mean there would be nothing available in the cheaper rate. If that was the case, she wouldn't take a single cabin; she absolutely refused to pay more, knowing that even a double-occupancy second-class ticket on the *Titanic* cost more than on other liners. She had chosen the *Titanic* because she had been saving for this retirement holiday for years and wanted to do it in style.

At three o'clock the purser appeared and announced that he himself would be guiding their tour. Forty-six people trooped after him as he led them from the deck into a passageway and up two flights of stairs, which brought them onto a promenade that ran half the length of the ship. The purser strode ahead, arms swinging, the rest of them hurrying to keep up, their shoes clattering against the deck. Stella was panting, she wasn't used to the pace. What was the hurry? This was a holiday, wasn't it? But she wouldn't give the purser, or herself, the satisfaction of slowing down. She steamed forward, past empty deckchairs and lifeboats snugged into their davits like giant snails. Finally the purser called a halt and waited for them to gather round.

"We will begin with the grand staircase," he said, and nodded to the steward who was waiting to hold the door. Flourishing a white-gloved hand, the purser directed his charges inside, marking the passage of each with a nod of his head, as if he was counting sheep. Once they were inside, he allowed them to stroll on their own while he stood, hands clasped behind his back, rocking on the balls of his feet, waiting for them to be impressed.

How could they not be impressed? The sweeping staircase and elaborate balustrade, the golden clock and candelabra, then further on, the unoccupied first-class stateroom with its gilded lamps and its tables inlaid with gold. So much gold, Stella thought in the bathroom, where she pocketed the bar of Vinolia Otto Toilet Soap beside the gold-plated tap. According to newspaper advertisements, this brand of soap was the best money could buy. From the stateroom they strolled through the reading and writing room at their leisure, and Stella was able to slip several sheets of notepaper and three envelopes into her purse, which she did nonchalantly in full view of three men standing nearby. Two floors down—she wasn't yet thinking *decks*—they were shown a squash and racquet court, a heated salt-water swimming pool, showers, saunas, an electric bath, and a room dimly lit with Arabian lamps. "I call this the sultan's harem," the purser said though there were no attendants, female or otherwise, in the room.

On their way back to their second-class quarters, they were shepherded through the Verandah and the Palm Court, where several ladies were taking tea. A splendid idea, Stella thought. She hadn't eaten since breakfast and intended to order tea as soon as the tour was concluded. After leading them along passageways, and up and down both elevator and stairs, the purser brought them back to their starting point, prompting a large balding man to say that a passenger needed a map to find his way around the maze of passageways and corridors aboard the ship.

When Stella asked to be directed to the second-class library, the purser wanted to know if she still wished to change her accommodation. "Not at present," she said. "I shall wait and see." While touring the first-class quarters, she had decided that she ought to spend at least one night in her assigned cabin: if the child was as agreeable as the mother said, it wouldn't be necessary to move to another double cabin where she might be expected to use the tandem or the upper berth. "As you wish," the purser said and told her where she might find the library.

Satisfied that the library's furnishings had been chosen with an eye to comfort and quality, Stella sat by the fire and ordered tea before settling down to write to her friend Lillian, who was still nursing at St. Vincent's. There was a tray of notepaper on the table, but she preferred to use the pilfered stationery. Lillian had not been able to join her on the trip, but she should at least be able to read a description of first-class accommodation written on first-class notepaper. When she finished her tea, she put the letter away and returned to the empty cabin, where she was pleased to note that the tandem had been made up. There was a wicker basket on top of it, while beneath was a cheap wicker case and an expensive valise. Mary O'Connor must have decided against using the upper berth, leaving it free for Stella's luggage—a scratched calfskin suitcase borrowed from Lillian, and her own mud-coloured carpet bag. Stella unlocked the valise and shook out two shirtwaists and hung them in the wardrobe beside a lace blouse and a fine wool skirt, which she thought were expensive clothes for a fireman's wife. She moved her nightclothes, toilet kit and books into the carpet bag before shoving the soap and silver-plated spoon she had taken during tea inside the toe of a shoe at the bottom of the valise. Then she took out the gold cord she had pinched in Cork the night before, and began winding it into a coil; at the same time chiding herself for having taken so much when she knew that she had to carry it across the Atlantic and back again. There had been four pairs of drapes in her room at the Savoy, each of them tied with a generous length of tasselled cord that she recognized at once as exactly what she had been looking for to trim the curtains that would separate her sleeping from her living area. (Having slept in nursing quarters for forty-five years, she found it satisfying to visualize furnishing the room she would move into upon her return from New York.) When she finished rearranging her possessions, she went along the passageway to the bathroom. There were no gold-plated taps here but an effort had been made to conceal the ugly black rubber sheeting in the shower bath behind an attractive chintz curtain. From the bathroom Stella went in search of the dining saloon. She was hungry, having passed up the raspberry tarts at tea because she had been saving her appetite for dinner. Fortunately, the dining saloon was on the same deck as her cabin, which meant that by following a steward's instructions, she found it quickly.

The saloon was enormous and splendidly appointed. As in the library the walls were panelled and the decor was a tasteful cream and gold. Noticing Mary O'Connor sitting by herself with the child at a corner table at the far end of the room, Stella chose an unoccupied table for two in the opposite corner, and sat with her back to the room, facing the sea, which was an oyster colour now that the sun was down. A waiter appeared and she ordered consommé, roast duckling and white asparagus—*gold*, it said on the menu—new potatoes, peaches in chartreuse jelly, a glass of rosé wine. She was well into the duckling when a jug-eared, robust man about her age introduced himself as Ernest Patcher and asked if he might join her. Without waiting for a reply, he sat in the opposite chair. A presumptuous man, restless too, judging by the way he kept glancing about and rubbing his hands. At once he began to talk, telling her that he recognized her from the tour of first-class quarters, and asked her name. Though she didn't say so, she recognized him as the man who had commented that the passengers needed a map to find their way around the ship. Mr. Patcher asked what she had thought of the tour and then went on to say that he had never seen such waste, that White Star had spent a fortune trying to entice the rich and famous aboard. He supposed the ladies wore jewels and silks to dinner. Nothing so ordinary as wool, he said, looking rudely at Stella's jacket. He made no inquiries about her, and in that way, at least, was her idea of the perfect stranger, someone who required nothing of her except forbearance. No one else sat at the table, which made it easy for her to gather a coffee spoon into her napkin and drop it into her reticule before leaving Mr. Patcher to himself.

After dinner, she read in the library and when she began nodding off—she had been up since dawn—she repaired to her cabin, where she knew from their breathing that Mary O'Connor and the child were asleep behind the closed curtain. She undressed, put on her night gown and climbed into bed, the sheets feeling stiff and cool against her flanks. Drawing the curtain, she lay in the dark listening to the thrumming engines below her, deep inside the ship.

Wan morning light seeped into the cabin. Opening her eyes briefly, Stella saw the outline of her body disappearing into a murky landscape of valleys and hills. Through the curtain she heard a hushed voice, rungs sliding along the metal bar, footsteps padding across the floor then a click of the lock and Mary O'Connor and the child were gone. How pleasant, how restful to lie here alone with only the hum of the engines to remind her she was aboard a ship, in limbo between continents and the imagined lines of distance that were no doubt changing as the voyage went on. It was a place—or was it absence of place?—in which many of her patients lived, suspended between sanity and insanity, wholly occupying one place or another. Ahead, on another continent, James, the brother she hadn't seen in twenty years, and his family waited.

The steward who brought Stella a pot of tea at midmorning (she had lain in bed an extra hour) was an entirely new face, which made it possible for her to slip a third teaspoon into her handbag without arousing suspicion. After she had eaten her toast, served the American way between a linen napkin, she began to read:

Once more on Broadway! Here are the same ladies in bright colours walking to and fro, in pairs and singly; yonder the very same light blue parasol that passed and repassed the hotel window twenty times while we were sitting there. We are going to cross here. Take care of the pigs. Two portly sows are trotting up behind their carriage, and a select party of half a dozen gentlemen hogs have just now turned the corner…

Here is a solitary swine lounging homeward by himself. He has only one ear; having parted with the other to vagrant dogs in the course of his city rambles. But he gets on very well without it: and leads a roving, gentlemanly, vagabond kind of life.

This was how Dickens had found New York seventy years ago and though the pigs were long gone and *American Notes* was out of date, Stella enjoyed it nonetheless. She enjoyed the fanciful turns and freewheeling jocular style, and she admired Dickens for his interest in those whom she thought of as the casualties of life. When touring America he had taken the time to visit hospitals, prisons and lunatic asylums and had a way of describing the insane that some might consider melodramatic, but which in her view was accurate, as far as it went: the gloomy picking of the hands and lips, the fierce wild face, the moping lunatic. She sometimes thought the word, *lunatic*, was an illogical way to describe the mad, if indeed madness could be described. Why should someone struck by the moon be regarded as unpredictable and insane, when surely there was nothing more predictable than the cycle of the moon; perhaps they were called lunatics because the moon created an illusory world where one could flit in and out of the darkness and light in a way that evoked the tormented existence of troubled souls.

Stella sat alone at luncheon, and once again Ernest Patcher sought her out. Today he was grumbling and plaintive: he had slept poorly, the steward had neglected to bring extra towels and he had waited a half hour to use the toilet facilities, of which there were too few in second class. It was obvious by now that he regarded her as some sort of receptacle for grievances, not because she was a nurse—he knew nothing about her personal situation—but because of her size. A large woman, she had throughout her life been expected to absorb all manner of cavilling and complaint. She thought that when some people looked at her strong shoulders and generous breasts they must assume she was the mothering sort, an assumption that was not only erroneous but aggravating. Ernest Patcher was going on about the *Titanic* not being a well-run ship. There were far too many stewards scurrying around as if they were lost, and only twenty lifeboats, which was hardly enough for the more than two thousand aboard. And why hadn't there been a boat drill; he would have thought that a boat drill would be mandatory aboard a ship, particularly a ship on its maiden voyage. Had Miss Flynn noticed that? No, she hadn't, but now that it had been brought to her attention and she remembered the regular fire drills at the asylum, she conceded that he was quite right, while at the same time thinking that she would avoid him at dinner by joining a group of jolly women sitting at a nearby table with one empty place. Eager to be off, she lurched to her feet, the wine she had drunk with the cream of celery soup making her unsteady, and returned to her cabin for a nap.

Mary O'Connor was waiting for her outside their door, letter in hand and as Stella came along the passageway, began limping toward her. "Miss Flynn, would you be able to stay with Annie Rose while I deliver a letter to my husband? I find it difficult negotiating my way around the ship carrying her. She's asleep and will be no bother." This pretty speech was carefully spoken, no doubt rehearsed. Mary O'Connor had the earnest, unaffected manner of a Dickens heroine, a guilelessness and sincerity that would have impressed the author but didn't impress Stella. Having persuaded herself that her cabin mate was thoughtful and unobtrusive, she had been caught unawares. The request was an imposition, but could hardly be refused; one could not refuse to help a lame woman with a small child.

"How long will you be? I have no experience with babies."

"A half hour at most."

"Very well. I will take you at your word."

"I am much obliged."

Stella opened the cabin door, then closed it with care and stood listening in case the click had awakened the child. Apparently not. Very well, she would sleep herself. Removing her hat, coat and shoes, she lay down but was soon on her feet again, peering through the narrow opening between the curtains drawn around the tandem. The child gave every sign of being asleep, her eyelids closed, her lips slightly parted, her wee hands curled around the blanket edge.

Comforted by the sight, Stella lay down and almost immediately fell asleep. An hour later, startled awake by the sound of her own snoring, she sat up and knocked her head against the upper berth. She had completely forgotten the child. Struggling out of bed, she again peered between the curtains and was relieved to see that the child—what was her name?—Annie Rose was still sleeping. Taking no chance that she might inadvertently waken the child, Stella went into the corridor to await her mother.

Mary O'Connor returned in considerable distress.

"I'm sorry to be late. I became lost and no one knew the whereabouts of my husband and the purser tried to dissuade me from leaving the letter with him, or with anyone else who might pass it on. Eventually I persuaded him to direct me to one of the supervising engineers who was more helpful, reviewing the list of firemen—there are more than two hundred aboard. Though my husband wasn't listed, the engineer told me that because firemen sometimes work under other men's papers, this was probably the case with my husband. He suggested that I leave the letter with him, and he would put out the word that there was a letter for Owen O'Connor. If no one claims it before we reach New York, he will return the letter to me."

"Are you absolutely sure that your husband is aboard?"

"Oh yes. As I told you, I saw him waving at me. He was black all over and was wearing a cap."

Stella didn't know what to make of this, but experience told her that her cabin mate was in some way deluded, that she might be one of these foolish, headstrong, romantic young women who altered reality to accommodate an irresponsible, unreliable man she imagined she loved.

That evening Stella dined with the Grimes family: two married sisters and their grown daughters. Merry and convivial, they welcomed her to their table, including her in their conversation and pouring her wine, though not enough for her to forget to slip a side plate into her handbag. After dinner she joined the women on the deck where they leaned against the rail staring trustingly into the dark. The cool air slid over Stella's skin, removing the wine flush, the smell of beef and Roquefort cheese, dispersing her warm, meaty breath. Talked out and subdued, the women spoke little, choosing instead to admire the splendour and magnificence of the night sky. Stella was the first to go inside.

Mary O'Connor and the child were conveniently asleep, and once in bed Stella settled down to read Dickens's account of prison inmates convicted of petty thievery, at no time connecting them to herself; she wasn't a thief but someone who merely helped herself to whatever was close at hand. She finished the chapter, turned out the light and when she fell asleep dreamed she saw a man in black waving at her from the top of a smokestack. He was sitting on the side and grinning at her, a manic, pop-eyed grin that when she awoke reminded her of a madman, who after sitting for several hours on the asylum roof grinning and swinging his legs, abruptly flung himself to the ground. The dream unsettled Stella and she lay with open eyes and a heaving chest listening to the thrumming engines. When she had calmed herself sufficiently, she fell into another sleep, this one so deep that she didn't hear Mary O'Connor leaving, and awoke midmorning to the realization that she had overslept. Regrettably, she had missed breakfast. Very well, she would take tea in the library and save her appetite for an early luncheon.

Stella was enjoying the *Titanic's* food; having eaten institutional food most of her life, she relished the variety and choice of the ship's cuisine. She had never seen such meals, and lacking a culinary imagination, had never realized that food could be so tantalizingly ingenious and complicated. She was impressed by the fact that cooks—aboard the *Titanic* they were called chefs—could transform ordinary vegetables, meat and fish into exotic and elegant dishes. Born to Ulster parents, she had been brought up on sausage and neeps, and as a child her favourite meal had been a raw egg stirred into a plate of mashed potatoes. At the asylum potatoes were usually boiled or fried. At today's luncheon, she ordered riced potatoes and sole poached with grapes. Who would have thought of serving grapes with fish? Or for that matter raisins with carrots, what the chef called *carrots Californian*. For dessert she ordered painted chocolate eclairs with chocolate gelato inside. For that evening's dinner she ordered lamb collets, cauliflower amandine, and minted peas finished off with orange surprise. Both these meals were eaten in the company of the Grimes family, who, unlike Stella, were no strangers to camaraderie. After dinner the women insisted she join them for cards in the smoking room. She had never played cards—it had been forbidden at home, along with dancing and drink—and she had to be taught how to play gin rummy. But play she did, gamely shuffling and dealing the pack when her turn came. By ten o'clock her head ached from sitting in a smoky room and from drinking too much wine. She excused herself and retired to her cabin feeling ill at ease. It had not been a productive day: she hadn't written a single letter, nor had she finished Dickens's book. Tomorrow she would write letters and read; Sunday was, after all, a day for contemplative pursuits.

As expected, Mary O'Connor and the child were asleep and Stella put on her dressing gown and, carrying her towel and toilet kit, went along the corridor for a shower bath, her first aboard the ship. She stood beneath the nozzle until the warm water eased her headache. Someone had left a tortoiseshell comb on the soapdish and after she had dried herself, she dropped the comb into her kit. She hadn't taken anything since yesterday morning and was satisfied that the day had not been entirely wasted.

In the morning, she met Mary in the corridor, returning from breakfast. "Did you hear from your husband?" Stella couldn't resist asking as she passed, wanting the answer without being drawn into conversation. "Not yet." Mary touched the baby lightly on the cheek. "But we expect to hear soon, don't we, Annie Rose?" Stella continued to the dining saloon, now only a quarter full since it was nine-thirty and most of the passengers had finished breakfast. She ordered a hearty meal of bacon and eggs which she ate near the window, watching tables being pushed aside to make way for the Anglican service. Stella stayed for the short, obligatory service: the *Lord's Prayer*, a scripture reading from Psalms and a hymn, "O God Our Help in Ages Past." Once it was over, she headed for the library, postponing an earlier intention to walk on the deck when the waiter told her that the weather outside was bitterly cold. Obviously the extreme cold had driven others inside because the library was full. In the far corner, near a reading lamp, she located one of the last seats and taking out the leather writing case that someone years ago had carelessly left on a park bench, she took out a sheet of first-class stationery and began writing her sister Edith, whose oldest son, a steamfitter with Harland and Wolff, had worked on the *Titanic*. Though he had no doubt acquainted Edith with the design of the ship, she would probably enjoy reading a detailed account of it written from a passenger's point of view.

An hour past noon, Stella broke off her correspondence and went into the dining saloon, once again sitting with the Grimeses though she would have preferred eating alone—their company was exhausting. She sat with them because she was avoiding the tiresome Mr. Patcher, and it was difficult to ignore the women gesturing and pointing to the empty seat. She ordered crepes Gruyère, cucumbers in dill sauce and melon compote. "No wine?" asked the oldest sister, who had ordered a glass of Marsala with dessert.

"I am spending a sober Sunday," Stella explained, "catching up on my correspondence."

"Can we persuade you to join us for cards?"

"Not today."

During the meal, Mary O'Connor passed their table holding Annie Rose, without giving any indication that she and Stella were acquainted. Her failure to do so bothered Stella, though she couldn't have said precisely why. After luncheon she returned to the library, finished her letter to Edith and took up the one she had begun writing to Lillian. At three o'clock Captain Smith appeared, a distinguished-looking man wearing sailor whites and a gold braided cap. Going from chair to chair he greeted passengers; he asked Stella if she was being well looked after.

A seafaring gentleman, was how she described him to Lillian: Ernest Patcher was a *professional pessimist*; the Grimeses were *obsessive optimists*; Mary O'Connor was a *wandering soul*. Stella had described her this way because she suspected the young woman had married beneath her and hoped to begin a new life in America. When she had finished the letter she sealed it, and after giving both letters, one containing the postcard, to the library steward to mail, she picked up her belongings and made her way to the cabin for a nap, after which she intended to change into a clean shirtwaist for dinner. According to the Grimeses, the chefs were determined to outdo themselves tonight.

At dinner she ordered baked haddock with sharp sauce, wine jelly and plum pudding with a dollop of American ice cream. Following the meal, the tables were cleared and a piano was wheeled in for an evening hymn sing. The Grimeses didn't stay for the singing but a hundred or more passengers did. The first hymn was "Lead, Kindly Light," which, it was explained, had been inspired by a shipwreck. People seemed intent on calling for sea hymns: "From Ocean Unto Ocean," "For Those in Peril on the Sea,"

"From Greenland's Icy Mountains." Stella couldn't carry a tune but she enjoyed singing. During a hymn sing no one cared if she sang off key. What she appreciated most about hymns was that they had been sung through the ages by multitudes, and that multitudes would go on singing them. She was moved by the fact that her voice, poor though it was, was joined with the voices of a host of others. She knew of no better way of expressing what the church called *fellowship* than by singing hymns together.

As the congregation dispersed, she noticed that several men had tears in their eyes. Not she, she had never been one for tears, but she felt expansive and—for the moment at least—tolerant of her fellow travellers. Passing the trolley of coffee and biscuits, she pulled on her hat and gloves in preparation for a turn around the deck. During dinner, one of the Grimeses had remarked that the wind had gone down and that apart from the cold, it was pleasant outside. It *was* cold, startlingly, brutally cold, and stepping onto the deck, she gasped from the shock. It was pitch black but once she had regained her breath and her eyes had adjusted to the dark, she noticed others' shapes. Moving toward them, she arched her neck and found herself looking up at the inside of a quilt of stars. She remembered how, as a young child, she had thought of the starry night as a gigantic black quilt fastened to the sky with gold nobbed pins that went all the way down to the edge, which in this case was the water. There was no moon and the air smelt musty and claustrophobic.

"What is that smell?" Stella's voice hung in the air.

A disembodied voice came out of the dark. "I'm told it's the smell of ice."

She was about to say that she couldn't see any ice, but the man had moved away. Though she couldn't see it, there was bound to be ice in the water; this was after all the North Atlantic. She leaned over the rail and saw candles of light from the portholes of the lower deck flickering on the water, which was as flat and smooth as a tabletop. Behind her the door to the corridor opened and shut, opened and shut, and soon she went in herself: her fingers and toes were numb and she wanted to take a hot shower bath before going to bed, but inside, looking at the lateness of the hour—it was 10:40—she decided against it and entering the darkened room where Mary O'Connor and the child were, as usual, asleep, she undressed and slipping into bed without turning on the light, reviewed her plans for tomorrow: directly after breakfast she would send a Marconigram to her brother in New York before returning to her corner in the library to finish reading *American Notes*. Following dinner she might join the Grimes for an evening of cards since tomorrow would be her last full day aboard the ship and she wanted to make the most of it. By 11:10 she was deeply submerged in sleep.

Half an hour later she was awakened by a thud—a muffled bump—and heard the thrumming engines abruptly stop; there was a rumbling sound and then the engines started again. After an interval, they stopped again but not for long; within minutes their familiar thrumming resumed, and Stella spiralled downward into sleep where she remained until she heard a loud banging on the door and someone calling out. She sat up and thrust her feet to the floor, nausea foaming in her throat as it had whenever she'd been awakened from a deep sleep during an emergency at the asylum. She unlocked the door and saw a steward standing in the passageway.

"What did you say?" She was coming awake.

"The ship hit an iceberg. There's no cause for alarm but the captain wants passengers up on deck as a precaution." The steward moved to the next cabin. "Wear your life jackets."

Stella shut the door, switched on the light, picked up her watch pin and squinted at the time: 12:30. She opened the tandem curtains and looked at Mary's drowsy face.

"Who was that?"

"The steward. The captain wants us on deck with our life jackets. The ship has hit an iceberg."

"An iceberg?" Mary sat up. "Surely not."

"That's what he said."

Stella looked around the cabin before remembering that the life jackets were stowed above the wardrobe. Calmly, methodically, she placed one life jacket on Mary's bed and the other on her own, and after using the toilet, began to dress. Remembering the cold, she put on a wool vest beneath her coat and pinned on her hat so that it covered her ears. All this while, Mary O'Connor was in bed, her back against the pillows, feeding the child who had come awake. Didn't she intend to heed the captain's orders? But of course it was more sensible that she feed the child in the privacy of the cabin than up on deck.

"While you are getting ready, I will go ahead and assess the situation," Stella said, picking up her reticule. "I will come back for you directly."

"Thank you," Mary O'Connor said. "I would appreciate your help."

Stella hurried along the corridor, meeting no one, which surprised her since one would have thought that it would be crowded with passengers hurrying to reach the deck. Perhaps there was no real cause for alarm. She took the elevator two floors up, went along the corridor and opened the door to the second-class deck. There were a few shadowy figures out there in the dark, nothing more. The steward must have meant the boat deck. Why hadn't he said so? Stella hadn't been on the boat deck since Thursday's tour but she remembered reaching it by way of a staircase from the second-class deck. She found the stair without difficulty and went up. As she opened the door to the deck, she heard the sound of music. A band was playing somewhere, ragtime music, she thought it was called. The situation couldn't be very serious if a band was playing. There were about a hundred people strolling about the deck, and it struck her that if there was an emergency far more people would have left their beds. Yet why had the deck lights been switched on? She moved to the rail and was surprised to see a life boat being lowered to deck level for loading, and when she looked overboard, that a half-empty lifeboat was being rowed away. She saw ice in the water, bits and pieces, nothing large enough to damage a boat, let alone a ship.

"Women and children first." One of the ship's officers was speaking through a horn. "On the port side."

Stella went up to him. "Which is the port side?"

He lowered his horn and pointed to the other side of the ship. "Over there is port side."

"What time is it?" She had forgotten to pin on her watch.

"12:50. You had better hurry, madam, and get into a life boat."

She hustled to the port side. A life boat containing about fifty passengers was hanging from a davit. She felt someone take her elbow. "Get in," an officer said. "The boat is about to be lowered."

She jerked away. "Later," she said, "after I have fetched a mother and her child."

"Very well, but be quick about it." The officer turned and urged a much younger woman to get into the boat, but she refused to get in without her husband.

"Sorry. Women and children only. Captain's orders."

As she made her way toward the door that would take her below, Stella was knocked off balance by a man hurtling past, and grabbed hold of the rail. As she edged along, she noticed that she was walking uphill—the deck was sloping slightly toward the stern. She saw more people coming onto the deck. She had reached the door, had in fact taken hold of the handle when a rocket burst from the ship's bridge. She saw a white comet soar upward, blaze through the dark then arc downward and knew that if distress rockets were summoning help, the ship must be in serious difficulty. She wrenched the door open and in her haste to return to the cabin, slipped on the sixth stair and tumbled the rest of the way down the staircase. She sat on the bottom step and examined her ankle, relieved that nothing appeared to be broken. Getting to her feet, she bumbled along the passageway toward the main stairwell, her ankle so painful that she knew she had sprained it. Two young women she recalled seeing in the library rushed past and one of them asked if she had heard that the ship had dropped a propeller.

"We're sinking!" Stella said. It was only when the words were said that she understood that her voyage might end between two continents. "Sure we are," the other one laughed. Though she heard herself muttering, "Just you wait," Stella had to admit that here in the stairwell, the ship seemed to be all right. She noticed people were coming up the stairs singly and in groups and took this as a sign that the elevator would be crowded and slow; otherwise people wouldn't be using the stairs. Holding on to the rail, she went down two floors, flinching with every step. She hobbled along the companionway toward D43.

Why was she returning to the cabin? She was under no obligation of help Mary O'Connor and it wasn't too late to go up to the boat deck and get into one of the boats. Why didn't she? This was a question to which there was no ready answer. All Stella knew for certain was that one had a Christian duty to assist those in need and that a lame mother with a young child was waiting her for. It was wicked—there was no other word for it—to see to one's own safety at the expense of others; as a nurse her life had been guided by this principle.

Mary O'Connor was sitting on the tandem fully dressed with that silly hat on her head, and staring straight ahead, paying no attention to the child who was lying quietly on the bed in her night gown and napkin, beneath a pool of overhead light.

"Bundle up the child and we'll go up on deck," Stella said.

"I won't leave the cabin," Mary said. "I'm waiting for my husband."

"We must hurry. They are filling the lifeboats now."

"Owen knows where we are. He'll come for us."

"Did you receive a message from your husband?"

Mary didn't reply.

"I asked if you received a message from your husband."

"No. Which means he is aboard."

"I think you are mistaken. Surely if he was aboard, you would have heard from him by now."

"Owen has his own ways of doing things." Mary said this resignedly, twisting her wedding ring on her finger, shaking her head as if she was talking about a mischievous lad who refused to co-operate or to explain his actions.

Stella slapped her, hard enough to leave an imprint on the cheek, which was what one did with catatonic patients. The slap frightened the child and she began to cry.

"You've upset her."

My mother picked me up and seeing the water brimming in her eyes, I cried harder, convinced that if the flood of tears continued, the bright blue circles in her face would float away. "There, there." She rocked me.

Stella sat beside her. "Listen to me, Mary. Your husband is not aboard to save you. The ship is sinking and we must save ourselves. There is not a moment to spare." Stella looked at her watch. It was 1:15.

"Do you understand?"

"Yes."

Tears spilled from my mother's eyes and fell on my chin.

"Where are the baby's clothes? We must dress her warmly."

Stella noticed the green valise and the wicker case by the door. She opened the valise and taking out a knitted sweater, leggings and a hooded bunting, gave the clothes to Mary. She heard passengers trooping along the corridor. "Hurry!"

"Babies don't like to be hurried."

An infuriating woman. No wonder her husband chose not to be aboard. Chiding herself for the unkind thought Stella waited until the child had been buttoned into the bunting before helping Mary into her life jacket. She opened the door and they went into the passageway, Mary holding the child and walking slowly so that people hurried past. There were more people on the stairs and Stella went first to clear the way. There was a family of six directly ahead, the children holding onto a string, following a steward like a taggle of ducklings.

The steward looked at Stella. "Are you ladies going up to the boat deck?"

"We are."

"Good. The officers have had a devil of a time finding women who will get into the lifeboats. Go to the port side."

Out on the deck, Stella led Mary toward the portside rail where a large crowd had assembled to watch a lifeboat being loaded. Suddenly a pistol shot rang through the air and an officer shouted, "Back! Everyone back!" and the women were pushed backwards by the crowd.

"This won't do at all." Stella steered her charges further along where there was a space near the rail. She looked over the side and saw two lifeboats in the water and another one pulling away.

"Come, Mary, we may do better at the far end," Stella said, though she didn't believe it. Everything was happening so fast and they were late.

But Mary refused to budge. "Listen," she said.

"Listen for what?" Stella shouted. What was she supposed to hear over the clamour and commotion?

"The engines have stopped."

It was true, the engines were silent—the ship's heart had stopped beating.

"That means the firemen are released. Now Owen will come looking for us."

"Mary. Listen to me." Stella put her hands on either side of Mary's face. "Your husband isn't aboard. You think so because you are in shock. What we must do now is find you a lifeboat that is being loaded. Think of the child."

"The child," Mary said.

Stella said, "Annie Rose."

Me.

I looked at her over my mother's shoulder. By now I was alert and without comprehending what it was, I knew something terrible was going on.

Stella took hold of my mother's arm. "Let us walk toward the music." The band was now playing a waltz.

While another rocket blazed overhead, Stella lowered her head and stumped forward, pain spiking her leg. She was mid-deck when she bumped—literally—into Ernest Patcher.

"Miss Flynn!"

"Mr. Patcher!"

"This is Mrs. O'Connor. I'm looking for a lifeboat for herself and the child. Are they loading from the bridge?"

"They were loading the last boat there five minutes ago. I'll go and ask them to hold it." he said. He turned around and padded in the direction from which he'd come.

We followed him down the slippery deck, passing a man throwing deckchairs overboard and musicians, who despite bulky life jackets, were continuing to play. Soon Ernest Patcher was running toward us. He slipped, righted himself but came gamely on and said that it was too late, the boat had gone down and the captain was calling for the life boats to return and pick up more passengers.

"What shall we do?" Stella said. "Is there nothing else?"

"I have been on both decks and to my knowledge all the lifeboats have gone. Some of them were half full. There's been no system, no organization. The ship is a madhouse." He looked at me. "Does the baby have a cradle?"

"She has a basket," my mother said.

"A basket will leak. We need something of wood, something that will float."

"I know something that will make the basket waterproof." Stella said. "I will fetch it and the cradle from the cabin."

"Where is your cabin?"

"D43."

"Midship. Good." Ernest clapped her on the back. "Go, woman, go!" he said. "We will meet you at the entrance to the boat deck on the starboard side! Keep to the stairs! Don't use the lift!"

Stella went off, half limping, half running, making her way between and around passengers, once taking hold of a man's arm to prevent herself from falling. The pain in her ankle was so intense that it brought tears to her eyes. She kept on, yanked open a door and went down one staircase and then another, barrelling along, she'd no idea she could move with such speed. She swept into the bathroom and pulling the black rubber sheeting from its rungs, dashed into D43 and picked up the basket. She was backing out the door with it when she asked herself how the sheeting could be secured to the basket. Of course, the gold cord. She went back inside and fumbling in her reticule, which in spite of everything, she still carried, she located the key and unlocked the valise, pawed through the jumble of stolen goods until she found the coils of drapery cord. She tossed these into the basket and wrestled it along the passageway and up the stairs, her heart thumping in her ears, and finally stepped onto the starboard deck.

It was 1:50. Ernest had timed her. Praise God, he and Mary were where he said they would be. Holding up a length of rope and a Swiss army knife, Ernest said, "I cut one of the davit ropes." He knelt down, pulled the rubber sheet around the basket and knotting the gold cord together, made the sheet fast. "Now for the baby."

My mother arranged me in the cradle cloths and reaching into her purse brought out napkins, a jar of water and a bit of bread wrapped in an embroidered handkerchief and put them beneath my blanket, saying that I would need them when a lifeboat picked me up.

Lifting the cradle, Ernest said, "Follow me, ladies. I only have forty feet of rope and we'll have to lower the cradle at the bow end where the deck is closest to the water. Hold onto the rail."

Bending their knees and clinging to the rail, my mother and Stella followed us downhill, easing their way toward the bow where the forecastle was now under water and the sea was minutes from the bridge. When we reached the forecorner of the boat deck, Ernest put down the basket and looping the rope through the handles, made a harness.

A rocket went up. It was 2:00 and the band had stopped playing. People were climbing over the rail and leaping into the water.

My rescuers looked into my basket, their pale faces hovering above me like fallen moons.

Ernest said, "You ladies will have to go down first, to steady the cradle when it lands on the water. It's not far to jump."

"I'll go." Stella dropped her handbag—how foolish to have carried it around this long—climbed over the rail, pinched two fingers to her nose, closed her eyes, clamped her lips and dropped. Down she plunged, then bounced up, gasping with fright and cold, but she was all right—the cork life jacket kept her afloat. Moments later, Mary surfaced a few feet away. Ernest swung the cradle back and forth, trying to clear it from the deck, then bit by bit swung it down until it landed on the water with hardly a splash. Before jumping in, he gestured toward a deckchair, which Mary swam over to and retrieved, towing it toward the cradle. Surfacing, Ernest cut away the rope from the cradle and, with Mary's assistance, eased it on top of the chair. "Now, we must get as far away as possible from the ship," he said and began swimming, guiding the chair with its cradle forward, Mary beside him murmuring to the child, Stella struggling behind.

She was finding it hard to keep up. The bulky life jacket made it difficult to swim and the best she could do was to bob along scooping the water aside with her arms. The sea was paralysingly cold and already she had lost the feeling in both feet. Behind her she heard splashes and plops as people continued jumping overboard. She passed a cello floating on the water among the debris of boxes, casks, suitcases and chairs.

There was no sign of the lifeboats though they were out here somewhere, swallowed by the dark. Now that Stella had moved beyond the reflected light of the ship, it was difficult to see anything clearly. Though Ernest and Mary were only ten feet ahead, all she saw was their fuzzy shapes. How many lifeboats had Ernest said there were? Twenty. They were bound to come upon one of them soon. She heard voices drift across the water, but it was impossible to tell if they came from lifeboats or from people like herself bobbing along in life jackets.

They were about a hundred yards away when they heard a horrendous tearing of metal. Stella turned and saw one of the ship's funnels topple over the bow. Snapping guywires, twisting pylons and exploding sparks, it crashed into the water sizzling and steaming as it sank. A wave rose in its place and washed over the deck, sweeping passengers overboard. The air crackled with their screams and those of passengers clinging to the rails, and from deep inside the ship came the noise of terrible wrenching as it was riven in two. The lights went out and a crescendo of voices, wails of desperation and panic rose with the ship and then were silenced as the bow slid underwater. The pitch of fear rose again as the stern tilted upward. But it was momentary and dropped to a low continuous moan as the stern knifed into the sea. It was 2:20. Now the voices were scattered and erratic; there were hundreds of them in all shapes and colours. It was a babble, a chaotic delirious speaking in tongues.

By now the wave had reached Stella and she was lifted up in the swell. "Mary?" she called. "Ernest?" She was breathing with her mouth open, making little clouds of steam, beads of frozen snot hanging from her nose.

"Over here."

Stella paddled toward Ernest's voice.

"Where is Mary?"

"By the chair," Mary said, but her voice was weak. How strange their voices sounded, as if they were coming from heads whose bodies had disappeared. Ernest waited until Stella reached him and then he said, "I see what might be a small ice pan off to our left and

I think we should put the cradle on it. It might be a while before we come across a life boat and when we do, with all these people in the water, it might be difficult getting the baby aboard. The child might do just as well on a flat bit of ice. Ice doesn't sink as easily as wood." Stella thought it a bizarre thing do, but no more bizarre than anything else that was happening.

"We should do it while we have the strength to lift up the basket," Ernest said and Mary and Stella paddled behind him while he continued to guide the chair with its cradle. They came to the ice pan which glistened faintly, an oily black. Ernest put a hand on it, examining the surface. "It's low and flat, just what the doctor ordered."The ice pan wobbled slightly and Stella thought about the underside, fearing that the ice pan might tip over, but she said not a word, knowing that in this ghastly floating battle ground strewn with the dead and dying, one mode of defence against the perishing cold was probably as risky as any other. While the women steadied the basket between them, Ernest heaved the cradle and chair on top of the ice pan and eased it away from the edge and Mary began to pray: *Hail Mary, full of grace. The Lord is with Thee; blessed art Thou among women and blessed is the fruit of Thy Womb, Jesus. Holy Mary, Mother of God, pray for us sinners, now and at the hour of our death.*

Tucked into my cradle I made no sound: I was listening to my mother. Beneath me I felt the ice pan move, and knew I was being guided forward by an unseen hand. I like to think it was my mother's. I like to think it was she who, while having her own life taken away, sent me on a voyage toward a life that however much she wished it, she could never have imagined.

Stella and Ernest were about thirty feet behind the ice pan, moving their arms to keep their blood circulating. Stella could no longer move her legs which hung below her, a dead weight. There was no sensation from the waist down and her heart beat sluggishly inside her chest.

"Yesterday when you were complaining about the ship's shortcomings, I thought you were suffering a depression." This was as close to an apology as Stella would come.

"You didn't like me."

"No."

"I put people off. I have all my life."

For a time neither of them spoke. Stella was becoming too tired for conversation but it was important to speak. Conversation shut out the panicked shouts, the tortured cries.

"What have you done with your life?" Ernest said.

A monumental question. What had she done?

"I nursed the insane. ... What did you do?"

"For the last five years I looked after my ailing wife. Before that I worked in insurance. Did you marry?"

"No."

"Too particular, were you?"

"I suppose." It seemed as likely an explanation as anything else. She *had* been particular. "I never saw any good reason why I should."

Ernest laughed. Odd to hear someone laugh when they were surrounded by sounds of terror: admonitions to God, wheedling, grovelling, pleading, weeping and praying. Stella could no longer hear Mary praying. She peered through the dark without seeing her, then paddled toward the ice pan. Mary was gone. Where had she gone? With a life jacket on, she wouldn't have sunk. Had she drifted away, become another anonymous head floating in the dark beneath the bloodless stars? "Mary!" Stella called. "Mary!" It was impossible to know where she had gone.

Ernest paddled over.

"Mary's gone."

It was 2:35.

"Mary!" Ernest called. He paddled in a wide circle but there was no sign of her.

Something was floating on the water. Stella picked it up and brought it close. Mary's hat, her ridiculous hat. She must have become disoriented and taken it off. Had she had taken off her life jacket too? Without knowing why, without even caring to know why—what did knowing why matter, after all—Stella handed the hat to Ernest who found the strength to reach up and place Mary's hat on top of the basket. There was no sound from the cradle.

I wasn't asleep. I had heard them calling, "Mary!" and was listening for my mother's voice, trying to pick it out from the wailings and moans of despair.

"She was a plucky young woman," Ernest said.

"She was."

Stella closed her eyes. "*Lead, kindly Light, amid the encircling gloom*." It took so much effort to push out the words that she thought she was bellowing, but her voice was faint.

"*The night is dark, and I am far from home*," sang Ernest.

"Were you at the hymn sing?" She no longer made the effort to look at him when she spoke but kept her eyes closed.

"I was."

"Do you think the lifeboats will return?"

"No, but the wireless operator sent out an SOS. A rescue ship is on its way."

"It won't come soon enough for me."

"Don't give up."

"I should have been kinder to Mary," she said, "but I was determined to enjoy myself." How surprising that she should be making this disclosure to Ernest Patcher of all people. How surprising that she and Mary had run into him on the boat deck and not the Grimes family. Providence had put a brave man in their midst.

"Did you enjoy yourself?"

"I enjoyed the food." She paused in drowsy remembrance. "It pleases me to remember what I ate tonight for dinner; lamb collets, minted peas, orange surprise. No, that was the night before." She was becoming muddled.

"I could have been kinder to my wife," Ernest said. "In the early days I used to bully her. She couldn't do anything right."

Stella wanted so badly to sleep. Her head dropped to her chest.

She felt Ernest tugging her arm. "Go ahead," she said, "break it off." She thought her arm could break off and she wouldn't feel a thing. Ernest was asking her something about the soul. He was asking her if she believed the soul left a body when a person died.

"I had a patient who believed he was tied to his soul..." She nodded off.

"Yes?" A second tug. "Yes?"

"...by an umbilical cord. He would unbutton his shirt and let it fly around the room. Sometimes he rocked it in his arms and talked to it."

"What did it say?"

"He was as mad as a March hare." She was mumbling.

"But do you believe your soul will leave your body?"

Another tug. "Do you?"

"I suppose I do," Stella said, and went to sleep. She saw a man dressed in black bobbing toward her across the water.

It was 2:45.

FOUR

THE HOME

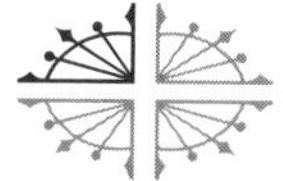

1989

Less than twenty-five miles from Cape Race, among the elderly residents of Ocean View Home, only vague memories of the *Titanic* remained. Didn't the Marconi station at the Cape receive an SOS before the ship went down? Didn't Hilda Sutton keep a deckchair from the *Titanic* that burnt with her house? Didn't one of the St. Croix brothers rescue a baby from the Banks who was thought to have been aboard? Or was it a fisherman from Nova Scotia? A fanciful story with no historical basis, said Cyril Gibbons, who was over fond of historical facts. Though Captain Coady disagreed, saying that the stranger the story the more likely it was to be true, he would have been astonished to discover that the woman who had been trimming his hair all these years was the baby Francis St. Croix brought home from the ice.

Whenever the subject of the *Titanic* came up, residents shook their heads and agreed that the disaster had been a terrible thing, yes it had. Then someone, most likely Captain Coady, would point out that what happened to the *Titanic* was no worse than what happened to thousands of ships wrecked off the coast, many of them right here in Trepassey Bay; it was no worse than the story of Newfoundland, which was one loss after another: boys lost to war, fishermen to the sea, sealers to the ice, not to mention a country lost to Canada. And it wasn't over yet: at the rate people were bailing out of Newfoundland, the leakage would never stop. In any case, there weren't any Newfoundlanders on the *Titanic*, Canadians, yes, but no Newfoundlanders. Except for the SOS sent to Cape Race, the *Titanic* story didn't really belong to Newfoundland.

Neither did the story of Amelia Earhart, the American pilot who spent three weeks in Trepassey waiting until the weather cleared so that she could fly across the Atlantic. This was in 1926, nine years before her plane ran out of fuel near New Guinea while she was circumnavigating the globe. Amelia made a name for herself all right, but it could hardly be claimed for Newfoundland. Cyril remembered Amelia. She stayed in the house next to his and complained the entire time she was in Trepassey about eating a diet of potatoes and fish. She didn't think much of using the outhouse and expected a woman to come in regularly and do her hair.

I understand the importance Amelia attached to her hair. Having at one time or another shampooed every resident at the Home, I know how a clean head of hair can imbue its owner with a sense of well-being. How easily hair forgives! How eagerly it picks itself up after being neglected and abused. With the exception of terminal balding, given half a chance most hair will obligingly restore itself and do its best to look lively and lustrous. I can imagine Amelia cooped up for weeks in a saltbox house, staring gloomily out the window toward the fogbound bay while she waited for a break in the weather, her bouncy hair becoming flatter and greasier day by day. She understood as well as I do how a double-rinse shampoo, followed by the use of Bride Sutton's curling iron and brush, would restore her melancholy hair to pert blond curls peeking optimistically from beneath her aviator's cap.

After Ocean View was restaffed a few years ago, hairdressing was all that remained of my caregiving duties. I was relieved that I had been left with this much since hairdressing is the part of my work I most enjoy. For me, doing hair, or barbering as the Captain calls it when he wheels in for a trim, is an expression of intimacy and goodwill, something I first discovered when I combed and brushed Merla and Francis's hair. I am touched by the innocent way residents lay their heads on the plastic support, trusting me not to hose water down their necks or get shampoo in their eyes. Such is their trust in me that they close their eyes while I soap their temples; and some even reward me with a blissful sigh or a rapturous moan. Residents count on me to be gentle and kind, to ignore scabs and discolorations, the bony protuberances and thinning patches, the deficiencies of illness and age. They count on me to turn them out looking better than when they came in. Since most residents talk while I'm working on their hair, they also count on me to listen. Cyril, the Captain and Brenda are the windiest talkers. Cyril—who considers it his job to educate me about the history of the Southern Shore—never tires of telling me that the Basque fishermen knew about the Banks long before the Portuguese and Bretons and for hundreds of years were Europe's chief supplier of dried cod. The Captain is fond of telling stories about the heroism of water dogs and the lives they have saved: 180 passengers from the *Despatch*, 177 from the *Harpooner*, and a modest nine, including the Captain himself, from his trawler, the *Elizabeth May*. My sister-in-law Brenda, who's been in the Home since Jerome died and needs a walker to get around, frets about her youngest son, Gary, who is a disappointment to her. Brenda says she understands why, with six teenagers clomping about the house, her daughter Fran couldn't cope with an invalid mother, but Gary, who lives alone, could have taken her in. Brenda claims that in her day a son's disrespect for his mother would never have been tolerated, and recounts how she took in her father, bully that he was, when she and Jerome were half starved and living in the Drook.

I was there the day Brenda's father put the boots to the dole inspector. This was during the thirties depression, when people were expected to live on six cents a day, and whenever the dole inspector hove in sight hid what little food they had in the woodpile. Those were the days when the country was run from Britain and Lady Hope Simpson threw candy to outport women as if they were children scrambling for birthday treats. Brenda contends that the only way Joey was able to get Newfoundlanders out from under the British was to sell them to the Canadians. Though Smallwood is nearly ninety and in no better shape than themselves, residents still refer to him as Joey—to them he'll never be more than a nervy schoolboy from upalong.

At Ocean View, the Confederation pot is always on a slow boil. Pugnacious and cocky, Cyril likes to turn up the heat, usually on Saturday nights when residents gather in the lounge for a singsong accompanied by Jack O'Brien on the accordion and the Captain on the ugly stick, a mop handle with bottle caps nailed on. After the wavering voices have made it through the "Ode to Newfoundland," Cyril calls for "O Canada," though he knows the only person who will join him will be Jack, the other resident besides himself who admits to being Canadian; Jack is more diplomatic about his allegiance than Cyril, claiming to be a Newfoundlander first and a Canadian second.

I am often present at these Saturday night singsongs. When she's short-handed, Marilyn, the Home's administrator, will call me in to help out; she knows that, living alone as I do not far down the road, I'm usually available at short notice. Though I linger for a while in the lounge after supper, I leave when the singing is finished, before Cyril can whip up a discussion. I know that after the political talk dies off, the conversation will turn to family connections, who's related to whom. Newfoundlanders thrive on such talk: your first cousin, Marge Sutton, was my Uncle Steve's second wife's sister, which makes you my aunt twice removed, by marriage—that sort of thing. The residents don't know that I was the baby rescued from the *Titanic*; to them I'm a St. Croix from the Drook, daughter of Merla Bevis of Clam Cove and sister-in-law of Brenda, a Martin from Long Beach. Out of respect for my privacy, Brenda never says a word and even if she did, residents would most likely tell her that it's just another story, of which there are hundreds along the shore.

I also prefer to avoid discussions about whether or not I'm a Newfoundlander. I've heard enough from my daughter, who has strong opinions on the subject and is suspicious of people who want to become Newfoundlanders because they naively regard the island as a panacea for troubled times. But even she admits that Newfoundlanders' overweening pride in being born on the island (not Labrador) gets shoved down the throats of newcomers. Though I've lived in Newfoundland since I was a baby, I still think of myself as a come-from-away. Given the circumstances of my deliverance from the ice, how could I think otherwise? I think that even as a babe in arms I was probably aware of my apartness and was waiting patiently for a sign that would portend how my life would unfold. Though I didn't recognize it at the time, I think the sign might have been given to me when I was being wheeled in a pram and saw fragments of ice floating in the sky.

March 6th, Cork

Dear Gran,

This will be one of my shorter letters written to accompany the photos of the house and garden which I took with the camera I bought with the Christmas money you sent. Sorry it's taken this long to get the film developed but I seem to be behind on everything these days. The garden looks a mess but once my boarders are gone and my courses are over, I'll have the time to put it to rights and begin painting again.

Keep well.

Love, Sheila

Brief though it is, I take Sheila's letter with me to read to Tom during the Catholic Women's League's spring sale and tea. Though he's been dead nearly twenty years I still find it a comfort to talk to him. I tell him things I would never tell another soul, which is one reason I've been able to maintain my privacy as well as I have. While people are inside the church hall drinking tea, I'm in the graveyard reading him Sheila's letter, sitting on a folding stool I bring along for these visits. His grave, which is near the road in a corner overgrown with sheep laurel and Labrador tea, bears an inscription I found in *The Book of Knowledge* beneath a picture of Jesus holding a lamp: *He was a Light to the World*. Nancy called it tacky and tried to talk me out of using it but I refused, pointing out that the inscription was exactly right for honouring her father's work. When I finish reading the letter, I tell Tom about our son-in-law's visit last week. I still think of Philip as a relative though he and Nancy have been divorced for years. The fact is I don't particularly enjoy his visits, but can think of no polite way to discourage him; I never know when he'll turn up on my doorstep and invite himself in. (A few months ago he arrived with his sister, a gaunt, bored-looking woman who poured whisky from a flask into her tea.) We never talk about Nancy but I'm sure she knows about the visits. Though I never discuss Philip with her, I have no qualms about discussing him with Tom. Once someone has passed away, dislikes and grievances don't matter any more. That's the exquisite symmetry of dying. When your soul passes over, there's a release of burdens and grudges.

When I'm talking to Tom I'm perfectly aware that I'm talking to myself, that if he were to speak to me his language would be entirely different from the one we use every day with its burden of purpose and information. Long ago, his voice would have changed into something as garbled and baffling as water running over stones, an intricacy of rhythm and sound that defies translation. Or his voice could be something as familiar and lonely as the cry of a gull. I could well be listening to him without knowing that I was. I tell Tom about Stanley, that he still spends all his time at work and never takes a holiday, that he'll be working in Halifax for another month. I tell him that Nancy is coming to see me this Sunday, without Gerry this time.

After their divorces, Nancy and Gerry Morgan began living together on the weekends. During the week she lives in her house on Dick's Square and he lives in his on Barnes Road. The arrangement wouldn't have suited Tom and me; until he entered the hospital, we slept every night curled around each other, turning together in our sleep, but the arrangement suits Nancy who claims she will never remarry.

Inevitably my conversations with Tom are interrupted by someone passing on the other side of the fence on their way to or from the church. When I see the Bennett twins coming along the road, as they frequently do, I fall silent and busy myself with the grave, pulling weeds, rearranging shells, or as I'm doing now, picking up ice crystals to encourage the few scrappy daffodils I planted last fall to poke through the gravelly soil. It isn't that I have anything profoundly shocking or scandalous to keep from the sisters, rather that the maintenance of privacy requires far more vigilance than the maintenance of a grave.

On Sunday Nancy arrives later than usual, in midafternoon. On the way down, she telephoned me from Renews to say that she would be late because she was interviewing Helen Farrell, whose Irish forebears emigrated from Waterford in the early nineteenth century. When I finally open the door to my daughter, I feel a spurt of parental pride at seeing her look so well in her belted blue jeans and brown leather jacket. As I never tire of telling Tom, Nancy has transformed herself into a confident and healthy woman. Gone is the beleaguered face, the widening hips and nunnish hair. Now her hair is dyed a chestnut colour, cut just above the shoulders.

"How are you, Mom?" She gives me the pink azalea she's holding in the crook of one arm; in the other is a brown paper bag containing a loaf of bakery bread. "It's cool now but it was warm when I picked it up."

"I'll slice some for tea."

We visit, as we always do, in the kitchen, the plate of buttered bread between us on the table. Nancy tells me that she's been approached by a publisher about adapting her doctoral thesis on migration patterns into a book.

"I think I'll take them up on it. What they have in mind is a coffee-table book made up of interviews interspersed with photos."

She tells me about being appointed to the board of a foundation that before she died, Tom's sister Maggie set up to preserve Newfoundland's heritage.

Maggie Hunt died in the house on Circular Road, where she hobbled about on canes, her back humped, her dark eyes hooded when she strained to look up. In her later years she became garrulous and tiresome, ranting on about the way Newfoundland's chances for independence had been ruined. She died when she hit her head on the iron replica of the Canadian wolf in the hallway, which the Hunts used as a boot scraper. It was thought that she tripped over a mat on her way to answer the door. The paper boy usually collected his money on Friday after school, which, the coroner estimated, was the time she died.

After tea we drive to St. Shott's, my window opened wide to allow an unobstructed view of the Barrens. Today they're a muted colour, not quite brown, not quite green. The colour is interrupted by islands of snow and frozen ponds that throw the light back to the sky. How soothing it is driving in silence, abandoning myself to the landscape as the car laps up the miles. Nancy drives southwest to the village of St. Shott's and parks the car beside the road while we admire the sweep of the ocean. I think about the tidal wave in 1864 that rolled the sea back so far that people could see the remains of the *Drake*, which had sunk forty-two years before. If the sea had rolled back further still, no doubt valleys and crevasses would have been revealed, canyons and plateaus imprinted with the archaeology of ships.

Stanley comes to visit on a sunny morning in June. It amuses me how he and Nancy take turns checking up on me, I'm sure at her insistence. Nancy expects chores—am I a chore?—to be shared fifty-fifty and it's probably true that if she didn't insist on visiting turn about, I would go a long time without seeing Stanley. My son is erratic, and left to himself might visit me as often as six times a month, after which, depending on his work, I might not see him again for half a year.

For the first time since Anna's death, he arrives on my doorstep with a woman. According to Nancy, Stanley has had what she calls "flings" with women when he's presented papers at conferences in Oslo, Lyons, Tokyo, Oaxaca, but nothing has ever come of these.

About eleven o'clock I see Stanley and the woman pass the side window on their way to my back door. As soon as he comes into the kitchen, he gives me one of his giant hugs while the woman stands looking on.

"Mom, this is Kate Bishop. Kate's a mainlander working at ERI."

I hold out my hand and she takes it at once, a small dark woman with hair cut short and tiny gold hoops in her ears.

"Kate's starting a job at the Cape. You know the Northern Radar project I was telling you about? Well, that's Kate's. She's an electrical engineer."

Amazing what women are up to nowadays; imagine this dainty-looking young woman being an engineer.

"We have to settle Kate at the Cape. I thought you might like to come. I brought a picnic lunch."

So it was business. What a shame. If there was anything romantic going on, Stanley wouldn't be inviting me along.

For years I wouldn't visit the Cape because I thought it would make me lonely for Tom. I am lonely for him, but because I enjoy solitude it's a manageable loneliness. During the past few years I've been out to the Cape several times and now I can visit it with the detachment of someone who has settled into another life, someone who has made herself over into someone else.

Stanley has brought the institute's truck in order to haul Kate's equipment and supplies. A truck is also needed to negotiate the road, which has been washed away in places and never repaired. The last time I was out here with Stanley, the muffler fell off the station wagon and he casually stopped to pick it up and put it in the trunk. The road is even worse today, and as he eases the truck in and out of ruts on Drook hill, he mutters something about it being faster to come out here by boat.

The sight of the Drook always lifts my soul, that part of me that's most deeply touched by sorrow and joy. Today it is joy. Today my soul is being lifted straight up then lowered gently into the valley, onto the shining pond and the stream pummelling seaward across sand glistening like obsidian. The Drook is now a weekend camp, a place to boil tea and have a cook-up after hauling wood or laying rabbit slips. Slowly, inch by inch, the landscape is taking itself back, reclaiming grassy patches and gardens. Albert and Lucy's house is a rubble of stone, as is Philip and Bride's. None of these houses were floated away; instead they were partly or wholly dismantled, board by board, wall by wall, by my brothers, uncles and cousins wielding the demolition crowbars themselves. Before Joey's resettlement scheme was under way, they'd heard the pendulum swinging and decided that it was time to take whatever could be salvaged from the wreck of poverty that the Drook had become and find another use for their houses rather than try to hold on to what had been irretrievably lost. Stanley didn't stop at the Drook or Long Beach, where barely enough pastureland remains for sheep to graze.

"The clouds look like nightgowns. The ghosts are out for a sail!" I say, trying to cheer up Stanley who I know by his silence is probably remembering when he and Anna were here. I'm excited by the sudden cliffs and yawning sea. The Cape is a place where I feel vulnerable and exhilarated, as if I could easily be scooped up by the wind, swept into the sky and upwards into space.

Our house at the Cape is now a bungalow, the second floor having been removed. The school is gone, the wireless buildings, the covered walkway, the mess hall, all those buildings are gone—they were taken away when we were living here. There are no families living here now, but someone is always on duty for a four-week shift. Only the lighthouse is the same, its lantern flashing a quarter-second between eclipses. According to Kate, the original Cape Race lighthouse is now in an Ottawa park where it is dwarfed by the Atlas rocket that launched John Glenn into space. She says that beside the rocket, the lighthouse looks like a barber's pole. Past the east landing, a half mile from the lighthouse, is a new bungalow, the place where she will live and work while a new story is grafted onto the Cape. The three of us sit at the chrome table in the bungalow kitchen eating ham and mustard sandwiches—it's too windy to eat outdoors—and Kate explains about ground wave radar. She points out the window to where the transmitting tower will be built, and where forty receivers will stand, spaced equidistant along the cliff, all of them hooked up to the computers downstairs. Seventeen thousand metres of copper wire will be buried along the cliff to make the ground conductive. Unlike conventional radar, ground length radar follows the curvature of the earth and is able to detect ice and waves two hundred miles offshore.

"We've come a long way since Marconi," she says, and I see a cloud pass in front of Stanley's eyes.

October 3rd, Daniel's Point

Dear Sheila,

Thank you for your letter written in the garden. I'm pleased to hear that you've had time to paint. I like the thought of you painting in the garden. I'm writing this in ours. I always think of the garden as ours since we worked on it together. No frost yet. The shooting stars are still blooming and the heather I planted near the tuck seems to have taken root.

I don't know if your mother has told you but there's a woman in your uncle's life. It was Gary St. Croix, not Stanley, who told me. I ran into him this morning when he was in Waddlington's buying a lotto ticket. He said Stanley was spending every weekend at the Cape with Kate Bishop. She's the engineer in charge of the radar project they have going on out there. I met her the weekend Stanley helped her move to the Cape.

You'll laugh when I tell you that I've begun making Christmas presents. With so many to make I like to get started early. This year I'm making wall icons that will use up the Christmas cards of the Virgin I've been saving for years. Each card will have a frame of wrinkled foil to look like beaten tin. On the foil I'll glue sparkle dust, glass chips and beads and other bits of jewellery. Everyone at the Home will receive a wall icon, including Nina Riggs, the Protestant who took Flo Kearny's bed after she passed on in August. I intend to complete a wall icon a day until I'm finished.

Keep well,
Love, Gran

In addition to making wall icons for the residents and staff of the Home, I'll make another dozen for the Holy Redeemer Christmas sale and tea; that means thirty-eight altogether. Before I finish I will be thoroughly bored by the repetition, the mundanity of busywork. Think of the books I could be reading, the walks I could taking! I vow never to undertake making Christmas gifts again, but I will, I will. I am determined to reuse every scrap of waste I come across, every button and bottlecap, every bit of plastic and foil, every inch of wool and string: it all finds its way into my box of odds and ends where it stays until I turn it into something else. Aggie Halleran, who's seen me carrying my bag along the roadside, calls me Trepassey's bag lady.

For last year's sale I took apart the grey suit that was once my city clothes and used it to cover a discarded bird cage, arranging the wool to look like a roofed tree stump; the roof itself was a rusted cookie sheet I found in Waddlington's trash. Inside the house were stools made from buttons and toothpicks, and bedsteads made from broken combs. The bird perch became a mouse swing and a Popsicle stick and an empty spool a teeter-totter. The mouse house was put up for raffle and, I'm pleased to say, earned $264.50 for the League's scholarship fund.

I heard the phone on the sixth ring, but was unaware of opening my eyes because when it began ringing I was dreaming about being wide awake in an emptied room. The clothes on the chair had disappeared, and the chair itself, the dresser, and even the bed beneath me had been taken away, leaving me suspended on a sea of air. These days I often wake to find myself hanging in the middle of nowhere, a sensation that leaves me bereft. I switch on the light and look at the clock. Five a.m. Who can be calling at this hour? I pad into the hall and pick up the telephone.

"Yes?"

"Gran, it's Sheila."

"Are you all right?"

"I'm fine. I'm phoning to wish you a happy birthday."

Is it that time of year again? Tom always insisted on celebrating my birthday along about now. Beatty would bake a cake and Tom would present me with a sweater or nightgown he'd hidden away.

"It really is your birthday, Gran. Your seventy-ninth. You were born December 10th, 1910. I've known this for three days, but was waiting until your birthday to tell you. Your birth name was Annie Rose O'Connor."

"You don't mean it."

"I know it's a shock."

Shock hardly describes it. There's a fluttering inside my chest.

"Ever since you gave me the handkerchief I've been trying to trace your birth parents, without getting anywhere," Sheila goes on. "I started with the list of passengers aboard the *Titanic*, which I obtained from Lloyds of London. There was no Roche aboard so I figured your mother must have been travelling under a married name, perhaps with your father. Remember when you told me about the oceanography student who visited the Cape when you were at the Drook?"

"Patrick O'Connor."

"I got thinking that your mother's married name might have been O'Connor. I checked the passenger list for that name and found a Kate O'Connor. She survived the sinking and moved to the States. In any case she had no child. I more or less gave up after that lead fizzled. But when I was in London with Kevin last week after Grandfather Palmer's funeral, I spoke to a man at the National Maritime Museum in Greenwich. He told me that a lot of the survivors aboard the *Titanic*, ninety-eight of them I think he said, weren't on the passenger list and that I shouldn't be deterred by the fact that no more O'Connors were listed. I knew that the ship had stopped in Ireland and as soon as I got back to Cork, I started looking through the church marriage records for O'Connor and found the marriage of Mary Roche and Owen O'Connor, March 23, 1909, the Church of St. Peter and Paul, Reverend Kelly presiding."

Imagine. My parents, my lost, mysterious parents found. Retrieved.

"After that, of course, finding your christening record was easy. You were born seventy-nine years ago today, probably in one of the Catholic hospitals. I think your mother was a Protestant. Kevin says that in those days most Roches were Prods. She would have converted, otherwise she couldn't have been married by a Catholic priest. Now that I've come this far, I'll see what else I can find out about her, and your father, too, of course."

I sit on the stool for a long time after I hang up the phone, waiting for the revelation to take hold and watching the faint glimmer of dawn lighten the water—from where I am I have a view of the bay through the front-room window. I think about the news of my birth date, my parents' names. Mary. Owen. Though they are common enough names, I say them over and over to get used to them. I think about the fact that I've had two sets of parents living on either side of the North Atlantic, that in a way my life has been a reverie floating between. I'm still sitting on the stool when the telephone rings again. This time it's Nancy who is perhaps even more astonished than I am by the news. Though I knew she never believed that I had been rescued from an ice pan, I didn't know that she had come to regard the story as a cover-up for an illegitimate birth in the St. Croix family that she had decided was better to ignore.

"Well, now that it seems likely that I was on the *Titanic*, it doesn't mean you can broadcast the fact. I won't have it, I won't have people nosing around asking questions. I made that clear to Sheila too."

"Mom."

"I won't have my privacy invaded." I'm surprised by the determination I hear in my voice.

"Mom."

"What could I say of interest? I was an infant when I was rescued."

"Mom's the word."

"Nancy, I want you to …"

"It's a joke, Mom. Don't worry. I won't say a thing."

I get off the phone, make myself a breakfast of cocoa and toast and go back to bed. Later that morning I walk to the graveyard and tell Tom the news. Fortunately no one passes on the road, which allows me to tell him the whole story without interruption. Afterwards I go into the church and after lighting two candles, pray for the souls of my parents.

December 10th, Daniel's Point

Dear Sheila,

I am very grateful to you for finding my birth parents. All these years I have been living with the knowledge that there was a piece of myself missing.

Now, thanks to you, the piece has been retrieved. I can't say that I suffered much for want of this knowledge (I was so very young when Francis first put me in Merla's arms) but I'm glad to have it, mostly on account of my parents. Today when I lit a candle for them in church I prayed for them, especially my mother who was with me that tragic night. I have no sense that my father was with me, but if he was on the ship he must have survived, otherwise he wouldn't have sent my stepbrother to the Cape. I think the knowledge of my father's existence was something I knew without wanting to know that I did. The fact is that I probably could have found him if I had tried. I could have written Patrick O'Connor in Woods Hole. If I had suffered, if I had lived an unhappy life, maybe I would have been compelled to find my father, but I wasn't compelled.

The truth is that I wasn't all that upset not to have met Patrick. Since you have been working so hard to find my lost parents, it may be difficult for your to understand why I didn't try to find them myself. As I said, because I wasn't unhappy with my life, I didn't want to go chasing after another. I may have been afraid what I would find. Also, I had become accustomed to letting my life be guided by chance, the result, no doubt, of my miraculous rescue. But now that you have retrieved my earlier self, I am eager to learn everything you can find out about Annie Rose and her parents.

Thank you again,

Love, Gran

P.S. I'll be spending Christmas and New Year's with Stanley and your mother.

I am someone who follows the rituals of Christmas, Easter and Thanksgiving. This year, for instance, I spent Christmas in Tors Cove with Stanley—Kate was in Ontario with her parents—and New Year's on the waterfront in St. John's with Nancy and Gerry. I believe these family rituals (the tree, the ham, the turkey) are temporal beads of prayer that deserve modest, though not slavish, attention. But Valentine's Day can no longer be taken seriously as a family ritual, since it has become too promiscuous to be regarded as an exchange between true lovers. In my view the indiscriminate use of valentines cheapens love. Every year on Valentine's Day, two or three girls from Stella Maris High School come to the Home to dispense valentines. These aren't handmade cards, or even cards chosen with care, but shabby bits of paper punched out of a book intended for youngsters and showing cartoon pictures of teddy bears, mice and sheep bearing the captions *I can't bear it without you. Please, Valentine, will you be my cheese? I've got it baaaad.* The girls, dressed in jeans and T-shirts, their hair tucked behind their ears, kiss each resident, leaving red imprints on foreheads and cheeks. They are scarcely out the door before I toss the insulting valentine into the trash. There isn't so much as a scrap of lace on it, not even a bit of redeeming foil.

Tom's valentine—he pegged the same one to the clothes line every year—is inside a tin sea-chest I found years ago washed ashore at the Drook. Long before I became the Widow Aurora, when during my years at the Cape I wasn't always up to being both wife and mother, I looked for solace in Brenda and Jerome's abandoned house. As such times I arrived at the Drook feeling shipwrecked, as if I had run aground on the rocks. It took days of walking, reading and thinking for me to repair the broken spars, before I was ready to make the journey back to the Cape.

I found the tin chest early one morning after I'd finished breakfast and was on the beach looking for bits of wood, shells, whatever the tide had brought in overnight. The sand was pristine, swept clean so that whatever came ashore was seen at once. The chest, which was at the far end of the landwash, was rectangular, a useful size, about three feet wide and two feet high with metal handles, metal trim and a metal lock corroded with rust. There were no identifying marks, nothing to indicate what might have brought the chest to this particular shore. It could have been something from the *Marianne*, the *Commerce* or the *Mab*. Or currents and tides could have brought it from further away, just as Louis's body might have been carried to the waters of Nova Scotia or St. Pierre. I dragged the chest across the beach and along the overgrown path to the house where I heaved it onto the weathered step and set to work scraping off florets of rust with a kitchen knife. The metal fixings were brass, the lock was the kind that requires a padlock but without one is easily opened with a knife. Inside was a handful of sand and a white periwinkle. It took most of the day to scrub away the rust and pound out the hollows and dents. Once it was cleaned up and straightened out, I saw that the chest had been finely made. I thought it might have been where a sea captain's wife stored her valuables. I kept it at the Drook for years, using it to store my wander books. Later I moved it beside the bed at the Cape and from there to Daniel's Point.

Tom had his own chest up in the light for keeping his blue scribbler and his favourite books. The light was where he went when he wanted to be alone; he didn't need to go as far as me and used to say that he could see the entire universe from up there. Before he died he asked me to bring the scribbler down from the light and put it beside the bed. Ill as he was, he sometimes wrote in it.

I saw Tom for the first time on July 15, 1917. The *Kristianiafjord*, a huge Norwegian liner with 1,117 aboard, had run aground on the rocks at Mistaken Point in dripping fog. I remember Merla shaking me awake in a blur of grey and telling me that a ship had been wrecked, that the passengers had been put ashore and now were hungry and that I must get up now and help Louis carry food to them. Francis had left hours ago taking Jerome and Ben in the dory to help evacuate survivors. Merla tied a kerchief around my head and instructed me to keep to the road, saying that when we reached the point, I was to take hold of my brother's hand because the cliffs were steep and I might fall off. Louis and I trudged through fog thick as porridge, Louis carrying the soup buckets and I, the bread.

When we reached Mistaken Point, he gave me one of the buckets, shifted the bread to beneath his arm and took hold of my hand.

We edged forward—it was impossible to see anything until we were right on top of it. We heard voices babbling in the fog—we were surrounded by hundreds of strange-speaking survivors. There was something disturbingly familiar about them though I couldn't have said why. Louis bumped into a suitcase—more than two thousand pieces of luggage had been brought ashore and piled on top of the cliff. Heads appeared and disappeared, most of them crewmen, and Louis spoke to one face after another, asking if anyone would like soup and bread, but no one understood was he was saying until a head floated toward us and spoke, wobbling slightly as if it had been knocked by a wave. It was a young man's head with a scarf wrapped around it and a lick of hair flopping in his eyes. "Over here," he said and before drifting away, took my brother by the arm and steered him to where some tables had been set up.

Years later, when I told Tom about this encounter, he was disappointed that I had seen him and he couldn't recall having seen me—he was disappointed even after I reminded him that in the dense fog he wouldn't have seen anything except the top of my head. Tom wanted to believe that we had met that day on the Barrens and no other; he believed that we were meant for each other, that it was inevitable that we had both gone berry-picking (which until we met he seldom did) on that particular day. I have never thought our meeting was inevitable; I think it was random, a stroke of good luck like Francis plucking me from the ice. Though I don't remember seeing any man except Tom picking berries, I could have met another man on the Barrens, a man I might eventually have married. (If he hadn't died, the man might have been Louis.) I counted myself fortunate that Tom had rescued me from the possibility of marrying a man to whom I wouldn't have been half so suited. How many men along the shore read poetry? How many men liked to spend a night listening to their wives read aloud? How many men would sit up in a lighthouse writing down their thoughts? Precious few. Lucky for me it was Tom who walked out of the mist that day looking like an anteater the way his head was bundled in a scarf, the same plaid scarf he wore the morning the *Kristianiafjord* ran aground.

Whenever I remember that morning I think that, young as I was, I must have recognized something in the face I saw floating in the fog. At the age of seven, what could I have recognized? Passion? Kindness? Intelligence? Nowadays I often see Tom's face floating in fog. Having been separated from him for so many years, this particular memory signifies both assimilation and detachment. Tom is here, there, appearing as an evaporating cloud, rain plinking from the roof, sea water slapping against a rock. It's always something transitory and diffuse.

The Widow Aurora isn't herself. I hate to admit it, but she's ill. What began as an innocuous cold has settled in her chest as pneumonia. Marilyn heard me coughing when I was helping out in the Home's kitchen and insisted on taking me to Dr. McCarthy who prescribed penicillin and told me to stay home, drink fluids and get plenty of rest. To make sure I followed his instructions, Marilyn escorted me to my door. Towering above me—she's close to six feet—she said, "You're not to come back to the Home until this cough has gone. You might infect the residents. We have to be careful." To which I reluctantly agreed.

I've passed the month since rereading *Moby Dick*, *Lord Jim*, *Typhoon*, musty, mouldy books whose covers are spotted from their years in the damp salt air. Confined to the house I've become increasingly out of sorts. When Nancy phoned to ask how I was feeling, I came close to telling her the truth. I almost told her that I felt plaintive and put upon, that all the goodness in me had trickled away. She asked if she and Gerry could bring his youngest daughter to Daniel's Point for Easter dinner. She said that they would do the cooking and I wouldn't have to lift a finger. I took her at her word and except for making a chocolate pie, did very little.

In my view the dinner was not a success. Though the food was delicious, Gerry's daughter claimed not to like any of it and was so bad-tempered that it was a relief when after the washing up, they took her back to St. John's.

On Tuesday morning I was well enough to return to my hairdressing job. I had no sooner stepped inside the Home than Marilyn invited me into her office. I see now that she must have been waiting for me, wanting to get the whole matter over with before I got to work. She may have thought inviting me into her office was considerate, but I didn't think so because I had hardly taken a chair when I was fired. She didn't actually use that word: she said I had been replaced by the young woman who had been doing my job when I was ill. It was nothing personal, but the residents, the women especially (she meant Aggie Halleran) preferred having their hair done by someone who knew how to colour and kept up with the latest styles; it was bound to happen sooner or later. Marilyn said she wanted me to continue helping with the residents, that they had come to depend on my cheerful good nature. Was I cheerful? Did I feel good? I did not. I felt useless and discarded, like a forsaken dory left to rot in the weeds. To make sure she knew I was displeased, I stayed away from the Home for a week.

Knowing I would feel better if I took matters in hand, I made an appointment with a lawyer whose name I found in the telephone book and took myself to St. John's where I signed the deed to my house over to my granddaughter and made out a will. My children didn't want my house: Maggie had left each of them a chunk of the Hunt money, which Stanley used to buy his house and Nancy to pay off her mortgage. After my business was concluded, I walked along Water Street until I came to the Hair Factory. After waiting half an hour, a hairdresser with earrings in his nostrils and a sea serpent tattooed on one arm looked at my flyaway frizzy hair and asked what I wanted done with my "glorious mane."

"Pardon me?"

"A woman's hair is her pride and joy."

As much as I believe in the efficacy of doing hair, even I wouldn't make such a ridiculous claim.

"Cut it short."

When he finished twenty minutes later, my hair had been cut within an inch of a shave, which he said made my head look like a delicate flower balanced on a stalk. "You look years younger."

Perversely, this claim cheered me up. If flattery and lies were what hairdressing had come down do, I wanted no part of it, especially after having to pay twenty dollars to have my hair removed. I left the Hair Factory and went along the street and in a shop hardly bigger than a closet, bought myself a beige-coloured felt hat—already I was feeling the draft. Further along the street, I went into a coffee shop and drank a cappuccino, the first one since Anna's death. I made no effort to telephone Nancy or Stanley, but did exactly as I pleased, and returned to Trepassey feeling like an entirely different woman than the one who had left.

June 6th, Cork

Dear Gran,

I have found your mother's home! Believe me, it wasn't easy because it's taken a while for me to twig to the fact that Mary Roche wasn't born in Cork City but someplace else. Once I came to that conclusion, I began looking in Roche territory outside of town. With no car, I had to rely on friends' cars to drive to churches and graveyards in Castlemanger, Mallow and Castletownroche to look for a record of Mary's birth. I finally found it yesterday listed in the parish record of the Church of Ireland in Doneraile. Mary Roche was born 100 years ago at Annakisha.

Annakisha is a sheep farm owned by a family named O'Keefe. Though Moira O'Keefe has two little kids and another one well on the way, she was kind enough to show me around. The O'Keefes have torn the back off the house and added a large modern kitchen, but the front of the house is unchanged. I think your mother might have been born in the large upstairs bedroom facing a meadow which Moira and her husband use. She says the house is Georgian, built in 1847. It's elegant with high ceilings and marble fireplaces inside and outside an orchard and what used to be a lawn. The Roches were rich, horsy people but now their stable is used as a sheep barn. There was once a glass room off the sitting room but it was torn down by the Rices who owned the house before the O'Keefes. I took photos of the house and grounds and Moira gave me two photos she found when she was cleaning. They had fallen behind the drop piece in a sideboard drawer. After I get them copied I'll send them to Mom by registered mail and she can bring them down. I want you to know, Gran, that finding my great-grandmother's house was important for me. To be honest, I think I did it as much for myself as for you.

I hope you are feeling better. I am painting every day.

Love, Sheila.

Now that the teaching term is over, Nancy spends most weekends on the Southern Shore. As a member of Maggie's heritage board, she's on a mission to reclaim the outport life erased by the decline in the fishery and Confederation, and has already persuaded the curator of the Memorial University Art Gallery to have a show of Merla St. Croix's mats. This summer she's been tracking down what she calls the Bay mats, those Merla hooked when she was living here with her sister Win. Apparently the show is to be organized according to place, and in addition to the Bay mats there will be the Drook mats and the Cape mats, most of which are hanging on my walls. I told Nancy that I remembered seeing the Bay mats inside Win's house, but that after the house was sold, they were scattered along the shore. In St. Vincent's Nancy and I found a mat showing a schooner entering Trepassey Bay that belonged to a woman who had bought it at a yard sale because she wanted something warm to stand on while she washed the dishes. In the school principal's office we found another Bay mat showing Holy Redeemer Church with Tom's corner of the graveyard on the upper left-hand side.

The third weekend in August, Nancy arrived at Daniel's Point carrying a bulky brown package. I was in the fairy garden, sitting with my back to the house, the beige hat on my head (my hair was slow growing back and ever since the pneumonia, when I'm outside I mind the breeze blowing off the bay), watching a rabbit feed beneath the toadstool while I drank my tea. As soon as Nancy appeared the rabbit bolted toward the tuck, where it crouched, watching her hand me the package.

"For you, from Sheila. Any tea left?"

While she went inside I opened the package, and a letter and two envelopes fell into my lap. Inside the bulkier envelope were colour photos of Annakisha. I lined up them up, eight altogether, on the table—a broken lobster trap with a board on top—and examined each in turn. Nancy brought her tea outside, and sitting side by side we looked at the photos, picking them up and handing them back and forth. Annakisha looked much as Sheila described it, a mansion with a stone stable and an orchard nearby. There were pictures of a meadow behind the house where two horses grazed and black-faced sheep faced the camera with defeated ears. Huge trees framed the meadow that even in the photo was an overwhelming green, except in the distance where it became a blurred, misted blue.

I opened the second envelope and took out two pictures the colour of milky tea. The photos were blurry and overexposed, but I could make out a stylish, imperious-looking woman wearing a high-necked dress and earrings that dangled above her collar. One of her hands rested on the shoulder of a young girl with long fair hair caught with a large floppy bow. The girl's head was tipped to one side and she seemed to be squinting against the sun. There were flowers taller than she, hollyhocks I think, growing in the background. I turned the photo over. Written on the back in a delicate sloping hand was *Emmeline and Rose, Annakisha, July, 1916*. The other photo showed the same woman dressed in black and wearing a broad-brimmed hat that shaded her face, making it appear circumspect and closed. She was standing in front of a large Victorian house, one hand on a wrought iron gate, the other on the crook of a parasol. On the back was written in the same delicate hand, *Emmeline, Salisbury, March 1925*.

I read Sheila's letter aloud, just as I read her letters to Tom.

"Dear Gran, thanks to an article in the Mallow Field Club Journal, I have Mary Roche's family figured out. The girl in the photo is Rose, your mother's sister, which makes her your aunt. The woman is Emmeline Ellsworth, your mother's aunt. She and your grandmother, Louise Mayne, were from Salisbury."

"Salisbury!" Nancy yelped. "They were English!"

"Your grandfather, Charles Roche, died when your mother was fourteen. Your grandmother, Louise Roche, remarried soon after to an Englishman, Harold Burke-Davis. Mary had two brothers: Thomas, a military man, and Will, a journalist who emigrated to the United States. So there you have it, Gran, part of your family tree on the Roche side. Now I'll see what I can find out about the O'Connor side."

So much information at once! What was to be made of it? Arrows of excitement were shooting through my chest. "Isn't Sheila amazing?" I said. "Isn't she amazing to have found all this?"

"She is," Nancy said. "She's the one thing Philip and I got right."

I am tunnelling downwards like a clam rediscovering a former trail. Back, back, I burrow until I am on the Barrens, berry-picking in the fog. I hear the sound of berries plinking against the tin bucket; I feel the cold metal against my legs. A bird with scarlet wing bars and a purple breast flies out of the mist and perches on my arm. I reach out to stroke its golden head but the bird flies away. A red fox comes out of the mist but when I hold a crust of bread toward it, it vanishes into the fog. A young woman, with long white hair and wearing a white dress, comes out of the mist. When I reach out, she too disappears. Who is that woman? Have I dug a circle and met myself?

November 2nd, Daniel's Point

Dear Sheila,

It's Christmas gift making time again. Since you've convinced me that you don't want my wedding dress, I've decided to use it to make Christmas fairies. I've cut 50 dresses from the satin and 50 sets of wings from the veil. The reason I've cut so many is because I was again asked to make a raffle item for the League. I'm decorating the dresses and wings with coloured stars and bits of jewellery given to me by residents at the Home, a rhinestone necklace and an evening purse made from tiny silver balls.

I've collected two more of Merla's mats. Now that Nancy is too busy at the university to do any collecting I've been making inquiries whenever I get the chance. I found two of the Bay mats practically under my nose in the pastorate. I'd never gone in there until Father Mahoney told me about the mats when he came to say mass at the Home. One of the mats shows a crowd of people standing beside the Bay, holding their arms toward a foundering ship; the other mat shows a crowd of people rising heavenward from the ship. In exchange for the use of the mats I gave Father Mahoney an old doorknob I've had since I was a maid. I've been trying to find a use of it for years. It being an artefact from the sea, I didn't want to mount it on an ordinary door, and when I saw the messy desk in the pastorate, I knew that it was suited to becoming a paperweight.

Love, Gran

November 27th, Cork

Dear Gran,

Just a quick note as I am in the thick of things here. Mostly I'm writing to tell you how sorry I am that I won't be able to come home for Christmas as I promised. I know you will be disappointed. Sorry that I won't be there to help celebrate your birthday. I will phone of course.

Love, Sheila.

There's to be a birthday party for me in St. John's. Although Nancy claims it will be a small family occasion, I suspect something larger is planned. There were the whispered conversations between my children when they were washing up after Thanksgiving dinner. There was the unexpected gift of a green silk dress and green shoes in November, which Nancy explained away by saying they were a match for my purse. There was Sheila's recent letter apologizing for not being able to spend Christmas in Newfoundland as she had promised, when in fact there had been no promise that she would. There is the way Aggie has been fussing over me all week, tugging my hand whenever I pass, bringing me tea and cookies. This is so unlike her that I know something is brewing.

On the morning of my birthday, I put on the green dress and shoes, brush my teeth, pat my hair then look at myself in the mirror over the bathroom sink. Apart from a quick glance every morning after I clean my teeth, I seldom look in the mirror. What is the point of looking when I'm not there? Since the day I took a long look at myself in the jagged kitchen mirror, I've understood the futility of expecting to see myself in a reflection. I know no more about my appearance now than I did then and have gone all these years hanging clothes on my serviceable body, putting socks and shoes on my wandering feet, without ever knowing what I looked like, and it hasn't made any significant difference to my life.

By noon Nancy and I are driving north at a leisurely pace, stopping at Tors Cove to drink tea from a thermos. When we reach Dick's Square, there are no signs of a party inside her house, not even a tell-tale bakery box on the counter—the cake would have to be bought, Nancy isn't someone who would bake a birthday cake. After carrying my suitcase upstairs, she insists that we drive out to the Gould's: she's forgotten to pick up seal flipper pie, she has to stop at the drugstore and the bank, and wouldn't you know it, there's bread to pick up from Mary Jane's. These errands explain the absence of party signs inside her house: we are stalling so that preparations can go on supposedly without my knowledge.

By six o'clock we're back in Dick's Square. Nancy parks the car and steers me toward the Star of the Sea Hall. So that's where the party is! How clever to have it across the street. Probably Nancy has a party dress stashed away over here. I allow myself to be led up the crumbling front steps, through one doorway and another until I'm nudged into a room decorated with streamers and balloons, beneath which a crowd of family and friends are gathered. "Happy birthday, Aurora!" they shout, people I haven't seen in years: Johnny and Beatty from Brigus and five of their grandchildren; Ben and Bridgit's sons and wives from the Cove; Ruth's daughter Cheryl, her husband and three children who have driven all the way from Corner Brook; Gary and Brenda St. Croix; Cyril and Captain Coady in his wheelchair, Marilyn, Jim, Aggie, Nina, even Billy Dodge who once worked at the Cape. Dr. McCarthy and Father Mahoney and Kate. Another surprise is Philip Palmer, who has brought his wife of two weeks. Philip has never mentioned this slender blond woman wearing dark glasses, but as I later told Tom, I hadn't seen Philip in months. One of the musicians on the small stage strikes up a drum roll and who should walk through a side door but Sheila with her black hair and black leggings. Who is the young man behind her? Why, Kevin! Now that is a surprise!

Gerry has cooked up a scoff: chowder, cod tongues, flipper pie, salmon and boiled potatoes, partridgeberry pie, but I'm too excited to eat. After the meal, the floor is cleared for a dance. I waltz with Stanley and Gerry, and Kevin, a tall, bony man with freckles and red hair. Not a handsome man, but then neither was Tom. Like Tom he has a quiet manner and an easy laugh. A self-effacing man, not at all what I had been expecting, which was a vain, brooding actor.

"You like him, don't you, Gran?" The party is over and Sheila and I are alone upstairs in Nancy's house. I'm already in bed and she's sitting at the end, knees drawn up to her chin. I assure her that from what I've seen, he seems a lovely man.

"We get on well together. That's why we won't marry. No offence, Gran, but we don't want to risk spoiling what we have."

"No offence. My views are more modern than you might think." Then I change the subject because there's something more important on my mind. "Tell me, do you miss Newfoundland enough to live here again?"

"Of course I miss it, that's why I paint it. I would live here, at least part of the year if I could afford it, but as you know Kevin and I don't have the money to give us that choice."

"You have a choice." Does God feel like this? "Fetch me my purse, will you? It's on the chair." The green leather purse had once been Anna's.

I open the purse and take out the deed.

"I had planned to give you this for Christmas but I've changed my mind."

Sheila lowers her chin and looks at me. From the time she was a youngster, she's had a way of looking through her lashes that makes her seem languid and at the same time canny.

"You knew I was coming."

"Oh, no." Why spoil a surprise?

"What's this?" She unfolds the deed. "I don't believe what I'm reading. Am I understanding this? Are you giving me your house?"

"That way you'll come back to Newfoundland."

"You are actually giving me your house."

"It appears so."

Sheila leaps off the bed, spreads her arms and whirls around the room, flapping the deed in the air. "Whooee! Thank you, Gran!"

"You're welcome, I'm sure."

"You're a sly one."

I tell her about the will, that I've set aside enough money to pay taxes on the house for ten years, and she goes downstairs to show Kevin the deed, leaving me mercifully, blissfully alone. Most of the birthday guests left hours ago and the remainder moved the party across the street to the room below my bed. I lie in the dark listening to the sounds float through the cracks of the old house. Someone, probably Gerry, is playing the spoons. I've no wish to join the crowd and am perfectly content lying here by myself. After a while I'm aware that the spoon playing has stopped and the party has launched into the "Kelligrews Soiree," a song we often sing at the Home though not with the same gusto as they are singing below. The light outside the Star of the Sea is still on which means the diehard card sharks and dart players are lingering inside. The light spills through the curtains and onto the quilt with an intimacy that brings to mind another light shining on another bed. This is a memory so distant, so elusive that it seems impossible to retrieve. I close my eyes and then open them again, and whether it's from excitement or fatigue, my eyelids continue to flutter as I drift between islands, between the latitudes of darkness and light until finally, I cross the meridian of sleep.

ISLANDS

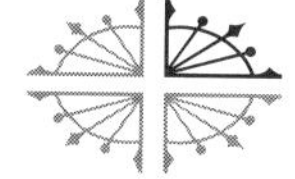

1990

If time allowed, when Stan drove down the shore he would sometimes drop by Daniel's Point to see his mother, but if Kate was spooked he always went straight to the Cape. Weeks would go by without Kate sounding the alarm, until the afternoon when she would telephone him at work, her voice low from the effort of trying to keep it steady: two boys yelling obscenities had been circling the house on RVs, and though she didn't want to risk the dog being hurt, she'd decided to put him outside to scare the intruders off, when abruptly they'd left. But they'd be back, she knew that because when they were here two weeks ago, they went off for a while only to return.

Or there was a weird-looking man with a gun who kept hanging around the receiving towers and was taking pot-shots at the fence; so far he'd missed but he was still here, and what if he came to the house and tried to get in? With a gun he could shoot out a window or maybe even shoot the dog. She didn't want to call the Mounties because if word got around that she was living out here alone, there might be trouble. In any case, Stan would get here before the police, who in her experience always arrived after the harm had been done.

After one of these calls, Stan would leave work early but by the time he arrived at the Cape, there would be no sign of the boys on the RVs or the man with the gun—whoever it was this time—and Kate would have supper waiting: Kraft dinner or wieners and beans heated in the microwave; she wasn't much of a cook. After they finished eating, they sat at the kitchen table drinking instant coffee and discussing work. She didn't want to talk about "the problem": all she wanted was for Stan to stay with her until she calmed down. When it was time to go to bed they went into separate rooms and Kate locked her door. She did the same thing during the week she worked out of the St. John's office and slept at his place in Tors Cove. She wouldn't sleep in town.

Three years ago when Kate was sharing a house in the city on Cochrane Street with four others, a stranger wandered in from the street, opened her bedroom door on the ground floor and stabbed her four times in the abdomen and groin with a geologist's pick before the student in the next bedroom pulled him off. In the confusion of looking after Kate, telephoning the ambulance and the police, no one prevented the attacker from slipping away. He was never caught. Kate didn't know who or where he was. Though the police called it a random attack and thought the man had probably left the island, she was terrified of meeting him, and there were days when she thought she should clear out of Newfoundland and head for New Zealand or the Faroes, find a job on a sheep farm, make a new life for herself somewhere else. Most days she dug in her heels; after nine years of university and two degrees, why should she be prevented from doing the work she liked? All of this had been related to Stan with astounding matter-of-factness shortly after she met him.

He installed deadbolts both at the Cape and Tors Cove and bought a German shepherd pup. He'd been intending to get himself another dog since Fram died, the year after he returned from the South Pole, of cancer, mostly likely caused by nuclear contamination—during the 1960s there had been a meltdown at the nuclear station at Scott Base—but the pup wasn't his; the whole point of buying him was to give him to Kate. Apart from the gift of the dog, all he could do was respond to her terrified calls, and wait. He was waiting for a word, a gesture, a look, a signal that it would be all right if he took her in his arms. That was what he wanted to do, take her in his arms and kiss the wounds. She was the first woman since Anna with whom he could imagine making a life. Sometimes when they were walking over the Barrens or throwing a stick to the dog or simply doing the dishes, she would take Stan's hand, but she would never hold it for long, and if he put an arm around her she ducked away.

At least he had work to keep him occupied. Nowadays he spent most of his time computer-modelling ice scour; using data collected from ancient Lake Agassiz and the Scarborough Bluffs, the Labrador Shelf and King William Island, he examined probabilities and made projections. Fortunately, computers made it possible to track a scouring iceberg from a safe distance. Stan had never boarded an iceberg in the process of scouring as it dragged itself over the seabed, grinding its way through sediment, sand and wreckage, gouging a trail across the sea bottom, its idiosyncratic bulk tacking erratically, driven by the forces of currents and wind. As the leader of the ice engineering group, he spent most of his time within the ERI's labyrinthine halls. He'd opted not to go the South Pole in January for ice-towing experiments, an opportunity he wouldn't have passed up ten years ago. He will never return to the Antarctic. Now when he remembers Scott Base, he thinks of it as a martyr's grave and has no desire to return to the place where he came close to doing himself in. But he did fly over Baffin Island and along the Labrador coast in May, looking for a low berg roughly one hundred metres long at the waterline and triangular in shape. This was after a publicist telephoned from

France to say that he was looking for an iceberg that could be carved into the shape of a whale. On the back of the whale ice sculptors would carve an elephant, a rhino, a tiger and a gorilla, afterwards towing it around until it melted as a demonstration of the gradual disappearance of endangered species. At first Stan thought the publicist was pulling his leg, and told him he should look for a berg in Witless Bay, but the man was serious and assured him that DBL Enterprises was prepared to pay ERI for its help. They would also provide experienced glaciologists and alpinists. Stan took the job. You never knew, some interesting fieldwork might come out of it, ice drilling, explosives, that kind of thing. He was also considering Yosh Akira's invitation to join next year's scientific expedition to the *Titanic* site that a team of Russian and Canadian scientists were putting together with an IMAX film crew. According to Yosh, a marine biologist Stan had met when he worked in Halifax, though Ballard had discovered the *Titanic* five years ago, there had never been a concerted attempt to undertake scientific examination of the wreck until now. There had been endless discussions about who had been responsible for the disaster and why the ship had gone down, but no one seemed interested in the fact that the ship had been hit by a relatively small iceberg—200,000 tons—or in how the wreckage affected the seabed. Yosh said he needed an expert like Stan on the team to investigate ship scour. Though Stan knew the investigation would require him to dive, and he hadn't been in the water since Anna's death, he was unwilling to pass up an opportunity to examine the wreck and told Yosh to keep him in mind.

The first Sunday afternoon in August, Stan drove to Trepassey and brought his mother to St. John's for the opening of the exhibition of Merla's mats. He and his mother arrived at the Memorial Art Gallery just as Newfoundland's premier finished opening the exhibit and was leaving the microphone. Nancy had invited the premier and several other dignitaries, including the lieutenant-governor, in order to be assured of a crowd. There were about a hundred people in the room.

Kate, who was working in St. John's that week, had been posted to watch outside the gallery door. "Your sister's been looking all over for you. Your mother is supposed to be up front."

Nancy caught sight of them from the podium but it was too late to signal their mother to join her, which was just as well. If she'd been told ahead of time that she would be part of the ceremony, Aurora might have refused to come. The curator, a tall man with a domed head and walrus moustache, came to the microphone.

"Ladies and gentlemen, I must clarify something at once. Despite the premier's generous remarks, I cannot take credit for this unique exhibition. Apart from offering advice on the organization of these wonderful mats from the Southern Shore, I did nothing. All praise must go to Dr. Nancy Palmer who, with the assistance of her mother, Mrs. Aurora Mulloy of Trepassey, assembled this exhibit. I merely provided the space."

Stan saw his mother duck her head; she had been caught unawares. Nancy took the microphone and began talking about the tradition of women's handwork in rural Newfoundland and Labrador. Knitting, sewing, quilting, crocheting, hooking, work that had originally been done out of necessity to provide warmth and comfort. The decorative aspect of the work had been secondary. During the last century, however, decoration had become a primary incentive as artisans sought to express their culture through various motifs.

When the lecture was over, a youngster wearing a blue dress and patent leather shoes appeared, carrying two bouquets, one for Nancy and the other for Aurora. When his mother was at the front receiving hers, Stan watched her talk to the little girl, then shake hands with the curator, the premier and the lieutenant-governor, smiling and nodding as if she was used to such occasions.

"Your mother's charming," Kate said. "But of course you already know that."

Aurora didn't stay long at the front and soon was beside Stan and Kate asking to be taken to ERI. "Nancy's being interviewed by the CBC, she won't mind if we leave."

His mother always found something to interest her at the Institute: pictures of icebergs, drilling platforms at sea, satellite photos of the Poles. She said she liked to keep up with Stan and Kate's work, to know what was going on in the natural world. She also liked returning to Trepassey with a bundle of facts for Cyril Gibbons, who was hard to impress.

Before leaving the gallery Stan told his sister where they were going and asked if she wanted to meet them there later, although he knew she'd decline. The fact was she wasn't interested in ERI and the only time she'd been there was after he'd shamed her into going. Nancy didn't share their mother's fascination with the sea and ice, which she called a contradiction, saying that she didn't understand how someone who wouldn't fly across the North Atlantic to visit her granddaughter could be captivated by it. Stan understood. He, too, was a captive and though he spent most of his waking hours studying the sea and ice, he hadn't set foot in or on either one for seven years.

As they were leaving the art gallery, his mother said. "As soon as we get to the Institute, these flowers should go in water. Tomorrow when I go home, I'll put them on Merla's grave."

It was Nancy, not Stan, who drove their mother home, intending to stay in Daniel's Point for the next few days because a week from now she would begin a four-month sabbatical in Cork. Knowing how much her mother enjoyed outings along the shore, Nancy took her to St. Peter's and St. Mary's and drove her over the Cape road as far as the Drook where they ate their lunch at a picnic table that had been washed across the road in a spring storm. They had another picnic at St. Shott's, sitting on the cliff top looking down on the sea, and another in Biscay Bay where, after watching youngsters playing with a dog on the beach, her mother said, "Sometimes when Stanley and Kate visit, she brings along her dog. She calls him Smudge." She laughed. "His fur does look like charcoal and chalk rubbed together. I had a grand time with that dog."

Without warning—she never saw this coming—Nancy jammed her fists against her mouth to stem a flow of tears. She used to do this as a girl whenever she was ambushed by feelings she didn't, and perhaps never would, understand. She turned and saw her mother's puzzled face. "It's nothing. I get emotional sometimes. It will pass."

What had brought this on? Her mother's wistfulness about the dog, or the thought that her mother would miss her when she was away? There was so much about her mysterious mother that Nancy would never know, that no one would ever know.

There had been a lot about Philip she had never known either, but he was far from mysterious. Unlike her mother, he didn't inhabit a strange terrain, and in her view turned out to be a rather predictable man. The most surprising thing about him was that he had married a blind woman, Selma, on whom he apparently waited hand and foot: shopping, making the meals, serving her breakfast in bed. It was hard to imagine him in the kitchen, a dish towel tucked into his belt, or carrying the tea tray upstairs. Though she had seen no sign of such a need during their marriage, Nancy thought that Philip had reached a point in his life where he needed someone to look after, someone less prickly and impatient than herself, someone less independent and ambitious, someone who would rely on him completely.

Not Gerry, who said that after years of being trapped in a suffocating marriage he wanted an independent woman. Nancy had no reason not the believe him. Gerry was a straightforward, plain-speaking man who was easy to know; there were no hidden agendas, which made her trust him in a way she had never trusted Philip. Sometimes she thought she might know Gerry too well. He certainly knew her well, knew when for no obvious reason she was seized by one of her fits of restless, unspecified anger and he had the sense to leave her alone.

After they'd returned to Daniel's Point, Nancy and Aurora sat in the car for a few minutes before saying goodbye. Nancy's bag was already in the back seat; she was eager to get back to St. John's and begin dinner; Gerry was coming over at six and it was her turn to cook. Her mother opened the door partway, then turned sideways and reached for her hand. "You enjoy yourself in Ireland," she said. "Don't trouble your head about me. I'll be fine."

Sheila saw her mother clear the baggage area of the airport before Nancy saw her. She was carrying a laptop computer in one hand and a small box in the other. She kissed Sheila on the cheek and handed her the box. "Your father wanted me to give you this."

"What is it?"

Nancy shrugged. "I don't know, but he wanted me to carry it on so it must be breakable." She looked around. "Is Kevin here?"

"He's parking the car."

While they were waiting, Sheila opened the box—she had never been able to delay opening a gift. Inside the box was a pottery bowl filled with dried flowers: pearly everlasting, purple asters and marigolds mixed with evergreen. She read the card tucked between the flowers. *Selma made this for you. Hope you like it. Love, Dad.* Speaking carefully, Sheila said, "I'm impressed that a blind woman could have made this." To which her mother replied, just as carefully, that the blind were said to have an exceptional sense of touch and smell.

When they reached the house on Lower Janemount, the flower arrangement was placed in the unheated dining room, which was seldom used because meals were taken in the kitchen. On the kitchen table was a pitcher of late blooming roses—in spite of the neglect, flowers still bloomed in what had been Kevin's mother's garden, pushing themselves up between the long grass and ivy that had taken over the iron fretwork beside the door.

Kevin's mother had left him the house and a modest annuity. She must have known better than anyone that her son had no interest in making money beyond what was required to keep a roof over his head. It had never been his idea—as Nancy had once thought—that Sheila take in paying students. Nine years ago when Nancy's first sabbatical in Cork was winding down and she was making plans to return to St. John's, Sheila decided that if she was to stay behind with Kevin, she would have to pay her own way, not because Kevin cared one way or the other but because she did. Since his house was close to the university, taking in student boarders was an obvious way for her to earn money. It was an easy job and had the advantage of being seasonal, allowing her the summer to paint.

Nancy's attic bedroom was the quietest and warmest room in the house. For her mother's last visit three years ago with Gerry, Sheila had bought a new double bed, and for this visit had added a table she found in a second-hand shop behind Coal Quay. It was pitted and warped, but sturdy enough to serve as a desk. She placed the table in front of the dormer window that had a view of the university and the trees following the Lee, St. Finbar's soaring above it all.

Sheila's first drawing class at the Crawford began the next morning, and by late afternoon of the same day her boarders had arrived: one new one from Macroom, the rest returning for a second year. Two days later Nancy began teaching a course at the university on Irish settlement in Newfoundland, as well as a seminar on Irish customs in Newfoundland. Most of these customs were in one way or another connected with the church: St. Bridgit's and St. Stephen's Days, St. Patrick's and Sheila's Days, Colcannon or All Souls' Night, when the souls of the dead flew about. This was the same night when the fairies were said to be on the lookout for someone who could be lured away and a changeling put in her place. Nancy didn't spend seminar time on fairies, mainly because she didn't want Newfoundland to be seen as an imitation of the tourist view of Ireland. Tourist fairies were linked with leprechauns and pots of gold, whereas Newfoundland fairies had a context uniquely their own. Moreover she was too much of a scholar to deny that Newfoundland was as much English as it was Irish. How infatuated with England she had once been! Her brother claimed that after four years of living in England she had returned to Newfoundland with a mid-Atlantic accent. She wasn't the only Newfoundlander, or for that matter Canadian, to regard England as a high-class finishing school, the place where one hoped to have one's rough edges sanded down and acquire a polish that would command respect, even envy, amongst one's colleagues.

After she had settled into a routine, Nancy telephoned her mother every Sunday, using the kitchen phone on Lower Janemount. After inquiring about her health and whether Stan had been down to see her, she gave the phone to Sheila, who chatted to her grandmother, usually about Ocean View. It amused Sheila that at eighty years of age her grandmother still helped out at the Home. Her Gran said that most of the residents in the Home craved attention, that much of her job—she still referred to it as a job—was little more than pampering. This Friday past she had helped with the baths because the Home had a new gurney for moving a resident from a wheelchair into the tub. Captain Coady, who was the first to try it, was so terrified of the thing that she'd had to hold his hand and remind him it was probably like sitting in a bosun's chair. Once he'd been lowered into the water the Captain sent her away, because he didn't want her to see what was "down below." She'd had a good laugh about that. Sheila was shaking her head when she put down the phone. "Gran hasn't lost her sense of humour," she said and went back to peeling potatoes. She was making potato scallop for supper.

It had been raining all morning. Through the window Nancy watched water dripping from the eaves. The house was so quiet she could hear the grandfather clock ticking in the hall. Kevin had already left for Galway—his play, *One Eye Open*, was in production—and except for Adair, the new student from Macroom who was asleep upstairs, Sheila's boarders were out.

"Do you know what baffles me about Mom?" Nancy said. When she was idle, she was inclined to brood over the inexplicable.

"I haven't the faintest idea."

"That she seems to be entirely without ambition. For such an intelligent, talented woman she could have made so much more of herself. Instead she's been content to stay down there on the shore, drifting along from one day to the next, waiting to see what will turn up. Living that way would drive me crazy."

Sheila suspected her mother's remarks were as much about herself and Kevin as they were about her grandmother. She jabbed the knife deep before launching a reply.

"All of us aren't driven by ambition the way you are. Some of us are satisfied with what we have. I think Gran has been wise to allow life to unfold in its own good time rather than try to live in a way other people think she should. I wouldn't want to end up at her age regretting the way I've lived, thinking that I'd spent my life pursuing the wrong things."

"Do you think I've spent my life pursuing the wrong things?"

Sheila ducked the question.

It was a question Nancy sometimes asked herself. By pursuing independence, a profession she enjoyed, the respect of colleagues, how much had she missed? She knew she had missed out on the spontaneous gifts of joy and wonder that were the early casualties of structured time. She had never, for instance, held up a jar of clear apple jelly to the window light, something she'd often seen her mother do; or come upon an amphitheatre of stone when she set out on a walk with no particular destination in mind; or sat on top of Drook Hill watching the recession of sunlight from the water. Nancy thought there might be time for idle reflection when she grew old, if she felt the need. For the present she had everything she needed. She was content with her life, but how long would the contentment last?

"Don't you ever wonder why Mom never once tried to find out if she had been on the *Titanic?*"

"Gran wrote to me about that," Sheila said. "She said she was happy with her life and didn't want to go chasing another."

"You would think at the very least that she would have written Patrick O'Connor. I was there when he came to the Cape. I remember him saying he had a summer job at Woods Hole. It wouldn't have been hard for Mom to track him down."

Although her Gran had admitted as much, Sheila was irritated to hear it coming from someone who until recently had refused to believe that her mother had been on the *Titanic*. Turning around and straightening her arm, she leaned against the sink, the grey light from the window making her look the way she felt, grumpy and tired. She looked at her mother.

"For me the question is why *you* haven't lifted a finger. As you said, *you* were there the day Patrick O'Connor visited the Cape. Why don't you write to him yourself?"

This wasn't the placid easygoing daughter Nancy knew. This was a daughter who reminded her of Philip on a rainy day in the rectory kitchen, telling his young wife that she would have to shape up.

"You have all the research skills from your work," Sheila continued. "Why aren't you using them to find out more about Owen O'Connor? God knows I've reached a dead end."

Exactly. Why wasn't she? Why wasn't she making the effort to find the man who had been her grandfather? Wasn't she the one studying and lecturing about connections between Ireland and Newfoundland? She told Sheila that she didn't have time, what with assignments to mark, books to read, lectures to plan, interviews and a paper to write. She intended to have the paper done before Christmas. Nancy heard the whine in her voice and abruptly, she stopped.

By the end of the week she'd phoned every O'Connor in Cork City without success. It seemed that like Mary, Owen had been born somewhere else. She consulted priests in four Catholic churches and was told more or less the same thing, that there had once been O'Connors near Mallow and Kanturk, but since the Troubles they had been scattered all over the world. One priest chided her, saying she should know that Irish Catholic families were raised for export. Undaunted, she placed an ad in the *Cork Examiner* and posted a notice outside the registrar's office at the university inquiring if anyone had information about an Owen O'Connor.

The third week in November, shortly after the winter timetables went up, Sheila called Nancy to the phone. A young student named Carmelita Coombs asked if she was the Nancy Palmer who was inquiring about Owen O'Connor. Carmelita said that she wasn't an O'Connor, but that her Aunt Ellie was and that if Miss Palmer wanted to speak to her, she would put her on the line. The telephone was handed over.

"I understand you are inquiring about Owen O'Connor." An elderly, cautious voice.

"Yes. My grandfather was thought to be Owen O'Connor."

The woman was amused. "Thought to be!"

"Yes."

"My uncle was Owen O'Connor, but of course he may not be the Owen O'Connor you are looking for."

"Was he married to Mary Roche?"

"I believe that was the name." The voice wavered, but not for long. "I recall my father saying that his brother's first wife was a Protestant girl who had gone down with the *Titanic*."

There it was.

It was ten o'clock on Friday night. Nancy asked Carmelita's aunt if they could meet at nine the next morning and Ellie Coombs gave her address: number 9 Summer Hill, next door to the Empress Manor, first-floor flat. She would ask Carmelita to leave the front door open when she went out.

Early next morning, beneath a sky that had the rinsed look of after rain, Nancy and Sheila left the house and walked down Sunday's Well Road and onto North Mall, the traffic carrying them along. Summer Hill Road bore the remnants of Victorian grandeur; crumbling walls and cornices, weedy terraces, the words QUEEN and EMPRESS stencilled on mouldy boards.

Ellie Coombs must have heard them come in the front entryway because she was waiting in the doorway of her flat, whose wainscoting, Nancy could see, was painted an ugly turd brown. A bony woman with fissured lips and glaucous eyes, Ellie was in a wheelchair, her arthritic hands gripping its arms. "Come in, ladies. Come in." With a flourish, she wheeled the chair inside the parlour and motioned toward the settee in front of the window. Like everything in the room, the red embossed wallpaper and drapes, the satin lampshades and Persian carpets, the velvet settee had seen better days. After they were seated, Ellie cupped her hands in her lap as if she was holding fragile shells, and said, "Now tell me about yourselves."

Nancy sat back while Sheila explained. There was a notebook and a tape recorder inside Nancy's shoulder bag, but she was reluctant to take them out: some interviewees didn't like being taped; even the presence of a notebook was enough to put them off. When Sheila asked Ellie about her family, she said she had been born in Macroom but had moved to Cork fifty years ago, after marrying Clifford Coombs, who worked on the railway. He had been dead eleven years, emphysema, God rest his soul. Ellie's parents, Susan Kielly and Eamon O'Connor, had been bakers in Macroom, and after they met started a bakery of their own, O'Connor's, which was there yet, run by Ellie's younger sister, Molly, who at seventy years of age still got up at three in the morning to start the bread.

"Owen was your father's brother?"

"His twin, though you'd hardly credit it, they saw so little of one another."

"Owen married Mary Roche."

"As I recall that was her name. There was a child, a girl, I believe."

"My mother."

"You're joshing me. Mary Roche and her baby went down with the *Titanic*. My father took them out to Cobh, Queenstown, as it was called in those days, himself. I remember him telling me that when I was a girl. He was sweet on Mary, I think."

Sheila told Ellie about Francis St. Croix rescuing Aurora from an ice pan and bringing her to the Drook.

"Holy Mother of God!" Ellie crossed herself. She nodded toward the walnut sideboard between the windows. "Fetch the Tullamore Dew."

Nancy went to the cabinet and took out the bottle.

"Three glasses," Ellie said.

Nancy put the glasses on the table beside a pair of china swans.

"I'm not supposed to drink, but I think even the doctor would agree that the occasion demands it. No water in mine."

They lifted their glasses and drank to Mary Roche and Owen O'Connor.

"You said your father took Mary and my mother to Queenstown," Nancy said. "Where was my grandfather?"

"In England. Owen never got on the *Titanic*."

Nancy swallowed a mouthful of whisky.

"Do you know why?"

"I couldn't say. He lived in England for some years. I remember my father speaking to him on the telephone after my grandmother—that's Annie O'Connor—died. Let me see. That would have been in 1922. Yes, she died four years after the Great War, and a year or so later Owen emigrated to America and worked in the building trade. Lived in Brooklyn. Married an Irish girl over there and had four sons."

"One of them was Patrick."

"How do you know that?"

"He came to Newfoundland when I was a girl. My mother was away at the time. He said he was looking for a woman who had been brought ashore as a baby after the *Titanic* went down. I remember Patrick saying that his father had seen an ad in an old newspaper about a baby being rescued."

"Patrick never told me that." Ellie wiped a dribble of whisky from her chin. "What did your father tell him?"

"That he couldn't help. He was mad at my mother for going off without telling him where she was."

"Glory be."

"I remember Patrick was handsome with dark curly hair."

"He favoured his mother. I have a picture of him somewhere in the house. It was taken when he came to see me, let me see, it must have been twenty-five years ago. He was the only one of Owen's sons who did. We still exchange Christmas cards."

"When she comes home, I'll ask Carmelita to have a look. I'll also dig out his address, which is probably upstairs in the linen closet with the Christmas cards. Drop by tomorrow and I'll have it ready for you. How's that?"

"Fine." Nancy lifted her glass. "Cheers."

That evening, Nancy was making tea in the kitchen on Lower Janemount when Adair came in and poured himself a glass of milk. Nancy asked him if he knew the O'Connor bakery in Macroom. Of course he did. He'd been there dozens of times buying bread. Everyone knew that O'Connor's made the best soda bread in the county.

On Sunday morning before Kevin awoke, Sheila went to her studio and began sketching in front of the window. She always made preliminary drawings before she began painting. Though she was a landscape painter, she never drew anything she saw outside the window. She drew the landscape of the imagination, what was taking shape inside her head, transforming what the inner eye saw, like watching clouds outside an airplane window drift over the sea, making reefs and kelp beds from shadow. Sheila drew the Cape—these days her imagined landscapes were invariably in Newfoundland. She drew the rocky cliffs, the lighthouse, the sea, the road running through the Barrens toward the light. A gowned woman floated from the lighthouse toward a man who was coming toward her. The woman was both angel and ghost, and like the man's, her feet barely touched the ground. When the sketch was finished, she painted the image quickly in blue and green, a few strokes of red, leaving the figures to paint in later. If she liked it, the painting would become part of a Newfoundland cycle she was painting about her grandmother. Sheila closed the studio door behind her, tiptoed downstairs and crawled into bed beside Kevin.

They were still in bed when Nancy got up. She made herself toast and tea and, as planned, returned to Summer Hill with her camera and a photo of Aurora, which she gave to Ellie, who claimed that it showed a remarkable likeness to her father, Eamon. Carmelita had found the photo, which showed Patrick as a young man not much older than the visitor Nancy had met at the Cape.

"You keep it for your mother," Ellie said. "Carmelita has written Patrick's address on the back."

By the time Nancy returned to the house on Lower Janemount, Sheila and Kevin had gone off somewhere. It was just as well. Kevin was away so much that when he was home Nancy tried to leave him and Sheila to themselves, partly out of consideration and partly because, being devoted to one another, they spoke in a way that made her feel excluded. In the Cape days Nancy had thought her parents' devotion to one another excluded her—which it sometimes did. She'd thought her mother wanted all of her father's attention for herself and for that reason had kept Nancy at arm's length. She'd also thought her mother had favoured Stan, that he'd got all the attention, that she might have let go of his carriage for that very reason. Nancy knew there wasn't much truth in any of this, that in fact she had demanded more attention than Stan, that very likely she had been one of those children who was greedy for attention, who could never get enough.

After a solitary meal of soup and crackers, she telephoned her mother, but she was out, either at the Home or off on one of her rambles—she still walked miles every week. She would try her again later on, after she returned from Cobh. She put on her raincoat and went outside into the swampy November air, walking downhill and along the river to Glanmire Road, where she caught the three o'clock train. When she arrived in Cobh she lingered for a time in the railway station to look at an exhibition of the diaspora: videos and soundtracks of storm-ridden coffin ships on their way to America and Australia, and a diorama of emigrants being waked before departure—a reminder that for those left behind a ship's disappearance over the horizon was a kind of death. There were photos of the *Titanic* and of the *Lusitania*, which had been torpedoed off Kintale during the Great War. Beyond the train station Nancy looked for the dock where her grandmother and her mother must have boarded the tender that took them out to the *Titanic*, but she found only rotting planks stained with algae and a light standard with the ubiquitous gull on top.

Before returning to Newfoundland she drove to Annakisha and walked around the outside of the house and into the meadow, as Sheila had done. She didn't stay long, not wanting the O'Keefes to return and find her poking around when no one was at home. She also returned to Summer Hill twice more, and on Christmas Eve when she, Sheila and Kevin went to visit Ellie bringing cake and wine, became tipsy and maudlin about leaving Ellie, of whom she had become fond. "You'll come back," Ellie said blithely. "Though I might not be here."

It wasn't until she was on her way back to Newfoundland, flying over the North Atlantic with her head cushioned against the seat, her mind in a drowse between waking and sleep, that Nancy recalled the opening of an installation show she had attended with Sheila in Cork one night before Christmas. The show had been entitled *Walking*. On the gallery floor there had been dozens of paired shoes: shoes made of leather, fabric, paper, straw, leaves, wood, all of them in different stages of disintegration, as if they had been walking for centuries through fields and meadows, forests and swamps, paths and lanes, streets and roads, walking over hills and by the sea. Sheila said she thought the shoes were meant to show ancestral continuity.

Until her daughter made this observation, Nancy hadn't understood what was happening to her in Ireland. It hadn't occurred to her that quite apart from visiting Ellie Coombs, while she had been walking around Cork, going to her office, to the library and shops, that she had been walking where her grandmother had walked (and what had she worn on her feet?), that their footsteps must have crossed and recrossed any number of times: beside the river, on the quays, in the park, in Cobh and at Annakisha. This might have been nothing more than a shifting of air and space, a rearrangement of moisture and dust on pavement and stone, an invisible exchange of atoms and molecules. Most people would think so. Most people, Nancy was sure, lived satisfactory lives without wanting to wear their forebears' shoes. Until Sheila had started her down the ancestral trail, Nancy herself hadn't been interested in following Mary Roche's footsteps, but now that she was she couldn't stop thinking about what she had missed. She regretted not knowing her grandmother's family, not knowing who and where they were. During the years she had lived in Salisbury, she might have brushed against her grandmother's family, she might have pushed Sheila's pram past Emmeline Ellsworth's house, she might have handed Emmeline one of Mr. Peake's prescriptions or taken the same book out of the library as her great-aunt Rose. She might have crossed their paths any number of times, but in the end it came down to little more than speculation and guesswork, because without recognition, without any knowledge of who the other was, she and her grandmother's family would remain as they always had been—invisible to one another.

THE GOOD SHIP ANNIE ROSE

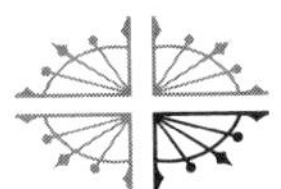

1991

For some reason—it may be the weather—I seem to be dreaming the winter away. It has been so windy and cold and my house so drafty that some mornings when I get up and see the exquisite frost crystals painted on my windows like the breath of stars, I go back to bed for a nap, idling between wakefulness and sleep. Increasingly I dream about being at sea. This morning I am in a boat of some kind, being held against a woman's shoulder while an immense black wall rolls toward me and I am powerless to move. I know I am dreaming memory, not fiction. Sometimes I catch a whiff of soap, sometimes I smell the woman's milky breath, sometimes I hear her voice. "There, little one, there," but I refuse to be consoled. When I dream like this I know I'm searching my memory, tinkering with the lock until I've released smells and sounds, fluctuations of cold and warmth, images that blink and fade before folding themselves away, never to be retrieved again in exactly the same way.

⸻

While his mother dreams, Stan is on top of Signal Hill looking out to sea, having driven here straight from the airport—he often comes up here when he wants to think something through. It's one of those rare winter days when there is nothing on the water—even at this slow time in the shipping year, there is usually some kind of vessel leaving or entering the Narrows: the *Oceanex*, the *Terra Nova*, the *Northern Princess*, but today there is nothing but an empty sea and an empty sky. It's as if the arctic wind has blown everything away except the automated light flashing across the water from the lighthouse at Cape Spear. Pulling his anorak hood over his head, Stan gets out of the car and is immediately punched in the face by the wind, but it's just what he needs to clear his head. He walks along the wall, past the place where Marconi received his transatlantic message from Poldhu in Cornwall, past the arrow reminding tourists how close they are to Dublin, London and New York; past the old powder magazine, walking uphill until he is standing in front of Cabot Tower, where the wind is strongest.

He's just returned from spending a weekend in Halifax discussing the Russian expedition to the *Titanic* with his friend Yosh Akira. It's been nearly a year since Stan told Yosh to count him in on the expedition, but beyond submitting a written proposal he's given it little thought—he's used to submitting proposals for projects that for financial or political reasons never go anywhere—and has avoided thinking about whether or not he'll be able to dive, though he's well aware that there's no point in his joining the expedition if he isn't prepared to dive. Well, now that the expedition is going ahead he's up against it and has to decide whether he's going to back out now, in order to give Yosh time to find a replacement, or follow through. During the weekend's discussions he gave no inkling of his ambivalence and talked about collecting data from the seabed around the ship and how it could be used to model calculations of ice scour. Yosh said that it was crucial that sample cores be taken from the area surrounding the wreck and was assuming, of course, that Stan would be inside the submersible when this was done.

Stan has no confidence that he'll be able to get himself into a sub and go two and a half miles below the surface of the sea. His doubt has nothing to do with the recent disclosure that his mother was on the *Titanic*, that his grandmother perished while his mother was saved, probably by ice, which had saved shipwrecked survivors before her from the waters of the North Atlantic. His doubt has to do with Anna. Though he wouldn't be required to dive in a wetsuit, Stan isn't sure that even inside a sub he wouldn't panic, wouldn't see her below, drifting past the eye of the sub—he still has nightmares of being below, her life bleeding away while he struggles to shorten the distance between them; he knows that panic could put himself and the other scientists inside the sub at risk.

In her quiet way, Kate has been encouraging him to go on the expedition, reading a draft of his proposal, finding copies of relevant papers and books for him to read. Before he went to Halifax she bought him an underwater camera, which at the time he interpreted as nothing more than a gesture of friendship. Over a year ago, he'd told Kate how he felt about her, told her that he was prepared to wait until she was ready to become more than a friend. Though it was true when he said it, it's less true now. He's unwilling to wait much longer, knowing he'll never get over Anna until he has another woman to love—Warren is right, he can't keep loving a ghost; he needs a flesh-and-blood woman. Stan hasn't talked to Kate about any of this, because he doesn't know how to tell her how he feels without making her feel like a replacement, doesn't know how to say that if she doesn't want them to become lovers, they will have to go their separate ways.

Later, when Stan telephoned the Cape to tell Kate about the meeting with Yosh, he didn't say a word about his fear of diving because it had occurred to him that by giving him the camera Kate might have been telling him that she knew how he felt. Instead he told her that he might take along his diving gear in order to take underwater photos with his camera.

The third week in February, while eating mussels in the Outrigger restaurant at the Hotel, Stan told his sister the details of the *Titanic* expedition. "I'll be gone most of the summer. There'll be briefing sessions in Halifax in May before we mobilize in Bermuda. That means I won't get down to see Mom for at least two months. Can you cover for me?"

"Of course. Have you told her about the expedition? Do you think she minds? I mean, the wreck is her mother's grave."

"She said she didn't mind and would like to visit it herself."

"Sounds like something she'd say. By the way, I forgot to tell you that I wrote to Patrick O'Connor."

"Who?"

"You know, Mom's half-brother in New York." Nancy had mentioned Patrick on the telephone when she was telling Stan about meeting Ellie in Cork, but it was apparent that he hadn't been listening. Lately he was often preoccupied.

Stan ordered another beer. What did his sister to expect to learn from this half-brother? It was quite a switch for someone who until recently had shown so little interest in their mother's origins.

"Last weekend when I arrived in Daniel's Point, Mom was making a rosary out of her wedding pearls and a necklace of black beads. She says she has to work on the rosary at home because if Aggie Halleran sees her, she'll recognize the beads as the present the residents gave Mom last Christmas." Nancy picked at her salad. "You'll never guess what else she said."

Stan shook his head.

"That there's likely a trail of pheromones between Gerry's house and mine."

"Pheromones?"

"Those hormonal trails animals are said to leave." Nancy gave her brother a sly look. "Likely there's a trail of them between Tors Cove and the Cape, too."

Stan laughed this off. "She didn't read that in *The Book of Knowledge*."

"She learned about it on the Home's TV. She also learned that though animals don't shed tears, they weep, and that eels return to the Caspian Sea to die. Also that there are monkeys who spend their entire lives in the tops of trees."

On Wednesday, soon after I returned from the Home, Nancy called me to say that she had news that couldn't wait until the weekend.

"I received a letter today from Patrick O'Connor. I don't think I told you that I wrote him after I got back from Cork."

It was just like Nancy to write Patrick without discussing it with me.

"I hope you warned him not to go to the newspapers with a story."

"Yes, Mom, I was extremely careful. I'll bring the letter with me this weekend. Patrick included photos of himself. I sent him one of you."

Did you now, I felt like saying in a tart, sarcastic voice, but I stopped myself as I sometimes do, by conjuring up the soothing image of our continents drifting close enough to touch.

On Sunday, while Nancy made the tea, I looked at the photographs. There was one of Patrick alone as a young man, and another more recent photo of himself and his wife, a short, stocky woman with a take-charge air. Patrick, a thick-chested man of medium height, looked nothing like the handwriting in his letter, which was slanted and looped.

February 27th, Brooklyn

Dear Ms. Palmer,

I can't tell you how amazed I was to receive your letter. Until I read it I had forgotten the day Lois and I went to Cape Race. As I recall I was in a hurry and didn't want to be there at all. I had only gone at the request of my father who, I thought, had sent me off on a hare-brained scheme based on a notice he'd found in an old newspaper that I seem to remember had been wrapped around his fish and chips. I was relieved when your father said he couldn't help. When I told my father that his lead had reached a dead end, he never brought up the subject again. He died in 1975 at the ripe old age of 87.

Now that I'm older myself, I have a different attitude about my father's request. You could say this letter is intended to make up for my youthful indifference. Judging from the photograph you sent, I would say that your mother bears a resemblance to my father.

As for the Titanic *business, you can be sure I will keep the contents of your letter to myself. I have not even confided in Lois though she would concur with your request. Thanks to an unscrupulous reporter, we were once badly burnt by the press. In any case both of us are unwell and have little energy these days to take on challenges.*

Please tell your mother that I would welcome a letter.

Sincerely yours,

Patrick O'Connor

"So you see, it's all right. Patrick will respect your privacy."

"For reasons of his own."

"Are you going to write to him yourself?"

"I might."

"It's interesting that Owen tried to find you. I wonder if he tried to get on the *Titanic* and failed."

"Sometimes I can smell my mother. She smells like Ivory soap. Did they have Ivory soap in those days?"

"I have no idea."

March 16th, Daniel's Point

Dear Patrick O'Connor,

I read the letter you wrote to my daughter. It does appear that we might be half-brother and sister. I should confess that I saw you that day you went to the Cape. I was on the roadside when you drove through the Drook. It was foggy and your eyes were on the road so you didn't see me.Yours was the only car I saw pass (to this day there are few cars on the Drook road) so that I am certain it was you.

Do you believe in the company of souls? This is not a question I would ask my children but at 81 it preoccupies me. I believe that after our death our souls swim in the universe like newborns, that we begin life anew as something else. I believe that is where our parents, my husband and other loved ones are. I believe that our souls are both inside and outside this world. I would be interested in knowing what you think.

My daughter has told me that you are one of four brothers. I hope you will write and tell me about them too.

Yours in confidence,

Aurora Mulloy

Stan has spent so many Mother's Day weekends at Daniel's Point house-cleaning that it has become a habit. When their mother bought the house and Nancy targeted this particular weekend for spring cleaning, he went along with it, and still does, though as far as he can see the house doesn't need cleaning. If he protests, he knows that his sister will say surely he must have noticed the grime (he hasn't) on the windows and floors. He also knows that the cleaning must accommodate Nancy's itinerary—that's how he thinks of the spring cleaning, as a chore that can be conveniently worked into her schedule, usually when Gerry is away. Stan goes along with the scheduling without rancour or resentment, knowing that spending a few hours once a year washing floors is an easy way to show gratitude to someone who has demanded so little from him all these years.

By the time he and Kate arrived at the house on Saturday,

Nancy had already cleaned the stove and was wiping down the cupboards. She was alone; their mother was working at Ocean View. Stan assumed that she wanted to be out of the way until the cleaning was done, but Nancy said that she was filling in for someone who was on holiday. While the women visited in the kitchen, Stan carried in the bags, noticing that his sister had put her suitcase on one of the twin beds in the front bedroom, leaving the double bed in the back bedroom for Kate and himself. He moved Nancy's suitcase to the back bedroom so that he and Kate could have the twin beds—let his sister think what she wanted. Once this was done, he got started on the floors while the women cleaned windows. By late afternoon the bull work was done and Stan put the lasagne in the oven to heat for supper and opened the wine, while Nancy set the table and Kate walked over to the Home with the dog to fetch Aurora. When she came into the kitchen, Stan could see that his mother was tired—she'd probably spent most of the day on her feet. He asked her about it and she claimed that it wasn't the work that had tired her out, she didn't do heavy work any more, it was the discouraging talk about the fishery decline. Had he heard the rumour that the fish plant would be closing? Stan hadn't heard, but he wasn't surprised, because nearly every day there was something in the *St. John's Telegram* about the inshore fishery shutting down.

After supper, when their mother had gone to bed, Nancy told Stan that she thought one of them should call the administrator at the Home and tell her not to expect their mother to keep helping out at the Home, that she was past the age of fetching and carrying or whatever it was she did nowadays over there. Stan was against interfering and said that if their mother found it satisfying to help out at the Home then she should go right on doing it.

In the morning his mother was the first one up. When he got up to use the bathroom Stan saw her drinking tea at the kitchen table, and remembered that Nancy had said she would take her to early mass, and that he had promised to have pancakes ready when they got back. He got dressed and made coffee, and after his mother and sister left the house, he and Kate sat in the immaculate kitchen drinking coffee, the dog stretched out on the floor. Now fully grown, he took up most of the space beneath the table. Stan reached down and rubbed his ears while Kate looked at Eugene Fitzgerald's plastic clock on the wall behind him. She seemed fascinated by the way the minute hand hiccupped whenever it passed twelve o'clock. Finally she stood up, took hold of his hand and tugged him to his feet.

"Come on." She pulled him into the bedroom; the dog following and closed the door. She stood in front of Stan, the top of her head level with his nose.

"Undress me."

"Are you sure?"

"Now, while there's time."

She wasn't wearing a bra. He traced a four-inch scar, red as a whip mark, across her right breast. There was a diagonal scar above her waist.

"Keep on."

He unzipped her jeans. She stepped out of the jeans and underwear and kicked them away. There was a twelve-inch scar down her hip to her groin. In the groin itself was a purplish scar, a puckered hole where the pick had gone deep.

He dropped to his knees and kissed the scar. "Kate, oh Kate."

"No pity," she said. "Pity will spoil everything."

They lay on the bed, where she stroked his unshaven cheek and he took off his glasses and held her with his myopic gaze. What he saw in her gaze was her view of him, which more than anything, was what he needed to see. Neither of them heard Nancy's car wheels on the driveway. The dog heard and ears pricked, he whined and barked then clawed the bedroom door. Kate opened the door and fled to the bathroom with her clothes while Stan struggled into his jeans. Smudge had his paws up on the window sill to watch the women walk to the kitchen door.

When Nancy came into the kitchen asking if the pancakes were ready, he stuck his head around the bedroom door and said no, they weren't because he'd gone back to bed. He heard the bathwater running.

"Oh." He heard Nancy say something about pheromones, and then she and his mother laughed. What was so funny?

After they had eaten, the three of them sat in the living room drinking the last of the coffee while Kate washed the dishes. When Stan stifled a yawn, Nancy smirked at their mother and asked if she would like to go to afternoon mass so that Stan and Kate could have another nap. "No, thank you," she said, "but I wouldn't turn down a drive along the shore."

Stan said, "If it's all the same to you, I think I'll stay here and mow the lawn."

"You've got to be kidding," his sister said. "There's snow on the ground."

"Well, I have to get it done while I'm here, what with everything I have to do before going on the expedition."

His mother said brightly—too brightly, Stan thought—"Come to think of it, if it's open, I'd like to visit the nature park in Salmonier. I can't think of a pleasanter way to spend Mother's Day afternoon."

"Let's go," Nancy said. "I haven't seen a moose for at least six months and I'm feeling deprived."

As they were going out the door carrying a thermos of tea, Stan heard them snorting with laughter. Let them go to it. He should go out and mow the lawn just to show his smart-ass sister that snow or no snow, it could be done.

May 15, Cork

Dear Gran,

This is just the weeniest note to let you know that I have my ticket in hand and will be arriving in St. John's June 18th. Kevin will arrive in early July after he finishes a workshop he is giving in Romania this month. If you can put up with us, we plan to spend all of July at Daniel's Point. I can hardly wait.

Love, Sheila

May 27, Daniel's Point

Dear Sheila,

I'm writing to you though the letter will be one long complaint about the weather. Every day it rains, a wintry rain that turns to sleet. I wouldn't be surprised if we skipped spring altogether this year. I usually enjoy weather of all kinds but I'm chafing this year because I want the garden to be at its best when you arrive. With the weather so poor and the ground still frozen and patches of snow here and there, it is in disarray. Only the grass seems to be growing.

This past month I've been helping out more than usual at Ocean View. They are short-staffed and need someone to assist at meal time and bath time. Your mother seems to think that the administrator is taking advantage of me, but I never say yes to doing anything unless it's something I want to do.

By the way, did you know that we are taller in the mornings than in the evening when our vertebrae are squeezed flatter?

Love, Gran

It wasn't until the first week of June that I could finally work in the garden. It was still raining off and on, but it was a milder rain, nothing that would keep me inside for long. It was midafternoon and I was walking along the road on my way home from Ocean View earlier than usual because Jerry Ward had agreed to meet me after school so that I could explain what I wanted done in the garden. I wanted him to pull out the weeds before they overtook the flowers, to mow the grass and dig a new flower bed for the Johnny-jump-ups and Jacob's ladders Marilyn promised to bring me after supper when she was finished at the Home.

The afternoon was mauzy with fog drifting across the bay like a fleet of phantom sails. Mist was falling, not much, but enough to hear the swish of moisture against the wheels of a passing car over the muffled blare of the Powles Head horn. Inside the pocket of my raincoat was a square of folded notepaper on which I had drawn a map of the garden showing where I wanted the new plants to go. I was carrying a dried-up chrysanthemum rescued from the lounge window, and I'd printed an x on the map to show Jerry where it would go in the rockery. Also in my pocket were packages of sweet alyssum and blue angel seeds for the fairy garden.

Listening to the foghorn I wondered if there were foghorns in Bermuda. I had forgotten to ask Stanley before he left on his expedition if fog existed that far south. I knew there was fog in the Antarctic—where there was ice there was fog—and that an iceberg had once been sighted off Bermuda, but I knew it was a freak, the island being far below the latitudes of melt.

By now the *Keldysh* had been in Bermuda several days—the expedition was leaving for the *Titanic* site from there. Before the expedition set out, Stanley said the crew would be spending a week on the island attending orientation sessions and checking equipment during the day, while at night the subs dived offshore, testing their deep-water lights. I didn't expect to see him again until July.

I reached my driveway and followed it around the side of the house to the back and started down the steps leading to the garden. Eugene Fitzgerald had built the steps from abandoned railway ties, which he used to make rectangular boxes filled with gravel. The steps were a roundabout way of reaching the garden, but I wanted to avoid wading through the shin-high grass at the front. I was three steps from the bottom when the lace of my left sneaker caught a large splinter on the inside tie. I pitched forward, sprawling sideways into the rockery and my head hit a large stone that I had put there myself.

When I eventually came to, the first thing I heard was the foghorn and I thought I was back in school in the Cove. I imagined the horn was Miss Kelland's voice calling out the roll, and she was expecting me to say, "Here. I'm here!" I heard a car pass on the road and was reminded that I was supposed meet Jerry Ward after school. I tried to push myself up with my hands, but the pain in my left hip made me faint. Was it broken? Several residents at the

Home had broken their hips, but I had never broken a bone in my life. But I had hurt something, that much was certain, and I knew I had to lie calmly until Jerry arrived.

I had fallen with my right arm crooked, my hand inches from my face. Slowly, gingerly, I brought my wrist up to eye level. It was 4:30. Surely it wasn't 4:30. Jerry had been going to meet me at 3:30. Where was he? It wasn't like him to be late. I called once, twice. "Help! Someone help me!" I listened for footsteps on the road. All I heard was the sound of passing cars. "Help! Help!" It began to rain, a soft rain, a gentle shower, a veil of minuscule drops fizzing against my ear. Usually I thought of mist as an embrocation for birds, spring bulbs and new grass, but not today because the mist was making me heavy and wet, seeping into my pores, penetrating deep into my flesh and bone so that my body trembled and shook with cold. "Help me, please!" Once again I tried to move, but the pain in my hip made me swoon. I closed my eyes and willed myself to float away.

The transforming magic was with me still. I rose above the rockery and grass, rose until I was above the house. I hovered briefly over the rooftop and then began drifting eastward over the Barrens toward the sea. Now I heard nothing but the calming sibilance of the mist until abruptly—rudely, I thought—I heard a shout.

"I found her! She's fallen!"

Marilyn's voice.

"Can you hear me, Aurora?" She was shouting into my ear and prodding my hip. Pain shot through my leg. I heard a groan.

"Phone the doctor, Lloyd! And bring the stretcher from the Home!"

Lloyd, who was Lloyd?

Something heavy and warm pressed against my forehead. I wanted to shake it off but it was too difficult to move my head. I willed myself to rise, high, higher, until I was above the pain. I drifted up and away.

I was floating over the Trepassey Barrens, over bogs and ponds and rolling downs. A herd of caribou were grazing peacefully by a stream, tugging at lichen and grass, unaware that I was looking down on them from above. I passed the road winding north, the rocky slope and signalling tower. I passed over swamps and marshes and came at last to the narrow wooded valley that was the Drook.

I heard voices and footsteps. Abruptly, the drifting stopped and I felt myself plummeting down, grounded by the pain in my hip. Something pierced my arm and when the pain ebbed away, I was airborne again.

I was picking berries on the Barrens above the Drook. In one pocket was a thick slice of bread and in the other my prayer beads—Merla never let me go far without my bread and beads. She had told me to stay on top of the hill where my white smock and white hair would be easily seen. I was about twelve, old enough to pick berries on my own. It was a mild August morning, months before Louis died. A wadding of pinkish fog lay on the water. It had been there for days, rolling back and forth with the tide. Bent over, moving from bush to bush, I picked blueberries, glistening blue globes with smoky skins. Every so often I popped a berry into my mouth, staining my tongue a purplish red. My pail was half full when I spied a bush laden with so many huge berries that after I had knelt down and stripped it, my pail was full and it was time to go. When I stood up, I noticed that while I had been picking, the fog had moved off the water and funnelled into the Drook. All the St. Croix houses had vanished, including my own, taking with them the voices from below—the shouts of my brothers going about their chores. The sea was silent and the landscape had become unfamiliar and strange.

I looked down and saw rabbit paths going every which way through the bushes. I began following the paths, one after the other, but they crisscrossed each other so often that I circled myself until I came to a wider path that I followed as it curved and dipped through the Barrens. The path seemed to end at a brook, more of a trickle than a brook, a narrow thread of brown bog water tumbling over rocks and around islands of moss. The water made me thirsty, and when I knelt to scoop up a handful from a small rocky basin I heard faint tinkling music, not of water but of glass, and in that instant, without warning, before I could drink, I was face down beside the brook.

I might have lain there indefinitely had it not been for the white pony that put its cooling nose against my neck, nuzzling me, nudging me to get up, which I did, though I made no attempt to mount him and he gave no indication that I should. Rather, he tossed his mane and trotted down the path, looking around once or twice to see if I was following. I hurried after him, looking neither right nor left until the path ended at the road, and I heard waves breaking on the shore. I knew at once that I was at the top of Drook hill. I heard my name being called.

"Aurora!" There was a yellowish glow below me.

I walked downhill, drawn to the arcing light.

Ben was on the road swinging the lantern back and forth.

"Where've you been?" He was in a crooked mood. "Look at me, Aurora!" The light was shining in my face.

"Berry-picking."

"Sure you have, girl. Where's your pail to?"

Where was my pail? Gone. Vanished like the pony.

"Do you know the time? It's half past seven. Mom is near out of her mind. You get inside quick. I'll tell the others you finally come." Ben looked at me with disgust. "You should see yourself."

I opened the door and stepped through the rubber sheeting. Merla was looking out the window that faced the sea. When she heard me come in, she turned and backed up slightly as if she was gazing at an apparition. "Blessed Mother! You're safe!" She came forward slowly and took my hand.

"What happened to you, maid?"

"I was berry-picking on the Barrens and got lost. The fog came in, and the next thing I knew I was standing on the road."

"Did you lie down and sleep?"

"No, but I fell into the water."

"Did you drink?"

"No."

"A good thing you didn't or the fairies would've got you."

Merla ran a hand over my head. "You're dry. And what's this in your hair?" She removed a bird bone and a stick from my hair and laid them on her palm. "What do you make of this?"

I could make nothing of it.

"You've been gone six hours."

Nor could I account for the time.

"You've been fairy led," Merla said. She took the lid off the stove and emptied her palm before washing her hand.

"But I wasn't afraid."

"That's because you took your rosary. You have it still?"

"Yes."

"Are you hungry?"

I took the bread from my pocket. "I'll eat this."

"We'll bless it first." She made the sign of the cross over the bread. "It saved you too. If it weren't for this bread and the beads, you'd be out there yet. Eat up, girl. I'll go tell your father that you're safe. When we gets back, we'll fill the tub and give your hair a good scrub. We don't want fairy matter in your bed."

"Aurora?"

I opened my eyes. Squinting against the overhead light, I looked around; I could see at once that it was night and that I wasn't at home but on a hospital bed in Marilyn's office. She was standing over me, arms crossed, breasts bunched together.

"What am I doing here?"

"I couldn't very well leave you alone at your house, now could I?"

"I suppose not."

"How do you feel?"

I didn't tell her that I felt like a bird whose wings had been clipped. "I fell and broke my hip."

"Yes." Marilyn was frowning.

"I was supposed to meet Jerry Ward."

"What time was that?"

"Three-thirty."

"I didn't find you until six when Lloyd and I delivered the plants."

Ah yes, Lloyd is her husband.

"I was floating over the Barrens."

"How is the pain?"

"Not so bad."

"I gave you a painkiller. The doctor's been in and ordered another shot in an hour. Are you thirsty?"

"Yes. I fell into the water, but I didn't drink. Merla said it was a good thing I didn't or the fairies would've got me."

"Well, of course." I knew she didn't believe a word. She held the straw between my lips so that I could drink, and when I was finished she put the glass on the desk beside a shiny metal bell with a button press on top, the same kind Miss Kelland used in school. "Ring if you need me. Your daughter will be here in the morning. Now you try to sleep." Obligingly, I did.

At first my sleep was intermittent because I kept hearing the foghorn and answering the roll call, but sometime during the night I fell into a deep sleep and didn't awaken until morning. What woke me was sunlight coming through the office window; I felt so much heat through the glass that I knew the fog had burned away. Lying there with the sun on my eyelids, I carried myself back to the Drook, to the inside of the house that Louis and I were making deep in the tuck.

I am about five or six; Louis is four years older but still willing to pretend. So far we've made a front room, a kitchen and a bedroom, all of it smelling of warm spruce, and I am waiting for him to bring back blasty boughs for our bed—he didn't want to cut away boughs from the roof protecting us from the rain. The rust-coloured floor is dappled with islands of gold where the sun pokes through. The islands shimmy when the roof is shaken by the breeze. After Louis returns and we finish the house, I'll drape Alice Marie's shawl over my head and, holding our rosary beads and kneeling side by side, we will marry each other.

"Aurora! Come here, maid!"

Merla is calling me inside. I hold my breath. "Aurora!"

I waited forever, but Louis never came back.

"Wouldn't it be wiser to take her to St. John's?"

Nancy was here.

"Dr. McCarthy says she's better off at the Home for the time being." I recognized Marilyn's voice. "He says that until the hip begins to heal, the less she's moved the better."

"Even so, I can't help thinking…"

"If it will put your mind at rest, you could arrange for Jackie Ward to work the night shift when I'm off duty. With her husband laid off, she could use the work."

Jackie was Jerry's mother. I should ask her why Jerry didn't come.

"It's too bad the hip can't be replaced," Marilyn said. "It made all the difference with my aunt. Ah, your mother's awake."

"Hello, Nancy. Why can't it be replaced?"

"Hello, Mom. Your age won't allow it."

"But I'm only eighty-one."

"I phoned the *Keldysh* this morning. The ship has left Bermuda and Stan knows about your fall."

"I don't want him worrying about me. The next time you talk to him, you tell him that and I don't want you worrying either. You should get some rest. You seem tired."

"Look who's talking," Marilyn teased, holding a needle behind her back.

"What's that?"

"Morphine."

"Ah." Xanadu. My pleasure dome.

I am on the sea. Am I following Stanley? How strange that I should be floating on the water, when as far back as I can remember I've been afraid of the sea. I'm not afraid now, perhaps because I'm imagining myself as a little boat toddling down the bay. I'm no bigger than a skiff, but I'm perfectly seaworthy and know how to mould myself to the water as the swells lift me up and down. I take my time, drifting into coves and tickles, inlets and bights, on my leisurely journey through the latitudes of melt, idling past capes and points and beaches in no hurry to reach the place of trespass, the bay of souls.

"I smell peppermints."

"They're Brenda's." Nancy is beside me, holding my hand. "She moved in with Aggie Halleran so you could have her room."

"That's very generous of Brenda. Please thank her for me."

"I already have."

"I never knew she liked peppermints."

"There's a bowl of them on the window sill."

"Is red still your favourite colour?"

"It is."

"I don't think I ever had a favourite. I liked them all."

Zippered into his anorak, Stan stood on the aft deck of the *Keldysh*, watching waves break against the stern. They hadn't been long out of Bermuda when they ran into this storm with its fifteen-foot swells riding over the deck, flinging spume as far as the bridge, where it clung to the windows like spittle. Stan was becoming drowsy from the ship's motion but was alert enough to keep a firm grip on the rail, determined to stay on deck as long as he could. If he gave in too soon, he could end up below where his cabin mate was curled up on the lower bunk, hands tucked between his knees, a waste bucket on the floor—the washroom was three doors along the companionway.

There was nothing fancy about the *Keldysh*, a well-equipped but spartan ship built with efficiency, not luxury, in mind. Except for the meals—they had been served watery corn soup twice a day since leaving Bermuda—the ship was more than adequate. The Russians might stint on the food but they hadn't stinted on the subs, and *Mir I* and *Mir II*, built by the Finns in exchange for Russian oil, were the most sophisticated and reliable manned submersibles in the world.

The sea was now running twenty feet and a wave washed over the deck as high as Stan's knee. It was time to go inside. He'd go down to the lounge where he'd find Yosh and the IMAX photographers, most of them a friendly crowd. But first he'd stop off at Yosh's fridge, where he'd stashed several bottles of Newfoundland vodka made from iceberg water, and a bag of iceberg bits, which the American photographers especially liked to put in their drinks. Stan got a kick out of watching them hold their drinks to their ear so they could hear the fizz of escaping air.

Because of the storm it took four days, twice the estimated time, for the *Keldysh* to reach the *Titanic* wreck site, 584 kilometres—

365 nautical miles—from Newfoundland on the southern end of the latitudes of melt, where the ruined ship lay in a canyon below the tail of the Banks and above the Abyssal plain. Because of the two-day delay, the Russians and the IMAX crew began diving as soon as the ship was on site. For reasons of safety a dive wouldn't proceed unless twenty-four hours of good weather was predicted—after eighteen hours below no one wanted to be aboard a sub surfacing in a high sea. Though IMAX booked all the early dives, both their cameras and the Russian cameras shot whatever Yosh and Stan wanted—Yosh intended to go down twice, Stan once; he would be making the expedition's final dive with his Russian counterpart. By the time the IMAX crew were finished—they would do fifteen dives in fifteen days—Stan would have become thoroughly familiar with the site from studying the photos taken on the bottom; he'd know what to look for and where to find it. Unwilling to wait until then to get in the water (waiting would only increase his anxiety), Stan suited up and dived into the sea as the first sub was being launched. He photographed the *Keldysh* divers with his underwater camera as they unhooked the sub and checked its hatch before it went below. *Mir I* slowly sank, Stan following it for thirty feet, shooting an entire roll of film before he surfaced, victorious that he had dived without being haunted by the memory of towing Anna's bloodied face ashore.

No one aboard saw the IMAX film which was taken ashore every day by speedboat for processing in IMAX labs. Instead, at night in the lounge they watched videos of *The Deep* and *The Abyss*. But the Russian film was processed aboard, and every morning after a dive there were new coloured stills tacked to the bulletin board. The photos were of artefacts scattered over the debris field below: a leather suitcase, a toilet bowl, a bedstead, a china plate painted with a white star. The photos had a subduing effect on the expedition; though the scientists sat around after meals talking and joking, no one forgot they were floating above a graveyard.

"Aurora!"

Someone is close, someone with a smoker's rattle.

"Aurora, it's me, Aggie."

My nemesis.

"I brought you some flowers. They're from all of us. We chipped in."

"Thank you." I can't seem to open my eyes, but I can push out the words.

"There's roses and carnations mixed together. The roses were the Captain's idea."

Roses. I've never been given roses, but I remember trying to grow mail order roses once.

"You get well. You hear?"

"I hear."

Is that Aggie sniffling? She must have a cold.

"Gran!"

Sheila. When did she arrive? She's early and the grass needs cutting.

"Gran, I know you hear me. We're taking you to the hospital in St. John's so you can go on a respirator. I'll ride in the ambulance with you. Mom will follow in the car. Squeeze my hand if you understand.... Good."

I don't want to go to St. John's, but what does it matter now? I feel myself being slid off one bed and onto another. I am cold, colder than I have ever been, colder than when I was in my cradle at sea. Behind my eyes is a picture of a white-haired woman covered by a white blanket being wheeled toward a white ambulance. The ambulance doors are open and I see myself being lifted up and slid inside like a tray of ice cubes into a fridge. I have become a captive of ice and soon my body will become an artefact like those I read about all those years ago. Strange to think that, all along, I have been a voyeur in my own life.

"Aurora, it's Beatty!"

Who? Oh yes, Beatty. Beatty moved to Brigus ages ago.

"I came to see how you're getting on. I brought you some lemon junket in case you feel like eating."

Bringing lemon junket is the sort of thing Beatty would do. I never told you much about Beatty, did I? Beatty was kindness itself. She was stalwart and loyal. Though we both kept to ourselves, I always thought of her as a friend.

"Johnny sends his regards. He couldn't make the drive."

Johnny's hooked up to a kidney machine. Or was that his father?

"Goodbye." Was that me? I meant to say hello.

"Nancy? Are you there?"

"I'm here."

"I want you to have my tin sea-chest. Stanley is to have the books and Sheila her great-grandmother's mats."

"Don't talk, Mom. You're not supposed to talk."

"There's to be no wreckage, no flotsam and jetsam washed ashore. Do you understand?"

She doesn't reply or squeeze my hand and I know I have been talking to myself.

Stan was inside *Mir I*, about a mile below the *Keldysh*, Jonah inside the whale. With him inside the sub were the pilot and co-pilot. There they were, Stan thought, three astronauts of the deep. Inside the untethered sub they had no more control over their fate than if they were inside a space capsule. They were here by the grace of gravity—if they got into trouble down here no computer could save them; they were on their own. Like Eriksson and Amundsen, Armstrong and Captain Bob, they were journeying to a place beyond rescue. The three of them sat in the dark, two of them in shirtsleeves—it had been 30 degrees Celsius when they left the top, but the temperature was dropping steadily as they slipped through the water. Stan leaned back in his seat, listening to a classical music tape, Mozart he thought it was, and thinking of his mother. Two weeks ago Nancy had phoned to tell him that Aurora had been taken to St. John's and was on a respirator; she had pneumonia and was having difficulty breathing and might not pull through. The problem was that she had to be kept flat on her back because of the broken hip. They were keeping her comfortable with morphine and everything possible was being done. Whenever Stan phoned the hospital from the ship, he was told much the same thing.

I see my mother's pale shining face hovering above me like an anxious moon. Once I believed my mother had the power to bend the tide, but that was when I was looking at her through long-ago eyes. Suddenly she drops from the sky and I hear a splash. I feel myself being lifted into the darkness and then I am being swung down, down, toward the sea. But my landing is soft, without a splash or even a drop of water sprinkling my skin. I hear my mother's voice. "There, little one, there."

Stan awoke with a start on the ocean bottom and reached for his jacket, tuque and gloves—it was five degrees. The lights were switched on and *Squid*—Stan's name for the sub—began manoeuvring across the sea floor toward the wreck. He crouched in front of his porthole window, looking up at the queen of wrecks. She loomed above, a ship that took ten thousand men three years to build, rising out of the greenish-black water like a haunted skyscraper covered in greyish silt, and this was only half of the ship; the stern was at the other end of the debris field. The sub cruised over the deck allowing the explorers to look at the crenellated battlement of the corroding hull, the lava flow of rust, the rivers and trickles of reddish gold, the stalactites and rusticles, the caves and caverns of rust, the wreaths and boughs, the forests and gardens. The wreck had the exotic beauty of a reef, an ephemeral reef that sent up an explosion of red powder whenever *Squid* grazed it. Stan had seen beauty in wrecks before, anemones and corals laying claim to what had settled on the sea floor, but it had seemed a natural transformation, whereas there was something unnatural and grotesque about this wreck of the Titans, something that had to do with the reddish gold, glinting in the light like Mammon's treasure, and with the white rattail fish, the whiter starfish, the bone-white sponges—so far from the sun, everything that lived in this barren graveyard was a sepulchral white. Stan remembered that Yosh had been surprised to find four species of fish near the wreck and twice as many sea plants. He said that it was worth coming on the expedition just to learn that the Gorgonian coral growing on a jagged metal spear had taken seventy-nine years to reach three feet. The *Titanic* was a time marker—when she went down, automobiles and airplanes were the newest technology and now submersibles and space stations were the frontier; at the rate bacteria were eating the ship, the wreck would be gone long before tourists landed on the moon.

The bow had fallen on an old landslide caused by an ancient earthquake. Over the gravel and rock was an overlay of soft mud, a bed of shallow silt that was nothing like the primal ooze of the

Abyssal plain, whose depths had never been fully explored. The rippled patches on the bottom caused by currents rolling over the ocean floor during the earth's spinning looked like the ribbing on a sandy beach. Having studied hundreds of photos, Stan knew exactly where he wanted the co-pilot, who was manipulating the articulated arms for him, to collect core samples and deposit them in the basket. As well as samples from the ribbed silt, Stan wanted cores from the mud line between the bow and the sediment so that he could verify the wreck's scouring, which he estimated to be less than the maximum depth of trenches caused by scouring ice.

I can no longer hear my mother. She has drifted away and I am left alone yet not alone, for I am surrounded by others, a requiem of voices moaning, weeping, pleading with God, believing until their final breath that they will be miraculously rescued from death. Though I do not comprehend their words, I have lost my innocence and can feel their anguish. My tiny heart swells with their grief. For comfort, I look upward to the sky and see the Big Dipper hanging low. Riding high are the three stars studding Orion's belt, the W stars of Cassiopeia's throne. I see a constellation I've never seen before, a man reclining just beneath the polar star, his head propped on his hand, the way Tom used to lie. The man takes my breath away. Can he be my beloved Tom? Has he come to rescue me? I try to reach out to him but I can't seem to move my hands. I try to call him to my side but I can't seem to speak; there is no escaping the chaos and the tumult, the piteous voices, the sound of unremitting despair. If only I could move, if only I could rise into the ether, where stars flicker like lanterns in windows, beckoning weary travellers home.

All the samples Stan needs have been collected, and the explorers have cruised the length of the bow on both sides at close range, and photographed the impact trough in the seabed; they have taken a long and careful look at the site's geology, and after eleven hours on the bottom are ready to return to the ship.

By now exhaustion is blurring Stan's vision, and he feels that he's not so much inside a sub as he is inside a vast pool of mothers' tears. He thinks about his grandmother who died in these waters. He thinks about the millions of lives the sea has claimed, hundreds of thousands in these waters alone. Upwards of twelve thousand ships driven onto rocks, overturned in high seas, smashed by waves and ice or inexplicably pulled under. Fishing boats, brigantines, schooners, skiffs, dories, longliners, trawlers, whalers and sealers; emigrant ships and ferries; liners and cruisers; ice-breakers; ships of war: destroyers, freighters, frigates, submarines. The sea bottom is a vast cemetery of unmarked graves, and all the time he's been down here he's been scouring a trough of sorrow far deeper than anything he has known.

The lights are switched off, and the water tanks, whose weight has been keeping the sub down, are emptied. Slowly *Squid* begins to rise through a darkness so opaque that looking through the porthole window Stan can't quite believe that two and a half miles above, daylight will soon begin as this part of the globe turns toward the sun. Now that his concentration has been freed and there is nothing to do but wait while he is lifted through an oceanic night, Stan has to fight down terror. Not once when he was on the bottom did he think that he was pushing his luck, that he was indulging in the kind of arrogance that took down the *Titanic*; not once had the claustrophobia of being inside a sub frightened him, but now it does and he can't stop himself from thinking about the sub's vulnerability in the immensity of the sea. He feels he's in a place between the living and the dead, that he might see Anna's face or even his grandmother's, a thought that has him fighting for breath.

And then he sees her, a flash in the porthole window, no more and no less than a borealic shimmer before she dissolves into the oceanic night; not Anna or his grandmother, but his mother, her face a phosphorescent green, her white hair and fluttering gown pulled sideways by the current; her eyes looking far away and her mouth shaped in that familiar joyful smile. In an instant her face fades and he knows that she's disappearing with the dawn, that she's taken that fantastic leap into the beyond where there are no maps or globes, where the untamed universe swirls with the essence of the born and the unborn in galaxies of unimaginable darkness and light.

ACKNOWLEDGMENTS

Grateful acknowledgment is made to the following for permission to reprint previously published material:

"Grief and the Sea," by Don McKay, from *Apparatus*, copyright © 1997 by Don McKay. Published by McClelland & Stewart, Toronto.

"Sing Around This One," collected and arranged by Eric West, from *Songs of Newfoundland and Labrador*, Vol. 2.

"Titanic," by E.J. Pratt, from *E.J. Pratt: Complete Poems*, edited by Sandra Djwa and R.G. Moyles. Copyright © 1989 by University of Toronto Press. Reprinted with the permission of the publisher.

The poems excerpted on pages 48 and 58 are by Gerald Manley Hopkins.

During the writing of this novel I was helped by archivists and librarians in Memorial University's Maritime and Folklore Archives and the Centre for Newfoundland Studies as well as the St. John's and Cork City libraries and the Provincial and the Historical

Society Archives. I was also provided free access to the library of the Centre for Cold Oceans Resource Engineering.

As well, I am indebted to many others:

Ita, Noel and Eugene Myrick, Tom Myrick, Francis Myrick, Eileen and Cyril Myrick; David Mulloy and Gerry Cantwell; Bernard Pennell and Andy Wilson; Jerome and Mary Devereaux.

Mike McCarthy, Frank Galgay and Captain Joe Prim; Donald Cameron, Charlie Randell and Greg Crocker; Chris Woodward Lynas, Fraser Eaton, Judith Whittick, Martha Drake, and Jack Clark.

Alan Clarke, Peter Roche and Ann O'Keefe; Gail Crawford and Peter Hart. Ellen and Dave Robertson; Nancy Strike, Edna Alford, John Perlin, Eric West, Don McKay; Barbara Reiti, whose book, *Strange Terrain*, informed this novel, and Ann Meredith Barry, whose paintings of the Southern Shore inspired.

Anne Hart, Bernice Morgan, Laurie Clark, Suzanne Brandreth, and Bert Riggs for reading various drafts. Dean Cooke for his invaluable encouragement and helpful suggestions. Diane Martin for her tactful editing and unerring hand.

Last but not least I am indebted to Steve Blasco, who in 1991 guided me around the *Keldysh* in St. John's, where this story began.

ABOUT THE AUTHOR

JOAN CLARK is the author of two previous novels, *Eriksdotter* and *The Victory of Geraldine Gull*, which won the Canadian Author's Association Award and was shortlisted for the Governor General's Award, and of a collection of short stories, *Swimming Toward the Light*. She has also written award-winning books for children. Joan Clark was born in Liverpool, Nova Scotia, and has lived for several years in St. John's, Newfoundland.